A VORACIOUS HUNGER

"Be still," Damon grated out.

Ravyn ignored him.

"Ravyn, stop it."

She began to buck, trying to throw him off her.

"Damn it," he muttered thickly.

Ravyn froze in surprise as he pressed the lower half of his body against hers. He was hard. She looked closer at his eyes and realized that what she had taken as anger was arousal. The perspiration beaded on his brow wasn't from exertion, but from trying to rein in his libido.

For a moment, they stared at each other. Ravyn's anger drained away and she lost interest in escaping. Instead, she arched her body against his, shifting her legs slightly so he was pressed where it felt best. She couldn't hear his groan, but she felt it rumble through his chest.

Damon's hesitation lasted no more than an instant before his mouth came down on hers. There was nothing soft or gentle about the kiss, just voracious hunger. His lack of control didn't frighten her in the least. She reveled in it. She didn't even care that she could feel the grittiness of mud on her lips.

RAVYN'S FLIGHT

PATTI O'SHEA

LOVE SPELL

LOVE SPELL

NEW YORK CITY

LOVE SPELL®

November 2002

Published by

Dorchester Publishing Co., Inc.
276 Fifth Avenue
New York, NY 10001

ISBN 0-505-52516-X

Printed in the United States of America.

For Mom and Dad, who always said I could do anything and meant it. I love you.

To Jenny Low, the high priestess. Thank you for nudging me back on my path, for reading the words hot off the computer and for your expert advice on the action scenes.

To Theresa Monsey, the synopsis goddess. Thank you for finding the holes everyone else missed, for pointing out where details were needed and for listening to me go on and on about the story.

To Maria Hammon, the HoF. Thank you for finding the little pieces of illogic, for proofreading and for your enthusiasm.

And to Mo Kearney, Karen King and Dolly Lien for the time they spent reading, proofing and offering encouragement.

RAVYN'S FLIGHT

Chapter One

The clock blinked 12:00.

The blue light from the numbers illuminated the otherwise dark room. Ravyn sat on the floor staring at the flashing digits, concentrating on them to keep from thinking.

She didn't want to remember what existed outside her door. Didn't want to recall what she'd seen. She couldn't let herself think of the bodies beyond her room, the bodies of people who'd been her friends. Ravyn didn't know why she'd been spared and she didn't want to think about that either. A shudder coursed through her and she focused again on the numbers, pushing aside the smoky fingers of comprehension trying to seep into her brain.

Even as she sought oblivion, she knew she wouldn't be able to maintain this state of numbness indefinitely. Pulling her knees tighter to her chest, she linked her fingers around them and rested her head on her legs. She focused on the clock.

Coward, coward, it seemed to accuse with each flash.

Ravyn knew she should do something, but she didn't know what. Never before had she been so aware of the isolation. The Colonization Assessment Team lived and worked light years from Earth. It had taken a month of space travel for the twenty members of the team to journey to Jarved Nine. The idea of being alone on an alien planet left her paralyzed.

She couldn't have said how long she sat, huddled in the corner, before a noise brought her back to full awareness. She held her breath. Maybe she'd made a mistake. Maybe she'd missed a pulse and one of her friends still lived. Reality intruded in a merciless wave. She'd seen what remained of the bodies. No one could survive the trauma, the blood loss. The mutilation. She swallowed back her nausea.

It must be the killer, she decided. There was no one else on this planet. Every cell in her body froze as she waited to be found, waited to die. Then she shook her head, ridding it of her fatalistic thoughts. She had to live; she had to seek justice.

Her heart pounded loudly and she placed her hand over it to muffle the noise. Sound would carry in the dead silence of the facility, she reminded herself, and winced at her unintentional choice of words. Soft sounds, sounds that barely carried to her ears, continued to come from the other room.

Did the murderer know the number of people assigned here? Would he look for her? Frantically she scanned her quarters, searching for somewhere, anywhere to hide. The spartan room left few choices. There was a small wardrobe that held her clothes, but with built-in drawers narrowing the space, she doubted she'd fit. Maybe she could stay unseen beneath the small, metal-framed cot. The room was dark and the stand that held the flashing clock was next to the bed, deepening the shadows. She heard a muted thump near the door and jumped to her feet.

Her legs gave out and she landed in a graceless heap back on the floor. She stopped herself from crying out as sensation rushed ruthlessly back into her limbs, but she couldn't prevent the thud her body made as it hit the ground. Frozen in place, she listened fearfully for any sound, no matter how slight. She detected nothing but the low hum of electricity flowing into the clock and the raggedness of her breathing.

He'd heard her. She knew it. If he hadn't, she would still hear movement in the other room.

Terror more acute than anything she'd ever imagined held her in its thrall. The faint sound of footsteps had Ravyn scurrying on her hands and knees for shelter. She crawled under the bunk and didn't stop moving until she reached the corner. Rolling into a ball, she could do nothing but hope the dim lighting concealed her. She heard the soft swoosh of the door and bit her bottom lip. He was in the room now. Prayers learned in childhood, prayers she'd thought long forgotten, rushed into her mind. Silently, she repeated them over and over and over.

He moved around the room, not trying to hide his presence, but not making much noise either. Ravyn closed her eyes as he neared the bunk. Foolishly, she hoped that if she couldn't see him, he wouldn't see her.

A hand, a big hand, closed around her ankle. Ravyn let out a startled squeak, too scared to even scream. The hand pulled and she could feel herself sliding out from safety. She tried to kick out with her other leg, but with most of her body still under the bunk, it lacked power. Then another hand imprisoned her free leg and she opened her eyes. She refused to die without looking her murderer in the face, without fighting till her last breath. As she cleared the bunk, Ravyn raised her fists, prepared to pummel her captor. The faint glow of the clock silhouetted a very large man and she recognized she didn't have a chance, but she pulled back her arm anyway, ready to strike.

He moved fast, so fast she didn't know how it happened. The next thing she knew, he had imprisoned both her wrists over her head and thrown a heavy thigh across her legs. She couldn't do more than wiggle against his superior strength. She'd been wrong if she thought she'd known the height of terror earlier. This shot off the scale.

The room held enough light for Damon to see the absolute panic in the eyes of the woman he had pinned to the floor. Considering what he and his men had found in the other room, he didn't blame her. Terror rendered her incapable of making a sound, and for that, he gave thanks. He would hate to muzzle her, it would only add to her fear, but he didn't heed a scream to bring all his men running. Six heavily armed soldiers bursting into the room would do little to calm the woman he held.

He pitched his voice so she could hear him over her labored breathing and muttered soothing noises. Words would be wasted at this point. It was difficult to hold on to her level of fright and gradually her breathing slowed, her body relaxed.

"It's okay," he said gently. "I'm not going to hurt you. You're okay." He repeated this until he saw the blind panic leave her eyes. He didn't loosen his hold. Now that her fear began to abate, the odds said she would go one of two ways. She would either start swinging or become hysterical. Right now, he figured it was a toss up which way she'd pick.

Damon kept his focus on the woman, but he remained aware of the coming and going of his men as they carried out his orders. The bodies had to be taken care of and the scene in the other room had to be documented, evidence collected. He trusted them to carry it out efficiently and meticulously.

He ran his free hand across her cheekbone, brushing her hair away from her eyes. He hoped the gentle touch would help her regain her senses. It did. She went limp under him and he released her. Crouching next to her, he helped her sit. She needed the side of the bunk to hold her up, but she had made progress. "Who—" her voice cracked. He could hear her swallow, try again. "Who are you?"

"My name's Damon," he told her. He knew that didn't really answer her question, but he doubted she could take in more information than that right now. "I'm not going to hurt you."

She nodded. The pale blue light fell across her face.

"What's your name?" They had nineteen bodies. It would be easier to identify the survivor than the remains.

"Ravyn," she whispered.

He nodded once. Ravyn Verdier was the team's communications specialist. Her job was, had been, to transmit and receive data from Earth as well as keep the comm equipment up and running. She must have been the one to activate the emergency beacon. From the position and condition of the victims, it was unlikely any of them had been responsible. It didn't appear as if they'd had time to do much of anything before dying.

Military maneuvers didn't often take place off Earth and never before on a yet-to-be-colonized world. It was sheer luck he and his men had been on the other side of the planet. They'd responded immediately to the call for help, but they'd been too late despite their rapid reaction.

Damon closed his eyes briefly, trying to rid himself of the feeling that he'd known these people. He hadn't. Reading some abbreviated files on the Colonization Assessment Team did not qualify as acquaintance. It had seemed so easy when they'd landed. Train for six weeks on Jarved Nine, spend two weeks evaluating the CAT team and report on their progress to his superiors.

He had a different kind of report to make now.

She shed no tears. Not yet. Shock still held her tightly in its grip. He took her hand and offered her the only comfort he had, the presence of another human.

A loud hum preceded the return of the lights. He watched Ravyn blink owlishly as she adjusted to the sudden brightness. Her eyes, a rare shade of light brown, appeared gold in color. With her dark hair and fair complexion, it made for a striking combination. It took him an unusually long time to shift his attention from her face. When he took in the rest of her, he realized blood covered her and saturated her clothes. Damon's gaze sharpened and he quickly, but thoroughly, checked her for injury. She appeared unharmed, but he asked, "Are you hurt?"

Her brow furrowed as she looked at him in confusion. Then she glanced down and saw the blood. As he watched what little color she had leave her face, Damon dropped her hand and slid his arm around her shoulders. "Breathe," he ordered harshly.

She obeyed, and although she sounded shaky, it kept her from keeling over. Damon let out a relieved sigh as the color crept back in her cheeks. He needed answers. Fast. He did not need his only witness to faint.

His relief did not last long.

"I need to shower," she announced and leapt to her feet.

She swayed precariously and Damon caught her before she fell. "You can't even stand unassisted," he told her, careful to keep his tone neutral. He knew she was hanging on by a thread.

"I have to shower!"

The hysteria he'd been hoping to avoid came through in every word. After weighing the options, Damon swung her up into his arms and carried her into the bathroom. He put her on her feet, briefly letting go of her to start the water, and then stripped her down to her underwear. Blood had seeped through the fabric of her clothes and dried on her skin. She broke his hold and stepped under the flowing water, but not before he made sure she had not been hurt. Damon turned away to give her what privacy he could. Her sob had him looking quickly back at her.

Ravyn had her gaze focused on the drain. When he saw the rusty-colored water, he understood her distress. His hands knotted at his impotence. There was nothing he could do to help her. He heard her take a wheezy breath and watched her tilt her head back. His eyes traced the arch of her throat, the curve of her waist and the sweet length of her legs before settling on the nearly transparent material of her bra.

When he realized he was staring at her, Damon closed the door to the shower sharply. It amazed and troubled him that he'd noticed Ravyn as a woman after what he'd seen in the other room. Damn, he thought, this wasn't the time or place to lose his edge. He couldn't allow this weakness, not with a killer running loose.

He returned to the other room and found clean, dry clothes for her to wear. Placing them on the counter in the bathing chamber, he rubbed the bridge of his nose with his left hand. They had a problem, a big problem.

Ravyn had not been responsible for the death of her team. She didn't have the physical strength needed to commit the mutilations. He and his men had only been on the planet six hours and had been together the whole time. No one had gone off alone. And there wasn't supposed to be another soul on Jarved Nine.

Who, then, had killed nineteen people?

Damon needed to check on his men and discover what they'd found, but he loathed the idea of leaving her alone. Someone or something had killed with inhuman strength.

He had to keep Ravyn safe.

He refused to fail. Not this time.

Ravyn brought the mug to her lips and sipped the hot, strong tea. Her hands shook a bit and her eyes felt swollen and sore from the tears she'd succumbed to in the shower, but she had herself under control. She watched Damon pour a cup of coffee and sit across from her. He moved easily, silently for such a big man. His presence soothed her. Something about him conveyed he could handle anything that arose.

With her training, she'd felt sure she could protect herself until she'd seen the carnage in the communal room. Until Damon had grabbed her and all knowledge of self-defense had fled her brain. She'd flailed, not fought. Ravyn let out a shuddering sigh and struggled to hang on to her control. She wouldn't cry again, she vowed. But she set the mug on the table before the hot liquid sloshed onto her fingers.

"Can you tell me what happened?" Damon asked.

Ravyn nodded and gathered herself. Captain Damon Brody, Western Alliance Spec Ops, had been remarkably gentle with her. Now the time had come to give him the answers he'd patiently waited for. "After dinner," she paused, swallowed hard and continued, "we all gathered in the communal room, but I left."

"Why?" he prompted quietly after several moments of silence.

She looked up at him, found understanding in his eyes and kept her gaze fastened there. "Sondra is, was, from Chicago and it . . . was . . . her birthday. I wanted to see if I could pick up the World Series broadcast. She was pretty excited that the Cubs had finally made it." Ravyn reached for her tea, but her hands trembled too badly to allow her to lift the mug. Instead, she fisted them on the table. "It took a while, but I thought I had the game. Then came this distortion."

"What kind of distortion?"

"I don't know." Ravyn shook her head. "I'd never heard anything like it before. I thought there might be something wrong with the equipment, so I shut it all down and ran a diagnostic. Everything in the comm room checked out."

She felt the warmth of his calloused hand on hers and she unclenched her fist, linking her fingers with his. He may not have meant to do more than pat her hand, but she needed to hold on to something, someone.

"Everything checked out, so what did you do next?"

"I, uh, turned the receiver back on, but the distortion remained. I decided I needed to find the problem and fix it right away. This is our scheduled morning to transmit to Earth."

Again, Ravyn stopped. She frowned as she tried to figure out what time it was, even what day. At some point, she had lost track. She considered asking Damon, sure he knew precisely, but decided she didn't care.

"The communications base systems are in the subbasement. I went down there to check out that equipment. I ran tests on every component I could think of, but nothing seemed out of kilter." That bothered Ravyn. She should have been able to locate what had caused the trouble.

"You couldn't find anything wrong?" the captain asked.

Ravyn shook her head. "I decided to ask Pyle, our electronics expert, to help me, but when I came back up, it was silent. I thought everyone had retired for the night. It was eerie because the lights in the corridors and the communal room are always on, but they weren't tonight, last night, whenever. I thought we'd lost power since only the emergency lights were working, but I could see other electrical appliances running. I didn't understand how that was possible."

She tightened her grip on his hand and he returned the pressure. The steadiness she could see in his green eyes anchored her, and after taking a shuddery breath, Ravyn said,

"I fell over the first body. I couldn't figure out what had tripped me at first, not with the poor lighting. Then my eyes adjusted and I could see . . . I could see . . ."

"Shhh, it's okay."

Ravyn blinked rapidly, trying to keep the tears from falling, trying to hide her weakness. He took her other hand and she looked down in surprise, but she could only see the bloodbath she had stumbled across. She talked fast, wanting this over. "Part of me, part of me knew they were dead. I mean, how could there be so much blood everywhere if they weren't? But I couldn't believe it. I went to their bodies, what remained of their bodies, and tried to find some sign of life, you know?"

"Did you see anything else?"

"Like the fiend who did it? No. I didn't hear any movement either, but I was scared whoever did this was still around. I wasn't thinking clearly," Ravyn admitted. The contempt she felt for her fainthearted behavior seeped into her voice. "I went into my quarters and cowered in the corner."

"Did anyone know you had gone to the sub-basement?"

"No. I didn't leave the facility, so I didn't have to report my movement."

"Do you know what time you went down?"

"A little past twenty-one thirty." Ravyn anticipated the next questions and answered them. "I had to walk through the communal room. Everyone was still there and fine."

He nodded. "How long were you down there?"

"I don't know," she whispered, her voice cracking. "Less than an hour. Maybe three quarters of an hour."

"When did you trigger the emergency beacon?"

Ravyn looked up at him again, confused. "I didn't trigger the emergency beacon."

"Are you sure? You didn't forget because of shock?"

"No. I never thought of it. All I could think of was finding somewhere safe."

"Shit." Damon freed his hands and reached for the radio at his waist. It stunned Ravyn that the military would send a Spec Ops team out with such ancient comm equipment. His unit even had cords connecting the receiver on his belt to the transmitter. She listened to the captain try to raise his men.

They didn't answer.

He reached his feet in a flash and held out a hand to help her up. "Come on," he ordered.

She thought he would release her as soon as she was standing, but he didn't. They moved slowly, deliberately along the corridor from the kitchen to the communal room. The sight of the weapon he held in his right hand had her adrenaline pumping. When they reached the room, it was empty, bloodstains marking the deaths of nineteen good people. She saw the wreath of white flowers lying in one of the congealing pools of blood. It had been in Sondra's hair. Until she'd fallen over her body and gotten her hand caught in the braided stems.

The urge to vomit came upon her suddenly and Ravyn swallowed hard. She couldn't be weak, not now. Something had gone wrong and Damon didn't need to be distracted by her. She could fake bravery for a little while, long enough, she hoped.

They proceeded methodically through the building, cautiously going from room to room. Ravyn remained silent and worked on keeping her breathing even. She had the same eerie sensation she had felt last night before her world had come crumbling down.

Something was very wrong.

Ravyn may not have been in the military, but she knew enough to keep her mouth shut and her eyes open. She even managed to keep from crying out in alarm when they walked into the communications room. All her equipment had been smashed. More than smashed, pulverized. Even the spares that she had stored on the shelves were a mass of tangled wires and components. She looked at Damon, trying to judge by his reaction if this was a new development. Only the tightening of his lips led her to believe the comm room had not looked like this upon his arrival. He appeared grim, but his stoicism reassured her.

They found no sign of the six men who had arrived with Damon on the first level. The basement was used primarily for storage and they searched there next. Even with all the lights ablaze, the many boxes and shelving units cast deep shadows.

Damon did let go of her hand now, but whispered almost silently, "Stay close."

Ravyn nodded. She could have told him he didn't have to worry. He could consider her his Siamese twin from now on. Before today, she had never considered the storage area to be scary, but now she found it downright terrifying. It was almost a relief not to find anything or anybody.

Almost.

"Where are the stairs to the sub-basement?" he asked, his mouth next to her ear, his words almost inaudible.

Ravyn swallowed and pointed. He gestured for her to follow. As if she needed the reminder. She practically walked on his boot heels as they went to the door. With fear warping her sense of time, it seemed to take hours to reach their destination. The supplies concealed the door to the sub-basement. It hadn't been intentional, but the most efficient placement of the various shelves had created a "hidden" doorway. No one unfamiliar with the facility would easily find it.

The door stood ajar. They remained there for a long time, listening, before Damon led the way down the stairs.

The small sub-basement required only one light fixture to illuminate the space. Ravyn knew it hooked into the emergency system. It had remained lit last night, keeping her unaware that the rest of the facility had been plunged into darkness. This room held nothing but more smashed communications equipment. Ravyn could have cried in dismay at the sight.

"We're getting out of here, now. Stay right behind me," he ordered urgently.

Squaring her shoulders, Ravyn nodded. If she had considered their movement earlier to be cautious, it was nothing compared to the vigilance and stealth Damon used now. Her nerves were ready to snap by the time they reached the first level once more.

His men were not inside the building. That left only one other place for them to be. Outside.

The rectangular structure had two entrances. Damon chose to use the one in front. She froze, afraid to so much as breathe as he listened carefully before opening the door.

Bright sunshine bombarded her. Ravyn knew the threat remained, but it seemed hard to believe anything bad could happen on such a beautiful day. They stood to the side of the door, listening intently before stepping outside. Slowly, they circled the building, but found nothing, not even a footprint.

She'd lived on Jarved Nine for months, yet suddenly, she was struck by how like Earth it was. It seemed surreal, as if this were an odd dream and she'd awaken in her bed. She pinched herself, but she still saw oksai trees, not oaks. Ravyn shook her head and forced herself to focus on where they were headed.

The three-sided structure that housed the team's land transports was set away from the facility. As they neared it, Ravyn could see all five of the rovers had been severely damaged and she stopped to stare. Damon snagged her hand once more and tugged her along. She forced herself to keep up. They had to check out the building, see if the vehicles could be repaired.

One cursory look was all she needed to know the rovers were not going to be working again. Ever. Up close, they looked like heaps of scrap metal. Damon checked each vehicle, but nothing could be salvaged. There was no sign of his men.

They continued to search the area around the facility. In the clearing on the other side of a small copse of trees, Ravyn spotted the Spec Ops team transport. It listed drunkenly to one side. Damon's grip on her hand tightened briefly as they cautiously approached it. There were huge holes punched into the fuselage. Ravyn bit her lip to keep from gasping.

This particular military transport had not only been designed to withstand direct enemy attacks on the ground or air, it also had the ability to enter and leave a planet's atmosphere. It was used to shuttle between the big space transports and whatever planet the troops needed to land on. It should have been impossible to puncture the skin of the craft with anything short of an armor-piercing laser. One set of landing rails had been pulled from the belly of the transport and twisted upward like the tip of an elf's shoe. Damon cursed softly.

Rounding the nose of the vehicle, they made their way to the entry. There were gaps where the pressure seal no longer touched the door. After a careful scan, Damon tucked his gun away and forced open the hatch. She could see his muscles straining as the door resisted his efforts. It finally gave with a groaning sound that made Ravyn wince. After taking another look around, Damon said, "Put your back against the hull and keep watch. I'll be quick, but if you see something, holler."

Ravyn nodded, and after a slight hesitation, the captain hoisted himself into the transport. She could hear him moving around, feel the craft sway. He wasn't gone long. When he dropped from the hatch to the ground, she saw his expression had become even more grim. "What did you find?" she asked.

"The inside looks worse than the outside, if you can believe that." He looked around. "Come on."

Ravyn tilted her head back and sucked in a silent breath for courage. That's when she noticed the deiril circling on the other side of the facility. Like the vultures of Earth, they scavenged the remains of dead animals. She caught Damon's attention and pointed. She didn't know how he kept from running. If it had been up to her, they would have raced to the meadow.

It seemed to take forever to reach the other clearing. And there, Ravyn saw exactly what she had feared. She quickly glanced away, but it was too late. She would have one more nightmare scene burned into her memory.

Damon's men lay lifeless in the field.

Chapter Two

Damon kept them behind the cover of the trees. Even from this distance, he knew his men were dead. Carefully, he scanned the surrounding area, watching for any movement, listening for any sound. His gut told him the danger had passed, but he confirmed it with his senses.

When he felt confident that no immediate threat existed, he turned to Ravyn. She had her back to the clearing, but she held her composure. His first inclination was to leave her where she stood while he checked the bodies. She didn't need to see any more corpses up close, but sparing her was out of the question. Separating was risky and too many people were dead to take any chances. Damn, he wished he had his assault rifle. Like the greenest recruit, he'd left it inside the CAT facility. Too late now, he thought, and put his energies toward what they had to do.

"Ravyn."

She angled her head toward him, but not far enough to see the clearing. Her body vibrated with small tremors.

"You're going to have to come with me," he told her.

For an instant she appeared blank, but as dread flowed into her eyes, he knew she understood what he asked of her.

He thought she would argue, but she drew a deep breath and nodded. Damon returned the nod and the concern he had over her reaction eased. He didn't have to tell her to hang close; she stayed right on his heels.

Damon didn't want to look at the bodies, but he pushed aside his aversion. It's no different than war, he told himself. "Watch my back," he said, his voice low.

Without waiting for Ravyn's agreement, he crouched down and examined the first corpse. Even with the eyes gouged out and blood everywhere, he recognized his second in command. He remembered how happy Spence had been that the training mission would be over in time to get them home for his daughter's first birthday. He thought of little Ginny with her shiny blond hair and her bright blue eyes. His goddaughter was going to be a heartbreaker when she got older. And she wasn't going to have a daddy to protect her. His hands fisted. He couldn't think like this.

Ruthlessly, Damon quashed his emotions and took a clinical look at the body. Along with the eyes, the tongue had been cut or pulled out, the chest ripped open and the heart removed.

Exactly the way the other nineteen had been mutilated.

It appeared the victims had been alive until their hearts had been torn out. A shudder he couldn't quite repress went through his body. It was a horrible way to die.

The idea of searching his friends made him balk, but survival, both his and Ravyn's, depended on it. Shaking off his dread, he checked for anything useful. After taking what he could, Damon picked up the chain resting on Spence's left shoulder and removed one of the two dog tags. The tag needed to be imbedded in the cranial cavity so that the body could be identified no matter what its condition when it was recovered. Damon hesitated, then forced himself to do it. He broke a tab off the tag, activating the nano-bore, and pressed it against Spence's head. The sound it emitted as it entered the skull nauseated him, but he ignored it. He heard Ravyn gasp and saw her look away, but she didn't say a word.

It didn't become easier to be dispassionate as he did the same thing with the other bodies. He tried not to think of who the corpse had once been. Tried to put thoughts of wives, children, parents, brothers and sisters out of his mind.

The bodies had been arranged in some type of order. Damon didn't understand the significance of the pattern, but he memorized its details. Later he would analyze it more closely. Some of the retrieved items he tucked into pockets, others he handed to Ravyn. She accepted everything he passed her without comment.

By the time he reached the last man, Carter, Damon moved quickly. Their exposure played a part, as did his need to finish the unpleasant task. Besides, Ravyn shook visibly now and looked a little green. As he straightened, he noticed Carter's vest remained intact and didn't have much blood on it. Respectfully, he removed it. The man hadn't been dead long enough for his muscles to stiffen, making the task relatively easy, but of all the things he'd done so far, Damon hated this the most.

"Come on," he said.

When they reached the bushes, about ninety degrees from where they'd entered the clearing, Damon took everything Ravyn held and arranged the items in the many pockets of the vest. Although none of the equipment had protected his men, he wasn't ready to write it off yet. With everything placed to his satisfaction, Damon took off his own vest and handed it to Ravyn. He knew he wouldn't get her to wear Carter's, so he didn't ask. "Put this on."

Silently, she complied, but he could see the relief in her eyes. Despite her height, his vest hung past her hips. He put on Carter's and sealed it. The sergeant had been about his size, maybe a fraction bigger, and the fit was comfortable. As long as he didn't think about how he had gotten it.

Ravyn hadn't fastened her vest. He started to issue an order, but her attention was focused across the clearing. Something about her expression stopped Damon from speaking, and he reached over and took care of it for her, then slipped a canteen strap across her chest.

Of the six men, only one had still had a pistol. He could only assume that whoever committed the mutilations had the other weapons. The ammunition, however, had not been touched and Damon had taken all of it. This oversight made about as much sense as anything else he'd encountered today.

"Damon." Ravyn had spoken his name in a soft whisper, but since it was the first word she'd said in a long time, she had his immediate attention.

"What?"

"Do you see the knapsack across the way?" She pointed directly to the other side of the clearing.

It took him a moment to locate it because shadows and long, sweeping branches concealed the drab green bag. The distance and placement made it appear the pack had been thrown. Although it was difficult to be sure, he suspected it was the comm gear that Lopez had carried. When he hadn't found it with his body, Damon had believed the killer had taken it. "I see it," he told her. "And yes, we need it."

The simplest, easiest way to reach it would be to walk across the clearing. Damon wasn't willing to give up cover again, however, so he kept to the woods. He half-expected to hear Ravyn start complaining, but she didn't and his admiration for her went up a notch.

The odds of the pack being a trap were low, Damon decided, but he wasn't taking any chances. He might have been more daring if he were on his own, but he wasn't. His jaw tightened. Putting Ravyn a safe distance behind him, he warily approached the knapsack and checked it out. When he felt sure everything was okay, Damon opened the pack and quickly scanned the contents. As he'd suspected, it contained the team's portable communications equipment. He couldn't tell how extensive the damage was, but they could figure that out later. He closed the pack and put it on, shrugging until it rested comfortably.

"Let's go."

Ravyn had passed uncomfortable hours earlier. The canteen she carried banged into her thigh with every step and the vest seemed to grow heavier with every breath. As much as she wanted to collapse, she didn't. She tried to close her mind to everything but following the man in front of her. It wasn't easy, but sometimes she could do it for minutes at a stretch. When her ability to endure weakened, she would remind herself that Damon carried a lot more than she did. And when that wasn't enough to keep her going, she would remember her family. She could almost feel them with her, prodding her forward.

Her father had been a scout. He had died doing the most dangerous job in the Alliance. It was a high-risk job today, but twenty years ago, it had been worse. Scouts were the first men down on planets able to support human life, and they determined whether a CAT team followed.

As her energy flagged, she reminded herself that few received a position on a CAT team and even fewer got off-world assignments. She had been given both. Ravyn forced her feet to keep moving. For a split second, she thought she saw her father nod his head in approval, but she blinked and he disappeared.

It was monsoon season in this area of Jarved Nine and patches of ground remained boggy from yesterday's late afternoon downpour. Damon went around the small patches of muddy earth, but when they hit a big spot that would take too much time to avoid, they went through it. The one they tromped through now seemed unending. The mud sucked at her feet, trying to trap her. She had to pull her boots out of the muck with each step. If she'd had the breath, she would have been cursing.

Sweat ran into her eyes, burning them, but she didn't have the energy to lift her hand and wipe her brow. Under the vest, perspiration soaked her shirt. Her muscles screamed, begging for her to stop. Maybe if she rested, just for a minute . . .

Marie Verdier Sullivan hadn't raised her daughter to quit when things got tough. Her mother had been a doctor on the front lines of the Oceanic Wars and in the thick of battle. She had tended soldiers with bullets whizzing over her head. Ravyn could swear she saw her mother, heard her urging her on. On another day, that might have worried her, since her mother had died with her stepfather twelve years ago, but not when it took all she had to remain on her feet.

Damon glanced over his shoulder, not breaking stride. He'd done that off and on to verify she still tagged along behind him. The heavy humidity made her feel she couldn't take a full breath. She gasped for air with each step, and he wasn't even breathing hard. The man wasn't human, she decided cantankerously.

No, he's Spec Ops.

Ravyn stumbled and caught her balance. She'd lost it. That voice belonged to her stepfather. Muscle fatigue must be bringing on hallucinations; that had to be why she heard and saw dead people. First her father and mother, now her stepfather.

A louder squish than usual had her looking down. She grimaced when she saw mud oozing to the top of her boots. It took extra effort to free herself and then she had to run to catch up with Damon. She felt a stitch begin in her side. Think about something else, she told herself.

She'd been so young when her father had died that, except for a stray memory or two, her only knowledge of him came from pictures and the stories her mother had written down for her. She remembered his smile and how he would sit for hours with her playing tea party, but not much else.

Her stepfather, Gil, was much clearer in her mind. He had been Spec Ops too. She made a face at Damon's back, still irritated by his tirelessness. Ravyn winced when she imagined she heard Gil laughing at her childish expression.

Mom had met Gil when he'd helped bring in the remaining members of an ambushed patrol. All of them had been injured. Gil had always downplayed his part in the rescue, but Ravyn had looked up to him with awestruck eyes anyway. No matter what he said, she knew he'd been a hero.

Just like her father.

They reached dry land again and Ravyn could have dropped to her knees and kissed the ground. Her heartfelt relief didn't last long. They started going uphill. It wasn't steep, the terrain around the facility was mostly flat, but after all her body had already endured, it might as well have been a mountain. The thick undergrowth grabbed her ankles and slapped at her body. Ravyn ducked under the branch Damon held for her and barely kept from groaning as she straightened. As soon as she was clear, he continued on. She bit back a whimper and followed.

Good girl.

Thanks, Gil. Ravyn decided to go with the hallucinations. They helped and she enjoyed "seeing" her family again anyway. Gil had been a great dad. She had been as devastated by his death as that of her mother. The only family she had left was Alex.

Thinking of Alex brought a smile to her face. Guilt quickly wiped it away. How could she smile? Tears started to fill her eyes and Ravyn blinked hard until she'd beaten them back. Think of something else, she told herself. She couldn't remember. Not now. Not when falling apart could endanger Damon's life.

Ten years her senior, Gil's son hadn't wanted a little sister. It hadn't taken long, though, before she'd had him playing dolls with her. If her stepfather was home, he would join in. Ravyn's lips twitched. Just thinking of sixteen-year-old Alex and Gil, the grizzled warrior, sitting on the floor with dolls in their hands made her want to laugh. When she recalled the time Alex's friends had shown up and caught him, she wanted to roar. He had been sitting alone, surrounded by all her dolls and their accoutrements, while she had run up to her room to get another outfit. She knew he'd been harassed unmercifully after that day, but he'd still played with her when she'd asked.

Big brothers like that didn't come along every day.

And eight years later, when her mother and his father had died, Alex had finished raising her. It would have been easier for him to let strangers take her. He had followed his father into Spec Ops and though they'd been between wars, there had still been skirmishes and clandestine missions.

She wondered if Damon and Alex knew each other.

Her smile faded completely as she questioned whether she'd see Alex again. Just as he was the last of her family, she was the last of his. It would kill something inside him if she died too. With renewed determination, Ravyn grit her teeth and followed Damon. She wasn't going to die. Not from physical exertion and not from some monster murderer. And when she heard Gil say "good girl" again, she nodded her head sharply and continued walking.

Damon looked at Ravyn and frowned. She lay flat on her back, taking deep breaths. The wheezing had stopped, thank God. He wasn't angry with her, but she sure as hell should have told him she was having difficulty. He'd pushed them hard, wanted them as far away from the carnage as they could get, but they could have taken a few rest stops along the way. When she hadn't complained, he had assumed she could handle the pace he'd set.

He should have known better.

He had a good eight inches on her. What he considered a brisk pace would have been close to jogging for her. And she'd kept up with him through the rough terrain without complaining, without whining, without slowing them down.

She was one hell of a woman.

"Think you can sit up now?" he asked when her breathing approached normal.

She did it without his help, but he didn't miss the way she flinched. Hell, he thought, he'd already screwed up and a full day hadn't passed. Apparently, he hadn't learned a damn thing. Wordlessly, he passed her his canteen. She sipped the water slowly. When she passed it back to him, he drank too, then put the cap on again.

"You should have told me you were having trouble." He kept his tone even with effort.

"We needed to put as much distance between us and the facility as possible."

"Yeah, we did," he agreed, "but we could have done it without pushing you to this point. You've got to be able to walk tomorrow."

"I will."

He admired her determination, but she'd be lucky if she could stand, let alone walk, by morning. Damon knew he wasn't going to push her any more today, even though they had enough daylight left to add a couple more kilometers to their total. Running a hand across his mouth and chin, he considered the situation. They needed food and they needed sleep. He took another look around and knew they couldn't stay here. There were too many ways for someone to approach them undetected.

He'd studied maps of Jarved Nine extensively before leaving Earth and had the big picture down, but he still wished he had a map now. Hell, there were a lot of things he wished he had. Nothing had survived the fury unleashed in the transport and it had been too dangerous to go back to the facility for any reason.

That nineteen people had been killed without one of them running away or having defense wounds was bad enough. CAT team members didn't have the training to deal with the massacre that had taken place. It was in the realm of possibility, no matter how slight, that they had panicked and been picked off like sitting ducks. His men, however, weren't just military. They were Special Operations and had received training far beyond the average soldier. His men had been in combat, not one member was green, and yet the death toll on Jarved Nine had gone up by six.

All of them had taken the situation seriously when the beacon had deployed. Especially after he'd mentioned he had a bad feeling about it. They'd gone into the building by the book and on full alert. There was a zone you hit in war, when sounds became magnified, vision sharpened and the rapport between teammates became nearly psychic. After finding the bodies, the seven of them had automatically switched into that mode.

His men had been finishing up in the communal room when Damon had walked with Ravyn to the kitchen. They'd stopped what they'd been doing out of consideration for her. All of them had seemed to realize how shaky she'd been. How long had it taken for the water to come to a boil for her tea? He knew it couldn't have taken much more than ten, maybe fifteen minutes for Ravyn to tell him what had occurred at the CAT facility.

He tried to recall when he had stopped hearing the sounds his men had made as they went about their duties but couldn't. There had been nothing to tip him off that there was a problem.

Damon scowled. He hadn't heard the comm equipment being smashed. No way could that have been done silently. He hadn't heard his men leave the building. The kitchen was on the side nearest the clearing. The prefab wall shouldn't have been able to block all noise, yet he hadn't heard his men being murdered. If they had managed to get a shot off before being stripped of their weapons, he hadn't heard that either.

How could he not hear anything, not see anything? How could he not realize there was a situation until Ravyn had told him she hadn't set off the emergency beacon? It didn't make sense.

Crossing one booted foot across the other, Damon tried to sort out his thoughts. The murderer had been close enough to lure his men outside, yet he hadn't searched the building. If he had, he and Ravyn would be dead now too.

Somehow the killer had made it to the sub-basement. The only stairs were in the kitchen, which meant he had to have been in the facility while he and his men were there. Yet no one had noticed anything. They'd searched the entire structure while he'd watched over Ravyn. Nothing should have been able to escape their notice. Somehow the killer had eluded his men. But how? They'd searched in teams and the layout of the place didn't lend itself to sneaking past anyone into an area that had already been checked out. He didn't like it. He didn't like it at all.

Damon rubbed his eyes. He was giving himself a headache trying to work this all out. What should have been impossible had happened. He wasn't going to be able to make sense of it, but he did have to factor all these puzzles into his plans.

He looked over at Ravyn again. She had her back propped against a tree and her eyes closed. How was he supposed to tell her that they had to walk a little farther? As if she felt his scrutiny, her eyes opened and she looked at him. For a moment, they stared, measuring each other, then Ravyn said, "What?"

Damon hesitated, hating to say the words. "We can't stay

here." He read the dismay on her face before Ravyn banished it. Then she looked around, and when she turned back to him, she appeared resigned.

"We need a more defensible position," she said.

"Yes."

"Damon?"

"What?" he prompted when she didn't continue.

"Do you have a destination in mind or are we just running?"

The corners of his lips tilted up in a slight smile. "We're heading for the Old City."

Ravyn's eyes widened. He didn't blame her. Even in a transport or rover, it was a long journey and they were on foot. It would take them days to reach it walking the quickest route and they weren't going to be taking any obvious paths.

"Come on. Let's find somewhere to settle for the night and I'll tell you why we're heading there," Damon said.

He held out a hand and she stared at him for a moment before accepting his assistance. He pulled her to her feet, doing most of the work to spare her overused muscles. Her knees buckled as soon as she stood and Damon quickly slipped his arm around her waist until she had her legs back under her. He could see the red flare of embarrassment across her cheekbones.

"My legs feel like cooked noodles," she told him, her voice apologetic.

"I know, sweet pea. I pushed you too hard today. Once we find somewhere safer, you won't have to move again till morning."

"Sweet pea?"

Now it was his turn to be embarrassed. Damon started walking, pretending not to hear her question. He didn't know where the endearment had come from himself. He kept his pace slow, despite his desire to be out of earshot.

She didn't say another word.

Ravyn frowned down at the comm equipment. Damon had lugged most of it for no reason. The transmitter was missing from the radio, so they couldn't send a spoken message to

Earth and the long-range emergency beacon was mangled, something that should have been impossible. The lightweight case consisted of an alloy stronger than steel, yet it had been crushed and twisted as easily as a piece of paper. She decided not to dwell on what had that kind of strength.

"Do we have any tools?" Ravyn asked, her voice subdued.

Damon was off on the perimeter, setting up the warning system. Each Boundary Alert System module, more commonly referred to as BAS, emitted a frequency connecting it to the next device. If anything crossed between them, the connection was broken and an alarm would go off. The four units they had didn't cover much ground, Ravyn decided as she eyed the small area. Anything trespassing would be on top of them almost before they could react. Not exactly a reassuring thought.

When he finished, he came over and crouched in front of her. He moved easily, while her legs felt like she had lead in her pants. Life was so unfair. Then she remembered how lucky she was to be alive and couldn't believe she was complaining about being tired. Any of the twenty-five people who had died would be more than happy to change places with her.

"What's the prognosis?"

"Not good," Ravyn told him. "The only thing that I may be able to fix is the short-range beacon."

"What's wrong with the emergency beacon?"

Ravyn pointed to the twisted metal.

"Hell."

Damon the Tireless started to look weary. Ravyn guessed she'd passed weary at least ten hours ago and edged on comatose now. Still, it was discouraging to be so cut off. The weak signal from the short range beacon could only be picked up by someone already on the planet.

He reached for the vest she had left lying beside her, and pulled out what looked to be an antique pocket knife. "No tools. This is it."

Ravyn took the gadget from him. She'd work with what she had and hope it was enough. "Does this thing have something I can use to undo the screws on the casing?"

Damon took the knife back and pulled out one of the components before returning it. "Screwdriver slash can opener," he told her, his tone matter-of-fact.

"Thanks. This looks old." She concentrated on removing the protective covering from the short-range beacon. The knife felt awkward in her hand. She was used to the sleek, small tools she usually worked with.

"It belonged to my grandfather. He gave it to me when I joined up."

When Ravyn was able to examine the beacon more closely, she grimaced.

"How bad is it?"

"It's fixable," Ravyn said, looking up at him. "It's going to take a while, though. The question is, do we want to fix it?"

"Yes."

"How long before help arrives on Jarved Nine?"

Damon sat facing her. "The emergency transmission we picked up was from the facility's long-range beacon. It takes approximately thirty-six hours for a signal to travel from here to Earth. They'll try to contact the CAT team by radio and my superiors will try to contact my team. It depends on how long they wait for a response before launching a rescue team. My guess is three to five days."

"It'll take them more than a month to get here." Sheer willpower kept the despair out of her words.

Damon smiled slightly. "Not quite that long. This will be a military operation and our ships move a little faster."

Ravyn figured that was an understatement, but didn't press for a more exact answer. She doubted she would get one anyway. "What about the ship you came in on? Won't the crew hear our distress call first?"

Damon shook his head. "We traveled on an automated cargo ship destined for Cymara. We launched the transport when we were close enough to Jarved Nine."

"And automated ships don't respond to emergency beacons."

"No point in it."

"No," Ravyn agreed. "How were you getting back?" Maybe a ship was already en route to pick up the Spec Ops team.

"Automated cargo ship from Cymara to Earth with a quick stop here to pick us up. The ship's not due for about two months. The rescue team will reach us first, but it doesn't matter. You saw how damaged the transport was."

So they waited for the rescue team. Even if the military had ships that could travel in half the time of the CAT team ship, and Ravyn would not be surprised if they did, help was still almost three weeks away. She looked down at the short-range beacon for a minute, then back up at Damon.

"I don't think we should trigger this until help is here."

"Why?" he asked. His voice sounded noncommittal, but Ravyn had the impression he agreed with her, that he wanted to hear her reasoning. It made sense he'd want to know how her mind worked. The more he knew about how she thought and how she acted, the easier it would be for him to predict her behavior in a crisis situation and that might save both of their lives.

A quick replay of what he'd seen of her so far flashed through her head. She willed herself not to flush in mortification as she remembered him finding her hiding under her bunk like a child. Wouldn't Alex have been proud of her if he'd seen her cowering in fear? Almost as soon as the thought crossed her mind, Ravyn knew it wasn't fair. Alex would want her to stay alive any way she could.

"Because I didn't set off the beacon at the facility. I think whoever killed the rest of the CAT team did it to lure in anyone else on Jarved Nine."

"And since he knows our communications systems, he could track us," Damon added.

"Instead of alerting our rescuers," Ravyn said, "this could be broadcasting our exact position to the murderer."

Chapter Three

She was calm.

Too calm, and that made him edgy.

He kept waiting for her to crumble, but it wasn't happening.

With one eye on Ravyn, Damon finished stowing the last of their meager equipment. He'd taken each item out of the vests, checked its condition and then tucked it away again. After jettisoning the broken comm equipment from the pack, he'd been able to make Ravyn's vest much lighter for tomorrow's journey.

Dusk encroached, but Ravyn, her brows furrowed, still worked on the short-range beacon. She muttered something under her breath and Damon fought a smile. He sobered quickly as he wondered if he'd become too desensitized. How could he find anything amusing after what he'd seen today?

Damon had been trained to compartmentalize. He had fought in the last Oceanic War and in various flare-ups since. He had watched friends, acquaintances and strangers die and he had been responsible for the deaths of others. As part of a team sent on an intel mission to one of the prison camps, he had seen men who had been tortured. And he had seen the bodies of men who had not survived the torture. His background gave him the ability to push aside what he'd witnessed until he had the time and safety to look at it. But even so, he found it disquieting that he could forget, even for a second, what had happened on Jarved Nine. Ravyn didn't have his experience. She shouldn't be this self-controlled. It made him wonder when she would break.

Maybe exhaustion numbed her.

It had been more than thirty hours since he'd had any rest and Damon knew, from her account of events, Ravyn was just as sleep deprived. Not that he wanted a sobbing woman on his hands, but her self-possession was unnatural.

Damon mentally cataloged their weapons. Two pistols and his Swiss army knife. Not exactly the firepower he would have liked, but he had a feeling an arsenal wouldn't be enough against this thing. Regardless, he still couldn't believe, he'd left his assault rifle in Ravyn's room. It was a rookie mistake.

"That should do it," Ravyn said, recapturing his attention.

"It's working?"

"Yes." She didn't spare him a glance, her concentration focused on tightening the screws of the casing. When she finished, she closed his knife and pushed herself to her feet, her movements slow and awkward, her walk resembling that of Frankenstein's monster. Her face revealed nothing, however, of her stiffness or achy muscles. Damon rose and crossed his arms over his chest, watching. He could have met her, saved her a few steps, but she'd glared at him when he'd stood. Stubborn.

Damon took the knife she handed him and slipped it in a pocket. She held the pack open while he put the beacon inside and sealed it. Ravyn stood in front of him, only an arm's length away, and he felt the oddest buzzing sensation in his body. Lack of sleep, he decided, quickly taking a step back and clearing his throat. "You hungry?" he asked.

"Do we have anything to eat?"

He passed her an energy bar. "We've got four of 'em. After breakfast tomorrow, we'll be eating what we can find."

Ravyn opened her bar and took a bite. She tried to conceal

it, but he caught the slight grimace she made.

"Yeah, they're not exactly delicious, but they're packed with nutrients. Have some water with it. That'll help."

She took the canteen he handed her, but sat down before opening it. Her lips thinned as she lowered herself to the dirt. Yeah, he thought, she'd begun to tighten up.

He waited until they had finished eating before asking, "How much do you hurt? Honestly."

"I'm stiff," she admitted. "I'll probably be moving slow when we first start out, but it'll wear off as we walk."

"You'll be even stiffer after sleeping on the ground tonight. Do you really think you'll be able to walk tomorrow?"

Her chin came up; her eyes flashed. "Yes."

Damon swallowed a smile. He knew she wouldn't appreciate it. "Okay, but don't play martyr on me again. When I'm pushing you too hard, you tell me."

"Yes, sir!" She managed a crisp salute, although the effect was blunted since she remained sitting.

This time he couldn't contain the smile. "Smart ass. Give me your feet."

"Why?" she asked, her eyes narrowing in suspicion.

"That's the problem with civilians," he said conversationally. "They don't know how to follow orders without asking a bunch of questions first."

He reached for her feet and untied her boots. Clumps of dirt scattered to the ground as he worked. He half-expected her to jerk her legs away, but she didn't.

"You know," she told him after he'd removed her right shoe, "I recall following orders all day without asking any questions."

"You did well." He didn't mention that shock had probably played a huge role in her obedience. There was no point in reminding her of the massacre. Damon got the second boot off. He figured he'd have his hands full with her now that she'd regained her hold on herself.

She leaned back on her elbows as he checked for blisters or cuts, anything that might cause trouble down the road. "Your feet are fine," he told her, relieved that her boots had been so well broken in. He put her socks back on and started to rub one of her feet. Damon had to admire her self-restraint. Her eyes closed, her entire body seemed to melt, but she didn't make a sound. At least not right away. When he switched feet, she couldn't contain a small purr of pleasure. After that, she relaxed totally, not even trying to remain propped up.

"Roll over," he told her, "and I'll finish massaging you."

Ravyn complied without arguing. Damon worked his way up her legs. He could feel when he hit a particularly painful spot and he took extra time and care then. She'd still be sore tomorrow, but he hoped his ministrations helped a little. When he reached her butt, he hesitated. Damon figured she ached there too, but man, it was a little personal to rub a woman's backside. Especially a woman you'd just met. Of course, it hadn't exactly been an ordinary day. Straddling her legs, he tentatively rubbed her glutes. When she didn't object, his touch became firmer, more certain. Ravyn murmured softly, sighed and went totally limp.

Damon made his way up her body. Now and then, she would make a little noise of appreciation, but by the time he reached her shoulders, those had stopped. He continued kneading her muscles even though he knew she'd fallen asleep. It was one of life's little ironies, he decided. Ravyn was utterly boneless, and he couldn't remember a time when he'd been harder. His lips quirked up sardonically, and he eased off to her side.

Wrong place, wrong time.

He had to keep this unexpected attraction in check. It was too dangerous to do anything else. Thinking below the belt left a man vulnerable, and they were in a situation that left no room for distractions. Damon ran a hand over his chin and sighed silently. Pursuing any kind of physical relationship with Ravyn right now would be dishonorable. She was still reeling from what had happened and she already relied on him, was grateful to him. He didn't want her for any of those reasons. And he didn't want her because she needed to reaffirm she lived.

Maybe when they were back on Earth and enough time had passed for her to get her feet back underneath her, he would look her up and see what they had. With his body back in control, Damon glanced over at Ravyn. Even dirty with tangled hair, she looked beautiful. Yeah, he decided, once they were back on Earth, he'd find her, see if she shared his interest. But for now, he would protect her, keep her safe, until help arrived. He refused to consider the possibility that they might not make it back to Earth.

He wished at least one of his men had survived. It would make protecting her easier if he had another soldier to keep watch. As it stood, he had to put his trust in his ability to wake if he heard anything out of the ordinary. Not that he knew what constituted normal here on Jarved Nine. Still, he had no choice but to rest; he needed the sleep. Damon moved farther from where Ravyn lay and settled down for the night. Although the sun had set, it remained stifling hot, the humidity high. He closed his eyes, forced himself to relax and fell asleep.

The Old City had been built approximately three thousand years ago. Its existence remained a secret to most people. The rulers of the Western Alliance were concerned there would be panic if it were known alien life not only existed, but had created an elaborate city this close to Earth. They believed society, as it was now, would topple. Ravyn thought their concerns misplaced.

Damon had never explained why they headed for the Old City and she hadn't asked, not when looking at him made her blush. He'd only been trying to help her last night, she knew that, but it made her uncomfortable to remember the sounds she'd made as he'd touched her. At least until she fell asleep. Man, she hoped she hadn't drooled or snored. Ravyn winced a bit at the thought. Besides she knew why they headed for the city. It was surrounded by a thick, high wall with limited access points. Buildings provided cover, shelter and places to hide. It was also somewhere the rescue team would think to look for them.

When she'd had free time and had been able to help other members of the CAT team, she had frequently worked with Jason, the team's archeologist. The Old City fascinated

Ravyn, drawing her to it in a way she couldn't explain. From the first day she'd set foot inside its boundaries, she'd dreamed of the place, of the people who'd inhabited it.

The stone buildings and everything within the walls remained perfectly preserved. Vegetation had not overgrown the city and animals had not moved into the abandoned complex. A phenomenon that had interested Jason endlessly, but Ravyn found the sheer size of the compound just as curious. At one point, there had been somewhere between twenty and fifty thousand inhabitants. From what she'd seen, it looked as if they'd just walked away for a moment and would be back. She saw no signs these people had abandoned their colony and returned to their home world.

Now Ravyn couldn't help wondering if the monster had played some part in their absence. But even as she had the thought, she decided she was being paranoid. Killing twenty-five people was one thing, but thousands?

Damon moved slower today, and she found it easier to keep pace with him. It remained hot and sticky, but the weather wouldn't turn cooler for months yet. Without the distraction of struggling to match his stride, it became more difficult to keep thoughts of her friends out of her mind.

When he'd given her a shake that morning to wake her, Ravyn's first inclination had been to close her eyes and go back to sleep. She'd never been a morning person, and while the sky had begun to lighten, dawn had still been a ways off. Then the memories had flooded her, brutal and painful. She'd wanted to wail, but was too aware of Damon's eyes on her. Digging her nails into her palms, she'd fought off her memories. She had to focus on one thing and one thing only.

Survival.

It had taken every ounce of willpower Ravyn had to push herself to her feet. Her whole body hurt. She ached in places she'd never realized she had muscles. But the soreness had given her something to think about besides her team. Damon, of course, had known she hurt despite her efforts to conceal the pain. He hadn't made any comments, but she could tell by the look on his face that he expected her to have a lot of difficulty today.

He was only partially right.

She was in much better shape than he knew. Alex had put her through her paces mercilessly before giving her his blessing to join the CAT team. He'd developed a training program much more rigorous than anything the Colonization Assessment Teams had expected of her. Granted, she had slacked off since arriving on Jarved Nine, but she'd kept up enough so her aches were a minor discomfort, not a debilitating agony. Now that they'd been walking for a couple of hours, she felt only twinges.

Damon moved with a fluid agility Ravyn could only admire. She'd never learned to walk with the stealth he displayed, but she did her best to emulate his movements. The concentration this required was another way to keep her thoughts at bay.

As the day progressed, it gradually seeped into her consciousness that Damon was hyper-alert. It puzzled her for a moment until she recognized he'd taken on the full burden of their safety. Ravyn frowned as she realized he had to. She might as well be on a nature hike. She had no military training, but she'd lived with Gil and Alex long enough to have some idea what to do. Already, she tread more silently; now she started to pay attention to her surroundings. Maybe she couldn't fight by his side, but she sure as heck could watch his back.

He had a gorgeous back.

Ravyn almost hummed aloud in appreciation before the thought registered. How could she notice Damon's looks when her friends were dead? When her life was on the line? And how had she missed noticing the man was too good-looking for words?

She gave her head a good hard shake. Okay, he'd come to her rescue, he was protecting her and she'd taken relief and gratitude and changed them into something else. Now that she knew what was going on, she could fight it. But when he bent over to duck under a low branch, Ravyn found it impossible to ignore the sight in front of her. She felt her body temperature rise. It was a good thing she was able to walk under the limb without difficulty. Now that she'd become aware of him, Ravyn couldn't seem to take her eyes off Damon.

She could have growled in frustration. Focus, she told herself, you're his backup. It took a great deal of effort, but finally she brought her attention back to Jarved Nine. Ravyn registered the sound of animals scurrying away from them and the soft rustle of leaves as the wind gently caressed them.

The fresh smell of flowers overpowered the faint odor of rotting vegetation. Ravyn took a deep breath and glanced up. The sun rode high in the sky with no clouds to temper the strength of the rays beating down on them. It had to be about noon, and although the daily afternoon thundershowers remained hours off, the humidity had become nearly unbearable.

Her stomach rumbled loudly and Ravyn put her hand over it in a belated attempt to muffle the sound. Damon looked back and she smiled in embarrassment, but forced herself to meet his gaze. Even at this distance she could see the humor twinkling in his eyes as he drew to a halt. Reluctantly, she stopped a few feet away and waited for some smart remark. Heaven knew Alex wouldn't be able to resist. Probably something about her stomach giving away their position, she guessed.

"How familiar are you with what's edible?" he asked.

Ravyn was so surprised by Damon's question that it took her a minute to answer. "I'm the one who transmitted the information and images that Sondra gathered. She was our botanist. I don't know how much I remember, though."

Mentioning Sondra brought home what she'd been trying so hard not to think about. It alarmed her how quickly she was able to refer to her friend in the past tense. Hastily, Ravyn looked away from Damon and regrouped. He needed her to hold together. She *would* hold together.

"We studied everything sent to Earth before coming here," Damon told her. "I know what's what, but I want you to watch closely. If anything happens to me, you need to know what you can eat and what could kill you."

Ravyn's first inclination was to deny anything would happen to him. She didn't even want to consider that possibility. But she knew he was right. If the unthinkable occurred and she was on her own, she would need every advantage to survive. She'd be the only one left to tell what had happened. If Damon planned to sacrifice himself for her, though, he'd better think again. She knew he'd do everything he could to protect her, to give her a chance to get away, but no matter the trouble she would never abandon him, she vowed fiercely.

When she focused on Damon again, she realized he was waiting for a response. "I'll pay attention," she said, "but you better not let anything happen to you."

"If the situation deteriorates, I expect you to follow orders." He scowled down at her.

Ravyn met the intensity in his eyes without wavering. He had a formidable presence, but she had experience with forceful men. She'd been around them her entire life. And she'd always wound each one around her little finger. When she smiled up at him sweetly, he cursed and looked away. But not before she'd seen the flare of desire in his eyes. It wiped the smile off her face.

Apparently, the attraction was mutual.

That made things more difficult. He fought it; she could see that by the rigidity in his body. She fought it, telling herself it was the circumstances. The timing couldn't be worse. They were running for their lives, possibly being stalked. Yet knowing he shared her interest set her pulse racing.

Like waves lapping against walls of sand, she knew it wouldn't take much to undermine their control. The desire she had seen in his eyes still had tingles coursing through her body. He didn't know it was mutual. Yet. But how long would it take someone trained to be observant to notice?

When he pointed to the first plant and started explaining which part was edible and which parts were not, Ravyn breathed a sigh of relief. If he hadn't broken the spell, she might have done something stupid, like sway toward him. She knew he'd be asking questions later, so she paid close attention as he led her from tree to tree, plant to plant, collecting food. It was the way Spec Ops were trained. They lectured first, then tested to make sure the information had been absorbed. Alex had done the same thing when he'd given her self-defense lessons.

Sure enough, as they ate, Damon quizzed her. Although she answered correctly, Ravyn couldn't work up any enthusiasm. Some of the fruit and vegetables they ate, she recognized from the dinner table at the facility. A lump lodged in her throat as she remembered how Jason liked to put sugar on the pink fruit she held in her hand. That Pyle poured ketchup on cooked lanurr roots. The team had supplemented the supplies they'd brought from Earth with local plants. Their availability would play a role in the final determination whether or not to colonize the planet.

Ravyn guessed Jarved Nine would not be colonized. She doubted the Western Alliance had ever been serious about that. Not with the Old City giving testimony of alien civilization. More likely the CAT team had been sent to check out the planet for the teams the military would send. With another war on the horizon, finding alien technology increased in importance. For various reasons, neither side had been invested enough resources in their militaries, but if the alliance discovered advanced weaponry and did some reverse engineering, they had the advantage without spending much money.

Even if the Alliance had been sincere, no one would be willing to come here now. Something about mass murder tended to put settlers off. She swallowed hard and clenched her hand until fruit juice started to drip from her fingers to the ground.

Desperate to get her mind off the deaths, she looked at Damon, studying him. Nothing except his size had registered until today. He wore his dark hair short. That was no surprise given his military affiliation, but he did wear it longer on top than regulations allowed. He had his eyes closed, concealing his alert gaze, but she could picture his moss green irises easily. With a little concentration she could even recall the gold flecks that made her think he had a wicked sense of humor. Someday, maybe there would even be something to laugh about again.

Unwilling to explore that maudlin thought, she moved on in her study of Captain Damon Brody. Ravyn knew it was cliché to use the word "chiseled" in relation to a person, but that description immediately came to mind when she considered his jaw. He had no stubble and she found that mildly surprising. Most men didn't bother to have their facial hair permanently removed.

His full lips tilted up slightly at the corners. She could almost feel his mouth on hers. A shudder made her aware of just how long she'd been staring, and she quickly checked to make sure Damon wasn't watching her watch him. His eyes remained closed and she sighed in relief. It would be too embarrassing to be caught staring. Still, she couldn't quite tear her gaze from his face. Even the slash of dirt across one high cheekbone added to his allure.

That smudge reminded her of where they were and she forced herself to stop ogling Damon. She looked down at the hands in her lap. Her fingers were dirty and sticky, her nails caked with dried mud. Rubbing did nothing to eliminate the grime, but she wasn't going to ask for water to clean up. Jarved Nine was full of fresh water, and at some point, they'd run into a huge pool of it. Then she could wash her hands, her body, and she grimaced, her clothes. It was alarming in a way to have nothing but the clothes on your back and what you carried in your pockets. To know she couldn't run to the storeroom to get what she needed.

Ravyn fought back the rising panic.

Why did she do that to herself? Didn't she have enough to worry about without letting her imagination scare her?

"Are you okay?"

Damon's voice cut into her thoughts and she took a deep breath, clearing her mind before she dared to look up. "I'm okay," she told him and even managed to sound convincing. She couldn't let him know of her cowardice.

"We need to get going."

Ravyn shoved herself to her feet. She couldn't move as gracefully as Damon, but she didn't hurt right now either.

They started walking and she was grateful not to be leading the way. Her sense of direction had deserted her. Damon, however, strode with the assurance of someone who knew his precise location.

They walked through the mercifully brief afternoon thundershowers and they kept walking until twilight. When Damon finally called a halt for the night, Ravyn let out a silent sigh of relief. She was tired. Bone tired. She wanted nothing more than to collapse on the ground as she had the night before, but refused to allow herself the indulgence. No way could she continue to allow Damon to shoulder the entire burden.

With care for her aching muscles, Ravyn slipped the vest from her body and let it slide to the ground. She felt cooler, lighter without that extra weight covering her torso. Her pants remained damp from the rain and she plucked the material away from her right thigh with a grimace. When she roused herself from her discomfort, Ravyn noticed that Damon had started setting the perimeter monitors again. She watched him for a moment, but figured her inexperience would be a detriment to their security. There was something she could do, though.

"Damon, I'm going to hunt us up some dinner."

He straightened in a hurry and scowled at her. For a minute, she felt sure he'd tell her to stay put. Then he seemed to reconsider and said, "Just make sure you stay close."

"I will," Ravyn promised.

At first she tried to stay within sight of him, but she couldn't find anything edible. She paused and decided remaining within hearing distance would comply with his orders. But as soon as she could no longer see Damon, she felt the panic begin to rise. Her heart pounded; her breathing became fast and shallow; her vision blurred. Ravyn stopped and forced herself to take deep breaths. Nothing indicated danger nearby so why did she react this way?

The answer came with a suddenness that almost jolted her. The last time she had been separated from the others, everyone else had died. When Damon had become separated from his men, they had died. Now she was separated from Damon.

"Okay, Ravyn," she whispered to herself, "get the food collected. The longer you dawdle, the greater the risk."

After taking a few more deep breaths, she looked around. This time her vision cleared enough to spot the purple fruit of the kahloo tree. Not only edible, but delicious. But the thought of moving twenty meters farther from camp paralyzed her.

It would take a while for the adrenaline to quit flowing, but that didn't mean she couldn't function through the fear. You did what you had to do. Ravyn knew that. How many times had she heard someone in her family say those very words? She had to get to the kahloo tree. Even though her legs shook, she took the first step. By the time she reached the tree, her entire body trembled. Ravyn wanted to wrap her arms around the trunk and sink to the ground until the spasms passed, but she knew that wasn't an option. Damon would come after her before too much longer and she didn't want him to see her lost in terror.

Wiping sweat born of fear from her brow, Ravyn reached up for the nearest kahloo fruit. She had to blink several times to clear her eyes enough to see it was undamaged by insects or animals. She had nothing to carry the fruit back to camp with so Ravyn untucked her shirt, and holding on to the tail with one hand, loaded their dinner in the concave depression the material made. When there was no more room, she turned to go back.

She froze. She didn't know which direction to head.

The panic bubbled up again, but she beat it back. People got into trouble by giving in to fear. She knew she wasn't far from camp and if she didn't return, Damon would look for her. Ravyn calmed herself and listened intently. The captain moved quietly at all times, but he wasn't completely soundless. She hoped to hear some rustle, some clue as to his direction. The idea of having to be rescued mere meters from where they were spending the night was too humiliating to contemplate.

Alex would rip her up one side and down the other for

being so careless. She knew Damon wouldn't be so harsh with her. He didn't realize she knew any more than what the CAT teams were taught, but he wouldn't let her go off alone again. And he would begin to view her not only as incapable of helping, but as a liability.

The idea of being regarded as an even bigger burden than she already was allowed Ravyn to push aside the hysteria and think. The ground, while not wet, wasn't all that dry either. There should be some kind of sign that she passed through. It only took a minute or two of studying the area around her before she spotted a slight impression from her boot. The relief she felt nearly overwhelmed her, but she ignored that too. Sometimes she had to look quite far before she spotted a footprint or a crushed plant, but she always managed to find some sign of which direction to take.

Ravyn was so intent on searching for the next marker, she almost didn't realize when she was within sight of Damon again. Almost. It was as if a sixth sense told her he was near. She could feel the tingling on the back of her neck, and when she looked over, there he was. He glanced behind him at the same time and their eyes met. "I'm almost done," he said. "Step carefully."

Ravyn nodded, but was afraid to say a word. She wasn't sure her voice wouldn't give her away. Even if it was only a slight wobble, Damon would pick up on it and question her. No way was she going to admit how helpless she had felt.

It took him only minutes to finish the job, but in that time, she managed to compose herself. He sat beside her, picked up one of the pieces of fruit she had collected and sliced it in half with his knife. He handed one section to her and took the other for himself. Ravyn accepted the juicy purple fruit without hesitation, but the dirt on her hands made her want to cringe. She knew better than to ask for water to wash up though. Water might be plentiful on Jarved Nine, but they weren't camped next to it now and there was no point wasting their drinking supply.

"Damon," she said, after finishing her third half of kahloo fruit, "I need a bath. I know we're not exactly on a pleasure trip, but what are the chances of cleaning up?"

Despite it being more dark than light at this time of the evening, Ravyn didn't miss the brief glitter of heat in his eyes. He tamped it down almost immediately, and they both ignored it.

"We need to refill the canteens tomorrow," he said. "You'll be able to wash your face and hands then, but I don't want to take the time for a full-scale bath. Not until we're farther away from the facility."

Ravyn nodded. "Okay. I wish I had clean clothes though."

He smirked, but said neutrally enough. "I do too."

"What's so funny?"

"Nothing."

Narrowing her eyes, Ravyn scowled at him, but he remained quiet. Out of the blue, a conversation she'd had with Alex when she'd been thirteen came to mind. She'd demanded to know why women weren't in Spec Ops and Alex had told her because they'd always want baths and clean clothes. Her head snapped up.

"Leave it to a woman to want to be clean in the jungle," she said to him. They weren't exactly in the jungle, but the sentiment was the same. If that wasn't what he was thinking word for word, she bet it was damn close.

"What?"

"That's what you find so funny, isn't it?"

Damon shrugged, but Ravyn knew she had her answer.

"Tell me, is this attitude trained into you Spec Ops types or do they recruit men who already have Neanderthal mindsets?"

"Ravyn, I know you're scared and want to release some of the tension, but I'm not going to argue with you."

"I hate that reasonable tone," she groused, but without much heat. She loathed that he had discovered her motives before she had realized them herself.

"Do you want more?" he asked, gesturing with the knife to the fruit.

"No, I'm full." It was an effort to keep the sulkiness out of her voice.

"Then go to sleep. It's going to be a long day tomorrow."

The thought of sitting up to spite him rolled through her

head, but Ravyn was smart enough to know the only person she would hurt would be herself. And she was tired. Tired to her soul, tired in a way she could never remember being tired.

Damon had arranged two piles of leaves a long arm's length apart. Insulation, she realized, from the damp ground. Picking one, she lay down, closed her eyes and tried to find a comfortable position. She could feel Damon's gaze on her for a moment, felt when he shifted it away. Closing him out of her mind, Ravyn pictured clear water and clean clothes.

She let her thoughts drift into the blackness of sleep.

Chapter Four

Ravyn stood in the sub-basement, staring at her equipment. There was a problem. She turned, looking for her tools, but they weren't there. Brow furrowed in thought, she shifted to study the comm base system again and gasped. It was smashed. What was going on here? *Even with tools, Ravyn realized she couldn't fix this. She wondered if Damon knew what was going on. Her frown deepened as she realized he wasn't nearby. She didn't want to leave the room, but she did anyway. She had to find him.*

She was on the stairs to the main level when fear hit her. The urge to retreat was strong, but there was nothing except an endless void behind her. She couldn't stay in that nothingness. It would consume her. Ravyn didn't wait for the door to slide completely open. As soon as she could fit, she squeezed through.

A deep sense of foreboding weighed her down. She could see nothing but shadowy shapes in the meager light, hear nothing but the blood pounding in her veins and her rapid breathing. Terror squeezed every cell in her body. She needed Damon.

The evil felt closer, and like the coward she knew herself to be, she ran from it. The dark left her disoriented and she slowed down, stopped. Indecision rose, adding to the wild-eyed terror. As she stood, torn about what to do, a sinister laugh echoed through the building.

Glancing over her shoulder, she broke into a trot, running until she reached the common room. She expected to find help.

But she didn't. It was as eerily empty as the rest of the building. Ravyn stumbled, losing her balance, and fell before she could catch herself. She didn't know why anyone was sleeping on the floor, but she rolled off, prepared to apologize.

The scream caught in her throat.

She was surrounded by bodies. The whole team was there, mutilated, lying in dark pools of blood. She lowered her hand to brace herself, but instead of tile, her fingers tangled in hair. As she jerked away, something came loose. Flowers. White flowers braided into a coronet and spotted with red.

Ravyn covered her eyes, trying to block out the sight. Her hands were wet with blood; it dripped down her chin before she could yank them away. Not just on her face, she realized. She could feel blood soaking through her clothes. Her shoes slipped in the wine red puddles as she tried to stand. She sensed the monster watching her, enjoying her struggle to regain her feet.

Damon! Damon would help her. "Damon, where are you?" she called and waited for him to answer. There was nothing but silence. She had to find him. She wiped her hands on the legs of her pants, then clenched them into fists. She would find him. She would. Ravyn went from empty room to empty room. The evil one found her search entertaining. She could feel his amusement. Ignoring it, she went to the next door.

What if Damon were dead? *He would never leave her unprotected if he weren't in trouble. Ravyn started crying. Impatiently, she brushed away the wetness, uncaring of the blood that mingled with her tears. All she cared about was Damon.*

She turned and found a door behind her that she had never seen before. It had an old-fashioned silver knob and her hand left a smear of blood as she edged it open. A waist-high, black stone altar dominated the room and there was a figure on it.

"Damon," she said on a breath of relief. She rushed to him, needing to touch him, feel his strength. Looking down, she froze. Where his lively green eyes should have been, there were vacant sockets. His mouth gaped open, empty. A keening sound started, soft at first, then growing louder as she saw his open chest. His heart was still there, but it wasn't beating.

"No!" she howled, unable to contain her despair. "Damon!"

Ravyn fell to her knees beside the altar, her forehead resting on his shoulder. There was nothing but desolation inside her. The laughter sounded again as the evil one took pleasure in her sorrow. It grew closer, but Ravyn didn't care. Damon was dead. What did it matter now if she lived?

She could smell the monster's fetid breath, but she didn't move. Instead she put her hand in Damon's cool hand and waited.

The killer grabbed her shoulder and Ravyn knew a sudden, absolute fury. The bastard had killed Damon.

Without warning, she turned and struck out.

Damon woke, instantly alert.

He remained still, listening for what had roused him. When it came, the source was unexpected. Ravyn whimpered again and moved. She was agitated, but still asleep. A nightmare, he thought. He forced himself not to go to her, to continue listening. When he felt confident the only discordant noise came from her, he relaxed a little.

Damon had been waiting for the wall she'd built around her emotions to collapse, and it made sense it would happen when her considerable will was relaxed. It was better this way, he knew. The longer she held her grief inside, the harder it would be, and the more time it would take, to heal. Another sound came, this one he couldn't put a name to, but it was heartrending. He didn't hesitate any longer. He moved to Ravyn, and putting his hand on her shoulder, gently shook her awake.

She came up swinging.

He missed catching a fist on the chin only because of his quick reflexes. Grabbing both of her wrists, he said, "You're safe. I've got you. Everything is fine. You're okay."

By the light of the moon, he could see when her eyes cleared and she realized it had only been a dream. "Damon?" she asked and he could swear her voice held joy.

"It's me, sweet pea. You're all right."

"Sorry," she murmured, pulling free and burying her face in her hands. He could see her struggling not to cry, but enormous shudders began convulsing her body and he knew she'd lost the battle. Now and then she would make a snuffling sound or pull in a shaky breath, but otherwise she was quiet.

Damon shifted uncomfortably. He was never sure what to do when a woman surrendered to tears. It sounded like Ravyn's heart was breaking and he couldn't sit by and do nothing. Uncertain, he slid an arm across her shoulders. Her reaction was immediate. She turned into his body, wrapped her arms around his waist and buried her face against his throat. He was nonplussed for a moment, then brought his other arm up to rub circles on her back.

Her tears felt warm and wet against his skin. She tried to stay as silent as possible, but occasionally she would muffle a sob against his chest. She gripped him tightly, as if she were afraid he would disappear if she didn't hang on to him with all her strength. Damon felt helpless. There was nothing he could do to take away her pain. No way to go back in time and prevent the carnage, no way to erase her memories. He could only hold her and let her know she wasn't alone.

It seemed to take forever before her weeping stopped. She kept her face hidden against him. He could hear the shaky, raspy breathing and feel the tremors that still coursed through her body. He didn't bother asking what her nightmare was about. He knew. They were in the middle of the damn nightmare.

This kind of emotional release had to be good for her. Part of Damon longed to join her, to throw back his head and howl. He'd lost his best buddy and five other friends. And he couldn't. His arms tightened around her briefly before he forced himself to loosen his hold. Until he had Ravyn safe, until they were off this hellish planet, he had to be in control.

"I'm sorry," Ravyn apologized, still hiding her face.

He knew she felt embarrassed by her tears, that she considered them a weakness, but Damon saw only Ravyn's strength, her ability to bravely endure all that had happened. The feel of her breath against his neck made his body shiver. Desire, strong and fierce, almost made him groan aloud. He wanted this woman more than he could remember ever wanting anyone else. The sudden switch in emotions from grief to lust was nearly dizzying and completely unexpected.

Off limits, he reminded himself.

When that didn't work, Damon tried to ease Ravyn back from his body. She held on tighter and he acquiesced. He couldn't keep his hands still, but he was able to restrict himself to comforting touches. Even rubbing her back, however, tempted him. He moved his hand to her hair instead. They didn't have a comb and he tried to gently work his fingers through her tangles. Tomorrow he'd have to come up with some sort of brush for her, he thought.

"Damon?"

"Hmm?"

"Did you fight in the Third War?" Her voice was muffled.

"Yeah." He didn't know why she asked, but he'd talk if that made her feel better. "I fought five and a half of the seven years." Damon kept his voice soothing, hoping it would help her relax. They both needed more sleep tonight, but he knew she wasn't ready to settle down yet.

"It was bad," Ravyn stated.

Damon didn't say anything.

"My mom told me people believed the turn of the millennium signaled the beginning of an age of peace."

"Yeah," Damon said, unable to keep the cynicism from his voice, "and in the forty years since then, there have been three wars and there's sure to be a fourth since nothing got resolved."

They both stayed quiet and Damon found himself thinking about fighting in another war. Dread welled up and he felt a stab of relief when Ravyn broke the silence.

"What I remember most about the Second War was the shattered look in the soldiers' eyes. Even the ones who stayed in the rear area had this feeling around them, as if their souls had been wounded. I heard the Third set new levels of barbarism."

"How do you know so much about the Second Oceanic War?" Damon asked, deciding to ignore the second half of what she said. He didn't want to remember just how barbaric those last years of fighting had been.

"My mom was a doctor. She was stationed on the front for the Second War and our quarters were in the rear area."

His hand stilled. "Your mother was a military doctor?"

"Yes. A surgeon."

"Which front?"

"Mexico."

"Hell."

"It could have been worse," she told him. "Mom could have been assigned to the Middle East Theater of Operations or the Southeast Asian TO."

"They also could have sent her to the European front," Damon countered. Although Europe had been the hottest area in the First War, it had been relatively quiet in the Second and Third. The Southwest front, however, had taken a beating in the Second Oceanic War as the Coalition forces had attempted to breach the United States by moving up the Pacific coast of Mexico.

Ravyn might have lived in the rear area, but he knew California had been hit in a number of air attacks. He remembered her age from the file he'd read, and doing some quick calculation, he figured out she would have been four when the Second War started, seven when it ended. Hell. Not exactly a peaceful childhood.

"Where was your father?" He hoped she had one civilian parent. If both were military, she would have spent a lot of time in childcare with other kids who had two parents serving.

"My dad died just before the Second War broke out."

Frowning, he untangled his hand from her hair and tipped her chin up so she looked at him. "You're telling me that your mother was on the front lines and she was your only parent?"

Ravyn must have heard the censure he tried to keep out of his voice. "She was an experienced surgeon, Damon. She'd been on the lines for the First War. They needed her at the front."

"You needed her."

Ravyn tried to turn her head away, but he kept hold of her chin. This explained why she was so self-reliant, why she thought she had to be strong. No child should have to live knowing she could be orphaned at any minute. The brass had tried to keep single parents out of the battle zone, but doctors were always at a premium. It probably would have merited some debate, but, in the end, if the doctor was willing, single parent or not, she would have been assigned to the front.

"It wasn't just the two of us. Mom remarried when I was five and then I had a stepfather and brother."

Something in Ravyn's voice made him suspicious. "Let me guess. Your stepfather was military too and on the front."

"Not quite."

"Why don't you tell me what I got wrong."

She hesitated, then shrugged and said, "Gil was Spec Ops."

Damon cursed. Just one word, but it conveyed everything he felt. Her stepfather hadn't been *on* the front lines; he'd been *behind* enemy lines. Memories of some of his more dangerous missions flashed through his mind and his regard for Ravyn went up again. She'd grown up understanding the fragility of life, the uncertainty of what the next day held.

"It wasn't that bad," she told him quietly. "Both Mom and Gil survived the war and I had my big brother to watch out for me. And believe me when I say Alex took the job very seriously."

Damon could hear affection in her voice as she spoke of her stepbrother and he forced himself to let the rest go. It had happened years before and his outrage wouldn't change her past. He should consider himself lucky Ravyn had the background she did. This situation was made a lot more tenable because of her behavior. The thought of trying to get through this with some spoiled princess like his brother's wife almost made him shudder.

He ran his fingers from her chin, along her jaw to her ear before letting her go. He moved a few feet over and settled back, both hands linked behind his head. "I'm sorry," he told her, looking up at the sky. "I shouldn't have commented on your family. It's not like mine wins any prizes."

And unlike his parents, he thought, Ravyn's mother had wanted her child near.

From the corner of his eye, he watched her wipe the remnants of her tears from her cheeks. He should have done that for her. She eased herself slowly to the ground and turned on her side so she could look at him. "Tell me about your family."

Damon stared at the stars and tried to think of something to say. They might be related by blood, but he didn't feel a kinship to any of them. Not since his grandfather had died. Their life philosophies differed drastically. His parents and brother lived to increase the family fortune, while money had never meant much to him. "There's not a lot to tell," he finally said.

"Do you have any brothers or sisters?" she persisted.

"Yeah," he said quietly, knowing she needed the sound of a human voice right now. "I have a brother."

"Are you close?"

"No." Damon knew Ravyn wouldn't let him leave it at that. "Maybe it's because he's five years older, but we've never had any common ground."

"Alex is ten years older than me," she said quietly.

Damon turned on his side, propped himself up on an elbow and looked at Ravyn. "Are you best buddies or is your relationship more parent-child than brother-sister?"

She was quiet for a long time before she said, "You're right. Alex was a parent to me in a lot of ways. After Mom and Gil died, he even became my guardian."

"I thought you said they survived the war?"

"They did." She let out a long sigh before saying, "When I was fourteen, they took a second honeymoon. The hotel they stayed at had a partial collapse in the middle of the night."

"The Vegas Alps disaster?"

"Yes." Her voice held the echo of remembered pain. "That was twelve years ago. I'm surprised you remember it. Most people don't unless I mention it."

Damon frowned slightly. She'd looked away from him, centering her attention on the ground in front of her. He wanted to reach out and touch her, to take away even that small remnant of hurt, but she'd put a distance between them without so much as moving a centimeter.

"I remember," he told her when her eyes finally shifted back to his. He debated whether to add more and decided to tell her the rest. "I was in my first year at Yale. A bunch of us had reservations at that hotel the following week for spring break."

Again, she was quiet for a moment before asking, "So where did you end up going instead?"

"The rest of them went to Florida, where else?"

"You didn't go?"

Damon shifted a bit farther from Ravyn. "I couldn't. It seemed wrong to go somewhere and have fun when people had died. When it hit so close to home." He just about groaned when he saw she had tears in her eyes again. Damn, he knew he should have kept quiet. The loss of her mother couldn't be easy to talk about even though it had happened so long ago.

"You were pretty sensitive for a teenager," she said thickly. Then she surprised the hell out of him by reaching out and running her fingertips fleetingly across his hand.

In his shock, Damon nearly jerked his arm back. Instead, he cleared his throat, uncomfortable with the idea that she thought he was sensitive. Soldiers were *not* sensitive. He opened his mouth, but closed it in a hurry when he realized how close she was. He wasn't quite sure how she'd managed to move without him being aware of it, but the thought went right out of his head when she placed two fingers lightly against his lips.

"I know," she said, her voice low, "you're dying to deny you're sensitive. To tell me you're a Spec Ops officer, not some sissy. I know you're tough, Captain."

He couldn't quite tear his gaze away from the soft smile she had on her face. Ravyn caught him flatfooted again when she pressed her lips against his cheek.

"Goodnight." She rolled away, her back to him, before he was able to gather his wits enough to react.

Slowly, Damon brought his hand up and briefly touched the spot she'd kissed. He could swear it buzzed. All he could do for quite some time was stare at her. When he realized her deep, even breathing meant she had fallen asleep again, he returned to his back and tucked an arm behind his head. He was going to have to watch himself. Her nearness had been too disturbing, her touch too exciting. Even now every cell in his body vibrated with pleasure and all from a simple, innocent peck on the cheek.

Damon willed his mind to still, his body to calm, but they didn't obey him. He'd had more control over himself in the middle of his first firefight as a green second lieutenant. The realization did not please him. Neither did the knowledge that he wouldn't be getting any more sleep that night.

With an effort, he managed to wrench his thoughts away from Ravyn. What came to mind was even more unsettling. He saw his team, his friends, in the clearing. Even with his eyes open, he could see them as clearly as he had when they'd found them. His jaw tightened until a muscle began to tic.

What had the power to disarm and murder six of the toughest men in the Western Alliance?

Damon scowled into the night. Crossing one booted foot over the other, he ran through what he knew again. It didn't take long. The list of unanswered questions took a lot more time. Most puzzling of all was the pattern in which the bodies had been arranged. What was it? He could sense it was important. Squinting, he brought the scene into his mind's eye and studied it.

A lightning bolt!

Damon sat upright in a hurry. Shit. His men had been arranged in a zigzag pattern that was supposed to represent a lightning bolt. Unfortunately, this bit of knowledge didn't make anything clearer. It just raised more questions.

He tried to remember the placement of the CAT team's bodies. It had been so damn dark in that room. Damon closed his eyes and focused even more intently. Nothing came to him and he shook his head. They weren't laid out in a lightning bolt, or even a series of lightning bolts. He knew that. Finally, he tried to picture the scene from an aerial view.

Damon opened his eyes and ran a hand over his chin.

That couldn't be right. No damn way.

He was dealing with a psycho. There was no question about it. Yet, he couldn't conceive of even the sickest being arranging nineteen bodies in a giant flower. Now that he'd recognized it, the image was undeniable. A giant flower complete with a stem and leaves. And all made out of mutilated bodies.

Silently getting to his feet, Damon paced the perimeter of their camp. Whomever, whatever, they dealt with, he didn't think the killer was human. Not with the choices he made defying any kind of logic Damon had ever learned.

What if the Old City wasn't really abandoned? What if this being was one of the original settlers? Or a descendent of the original settlers?

He stopped and settled back against a tree. The night sounds of Jarved Nine soothed him. The low hum of insects; the slight scurrying of nocturnal animals. As long as he heard those sounds, Damon was sure there wasn't danger present.

Before he could block it, thoughts of his friends filled his head in a kaleidoscope of images. The look in Carter's eyes as he'd taken his wedding vows. Lopez beaming with pride as he'd shown off pictures of his kid's first day of school. Eng, normally Mister Calm, worried about proposing to his girlfriend. Bauman full of plans for his folks' ranch when his enlistment was up in a few months. Petrelli grinning from ear to ear as he'd told the team his wife carried twins. And Spence changing his mind every five minutes on whether his daughter's birthday cake should have teddy bear decorations or cartoon characters.

Damon leaned his head back and stared up at the moon. How was he going to tell their families about the deaths?

He'd left them in the clearing. The thought pierced through his heart. Scavengers would get to the bodies. The pain in his knuckles made him realize how tightly he'd clenched his hands. He forced himself to relax finger by finger.

The families weren't going to have much to bury, but there had been no other choice. His first responsibility was to protect Ravyn, to get her safely back to Earth.

But he wasn't leaving Jarved Nine without getting justice for his friends. Damon straightened. He would hand Ravyn off to the rescue team and then go hunting. He'd been trained to track, trained to kill and that was exactly what he was going to do.

"An eye for an eye," he vowed quietly.

Chapter Five

"You ready?"

Ravyn started slightly at the brusqueness in Damon's voice before nodding. It was a wasted effort since he'd already turned and picked up the pack. He didn't look back before starting off.

So that's the way it's going to be, Ravyn thought. She wrinkled her nose at his back before obediently trotting after him. She should have guessed this would happen. If the subject ever came up again, she'd remember to pick a different word than "sensitive." Something more manly. Biting back a smirk, she decided the best course of action would be to act as if nothing were amiss. It would confuse him if she didn't seem to notice a difference in his behavior. She loved keeping Alex on his toes and it looked like she was going to have the same fun with Damon.

He turned to check on her and caught a smile on her face.

"Beautiful morning, isn't it?" she said as a diversion.

With a grunt, he looked forward again.

Actually, it barely qualified as morning. The sun wasn't quite peeking over the mountains yet. Technically, she knew they were hills, but they looked like mountains to her. They'd reach them today, no doubt, and the thought of hiking through them was daunting. Still staring off in the distance, Ravyn stumbled over an exposed tree root, making enough noise to capture Damon's attention. He stopped and raised his eyebrows.

"I'm fine," she told him, blushing slightly.

His eyes traveled the length of her body, then he nodded and continued walking.

Ravyn made sure to watch where she put her feet this time instead of worrying about the terrain ahead. At least here the ground wasn't clogged with undergrowth the way it had been most of yesterday. The easier walk was a relief.

For a second, Ravyn thought she smelled coffee. Her mouth watered before she realized the odds of finding coffee brewing on Jarved Nine were about on par with waking up and finding the last few days had been a bizarre nightmare. She turned her head to examine the path they traveled, to distract herself, but the first thing she saw was a patch of sinestas. The flower Sondra's wreath had been made from. She could still see them spattered with blood.

The reminder of her dream sent a quiver of desolation racing through her body. It hadn't been a replay of when she'd found her friends' bodies, although some of it had really happened. This time Damon had been killed, laid out on an altar as a sacrifice. She was still shaken by the depth of pain that image evoked. Just thinking about anything happening to him . . .

Ravyn shuddered. Only the embarrassment of breaking down again kept her from wailing. She struggled to close the door on her memories and finally visualized erecting a brick wall to keep them contained. She watched the ground, focused on putting one foot in front of the other. This time she couldn't block her thoughts. Flashes kept sneaking past her barriers. She'd no sooner banish the image of the bodies, when she'd recall yanking the flowers from Sondra's hair or the feel of blood coating her.

Somehow it was worse, though, when she thought of how she'd seen Damon in her dream. It made Ravyn feel guilty.

After all, she'd only known him for a few days and she'd known her teammates for months, and in some cases, years. Yet her soul felt ripped apart when she thought of anything happening to the captain.

Her hands curled into tight fists, her nails digging into the palms, as she fought against the tidal wave of remembrance. Even with her eyes open, though, she couldn't focus on the vibrant life surrounding her, only the emptiness of death.

Surreptitiously, she wiped her eyes. Her thoughts slid to Sondra's birthday party. The guys had been giving her a hard time about turning thirty. Ravyn smiled slightly even as more tears fell. Sondra had laughed and told them all that getting older was better than the alternative. Ravyn turned a sob into a cough, hoping Damon wouldn't notice.

The evening had been boisterous and full of laughter. After dinner, they'd gathered in the communal room to watch movies and that had been when she'd slipped away. Ravyn bit down hard on her lower lip, hard enough to draw blood. She wasn't aware that Damon had stopped, that she had automatically stopped as well, until he took her by the shoulders and gave her a gentle shake.

"Come on, sweet pea, snap out of it." The insistence in his voice made her curious how many times he'd tried to get her attention before this.

The second shake wasn't quite as gentle and she blinked up at him in surprise. The sun was up now and Ravyn guessed she'd been lost in thought for hours. Finally, she focused on Damon and realized he was concerned. "I'm okay," she assured him, but the shakiness of her voice did not inspire confidence.

The warmth of his touch anchored her and she brought her own hands up, gripping his forearms almost desperately. Ravyn could feel the play of his muscles under the long-sleeve shirt and that distracted her. She stared at his tan throat, watched his pulse beat. For the first time, she noticed his ears stuck out a little bit. His hair was disheveled, standing straight up and sticking out in different directions. It was sexy as hell. A squeeze of her shoulders had her finally looking into his eyes.

"I need you with me," he told her.

Ravyn nodded, knew exactly what he meant. He needed her in the here and now, not in her head. She had to be aware of her surroundings, had to at least be of minimal help. "I know. I'm sorry. I don't know why I can't stop remembering."

"You're tired. It's harder to push the memories away when you're not rested, but I need you to do it anyway." He looked around before bringing his attention back to her. "Do you feel it?" he asked.

For a second, Ravyn thought he meant the attraction between them. Oh, yeah, she felt it. In every cell of her body. Then she realized he wasn't talking about that. She closed her eyes, letting her senses gather information. The air felt heavy and there was a muted quiet, as if the normal noises of the planet were muffled by the heaviness of the atmosphere. It was hard to breathe and even the scent of flowers seemed smothered. Opening her eyes, she said, "There's a huge storm coming."

Damon nodded. "That would be my guess. We need to eat something and find water and shelter before it hits. Don't think about anything else, okay?"

"Okay," she agreed and stopped clinging to his arms.

"Good. We're going to have to split up. There's food here. Gather up enough for the entire day. I'm going to scout ahead, try to find us some water and somewhere to ride out the storm."

The urge to grab him again was strong, but she refused to give into her weakness. He said he needed her; she wouldn't let him down. Taking a deep breath, Ravyn nodded. She tried not to be scared, but it must have been written on her face.

"Believe me," he assured her, "I wouldn't leave you if I wasn't positive you'd be safe."

"You mean safer than with you."

Damon looked away briefly, then locked his gaze on hers. "We did some circling as we walked. Our rear and flanks are clear. For now. But I don't know what's ahead of us."

"And you can move faster without me."

"We'll save time if we split what needs to be done. I won't be gone long, I promise."

She straightened her spine and gathered together all the determination she could muster. "I'll be fine."

He gave her a two-second smile. "I know you will. Don't wander off," he ordered. Then, shocking her, Damon pressed a kiss on her forehead and disappeared into the trees.

Ravyn wasted about ten minutes trying to figure out what that kiss meant before she could shake herself out of her stupor. All the impetus she needed was to think of Damon returning to find her standing where he left her. Now that would be pathetic.

He'd left the pack, a fact she didn't discover until she almost fell over it. Man, she had been out of it, Ravyn thought as she surveyed the area for fruits and vegetables. She gathered a variety, storing them in the pack when her arms got too full. She didn't stop until she had filled it. If the weather got really bad, one of the huge hurricane-type storms that could roll through, they might be holed up for days. She wasn't sure where they were, but the area surrounding the Old City was particularly susceptible to big storms. One of the enigmas of the settlement was why they had chosen to build there.

Without warning, the hair on the back of her neck stood up and Ravyn held her breath, afraid to move. Someone was watching her. Forcing herself to breathe, she considered her options. Two came to mind. Run like hell or wait and hope it was her imagination. Only she'd always had a fairly reliable sixth sense about these things and her abilities had grown stronger since she'd arrived on Jarved Nine. She didn't doubt someone was there. The captain had said their back and sides were clear. He'd said to wait here for him. Her hands shook and she tightened them into fists to keep them still.

As she debated what to do, movement caught her eye. She whirled to face the threat and almost laughed in relief. Damon. She brought her hand to her chest, covering her pounding heart. Damn the man was quiet. She took a few deep breaths. "I'm ready," she said, in control by the time he reached her. "Why are you carrying a branch with a porcupine cone?"

"Later." He hefted the pack onto his shoulder. The small grunt he gave had her lips quirking at the corners. "Come on."

They didn't go more than a kilometer before Damon stopped, but most of it was uphill. Ravyn almost bumped into him, but caught herself in time. She went up on her toes to look over his shoulder and then had to fight back the temptation to push him out of her way. Never before had any body of water looked so beautiful to her. It was a small river, barely more than a creek, but there was fresh, clean water and she wanted it.

"Wait here," Damon said quietly.

She knew caution was necessary, but she still shifted impatiently from side to side. The river called to her like a siren song. Ravyn looked away from the water and admired the small clearing the creek wound through. The grass here was short, maybe ankle height, and it added to the appeal. The little patch of land seemed like an oasis ringed with trees, bushes, tall grass and sprouting wild flowers.

When Damon gave the all-clear sign, Ravyn barely kept from running. It took more self-discipline than it should have, but she managed to fill her canteen and wait for Damon to fill his before rolling up her sleeves and plunging her dirty hands in the water. She rubbed at the grime, but she still didn't feel clean. As she scrubbed, she watched him take the canteens and drop a small tablet into each. She hadn't even thought about microorganisms.

Ravyn perked up when she remembered there was a plant that grew near water in this area with a soaplike sap. Pulling her hands out, she dried them on her pants and looked around. When she spotted the thick, flat protrusions of the plant she wanted, she smiled. "Can I borrow your knife?"

It was a measure of trust that he didn't ask what for, just handed it to her. She flipped open the blade and cut some limbs from the plant. Kneeling at the edge of the river, she sliced open one of the fleshy leaves and used the soap to clean her hands. Catching Damon's curious gaze, she said,

"Soap plant." She gestured to the pile beside her. "Help yourself."

"You can't remember which plants are edible, but you know which one can be used as soap," he commented wryly.

"It's a matter of priorities." Ravyn said and submerged her head. She split open another leaf and washed her hair and face.

When she finished, she noticed Damon had removed both his uniform shirt and the T-shirt underneath. Her eyes widened as she admired the sight. Only a scar high on his left arm marred the perfection of his body. His shoulders had looked broad in fatigues, out of them, they seemed impossibly wider. He had a light dusting of hair across his pecs. She followed the line to his ripped abs, drooled over them briefly, before continuing down to the waistband of his pants.

The tips of her fingers itched to touch, to stroke that warm skin and the hard muscles beneath it. She could almost feel the crispness of his chest hair. Her lids slid half-shut as she tried to decide where and how he'd like to be touched. A drop of water traveled from his neck to his left nipple. She wanted to push his dog tags aside, press her mouth to his skin and lick it.

Ravyn nearly hummed aloud before she realized he was getting half a bath. "Hey!" she squawked. "That's not fair!"

Damon looked over, a smug smile on his face. It was a dare, plain and simple, she decided. It was stupid, but she'd never been able to turn down a challenge. Pulling out the tails of her shirt, she started unbuttoning. She could feel his eyes on her.

Playing a game of chicken with a Spec Ops officer ranked as one of the dumbest things she had ever done, but that didn't stop her. When she undid the last button, she slowly separated the edges of her shirt. Ravyn knew the slowness came across as teasing, but she was waiting for him to turn his back.

Her hands started to tremble. He was going to call her bluff and pride wouldn't let her back down. At least her bra was black, she thought and hesitantly slipped the fabric from her shoulders. As soon as she discarded the shirt, she started to bring her arms up to cover herself, but stopped before they moved very far. She wouldn't give him the satisfaction of knowing how uncomfortable this made her feel. She shifted so her wet hair fell forward and concealed the blush she knew stained her face.

Her body responded to his nearness, adding to her embarrassment. Even with the black bra, he wouldn't miss her reaction. Without so much as a glance, she knew she had his complete attention. His stare burned her. She fought back a shakiness that seemed to start at her core and swallowed hard.

Doing her best to ignore him, she leaned forward and used her hands to wash her upper torso. She tried to be careful, tried to keep her bra from getting wet, but she wasn't entirely successful. When she straightened, she could feel water wend its way down her chest. Her nipples hardened further. Whether it was the cool water or the heat of Damon's eyes, she didn't know.

A choked off groan startled Ravyn enough that she finally looked at him again. He hadn't been trying to call her bluff, she realized belatedly. His eyes were hot and glued to her breasts. Mortified, she dropped her gaze only to find herself staring at his growing erection.

Now it was Ravyn's turn to choke. That part of him appeared to be in proportion to the rest of his oversized body. A flare of arousal shot through her at the sight and brought her back to her senses. They couldn't do this. With more speed than grace, she grabbed her shirt and pulled it on. She shook so badly, it took twice as long to fasten the buttons as usual.

This time Damon stuck his head in the water.

Ravyn moved from the edge of the river, and averting her eyes, took deep, calming breaths. When the trembling abated, she ran her fingers through her hair, trying to work the snarls out.

"Here," Damon said, sneaking up on her again, "use this."

He handed her the porcupine cone and didn't waste any time moving a safe distance away. The cone was part of the tree branch, but was oval with spikes coming out of it. As she held it in her hands, she realized at some point Damon had blunted the sharp quills so she could brush her hair without hurting herself.

"Thank you," she called. Ravyn didn't dare comment on how thoughtful he was, not when he had just managed to get over her mentioning his sensitivity last night.

Starting at the ends of her long hair, she worked the cone until she had all the tangles out. It felt good to have her hair clean and smooth again, but it wouldn't last long. Probably just a couple hours would have it all knotted up again, especially with the breeze picking up. Ravyn looked around and saw dark clouds close on the horizon. She couldn't guess what direction that was, but it didn't matter. The storm was heading their way.

Pushing herself to her feet, she went to Damon. He had his T-shirt on; his fatigue shirt had been washed and was drying on a nearby bush. She grimaced over her own filthy top, but this time kept her mouth shut. "Thanks again," Ravyn told him, handing him the porcupine cone. "It feels good to have my hair untangled."

She watched him stow it carefully in the pack with their food supply before he straightened and held out a shortened boot lace. "If you want to tie back your hair, you can use this," he said roughly.

"Good idea," Ravyn said, taking the string. She sat next to their pack and vests and tried to braid the damp mass of hair. It was a struggle. Her mom had braided her hair for her when she was younger; she'd never done it herself. At least Damon had moved off so he wasn't right there while she fumbled. The third time the damn thing fell apart on her, Ravyn started cussing under her breath. Growing up the way she had, her repertoire was extensive.

After several more failed attempts, she reluctantly admitted there was no way she was going to be able to braid it herself. Ravyn turned her head until she spotted Damon. He wasn't looking at her, but the smirk on his face led her to believe he could hear her cursing. He'd tied his damp shirt around his waist and that had to mean they'd be moving out soon.

"Damon."

"Yeah?"

"Could you come here for a minute please?" she asked in her sweetest voice.

He studied her suspiciously for a moment before joining her. "What?"

"Would you do my hair for me? Please?"

"You're kidding, right?"

"I'd keep trying myself, but we have a time constraint."

He considered the sky for a moment before settling behind her with a sigh. "Give me the tie," he ordered.

"Thank you." Ravyn handed him the lace.

Damon snorted. "You're just lucky I used to braid my horse's mane when I was in prep school."

Ravyn knew hair didn't have nerve endings, but the feel of Damon's hands on her tresses got her all hot and bothered again. She could feel his breath on the nape of her neck and fought to control the shiver of lust that wanted to go through her body.

She didn't think he was unaffected either. His breathing sounded harsher to her, louder than it had been when he started. Then there was the fact that the very graceful Captain Brody was suddenly all thumbs. By the time he had tied off her braid, Ravyn wanted nothing more than to sink back against him.

His hands came up, rested on her shoulders briefly before he trailed them down her arms to her wrists. He never touched bare skin, but it was the most erotic thing she'd ever known. She could feel the hardness of his chest against her back, the warmth of his body wherever they touched.

This isn't smart, she thought, leaning into him.

"Tell me to stop, Ravyn," he whispered near her ear.

"Don't stop."

"This is stupid."

"I know."

He wrapped his arms around her, pulling her closer. She felt enveloped by his strength, protected, wanted. Ravyn turned toward him, raised her lips and watched as he lowered his head.

The first raindrop hit her in the middle of her forehead.

They barely had time to untangle themselves from each other before the sky opened up.

Damon stood at the mouth of the small cave, his hands pushing against the rock over his head, and watched the rain sheet down. Their shelter wasn't roomy. It barely had enough space for them and the pack and vests. He would just fit when he stretched out to get some rest. That didn't matter, though. All that mattered was it was dry and safe. They were on the highest ground in the area so he wasn't overly concerned about flooding.

Behind him, Ravyn slept. He knew he should lay down too, try to rest. They'd both been running short on sleep since the incident and this was a good time to catch up. It was unlikely anyone, no matter how determined to kill them, was out in this weather. But he stayed put. There was nowhere he could go inside the cave that didn't put Ravyn too close. He was no longer positive he could stop himself from touching her, tasting her. And now he knew she felt the attraction as strongly as he did.

Or at least she felt something. He still thought their situation played a big part in her response to him. Why couldn't he have met her on Earth when he could be sure it was him she wanted and not just another human being?

He shifted, impatient with his thoughts and then grimaced. His clothes were soaked. Normally, he would strip down and hang them to dry, but not with Ravyn there. Damon sighed and couldn't keep from looking over his shoulder at her. He definitely needed every barrier between them he could manufacture and that included soggy clothes.

The rain began to ease up, but he wasn't fooled into believing the storm was ebbing. It had done this several times before starting up again full force. Damon pushed away from the entrance and sat down, his back resting against the cave wall.

Ravyn hadn't moved since she'd fallen asleep. Exhaustion would likely keep the nightmares at bay tonight, but she would never forget what she'd seen. He ached with the need to lie down beside her and gather her in his arms. He didn't need to make love to her, just hold her. But he didn't dare. Damon snorted in self-derision. His much vaunted self-control was all but nonexistent when it came to Ravyn. He went up like dry tinder with the simplest of touches.

His eyes drifted shut as he thought about what she had on underneath her clothes. Knowing he'd been the one to pick out her undergarments teased at him. He knew her panties matched the bra, that they were lacy and cut high. Damon opened his lids far enough to eye her long legs.

Ravyn had been uncomfortable when she'd taken off her shirt in front of him. She had tried to hide it, but the signs had been there. He guessed she'd forgotten he'd seen her in less than what she'd had on by the creek. But then she had been in shock, desperate to wash the blood off her body.

He wished he could forget as easily.

And he wished he were a better man.

A better man wouldn't be sitting here fantasizing about the woman sleeping next to him. He wouldn't be imagining what it would be like to slide all those clothes off her body and caress her, taste her bare skin. A man of true honor wouldn't be thinking about being naked himself or about burying himself inside her, while she had those sexy legs wrapped around him.

He was getting hard just thinking about it. The knowledge that Ravyn would be willing made it even more difficult to curb his desire. She would return his kisses and caresses; she would make room for him between her thighs. And when they got back to Earth, if they got back, and she recovered from the trauma, she would hate him for taking advantage of the situation.

He didn't want her to hate him.

Resting his elbows on his knees, Damon dropped his head into his hands and groaned. He made sure to keep the noise low so he wouldn't wake Ravyn, but he had to give voice to his frustration. If he thought it would help any, he'd walk out into the pouring rain, but he knew nothing was going to cool his hormones.

Pulling his eyes away from the woman sleeping next to him

was a lot harder than he wanted it to be. He stared out at the darkening sky. If this storm didn't let up soon, they might not be leaving tomorrow morning. The ground needed time to dry out before they could travel on it. After another hour or two of rain, it would be too dangerous to hike through the woods for at least one more day.

Being confined in this minuscule space for an extended period of time with a woman he wanted more than his next breath might be more than his good intentions could stand.

Damon felt considerable relief when he heard the rain ease and then stop about fifteen minutes later. He'd check in the morning, but he thought they could continue to the Old City.

He'd been fascinated by that place since the first time he'd heard of it. His biggest disappointment about the training mission on Jarved Nine had been that he and his team wouldn't be going anywhere near the city. Even then part of him had itched to reach it, to wander the paths that had been laid down more than three thousand years ago. Now he was concerned about how strongly he felt drawn to a place he'd never been to before.

It was almost spooky.

A sound caught his attention, stopped his thoughts in their tracks. Damon cocked his head, trying to hear it better. It almost sounded like an old supply train drawing closer. He hadn't heard one of those since the early days of the Third War.

Standing, he drew his pistol and stepped to the mouth of the cave. He didn't see anything moving out there, but the noise came closer and he didn't like not being able to identify it.

He shifted back and crouched beside Ravyn. He hated to disturb her, but if they needed to move fast, she had to be ready. "Ravyn, wake up."

Her eyes opened, but he could see she was groggy. Damon hoped they didn't have to make a run for it or he might be carrying her. As tired as she looked right now, she'd probably walk into a tree or over a cliff.

"What?"

Even though he was worried, Damon couldn't help the small smile at her querulousness. "I hear something," he said, keeping his voice low. "Be ready to go if I give the signal."

"What is it?"

She instantly became more alert, but even so he doubted she'd be able to move very fast. He shrugged his shoulders at her question. He still couldn't identify it.

Ravyn sat up and rubbed her eyes. He stood, and with only the smallest of hesitations, held his hand out to help pull her to her feet. His body reacted to her nearness, uncaring of any danger outside the cave. Damon squelched his desire, forcing his attraction aside. He was a professional and he'd be damned if he would endanger either one of them because he couldn't keep his mind off sex.

He moved back to the entrance, watching for heaven only knew what. He didn't have much time left to make a decision. They either were going to have to outrun whatever it was or stay here and take their chances in the cave.

Ravyn stood beside him and he glanced down at her. "What do you hear?" she asked again.

How could she miss it? "You don't hear it? It sounds like a train."

He hadn't realized how tense Ravyn was until she relaxed beside him. She smothered a chuckle, but not before he heard it. Damon narrowed his eyes and demanded, "Okay, what is it?"

"What you're hearing is a huge swarm of contilla. The closest thing we have to them on Earth would be the common housefly. The contilla migrate after heavy rain storms like this in groups that can number in the millions."

"They're not dangerous then?" he asked, trying to remember the facts he'd studied.

"No. Even if we ended up in the middle of the swarm, we'd just be irritated by their landing on us. They don't bite or sting or anything."

Damon tucked his pistol away and put some distance between them again. Contilla he could handle.

Ravyn was another story.

Chapter Six

Alex had been worried about Ravyn.

Twice a week the Jarved Nine crew sent encrypted messages to their families on Earth. His sister hadn't missed an opportunity in the entire eight months she'd been off planet. That two chances had gone by without her making contact, concerned him.

Now he was flat out terrified.

From the time Ravyn had been small, he'd always known when she was in trouble. That sense had been lost when she had gone off planet, and he cursed the distance preventing the connection. He needed to know she was okay. He needed to do more than sit here cooling his heels.

He studied General Bouchard with well-disguised dislike. As a career soldier, Alex knew how to keep his thoughts to himself. Blowhard, as he was not-so-lovingly known, was pompous, concerned only with his own image, and he homed in on the press like a heat-seeking missile after its target. What the man lacked in military aptitude, he made up for in ego. Alex eyed the two stars on the general's shoulders. The man had to have incriminating pictures. That was the only possible way he could have moved so high in the ranks.

When the summons had arrived, Alex hadn't been able to imagine why the general wanted to see him. The man had nothing to do with Spec Ops. Then he'd remembered Bouchard played military liaison to CAT Command. That had prompted Alex to move faster. How he'd managed to keep his face impassive as Blowhard had informed him the emergency beacon on Jarved Nine had been activated, he would never know. He'd barely recovered when Bouchard gave him his orders.

It had been a blessing when the call had come through for the general. It had given Alex a chance to compose himself. He needed the time to grasp that he was leading the rescue team. It had surprised the hell out of him until he realized Bouchard hadn't gathered even basic information. One cross check of the records between the J Nine team and his personnel file would have shown he had family there. Ravyn was his next of kin. It seemed Blowhard's only considerations had been rank and availability.

His patience began to wane as the general's consultation with his tailor continued. It had already been a half hour of minutiae. The lack of consideration was part and parcel of Blowhard's personality, but Alex was about ready to go over the desk and end the conversation himself. The idiot didn't think the problem on J Nine was critical.

Alex knew different. He could feel it in his gut.

It took all his training to sit as if he didn't want to put his fist through the wall. Or into Blowhard's soft mid-section. He reminded himself the beacon had been triggered four days ago. That it would be another two days before they'd be ready for launch. A half hour cooling his heels in the general's office wasn't going to make or break the mission. All the logic in the world didn't mean a damn thing, though.

Ravyn was in trouble.

Alex didn't need to close his eyes to remember the big-eyed little moppet who had become his stepsister. He'd resented the hell out of her when he'd learned of her existence. She was one more person to take up his father's time and attention, but he hadn't been able to hold out against her long. She had looked up at him with adoring eyes, smiled and said, "I love you, Alex."

That had been it.

When his dad had been too busy for him, Ravyn had dogged his heels, begging to be included. When his mother had cancelled visit after visit, Ravyn had been there telling him she was a big dummy. He had ten years on her and she had still tried to keep up with him. And had done a good job of it for such a pipsqueak.

Alex barely kept the fond smile off his face. It would be as inappropriate for him to grin as it would be to show his disdain for a superior officer. He continued to sit stiffly in the chair and waited for the conversation to wrap up.

The plush office offended Alex. There were so many things the troops needed far more than the general needed an office better suited to a big business robber baron. The desk alone must have cost more than an enlisted soldier made in a year. The highly polished surface held nothing work related except two short stacks of file folders.

They fought with the same weapons his father had fought with because the military claimed it didn't have enough funds to develop new, advanced rifles and other systems. The only saving grace was the other side spent the same pitiful amount to arm their troops. It galled Alex that money could be brazenly wasted on such unnecessary extravagance.

He bit back a sigh. The fault didn't lie solely with the military. The government shared a big part of the blame. Career politicians unwilling to shift necessary funding to the Defense Department. Citizens unwilling to sacrifice even one luxury item so resources could be diverted to weapons production. He gave a nearly imperceptible shake of his head and refocused his attention on his surroundings. With the American flag behind the general's left shoulder and the Western Alliance flag behind his right, even Alex was forced to admit it made a splashy backdrop. He just couldn't figure out who needed to be impressed that much.

"Now where were we?" Bouchard asked, finally finished.

"We were about to discuss personnel for the Jarved Nine rescue mission, sir."

"It's not a rescue mission, Colonel, and you will not refer to it as such. Officially, it is a fact-finding mission."

"Yes, sir," Alex said impassively. He would call it a pleasure cruise as long as he received orders to go to J Nine.

"Good. You'll have a full-sized K-110 transport ship for this mission. Two crews of military pilots will be flying. CAT Command wanted to send one of their own ships, but I convinced them we could get there faster."

Alex nodded and tried to look appreciative of the general's supposed brilliance. Evidently the performance was good enough.

"You're in charge," Bouchard continued. "Pick five men. I imagine you'll choose from Spec Ops since you are most familiar with personnel in that group. CAT Command will supply the communications specialist and the team doctor."

"General, I believe this mission will run more smoothly with all military personnel."

The general's expression of a pleased and benevolent leader disappeared. "Colonel, the emergency call came from a CAT base, not military. You're lucky you're not shipping out on a Colonization Assessment Team transport."

"Yes, sir." Alex hid his frustration. Of course, CAT Command wanted to handle this themselves. Unfortunately for them, the charter of the organization threw this set of circumstances squarely in the military's lap. Grudgingly, he had to concede the general had done a good job limiting the CAT personnel to two.

"I have one more piece of information before you're dismissed. A Spec Ops team was on a training mission to Jarved Nine. They were scheduled to land on the planet mere hours before the beacon was triggered. Not only has CAT Command been unable to raise their team, we have been unable to raise ours."

Alex stiffened. His heart had stopped when he'd heard the CAT team had not responded, but for a Spec Ops team to be unreachable at the same time meant trouble greater than he'd imagined. "Who was in command of the team, General?"

Blowhard pulled a folder from one of his stacks, opened

it and flipped through several pages. "Brody, Captain Damon Alan, Team Two Spec Ops. Do you know him?"

"Yes, sir. Team Two is one of our finest. They would have responded to the CAT base as soon as they heard the emergency beacon. I'm concerned that we have not been able to establish contact with them. We need to send in several Spec Ops teams."

"Colonel, there will be no additions to your team. You have your orders."

"With all due respect, General, I believe the situation on J Nine is more serious than you believe."

"What are you basing this insight on, Colonel? The fact that a Spec Ops team is late reporting in?"

Outwardly, Alex remained cool, but his frustration started to rise. Blowhard didn't work with Spec Ops enough to know, but the only way a team wouldn't have made contact in a situation like this was if they were incapable of it or it would endanger them to do so. On a personal level, Alex didn't like Brody, he never had, but professionally, the man had become one of the best officers they had and he led a top-notch team.

"Yes, General, that is what has me concerned."

"It's probably a communications glitch. There's never been a serious problem at a CAT base in the history of the program." Bouchard leaned back in his chair, clearly unconcerned.

"Jarved Nine is only the third planet to have a CAT team assigned. Just because nothing happened on Cymara or Rotesen, doesn't mean the situation isn't critical on J Nine, General," Alex persisted.

Blowhard straightened in his chair, his face mottling in anger. "Colonel Sullivan," he said, his tone brooking no further argument, "this is a low-level assignment. The only reason Spec Ops personnel are being allowed on this mission at all is because amateur comm operators picked up the distress signal and the press is about to run with the story. You have your orders. Your only options are to follow them or think about the penalty for disobeying a direct order. Am I making myself clear?"

"Yes, sir."

"Do you have anything else you want to add?"

"No, sir."

"You're dismissed."

Alex stood, snapped off the required salute, and when it was returned, headed for the door.

"Colonel, see my assistant on your way out. She has a file of compiled information for you."

Alex didn't rely solely on the general's information. He gathered his own. Both flight crews assigned to this mission pleased him. Their selection probably had more to do with the media coverage than any concern Blowhard had about the success of the rescue, but Alex would take them any way he could get them.

The five men he'd personally chosen for the mission came from Spec Ops as the general had predicted they would. But not for the reason the general had thought. No, Alex had choosen them because he knew beyond doubt the situation on J Nine was bad and Special Operations had the best warriors in the military. He'd worked with all five men before, assuring that they could function well as a team.

The doctor CAT Command had assigned came as a pleasant surprise. Gwen Mitchell was ex-military. She had, in fact, trained under his stepmother, Marie. The doctor had joined CAT after marrying a biologist already with the teams. In her forties, she'd had excellent reviews for her entire career and Dr. Mitchell wouldn't be useless if the situation deteriorated and she was forced to pick up a weapon.

His communications specialist was another story. Stacey Johnson from Podunk, Iowa. She was Ravyn's best friend and his sister had talked about her constantly, but he'd only met her once at comm school graduation. Although she had six years on his sister, Ravyn had seemed more assured, more confident. Stacey hadn't even been able to look him in the eye for more than a couple of seconds at a time.

Alex ran a hand over the top of his head. With no training, no experience handling hot situations and no knowledge of military comm procedures, she'd be a liability. He'd have to watch over her every minute to keep her from getting herself or someone else killed. Unless he could convince her to withdraw from the team. He'd found a comm spec on the CAT roster who had military time in. Granted, his record hadn't been stellar, but at least the man would be able to pull his own weight.

He mulled over what he knew about her, which was a lot thanks to Ravyn, then pushed himself to his feet. Stacey Johnson was the type who was fifteen minutes early for everything. The rest of the team wouldn't appear until briefing time. If he hustled down to the room, he'd have a good ten minutes to convince her it was in everyone's best interest to withdraw.

Alex barely slowed long enough to return salutes on his trek to the meeting room. Sure enough, there was one woman sitting alone in the room when he arrived. He had only a vague recollection of his sister's friend, but he would never forget that striking shade of strawberry blond hair.

He hesitated for a moment, trying to think of the best way to accomplish his goal. Before he could formulate a plan, she turned and caught him staring. Alex moved into the room with a casualness he did not feel.

"Hello, Stacey Johnson. I'm Alex Sullivan. I don't know if you remember, but we met at Ravyn's graduation." He held out his hand. Her hesitation was brief, but he caught it. When her hand met his, it was ice cold and damp. Talking her off the mission would be a piece of cake. She was already nervous and they hadn't left Earth. Hell, they hadn't even had the briefing yet.

"It was my graduation too," she pointed out.

The assertion had Alex mentally stumbling for a second before he said, "Yes, of course." He wasn't used to being off balance, but with one, declarative sentence this woman had managed it.

Alex decided on the direct approach. Something in her clear, hazel eyes led him to believe she had a low tolerance for manipulation. He leaned his hips against the table across the aisle from her and crossed his arms over his chest. "Stacey, let me be frank with you. The situation on Jarved Nine is not good."

"I understand that. I've seen General Bouchard almost continually on the news for the last twenty-four hours."

Her guarded tone made Alex wonder what she thought. He studied her, trying to put the pieces together. She'd fastened her shoulder-length hair back with a clip. She wore no makeup and kept her nails short and unpolished. He'd describe her clothes as functional, although it took Alex a second to suppress the desire to smile. With all the khaki she wore, she looked prepared to go out on safari. All she needed was a pith helmet.

"This mission," he said seriously and leaned forward to add emphasis to his words, "isn't an adventure or a lark. The emergency beacon on J Nine was activated five days ago. It didn't remain on long before being deactivated, but there has been no communication between Earth and the CAT team. Even more alarming, there has been no contact with the Spec Ops team training on the planet when this incident occurred."

"That's why you need me. I'm as good as Ravyn when it comes to communications. I'll be able to fix any problem with the equipment on Jarved Nine," she said, her determination obvious and Alex readjusted his thinking. So much for easy, he thought.

"If you're as good as Ravyn, then it follows she would have fixed any problem that cropped up. No, something much more dangerous has happened than an electronics glitch. I need someone who doesn't require a babysitter." Alex straightened away from the table. "I'm going to have you pulled from the team."

Stacey was out of her chair before he took a step. "If you try to have me pulled, I'll talk to General Bouchard. How long do you think you'll be assigned to lead the rescue once he finds out your stepsister is on Jarved Nine?"

"Blackmail?" Alex asked coldly. He couldn't quite reconcile this threat with what he knew about the woman.

"Whatever works," she asserted. Her mouth trembled slightly, but she firmed it and stared resolutely up at him.

Alex didn't have to manufacture his most intimidating look. He was furious. She swallowed hard, but didn't back down even when he took a step closer so he could tower over her. Stacey raised her chin defiantly, and her eyes didn't waver from his.

Since she held all the cards, he conceded the battle to her and moved to the front of the room. If Blowhard found out about Ravyn, he would waste no time pulling him from the mission. And there was no way Alex was leaving Ravyn's fate in someone else's hands.

The ship vibrated almost violently and the acceleration pushed her body against the high-backed chair. It wouldn't get any better until the pilots switched from maneuvering speed to full velocity. Stacey held on to the arms of her seat with more strength than necessary. The idea of traveling in space didn't leave her white knuckled, but Alex Sullivan sitting next to her made her nerves tap-dance.

He'd remained coldly furious with her since she'd issued her ultimatum, but he had also made himself her partner. Or babysitter, she corrected with a frown. Alex definitely did not consider her an equal, let alone a valuable, member of his team. Still, he hadn't left her side since they'd gathered this morning. He'd even sat beside her on the transport off Earth to the full-sized ship docked at one of the space stations.

Well, she'd dreamed someday Ravyn's brother would notice her, but she'd always imagined it in a positive way. This definitely fell under the heading "be careful what you wish for." Right now, she wished he would go away, but until the ship hit open space, they had to remain strapped in their seats.

"Relax," he told her, "or you'll burst a blood vessel."

"You wish," she said. *Oh, good comeback, Stace.* She should have ignored him, but Alex had been poking fun at her for more than twenty-four hours and she was sick of it.

"It's too late to get a replacement," he said laconically.

Since they were nearly out of controlled space, she guessed it was. Why couldn't he accept she was part of the team?

Stacey didn't realize she'd spoken aloud until he looked at her and said, "I've had no choice but to accept you, but by forcing yourself along, you're siphoning off manpower. Instead of focusing on the J Nine situation, I'm going to have to keep an eye on you."

They'd been over this before, Stacey thought and sighed. She'd love to tell Alex he was sexist, but it wasn't true. He had no problem with Dr. Mitchell or the two female members of the flight crew. Just her. Her lack of military training didn't mean she'd be a detriment. He assumed something catastrophic had happened. General Bouchard had said onscreen there had never been a serious incident at any CAT base. Stacey refused to believe anything had changed that safety record.

Alex was overreacting because Ravyn was there.

The ride smoothed out and Alex released his safety harness just before the chime signaled they were out of Earth's control sector. Evidently, he couldn't wait to get out of her vicinity. Stacey watched him walk away. The man was too everything. Too tall, too intense, too intimidating, too arrogant, too sexy. Too gorgeous. She had taken one look at him when Ravyn had introduced them six years ago and fallen in love. She doubted the experience had been as memorable for him. When he hadn't been doting on Ravyn, his focus had been on the beautiful ice blonde that had accompanied him. He'd barely noticed his sister's best friend.

Not that she blamed him. She was average in every way. Nothing made her stand out from the crowd. She didn't want to be flashy, but she didn't want to be ignored either. Stacey slumped back in her seat and closed her eyes. She had been too excited to sleep last night and now tiredness caught up with her. She'd almost drifted off when the feeling of being watched made her slowly open her eyes. Alex stood towering over her, his muscular thighs spread so he had a foot on either side of her extended legs.

Stacey didn't say a word, just drank him in. His light brown hair was liberally kissed by the sun and cut ruthlessly short. That particular military requirement was a shame, she thought dreamily. Alex would look good with longer hair. His face and hands were darkly tanned and she wondered how much of the rest of him was the same shade. Her eyes trailed over heavily muscled flesh, admiring the fit of his camouflage fatigues. He had big hands, she noticed, wondering if it was true what that implied. Her lips curved at the thought.

The sound of a throat being cleared had her glancing up in question. She didn't miss the humor on his too handsome face or the fact that his brown eyes glittered with amusement. "If you're done ogling my body, I want to go over this with you."

Stacey colored in mortification. How could she have forgotten, even for a moment, that this was the real Alex Sullivan and not some fantasy? She couldn't hide the fierce blush that burned her face, but she was able to ask normally enough, "Go over what?"

He waved the paper he held and Stacey felt her blush deepen. She hadn't even noticed he had something in his hand. The mission had barely begun and she'd already blown her appearance of disregard. Darn it. "What is that?" she asked.

"This is a schedule. You may have forced yourself on this mission, but I don't have to accept your incompetence."

Stacey furiously tried to push herself to her feet, only to be stopped short. She'd never unsnapped her safety harness. He managed to laugh at her without emitting a sound or changing his facial expression. Which only incited her anger further.

Deliberately, she opened the catch and stood. Alex didn't move, which left her standing too close for her peace of mind. "I am not incompetent," she got out between gritted teeth. She had a strong urge to give him a hard shove, but she knew better.

He ignored her assertion, and after folding the paper, slipped it in one of her pockets. "This is your training schedule. I have fifteen days to get you whipped into shape." His eyes ran down her body, then up again. "Don't be late. We'll need every minute."

He left Stacey sputtering.

* * *

"How can you say the curse hasn't been lifted?" Carmichael demanded. "The Cubs played in the World Series."

Alex didn't stop. He kept walking past the members of the team gathered in the lounge.

"They lost, man! Up three games to none and they dropped four straight." Baxter sounded every bit as vehement.

Voices rose and ran over each other until he couldn't tell who said what. The sides seemed to be equally divided on whether or not the jinx was over. The idea that a hex existed was never questioned, he noted, shaking his head in disbelief. The group did finally manage to agree, however, that there was no telling how long it would take the Cubs to make it to the Series again.

Alex settled himself in a chair off in the corner and tuned them out. He didn't believe in bad luck or voodoo and he didn't want to get pulled into a discussion about it.

He had other things to consider.

Like the fact that a certain wasp-tongued little hick wanted in his pants. Given the look of complete lust in her eyes, he figured she'd fantasized about that very thing a time or two before. He didn't have to think hard on how he felt about it.

The twitch in his shorts said it all.

It didn't matter how much that particular part of him throbbed; it wasn't getting relief anytime soon. Even if the timing didn't stink, even if he weren't leading the team, he still wouldn't act on it. Everything he knew about her indicated Stacey didn't have sex; she made love. And Alex didn't invest that much of himself in relationships with women. Not anymore.

"Alex, may I sit down?" Dr. Mitchell asked, interrupting his thoughts.

"Of course." Alex stood until the older woman was seated and then took his chair again.

"I know Ravyn is on Jarved Nine. Are you okay?"

"Sure."

She didn't say another word, just lifted one brow.

Alex held his silence for a few seconds. Gwen Mitchell had

been a frequent visitor to the Sullivan household when he'd been a teenager and he knew there was no stonewalling her. "Okay, so I'm worried. I've got a bad feeling about what's going on."

"So do I," Dr. Mitchell said solemnly. "Ravyn isn't the only person I'm concerned about. I don't know if you realize how close CAT team members are to each other. We become like family even before going off world."

"Ravyn's mentioned something to that effect," Alex said.

Dr. Mitchell stared at him, taking his measure. Fifteen years ago he might have squirmed under her steady regard, but not now. Alex knew who he was, knew his abilities and his weaknesses and he was comfortable in his skin.

After a moment she nodded. "One of the theories, probably your lead theory, is a member of the team lost it up on J Nine. That the isolation and seeing the same faces day after day made them snap. Maybe this person destroyed the comm equipment; maybe he even hurt some of the other team members."

"It's the most logical supposition."

"I don't think so."

"Closeness doesn't guarantee someone wouldn't hurt the other team members. Look at how many murders are committed by family members," Alex argued quietly.

"I know. I won't bring up the battery of psychological tests each person went through before being accepted into CAT," the doctor said, "although you know how extensive it is."

Alex nodded. He knew. Ravyn, chatterbox that she was, had told him everything about it. "What is your reasoning then?"

Dr. Mitchell leaned forward. "We both know how that Spec Ops team went into the facility. Do you honestly think some out-of-his-head CAT member was able to ambush them?"

"No." Alex pinched the bridge of his nose.

"Ravyn mentioned how much extra training you put her through before she joined the program." The doctor laid a hand on his arm, offering sympathy and support. "If it was one of the team, she could have taken care of herself."

"And that's why you think it's my favorite scenario."

"Yes. Alex, you're leading this mission, you need to be prepared."

"What do you think I need to be prepared for?" He lowered his arm and the doctor withdrew her hand. Alex didn't think he wanted to hear this.

"At first, I thought it might be a virus, something the team members had no immunity to. I discounted that. If that had been the case, your Team Two would have had enough time to send a message and warn others even if the CAT team didn't."

Alex was damn glad to hear she didn't think it was a virus. Ravyn would have been as helpless as anyone else on J Nine if that was what had happened. "So if you don't think it was a CAT team member gone mad or an illness, what does that leave?"

He watched the doctor take a deep breath. Whatever it was, she was reluctant to bring it up. Finally she asked, "What was a Spec Ops team doing on Jarved Nine?"

"No." Alex stood, refusing to believe what her question implied.

"Have you heard of another training mission to a planet that hasn't been colonized?" The doctor stood too and looked at him.

"Why would you think Team Two was sent there to eliminate a CAT team for heaven's sake?" Alex kept his voice low. He didn't want the others to hear this. A quick glance told him they remained occupied with their own discussion.

"The Old City. What if the team found something the Western Alliance doesn't want anyone to know?"

That stopped Alex short. He knew the Alliance leaders weren't above something like that. His stomach began to churn.

"That doesn't make sense," he insisted. "Why launch this rescue mission with Spec Ops personnel if that's what happened?"

"You know as well as I do the freelance comm operators picked up the emergency beacon. Public pressure was beginning to build and would have gotten worse once the press started covering it," the doctor said, her tone calm.

"No," Alex said again. "I know one of the men on Team Two. He would never follow those orders."

"It's something you need to consider, Alex," the doctor said quietly before walking away.

Alex left the lounge and went into his quarters. He sat heavily on his bunk and leaned forward until his hands dangled between his knees. He stared at the toes of his boots and thought about what Gwen Mitchell had said.

It was possible. But that wasn't what had happened.

If it were any other Spec Ops team, he wouldn't be this sure. There was no way Command could present it, no spin they could put on it, that Brody would buy. He was too smart to fall for a bunch of lies and too principled to carry out orders that went against his morals. Alex released a long breath and straightened.

It was a helluva thing when a person had to put his trust in the honor of a man he despised.

Chapter Seven

Ravyn hated mud.

After two days of incessant showers, the sun had finally made an appearance. But it would take more than a few hours of sunshine to dry out the sodden earth, and now the humidity had reached nearly unbearable levels. Between sweat and rain, Ravyn had gotten used to damp clothes, but she couldn't tolerate the dirt ground into the fabric.

Days of slogging through mud had left her pants coated below the knee. She'd wiped her filthy hands on her thighs, her butt, her shirt, everywhere, spreading the muck to new locations. Ravyn didn't want to think about how many times her grimy hands had touched her face. Her hair felt plastered to her head. Strands escaped the braid and continually fell into her face. Every time she pushed them back, she cringed, knowing she deposited more dirt.

So far Damon had found them dry places to spend the night, but Ravyn hadn't gotten much rest. Whenever she shut her eyes, all she saw was blood. The nightmares hit her relentlessly, but at least she hadn't disturbed Damon again. He wasn't the type of man who would fake sleep in the face of her anguish, even if he had become cold and abrupt.

Ravyn made a face at his back, but didn't slow her steps. His remoteness added to her ill-humor. The only thing that had made this ordeal bearable had been talking with Damon. Now she didn't even have that. He spoke only to issue orders.

They took frequent rests because of the draining humidity, but she really wanted a nice, hot bath. She focused on thoughts of a deep tub full of scented bubbles as she walked. At times she would imagine champagne and strawberries, but mostly she pictured soap and shampoo. She bit back a sigh of longing. Never again would she take being clean for granted.

The wind gusted, rousing Ravyn from her fantasies. She watched Damon duck under a low tree branch draped with thorned vines. The breeze came again even more strongly and one of the trailing vines whipped across his arm, just below the sleeve of his T-shirt. She winced as she watched a jagged barb rip at his skin. It didn't cause so much as a hitch in his sure stride. Cautiously, she held the vine up and edged under it. Even with the mud covering him, she could see several drops of blood well before they crawled down his biceps. She'd asked yesterday why he'd tucked his long-sleeve shirt in the pack, but hadn't received an answer.

At last, he glanced down at the cut, but there was no other reaction, not so much as a curse. Ravyn couldn't see his face, but she guessed his expression remained stoic. This robot warrior persona drove her insane.

He was as covered in grime as she was. His camouflage fatigue pants appeared more brown from dried mud than any other color as did his once olive T-shirt. Yet the scrapes and dirt made him appear even more ruggedly handsome while Ravyn knew beyond doubt she looked pathetic.

It was so unfair.

The self-condemnation rose then, as it did anytime she felt sorry for herself. She knew she was lucky to be alive, lucky to be this miserable. It was just hard to remember that sometimes. Instead of soothing her surliness, the feelings of guilt added to it.

They started up a steep incline and Ravyn had to concentrate on keeping her balance. The mud here was thin and slippery, with no grass of any kind to hold the ground together. Her feet slid out from under her and she grabbed a bush to keep from falling. Cursing softly, she pushed herself upright. The swearing became more vehement when she realized she'd sustained several small, stinging cuts on her hands. Damon never even turned to see how she fared. She scowled at his back. Evidently, Captain Android couldn't exhibit even token concern for the troops.

When she reached the top of the ridge, Ravyn paused to catch her breath. If anything, the descent appeared steeper than it had been going up. And it looked muddier. There must have been a landslide recently since there was a path down the middle of the hill where the otherwise heavy vegetation had been replaced by a sweep of sludge. Great. Damon hadn't stopped, but she didn't worry about it. Despite his demeanor, she felt confident he wouldn't let her get too far behind him.

Taking a deep breath, Ravyn picked her way carefully down the hill. It was even tougher going than she'd thought. Despite her caution, she slid in several places before she could catch herself. Each time more wet earth sloshed onto her pants. She kept her legs slightly bent, but her knees still took a beating.

The third time she slipped, she couldn't regain her footing. With a plop, she landed on her butt and her weight and gravity had her sliding down the hill. The speed kept her on her back and she tried to use her legs to stop her rapid plunge.

It seemed to take forever before she lurched to a stop. Ravyn didn't move as she took inventory. She was unhurt, she decided, but she could feel mud oozing on her backside from the top of her head to the heels of her feet. It had even oozed under the protective vest she wore. She could feel it permeating her clothes, her panties. Something scratched her neck. She reached up and pulled out a twig. She probably had more foliage stuck in her hair. Gingerly, she pushed herself into a sitting position and saw Damon standing just below her.

He didn't inquire if she was okay. If he had, she would

have asked him to help her up. If he had laughed, she would have laughed with him. She may be humiliated, but she wasn't blind to how funny she must look. But Damon did neither of those things. He just stood there, face impassive, and didn't say a word. It was the last straw. She'd had all she could stand of the robot warrior act. Ravyn's temper ignited.

Without giving it any thought, she picked up a handful of the mud that surrounded her and threw it at him. Her aim was true and she caught him in the center of his chest. His eyes narrowed, but there was no other reaction.

His lack of response fanned the flames of her anger.

She pelted him with another, bigger, mud ball. She'd knock the man-of-stone persona out of him no matter what it took!

This time he appeared slightly surprised as the wet earth plopped to the ground from his chest. He still didn't look too terribly upset, but when she watched him shrug off the pack, Ravyn knew she'd succeeded in irking him. Scrambling hastily to her feet, she unzipped the vest and tossed it aside. He was bigger, stronger and better trained, but she welcomed the confrontation she knew was coming. She widened her stance, balancing her weight the way her brother had taught her.

As he took off his own vest, Ravyn flung another wad of mud at him. This time she hit his shoulder. When he turned, she knew from the look in his eyes that she'd managed to really piss him off. She smiled, baring her teeth in a feral grin.

Damon continually underestimated her, so she wasn't the least bit surprised when he rushed her. She moved to the side at the last minute, easily evading his charge. His momentum carried him past her and Ravyn shifted until she faced him again. Just for the hell of it, she tossed her last handful of mud.

This time he sidestepped and her missile fell harmlessly to the ground. Obviously deciding her evasion of his frontal assault was a fluke, Damon tried again. He must have played football, she guessed. With his arms outstretched, he looked like he was trying to tackle her. Once more Ravyn easily dodged away. She thought it insulting to be so underrated even though it gave her a very slight advantage. At least momentarily.

She didn't care that she needed all the help she could get. After nearly a week in her company, Damon should know she was more than just some helpless woman.

"Is this how you fought in the Oceanic War?" she jeered, hands on her hips. "It's amazing you survived. But then maybe you didn't have to fight anyone hand to hand."

"Ravyn, don't push me," he warned.

Blithely, she ignored his menacing tone and crouched quickly to scoop up more mud. Almost not fast enough. He nearly reached her before she could straighten and jump out of harm's way. Ravyn barely suppressed a shriek at her close call.

Warily, she and Damon circled each other. That wasn't easy, not with the mud slick as grease beneath their feet. Options flashed through her mind. She tried to guess which moves Damon was likely to make and figure out her best way to counter each one. Alex hadn't trained her to just react. He'd taught her to use her head, telling her it was her greatest asset.

Ravyn wasn't foolish enough to think her strength was any match for his, no matter how hot her temper. Still, there were ways to win a battle other than an all-out attack. Right now, her best weapons were the mud in her hands, her agility and her ability to think under pressure. And she could taunt him until he became so mad, he forgot his training. That was unlikely, she admitted, but there was always a chance.

"Geez, Brody, how did you ever get into Spec Ops if you can't even take down a woman?"

Gleefully, she watched him lunge at her and miss. It cheered her considerably to see him land face first in the mud. Just to add insult to injury, she caught him on the seat of his pants with two mud balls. She didn't have time to rearm before Damon regained his feet.

Uh-oh. She took an instinctive step back before stopping herself. The fireworks in his eyes contrasted sharply with the mud covering his features. He wasn't going to take it easy on her any longer. As she watched, a mask came down over his face and she knew he'd gone into warrior mode. Ravyn didn't waste any more breath on insults. It was just a matter of time until he bested her, but that didn't mean she was going down without a fight.

It was almost a dance, as he took the offensive and she countered his tactics, dodging and ducking. Once he nearly had her, but she managed to slip away thanks to the slick coat of mud on her back. Ravyn didn't dare take her eyes off him for a second, not even to scoop up more mud. Each time she escaped him, he came back with an even more difficult maneuver. He lunged less and used more of his strength against her moves. If she even blinked, she knew it would be over in short order.

"Not so arrogant now, are you sweet pea?" he gibed. The knowledge of impending victory glowed in his eyes; his smile was insolent. He didn't seem to have any doubt she was on the ropes.

That rekindled her waning anger. Ravyn lifted her chin imperiously, but didn't respond. Instead she focused her energy on keeping her footing. Their little two-step had churned up the ground, making it muddier and even more slippery. Damon was handling the slick conditions better than she was. Experience, she supposed.

And, in the end, that was what defeated her. Damon feinted, she reacted before he committed himself and found herself caught. Desperately, she twisted away and lost her footing, going down face first. She rolled over quickly, but Damon already stood over her, his triumphant expression insufferable. She fired off two quick shots of mud before he covered her, pinning her hands over her head.

Then the man had the nerve to laugh at her.

If he thought he'd won this easily, he'd better think again. She had more tricks up her sleeve. Ravyn's legs were free and she used them to flip him over on his back. As she gazed down on him, her laughter echoed his earlier mocking amusement.

For an instant, he lay there stunned. Unfortunately, that didn't last long enough for her to savor the situation or solidify the advantage. Their positions were reversed so fast, she was almost dizzy, and this time he didn't make the mistake of leaving her legs free.

His heavy body pushed her deeply into the muck, but she still wasn't ready to concede defeat. Staring defiantly into his green eyes, she tried to wriggle out from underneath him. As she struggled against him, she was pleased to see sweat gather on his brow. At least she was making him work to keep his hold on her.

"Be still," he grated out.

She ignored him.

"Ravyn, stop it."

She began to buck, trying to throw him off of her.

"Damn it," he muttered thickly.

Ravyn froze in surprise as he pressed the lower half of his body against hers. He was hard. She looked closer at his eyes and realized that what she had taken as anger was arousal. The perspiration beaded on his brow wasn't from exertion, but from trying to rein in his libido.

For a moment, they stared at each other. Ravyn's anger drained away and she lost interest in escaping. Instead, she arched her body against his, shifting her legs slightly so his erection pressed where it felt best. She couldn't hear his groan, but she felt it rumble through his chest.

Damon's hesitation lasted no more than an instant before his mouth came down on hers. There was nothing soft or gentle about the kiss, just voracious hunger. His lack of control didn't frighten her in the least. She reveled in it. She didn't even care that she could feel the grittiness of mud on her lips.

Ravyn tugged at her hands and Damon released them. She wrapped her arms around his neck, pulling him closer to her. He nibbled at her lips and she opened for him. Her eyes drifted shut and she gave herself totally to him. There was nothing for her but the feel of his body against hers. Nothing but his mouth, his taste. He nudged her legs farther apart and Ravyn made room for him. It felt even better and she muffled a moan against his lips. His hand ran down the outside of her thigh until he reached her knee, guiding her leg around his hip and bringing her body even tighter against his.

Without being told, Ravyn brought her other leg up, cradling him against her heat. She felt his hands at the buttons of her shirt as they continued to devour each other's mouths. Even that small separation made her ache. She didn't realize he'd finished unbuttoning her shirt until she felt the warmth of his hand through the nearly sheer fabric of her bra. This time she tried to press the upper half of her body closer to his touch.

Ravyn moved her arms until she could grab fistfuls of his T-shirt, then began to pull it over his head. She wanted to feel his bare skin against her, touch those hard muscles, feel that crisp hair. It was a slow process since she kept getting distracted by his clever fingers and his hard, hungry kiss.

When she had the shirt up to his shoulder blades, she left it and ran her hands over the skin of his back. He was burning up, but then so was she. At that moment, she didn't think she could ever get enough of him.

The thought barely formed when he pulled away, his body suddenly tense. Puzzled, Ravyn opened her eyes in time to see Damon bring his hand down over her mouth. His pupils were still dilated, his chest heaving even as he tried to breathe soundlessly, but his attention was definitely not on her.

It took her a moment to process the information. Something worried him and he wanted her to be silent. Okay, she got that, but his method of keeping her quiet made it difficult to breathe. She pushed her tongue out sharply against the palm of his hand.

Startled, he glanced at her. She knew he got the message when he stopped muzzling her. Damon shifted slightly, inaudibly, and his hand emerged with a pistol. Ravyn moved slowly, trying to minimize the noise, but she knew she needed to get her legs down. He couldn't afford to be impeded by her and there was no way he could react fast with her wound around him.

What if it was the killer?

Ravyn tried to think of where they'd left their things and

couldn't remember. She could only hope it wasn't where they would be seen. Fear rose in her throat, but she relentlessly pushed it back. She couldn't be her usual cowardly self, not now. Damon might need her.

She kept her eyes on him, knowing he was her best gauge of how serious the situation was. He was intent, but not poised for battle, so she figured they weren't in imminent danger. Ravyn still didn't know what had caught his attention. She didn't see or hear anything unusual.

Her first clue came less than a minute later. The stench made her think of rotting flesh, and she swallowed hard to keep from gagging. It took an effort, but Ravyn forced herself to remain calm, to keep her breathing slow. That became harder to do when she heard the sounds of something large moving quickly through the undergrowth. She couldn't judge from which direction the noise came, but it sounded too damn close for her peace of mind.

Damon remained watchful and that helped her stay steady. Whatever it was couldn't be as close as she feared or he would be taking some kind of action, not calmly waiting. Gradually, the sound became more distant and the odor dissipated. Ravyn felt herself begin to relax, despite the continued vigilance of the man poised over her. It humbled her to know he would protect her with his body if necessary, and it made her worry again. She didn't want him dying for her.

Finally, after what seemed like a million years, he tucked the weapon away and stood. Damon was covered in mud, she realized. There wasn't an inch of him that wasn't coated. That had her looking down and taking in her own appearance.

She looked as if she'd been rolling in the mud. Which, she supposed, she had been. With shaking hands, she started to button her shirt again. She tried to keep her laughter in check, but between her relief at being safe and the sight of them covered in muck, she wasn't having much success.

"I don't suppose," Damon said, "your team forgot to report they'd found animals the size of a bear on Jarved Nine during their study of the wildlife?"

Ravyn sobered quickly. "No. We didn't find any animals over about ninety pounds on this planet."

"That's what I was afraid of."

"It was the murderer then?"

"Maybe," Damon said, finally looking at her. "Whatever it was, it was a hell of a lot bigger than ninety pounds."

Chapter Eight

He'd lost his mind.

What other reason was there? Yeah, he'd pushed them hard to get out of the vicinity where they'd nearly encountered whatever it was. And this lake *was* in a very protected location. Surrounded by sheer rock face with only a narrow entry, nothing could come close to them without him seeing it and being able to pick it off with his pistol. But it was still an indulgence. Okay, so he felt better after a bath and he didn't mind the chance to get his clothes clean. Plus there were a few other bonuses.

Damon watched Ravyn walk from bush to bush, checking on their drying wardrobe. With the high humidity, the best they could hope for by morning was damp clothes. The sound of her humming would reach him now and then. Idly scratching his bare chest, he counted her happiness as a benefit.

The last six days had been hard for her. He didn't know if the nightmares still gripped her, but it was obvious she wasn't getting enough sleep. If nothing else, this early stop would get her some needed rest. The other pluses were purely selfish. He'd peeked while Ravyn had taken her bath.

Damon's lips quirked at the memory. He should feel guilty. After all, he had been standing guard and she'd trusted him to behave like a gentleman, not a randy teenager after his first glimpse of a naked woman. He couldn't find even a hint of remorse.

She finished checking the clothes and walked toward him. Damon swallowed hard, her beauty hitting him like a fist. Her dark hair fell past her shoulders in waves. He wanted to sink his hands in it, hold her close while he explored her mouth. He wouldn't be in such a hurry this time. He wouldn't be so rough.

Her legs went on forever. He swore he could still feel them wrapped around him. The sensation had Damon shifting, trying to ease his sudden discomfort. With only his shorts on, he had no way to hide his body's response to her. He tried to keep his face, even his eyes, impassive. Ravyn had pulled back since their interlude in the mud and he didn't want to frighten her.

She sank gracefully to the ground when she reached him. Not too near he noticed and hid a smile by rubbing a hand over his mouth. He didn't blame her for running scared. He'd been all over her; there had been no wooing, no gentleness at all. He was lucky she hadn't fled in the other direction.

"Thanks again," she said, fingering the tail of his shirt.

This was his number one bonus. The sight of Ravyn wearing nothing but his fatigue shirt. She had the sleeves rolled up so the cuffs wouldn't hang past her hands and the hem of the shirt fell almost to her knees, providing more than adequate coverage. It didn't matter. Seeing her dressed in an article of his clothing caused his chest to ache. He had to clear his throat before he could answer her. "No big deal."

"It was, Damon." She started to reach out to him, but pulled her hand back before making contact. "I don't have to see all the scratches on your arms to appreciate what you did. I can't believe you kept the shirt in the pack just so I would have something clean to wear when we waited for our clothes to dry."

"How are the clothes doing?" he asked to change the subject.

Ravyn paused briefly, then said, "They're drying about as well as they can. At least the breeze is helping."

"Good."

"I know you don't want to hear this either, but thanks for stopping. I really needed this bath."

"Don't thank me, Ravyn. We both know we should have kept moving. This lapse of common sense could put us in danger."

The reminder made him scowl. He'd committed more errors in judgment today than he had in years. The last time he'd made this many mistakes . . . Damon shut the thought off. He couldn't think about it. Not with their close call so fresh in his mind.

First of all, he should never have let Ravyn goad him into wrestling her in the mud. If he had turned and walked out of firing range, the situation would have been resolved. Secondly, he shouldn't have kissed her. They were lucky his unprofessional behavior hadn't gotten them killed. But what made him sweat was if he had it to do all over again, he'd still kiss her. He'd enjoyed it too much to believe otherwise. His third mistake troubled him the most. When they'd spotted the lake, she'd turned to him and asked if she could have a bath. The need to please her had been so strong, he hadn't hesitated more than a second to consider their safety before giving in to her plea.

What was she doing to him?

He'd spent the last two days trying to put distance between them. Ravyn had hated it. Even so, it had been tougher on him. Somewhere along the way, talking with her had become more important to him. Cutting her off or answering in monosyllables had been almost torturous.

"Damon."

Ravyn's voice snagged his attention and he looked over at her. She appeared worried. "What's wrong?" he asked.

"I'm sorry I asked to stop. I don't want you to beat yourself up over it."

"That's not the only thing I've been thinking about," he

admitted. "Since we've met, you continually surprise me. Where did you learn hand-to-hand?" Hell, he should have asked that question hours earlier. The woman screwed up his head and his control. He'd always had total command over himself. That had gone out the window almost the instant he'd found her underneath the bunk.

"My brother taught me," she said with a fond smile. "He didn't think CAT training was sufficient. Alex said he wanted to be sure I could take care of myself no matter where I was sent."

"What else did your stepbrother teach you?" Damon didn't want any more shocks.

"Lots of stuff." She shrugged. "He taught me to shoot."

"You haven't asked for one of the pistols."

"I thought about it, but decided we were better off with you hanging on to both weapons. I'm not exactly a crack shot, and I'm sure you're almost as proficient left handed as right."

"How bad are you?"

Ravyn wrinkled her nose. "Bad enough that Alex strongly suggested I never buy a gun."

"In other words, if you're armed, I better make sure I'm directly behind you?"

She laughed. "Not quite that bad." Sobering, she added, "But if you need me to shoot, I will. I'm not afraid of guns."

Damon studied her resolve. He knew then, without a doubt, he could rely on her. Part of the weight he'd been carrying on his shoulders seemed to fall away. He wasn't alone. He had a partner. For the first time in six days, he felt a full and wholehearted smile cross his face. "That's good to know," he told her, "but I'll hang on to the pistols."

Her laughter made him feel good, made him feel ten feet tall. Damon chuckled along with her. In that moment, despite everything, he realized he was happy.

By the time the sun set, Damon knew exactly what Ravyn was attempting to do. He'd used aloofness to put distance between them, a plan he'd willingly relinquished earlier today.

She was trying to distance them with a "we're just friends" approach.

He suppressed a smile. He suspected a lot of men had found themselves "just friends" with her before they'd known what had happened. Once in that category, it became nearly impossible to develop a romantic relationship. Ravyn didn't seem to realize while they were already friends, it was far too late for them to be "just friends." He felt torn between stopping her chatter with a kiss or reminding her that if Godzilla hadn't stumbled near them this afternoon, they'd already be lovers. Damon resisted both choices and enjoyed their conversation instead.

She needed space and he would give it to her no matter how hard it was. His effort to keep her at arms' length had made it two days. He didn't think Ravyn would last much longer than he had. And at least with her method, they would continue talking, something he'd missed desperately. Damon wondered if Ravyn realized the more they spoke, the closer they'd become. The physical attraction between them was stronger than anything he'd felt before. That was difficult enough to combat. Attraction and affection would be a nearly irresistible combination.

If he could manage any kind of control, they wouldn't become lovers until they were on Earth, but it was a forgone conclusion where they were headed. For now though, he needed to find that control fast. He wouldn't jeopardize Ravyn by being so tied in knots he couldn't see danger coming up on them. He refused to watch another person's blood run from their body because he'd failed.

"Ravyn," he said, interrupting her story, "it's getting late. We both need some sleep." He saw trepidation pass through her eyes and knew then she continued to have nightmares.

"Sure, you're right," she said.

If he hadn't seen the flash of alarm, he would have bought her calm tone. It bothered him that he couldn't fix this for her, couldn't stop her terror. The only possible solution he had involved torture. For him. He made the choice without thinking twice. Damon settled himself on his side and patted the ground beside him. "Come here, sweet pea."

He could read the internal debate on her face. He didn't say another word or make another movement. It was up to her.

After a long minute, she complied.

The feel of her body lying next to his drove him to the edge, but he hung on. He ignored that they both were mostly undressed, that he could feel the softness of her bare legs against his. He was as stiff as lamordite crystals, but slowly, gradually, she relaxed against him, even resting her head on his shoulder. Wrapping his arms around her, Damon murmured, "I'm here. Nothing is going to hurt you."

The soft whisper of her breath against his chest had his heart twisting. And when he knew she slept, he felt as satisfied as if he had won the Third Oceanic War single-handedly.

Damon hoped their sleeping arrangement kept her demons at bay. As agonizing as it was to have Ravyn in his arms without going any further, it was the sweetest torment he'd ever known.

Hmm. Ravyn stretched, pressing herself languorously into the warmth beside her. She snuggled closer, her fingers kneading hard muscle through soft cotton. Her left leg rested over a set of masculine hips. An intriguing bulge pressed into her thigh and she rubbed against it.

"Hmm." Her voice purred from her chest. Contentment curled her lips into a sleepy smile. Two nights sleeping within Damon's protective embrace, two mornings waking up in his arms and it felt like it had always been this way.

Her hand stroked and circled, easing lower with each motion. Through her fingertips she felt a rumble and her smile deepened. He liked this too. Her hand encountered the waistband of his pants. For a while, she satisfied herself by exploring the ridges of his stomach. Then she slid her hand back up, tracing the muscles in his chest. Feeling Damon react to her touch increased her enjoyment.

"Ravyn, open your eyes."

Drowsily, she complied. His molten gaze captured hers. Satisfied with his response, she pressed her lips to his chin.

"Hell," he muttered, his voice as rough as ground glass.

He shifted until she was on her back, his body poised beside her. She read the intent in his eyes and Ravyn parted her lips, ready for his kiss. She thought she knew what to expect, but Damon surprised her. Instead of taking, he teased.

He nibbled at her mouth, first nipping her upper lip, then sucking the lower one. She gasped at the sensation. Damon broke the kiss and his hands framed her face, his calloused fingers caressing her jaw, her cheeks. And all the while, their eyes were open, gazes locked. It was the most intimate thing Ravyn had ever experienced. It went far beyond a physical connection and became a mating of souls. Lost in a world of gentle arousal, she knew no fear of this bond.

He came back for a second, leisurely kiss before he teased his way to her ear. Damon's tongue traced the shell, then his teeth nipped at the lobe. Ravyn moaned softly as he soothed the sting. Before she quite realized it, his lips were at the pulse point in her throat. She turned her head to give him better access and her eyes drifted shut. Finally, unable to stand it a second longer, she guided his mouth back to hers. Ravyn ran her hands through his hair, trailed her nails softly across his nape.

With a rumble of approval, Damon lifted his mouth from hers. "Look at me," he ordered.

Ravyn obeyed and gasped at the intensity she saw on his face. She couldn't look away from his eyes, caught by the heat she saw there, captivated by the tight leash he had on his desire. He smiled down at her, one big hand cupping the back of her head, angling her for another kiss. Impatiently, she waited for him to take their kiss further. He didn't. And when she tried, he eased back just far enough to foil her attempts.

"More, Damon," she demanded, frustrated by his restraint.

He deepened the kiss, but continued his leisurely pace. She shuddered as his tongue stroked the roof of her mouth. Soon, though, this lazy exploration had her wanting even more. She didn't get it. He began easing away, retreating, and Ravyn growled in objection. She tried to pull him back to her, but didn't have the strength. Her pleas for him not to stop fell on deaf ears. Finally, his forehead resting against hers, Damon rubbed her ear lobe between his thumb and forefinger.

"Good morning, sweet pea," he said, his voice husky.

"You're a tease, Captain."

He grinned at her and pushed away. "We need to get moving," he said, leaving her on the ground.

Ravyn sighed and sat up. This pretty much shot her friendship scheme out of the water, but she felt relief, not disappointment. Still, the fact he'd kept his control, while having her begging, cried out for retribution. With a contemplative smile, Ravyn climbed to her feet.

She was going to enjoy getting even.

Damon rubbed his fingers over his eyelids, trying to wake himself up. Two nights with Ravyn pressed against him had taken its toll. It was worth it, though, and not because she tended to drape herself all over him while she slept. And not because of the kiss they'd shared this morning.

He knew she hadn't had a nightmare since he'd invited her to sleep next to him. His hands reached for his canteen as his gaze sought her out. Ravyn sat atop a flat boulder, munching on a piece of fruit. She looked much more alert and rested. Yeah, it was worth it, he thought, sipping the tepid water. And he'd gone with less sleep than this.

They should get going. He'd been feeling vaguely uneasy since morning and he knew better than to discount his sixth sense. It had always been eerily accurate. Still, the feeling wasn't strong enough to concern him, not yet, and there hadn't been any sign of pursuit in the last two days. Five more minutes, he decided, then they were out of here.

Recapping the canteen, he joined her on the rock. She gave him a friendly smile, but it was more than that. It held an intimacy, a welcome that warmed him. No one, Damon realized, had ever smiled at him in quite that way.

"You know," Ravyn said, "you never talk about yourself."

"Who can get a word in," he said deadpan.

He watched her roll her eyes and grinned.

"Just what I need, another comedian. I can tell already you and Alex will be great friends."

The knowledge that she thought about him meeting her family had his heart skittering. He took a deep breath to settle his pulse rate. Don't read too much into that, he warned himself.

"No," Ravyn said when he opened his mouth, "don't say another word. You'll just get yourself in trouble."

"You do seem to have more to say than the average person," Damon offered diplomatically.

She shifted slightly so she was turned toward him. "Didn't I tell you not to say anything?"

Since she didn't sound angry, he decided not to worry about it. "Every word you've uttered has been fascinating," he said, tongue firmly in cheek.

Ravyn gave his shoulder a companionable shove and laughed. "You know what? I like you, Damon Brody," she said, still smiling, "but that doesn't get you off the hook. Start talking." She circled her hand in a "let's go" motion.

Damon rolled his shoulders to ease the tension that had developed there. He could see Ravyn sitting expectantly, but he let the silence drag on. It wasn't that he was opposed to talking, he just preferred not to talk about himself.

Her huff of exasperation sounded loud in the silence of the clearing. "You Spec Ops types are all alike," she muttered. "It's like pulling teeth to get any personal information."

He opened his mouth to ask how many Spec Ops "types" she knew, but before he could say anything, Ravyn continued.

"Why don't I ask you questions and you answer? Does that work for you? Keep in mind, I'm nothing if not tenacious."

"So I'm learning," he said softly. "Go ahead, ask."

"Where's home?"

"I'm stationed in California."

She heaved a sigh big enough to draw his attention to her breasts. Damon knew that wasn't her intention, but enjoyed the view for a moment before looking back up. Her expression screamed, why me?

"What?" he grumbled.

"I didn't ask where you were stationed, I asked where your home was."

"My home is wherever I'm stationed," he said reasonably.

"Okay, let's try this another way. Where did you grow up?" she asked with forced calm.

"All over." Damon hid a smile. He didn't realize how much fun it could be to rile Ravyn up this way. He reconsidered that idea when she dug her nails into his thigh. "Ouch." He pried her fingers off his leg. To be safe, he kept hold of her.

"Oh," she asked innocently, "did that hurt?"

"Not at all. I've always walked with a limp."

"I'll kiss it and make it better if you tell me what I want to know." Her smile appeared feline.

He realized she'd heard him gulp when her grin widened and smug satisfaction filled her eyes. "Be careful what you promise, sweet pea. What would you do if I took you up on that?"

"Why, Damon," she purred, her eyelids lowering half way, "I've always been a woman of my word."

Where had this side of her come from? Stunned, he loosened his grip and she slipped her hand free. Wary, he braced himself for her next move. He didn't have long to wait. Her fingers found the place she'd gouged. Expecting more pain, he froze when she made gentle circles around the injured area. A groan escaped before he could swallow it, but his lapse brought a reward. Ravyn began to run her fingers slowly up the inseam of his pants.

Damon could feel the blood rushing from his brain. He propped himself up on his elbows, eyes drifting shut, and moved his legs farther apart. Just when she seemed to make a little forward progress, her fingers would slide back down, before easing upward again. Anticipation zinged through his blood. He had reasons for not wanting to make love yet, but he was damned if he could remember what they were anymore. Finally, her touch was almost where he needed it, where he wanted it.

And then she teased her way back down.

"No," he protested, his eyes popping open. "Touch me."

"Damon," she said. She was short of breath and it got him

hotter to know touching him aroused her. "Remember this morning when I asked you for more?"

"Yeah?"

"Payback's a bitch."

It seemed childish now, her need to even the score. For a minute this afternoon, she had feared Damon would strangle her and she wouldn't have blamed him. She hadn't meant things to get so out of hand. She'd only wanted to tease him a little. It seemed her brain had left her body the instant she'd felt the hard muscles in his thigh. She'd loved touching him. He'd been silent since, probably thinking up ways to kill her in her sleep. Ravyn's lips quirked at the absurdity. Damon would never hurt her. Torture her, maybe. A girl could only hope.

Ravyn knew she owed him an apology. After a moment's consideration, she picked up her pace so she walked beside him. Damon glanced over at her, eyebrows raised.

"I'm sorry," she said, "about earlier."

"You mean you weren't out for revenge? I know better."

Ravyn smiled up at him. She couldn't help it. "Well, yeah, I was. I just didn't intend for things to go as far as they did. And I sure didn't want you mad at me."

"I'm not mad at you," he told her.

"You're not even looking at me."

He stopped then and met her eyes. "I'm not mad at you," he repeated. "Frustrated, yes, but I'm mad at myself."

"Why?" Ravyn didn't doubt him, but the fault was hers.

He let out a long breath and his gaze scrutinized the area before he looked at her again. Something about him seemed more alert, more tense than usual. "I want you, Ravyn," he said.

Her body heated at the intensity of his gaze. With just a few words, he had every cell in her body ready, willing and able.

"I'm always thinking about you," he continued, "when I should be concentrating on keeping you safe. I've been able to put aside the deaths of six friends, but I can't keep the door shut on my desire for you. I'm not used to this kind of weakness. I've always been able to compartmentalize before."

Ravyn glanced down at her boots, the toes just inches from his. She tried to come up with something to say, but couldn't. As she watched, his boots moved closer and she felt his hands on her arms. Surprised, she looked back up at him.

"I have very little control with you," he confessed, reluctance in his voice. His hands caressed her shoulders.

"That scares you," she managed to choke out.

A humorless smile chased across his face. "Yes, it does. How am I supposed to protect you when half the time my attention is on what we could be doing together? I'm scared my distraction is going to get us killed. And it's getting worse, not better."

Reaching up, she cupped his face in her hands. She watched him flinch, before he settled. She knew he wasn't lying; his response to this simple touch underlined what he'd just said.

"I trust you," she told him. He tried to jerk away, but Ravyn held on. "Now trust yourself."

This time when he pulled back, she let him. He cleared his throat roughly and scanned the area again. "We need to keep moving," he said and started walking.

Something was bothering him she realized, something more than what was happening between them. Ravyn fell into step beside him, but didn't stay there long. He picked up speed and she dropped behind. She sighed, but let him have the space. At least she could enjoy the view from back here.

She didn't know what he was thinking and wasn't sure she wanted to know. Not with that grim look on his face every time he glanced back. She was as scared by this as Damon. Somehow, when she wasn't paying attention, he had become important to her. Impatiently, Ravyn pushed the thought aside. She didn't want to think about it. The forest had given way to scattered trees, she noted, but their surroundings couldn't hold her interest.

Her eyes kept drifting back to Damon and finally she let them stay there. She imagined sliding his T-shirt off, measuring the breadth of his shoulders with her fingers. In her mind, she reached for his pants, opened them and pushed them down his legs. She pictured him naked, fantasized running her hands and mouth all over him. And she knew exactly what he looked like without clothes. He'd trusted her to stand guard while he'd taken a bath in the lake, but she hadn't been able to resist peeking at him.

The man's body was a work of art.

Ravyn unzipped her vest and reached for the front of her shirt. She fanned it back and forth, trying to cool her burning skin, but it didn't help. Not when she had such a great view of Damon's tight rear end. She licked her dry lips and decided she might be struck dead for all her lustful thoughts.

A loud crack of thunder made her jump.

"Coincidence," she murmured, but peered cautiously over her shoulder just in case.

What she saw behind them froze her. The sky was dark and foreboding. Lightning flashed from the clouds as she watched and there was another sharp report of thunder. Her heart took flight in her chest. She was accustomed to gentle, rumbling thunder on Jarved Nine, not this. The storm was heading right for them, Ravyn realized. She looked around and saw Damon hadn't stopped. That broke her paralysis. She zipped the vest again and ran to catch him. They had to find shelter fast. It wasn't smart to be out in any electrical storm, but wandering around with what looked to be a tornado bearing down on them was beyond stupid.

The wind picked up, whipping her hair loose from its braid. It felt like she wasn't gaining any ground on Damon no matter how fast she moved. The first drops of rain hit her skin and Ravyn turned to see the storm was almost on top of her.

"Damon," she called, but the wind grabbed her voice and carried it away. The lightning seemed to surround her now and she felt desperation well up. Ravyn picked up the pace and finally caught up with him. When she reached his side, she grabbed his arm and said, "We have to find shelter."

He stopped and she watched him study the low bank of clouds before he shook his head. "No, we have to keep going."

"We can't," she argued and about half a dozen bolts of lightning streaked out of the clouds in emphasis. It startled her so badly she almost leapt into Damon's arms. She waited for the deafening peals of thunder to finish, knowing she wouldn't be heard over them. "Did you see that?" she asked when it subsided. "If we don't get out of this, we're going to be toast!"

It began to rain harder and Damon pushed his wet hair back. "Ravyn," he said earnestly, "he's on our trail again."

Nervously, she looked around, but could see no evidence of danger, except the encroaching bad weather. "Did you hear something? See something?" she shouted to be heard above the wind and now driving rain.

"No, I just know. Come on," he said, taking her hand and tugging her along behind him. For an instant, she dug in her heels. He pulled harder and she acceded.

It seemed impossible that anyone would be able to track them through a storm like this, but Ravyn believed in instinct and didn't doubt Damon's was honed beyond that of most people. If he said the killer was on their trail, she didn't question it. But with the storm upon them and lightning flashing almost continually, she thought the weather was the greater threat.

They were going uphill she realized belatedly and wondered what Damon was thinking. She wasn't an expert by any means, but she was sure the higher you were, the greater the risk in an electrical storm. Especially when there were lone trees scattered here and there all but begging for a lightning strike.

The rain came sideways. Ravyn lowered her head and aimed herself forward. She was grateful for the warmth of Damon's hand around hers. The assurance and confidence he conveyed with his touch grounded her, calmed her. A sheet of lightning hit so close, the hair on her arms stood up. His grip tightened and she realized he wasn't downplaying the severity of the weather. Her fear increased. If he thought the greater danger came from the killer, then it was more serious than she'd assumed.

It became harder to walk. Ravyn looked down and saw the

rain running down the hill, taking soil with it. She grimaced at the thought of more mud, but didn't stop putting one foot in front of the other. Damon let go of her when they reached the top, and he used both hands to push his dark hair out of his face. They both dripped with water, their hair and clothes saturated. She bet he wished for a buzz cut right now.

She tried to smile, but couldn't manage it. It made her uneasy standing on the highest point around, like they were asking for trouble. Ravyn let out a short, startled shriek when a bolt of lightning hit a nearby tree. It crashed to the ground and smoldered there. Her feet tingled and she knew that was not good. Damon glanced at her when she screamed, but didn't say anything about it. She didn't need him to. If the murderer was on their trail, he might have heard her. She could have given their position away with her cowardice.

Part of her wanted to run, to seek shelter out of the elements. But she wouldn't. Not without Damon. She'd stick with him even if it killed her. And there was no humor or irony in the thought. It held nothing but truth.

"Come on," he ordered and started down the other side of the hill.

He moved quickly and Ravyn followed. They both slipped and slid in the mud. She frowned fiercely. Why did she even bother trying to stay clean? When she returned to Earth, she was living in the desert. Somewhere the rainfall was about a millimeter every two years. Cactus plants and sand. That was a climate.

The heavy rain made it difficult to see more than a few feet in front of her, while the roar of thunder and the brief flashes of lightning told her the storm showed no signs of letting up. She jumped at the nearness of the next rumble and lost her footing momentarily before regaining her balance. It didn't matter how precarious she thought their position, she would bite her lip bloody before she let Damon down again.

She tilted her head up to the heavens. "What if I promise to repent and sin no more?" she asked.

Another burst of lightning nearly blinded her and Ravyn

smothered a yelp. As the storm continued unabated, she realized she'd received her answer. It was for the best. She couldn't stop wanting Damon even if it would end this squall. Ravyn set her lips and kept moving. Her legs hurt from the weight of her wet pants and the effort of pulling her feet out of the deepening mud. She didn't dare stop. Damon was way ahead of her and she still had to make it to the bottom of the hill.

She had her eyes glued on him when it occurred. She wasn't sure if lightning or wind caused it, but a tree began to topple over. Time moved in slow motion. Ravyn could see it happening, but couldn't prevent it. She screamed at him, not concerned if the killer heard. The wind gusted, obscuring her vision with rain. By the time it cleared, she could no longer see him, but the tree was on the ground. Ravyn ran down the hill, uncaring of the distance she slid with every step. She stopped worrying about the storm, about the lightning. Only one consideration filled her mind: Damon.

She screamed his name as she got closer, trying to be heard above the ravages of the weather, but there was no response. She reached the fallen tree, but still couldn't see him. Ravyn fought back the panic. The tree had fallen into an area with flood water rushing through it. Even as she watched, the newly formed creek widened. She didn't hesitate. Backing up to give herself a running start, she leaped across the rising water.

She spotted him instantly when she reached the other side.

Damon was on his back and the only thing keeping his head out of the water was the pack strap caught on one of the tree branches. Ravyn gave thanks and jumped in. Immediately, she grabbed him, holding his head up as the water continued to rise. She slid the strap loose with no trouble.

His eyelids fluttered, so she didn't think he was unconscious, but there was no doubt the man had suffered a severe blow to the head. Ravyn braced herself on the bottom and pulled at Damon to free him. She felt his body give before her feet slid from under her and she dunked both of them in the muddy, fast-moving water.

She surfaced, sputtering, but propped Damon up instead

of wiping her face. Ravyn had to find some leverage. Her brain worked frantically, considering options. She decided he wasn't trapped by the tree, just tangled in its limbs, because she'd felt movement as she'd pulled him. The cord from his comm device was snared in the branches, and she struggled to unhook it with one hand. A snapping sound startled her and the cord slipped from her grip. She watched it disappear beneath the roiling water for a moment before turning her attention back to the more pressing situation.

Some of the tree's roots were still sunk in the soil, giving it a measure of stability she thought she could use to her advantage. Ravyn hugged Damon, then put her right foot on the tree trunk. She pushed with all the strength she had. It worked. They rolled clear of the tree branches, out of the deepest water, to an area that was a bit shallower, where the runoff didn't rush so hard and it was easier for her to maneuver them onto land. For a moment, she lay there panting, thankful to be on stable ground, even if it was muddy.

A bright flash penetrated her closed eyes and roused Ravyn. She slid out from underneath Damon and checked him for injuries. The gash above his temple scared her. It had already covered half of his face with blood. She bit her lip and ran her hands over his arms and legs, checking for broken bones.

Her limited medical knowledge worried her. Why hadn't she volunteered to receive comprehensive first-aid training when it had been offered? All she knew was what she'd picked up on her own. She needed a compress to stop the bleeding on his forehead and the only clean or dry piece of clothing they had was the fatigue shirt in the pack. She tried to lift him to get the pack off, but he didn't budge. "Damon," she said, leaning over him.

His eyes slowly opened, but that didn't offer Ravyn any comfort. His gaze was unfocused and she knew he was still out of it. At least his pupils were equal and of a normal size.

She pulled her shirt from her pants, opened the three bottom buttons and shifted to his injured side. She rolled the material from one tail and pressed it against his wound. His eyes drifted shut once more. Ravyn lost all track of time as she continued applying pressure. The storm started letting up, moving past them, but her focus was solely on the man lying on the ground.

When the water's path widened and threatened to wash over his feet, Ravyn wedged herself beneath Damon again and tugged. And tugged and tugged. The man weighed a ton, but she finally got him farther from the water. Her backside was covered with mud again, but she had more important matters to focus on.

Blood continued to seep out of the wound. She tried to guess how long she'd applied pressure, but had no way of judging. At this point, she didn't know what concerned her more, the bleeding or Damon's continued insensibility. Leaning down, she studied the gash. It was deep, but only a couple of inches long. She realized she was crying, and impatiently, wiped at the tears. "Take care of Damon," she whispered, "and fall apart later."

There was a good chance he had a concussion since the area around the cut was already discolored and swollen. She needed to wake him up to make sure it wasn't worse than that. "Damon," she said insistently, "look at me."

He groaned. It was the most response she'd gotten from him so far. "Captain, open your eyes and look at me," she ordered. That particular ploy didn't work and Ravyn blinked back the new tears gathered in her eyes. "Damon, I need you here with me," she said coaxingly. She ran her thumb gently across the uninjured side of his face. "Come on, honey."

His eyelids fluttered, then opened, but his stare was glassy and dazed. She shifted so he looked right at her, but she knew he didn't see her. Her concern increased. "Damon, focus on me," she pleaded.

It hurt her to watch him fight the pain, the confusion, but he did it. She saw awareness return to his gaze and sighed in relief. That didn't mean there wasn't a problem, but she took his new expression as a good sign. Smiling, she pushed a few strands of hair off his forehead and pressed her lips softly to his.

As she drew back, her eyes locked on his, and Ravyn's

heart stopped. There at the bottom of the hill, kneeling in the mud as rain fell gently down, realization exploded in her brain.

She'd gone and fallen in love with the damn man.

Chapter Nine

No! The denial came quickly and instinctively. It was the situation, not the man. She wouldn't let it be more. Ravyn looked away, sure if she didn't, he would read her turmoil despite his head injury. She shook her head, trying to ignore her emotions. She couldn't waste time thinking about this now. Damon needed her.

"Ravyn?" His hoarse voice brought the tears back.

She knew what he was asking with that one word. "I'm fine. You're the one who got hurt." She kept her voice soft, sure he had a huge headache. "Does anything hurt besides your head?"

He frowned and Ravyn guessed he was taking inventory. "No," he finally answered, "not really."

"What do you mean 'not really'?" She asked gently, although she couldn't prevent the tightness in her voice.

"Bruised," he said, "not hurt." Damon tried to push himself into a sitting position. "We've got to go. Help me up."

"Are you crazy?" she demanded, forgetting to speak softly. He sat up without waiting for her assistance, although he had to struggle to do it. If he hadn't already taken a blow to the head, Ravyn would have bopped him for sheer stupidity. "Damon," she said, trying to remain reasonable, "you're hurt. We can't go anywhere yet."

"Ravyn, he's close, I can feel it. We have to find a more defensible position. Now help me."

She frowned, trying to decide what to do. She couldn't write off his instincts, not when she inexplicably knew things herself. But she didn't want him moving until they discovered how badly he was injured. Blood still seeped from his wound.

On the other hand, if the killer was close, they were sitting ducks. But was Damon right? He'd taken a hard hit to the head. Ravyn had to make the decision fast because she knew he wouldn't wait much longer. She stared at him, trying to read his state of mind. What she saw worried her. His eyes seemed to go out of focus frequently and the set of his mouth spoke of pain. Despite all this, Ravyn decided to trust his instincts.

"How many fingers do you see?" she asked, holding up her index finger.

"One. Now can we go?"

Ravyn nodded and crouched beside him. "Lean on me," she said, slipping an arm around his waist. He did, a little too heavily, and they both ended up sitting in mud. Shifting to her knees, Ravyn took a deep breath and said, "Let's try again. This time, though, use my shoulders to push yourself up."

This worked better. Damon made it to his knees before he started swaying precariously. Sweat ran down his face from the effort, and Ravyn bit her lip to keep from saying anything. They stayed that way a few moments as he fought to steady himself.

"Ready?" he asked, eyelids more closed than open.

"Yes." She spoke aloud because she didn't think he would see if she nodded.

Ravyn winced, pressing her lips together to keep from gasping. She knew Damon would be appalled if he realized his weight hurt her shoulders. It took him a long time to stand and even then, he kept a tight grip on her. Finally, when she didn't think she could bear it anymore, the pressure eased. She blinked rapidly a few times to clear the tears from her eyes.

Damon was gray. She kept a hand on him as she rose. When she reached her feet, he slid his left arm across her shoulders. Ravyn took the hint and put her arm around his waist. She waited for him to start walking, unsure if he could move.

Chalk one up for stubborn determination, Ravyn thought as they inched along. He'd instinctively left his right arm free so he could draw the gun if he needed to. She knew, however, he was incapable of protecting them, that it was up to her.

They hadn't gone far when he started talking. The words were mumbled, but she picked up enough to know he was issuing instructions on what constituted a defendable position. It was a good thing Alex had already taught her this stuff because she never would have figured it from the few words she was able to understand. His slurred speech scared her witless, but she knew Damon wouldn't let her stop until they'd found a good place to hole up. Ravyn hoped she spotted something soon.

He slipped in and out of awareness. When he lost full consciousness, Ravyn had to support all his weight. More than once, they fell in the mud. Footing was treacherous and Damon was a heavily muscled six foot four. Falling was inevitable.

Hitting the ground always seemed to bring him to his senses. Wordlessly, she'd help him to his feet and they'd continue. Ravyn tried to pay attention to their surroundings, tried to keep her ears open in case the killer closed in. She could only hear their labored breathing and the water dripping from tree leaves. The rain had stopped, but the sun's return had the area steaming. Weariness left her uncaring that, once again, the two of them were covered in mud from head to toe, front and back.

They continued plodding along, one shaky step after another. Ravyn didn't know how Damon managed. The thought no sooner registered when, without warning, she had all his weight again. She twisted as they went down so that she took the brunt of the impact. Damon couldn't afford another bump on the head.

Ravyn couldn't move, couldn't breathe. She didn't even try. She'd had the wind knocked out of her and two hundred plus pounds of male continued to squeeze the oxygen from her lungs. She closed her eyes and focused on recovery. When she could take in air again, she realized Damon wasn't moving. Now she panicked. Every other time, he'd been ready to go before she was. Carefully, she rolled him onto his back, one hand bracing his head.

As she looked down at him, Ravyn realized it didn't matter any longer if they were being tracked, it didn't matter if she hadn't found the perfect sanctuary. She'd have to settle for the best position she could find nearby. Damon couldn't continue. If he wasn't unconscious, he was close to it. She buried her head in her hands. What if he had a brain aneurysm or a skull fracture? She had no way of knowing and none of the skills necessary to to treat either condition.

Getting a grip on herself, she leaned over Damon. Blood still dripped from the gash and Ravyn had to remind herself that head wounds bled a lot. Still, it couldn't be good for him to have lost as much blood as he had. Some of his hair had fallen into the laceration and Ravyn gently brushed it aside. "Stay with me, Damon," she murmured. "Don't leave me by myself."

She didn't like the color of his skin beneath the tan, didn't like the look of the injury, and she hated that he was unresponsive. Ravyn pushed her own hair out of her eyes, uncaring of the mud she deposited there. It didn't matter what it took, she wasn't losing him.

Damon bit back a groan. It felt like someone had buried an axe in his head. He remained still, kept his breathing deep, and tried to ascertain the situation. Something was tied tightly around his head, and he wondered if that was what caused the pain. He didn't hear or sense anything that alarmed him and slowly he opened his eyes. The dim light could have been either dusk or dawn, but even the weak glow added to his discomfort. He forced himself not to close his eyes, concentrating instead on beating back the pain. He needed to think, had to get his bearings.

Gingerly, his hand brushed the throbbing ache over his left temple. He felt cloth tied around his head and pushed it away before realizing it was his fatigue shirt. Carefully, he touched the wound. His fingers came away sticky with blood. *Oh, yeah.* His memory was spotty, but he remembered telling Ravyn they couldn't stay where they were. He remembered leaning on her, letting her help him, but he didn't recall how he'd gotten here.

Ravyn! Damon sat up. The axe became a sword, stabbing through both temples, and he clenched his hands. His head swam, but he fought it off. He had to locate Ravyn. As his vision cleared, he could see he was under some kind of rock overhang. It wasn't deep, but it was big enough to offer cover to his entire body. Damon didn't relax until he spotted Ravyn sleeping at the entrance. The knowledge that she had put herself between him and danger in order to protect him stopped his breath.

He could only see the back of her head and he eased forward, jaw clenched, to get a look at her face. Damon needed to know for sure she was okay. Exhaustion etched her features, despite the mud obscuring his view. Her sleeping countenance touched him, but what squeezed his heart was the sight of the pistol clutched in her hand. Though sound asleep, she hadn't relinquished her hold.

Even as muddleheaded as he felt, Damon knew better than to startle Ravyn by touching her. He didn't want to disturb her, but he had to. He needed her to fill him in on what had happened. "Ravyn," he said, wincing at the noise. Unfortunately, it wasn't enough to rouse her and he had to speak louder.

He'd never seen her wake up so quickly before, instantly on alert. And she reacted exactly the way he thought she would, sitting up and taking aim. Luckily, she pointed the pistol out into the forest and not at him. He waited until she finished scanning the area outside the overhang before saying her name again.

"Damon! Are you okay?"

When she turned to him, her face filled with concern, it was all Damon could do to answer. No one, not in his entire life, had ever looked so distressed on his behalf. "Okay is a relative term," he kept his voice low.

Immediately, she moved to him, zeroing right in on the gash. He could see her anxiety increase as she studied it. She lay the weapon off to the side so her hands were free, and lightly her fingers brushed beneath the cut. "What is it?" he asked.

He could see her debate whether or not to worry him. "That wound hasn't stopped bleeding yet. I put pressure on it for more than an hour last night and finally I tied the shirt around your head hoping that would take care of it, but every time I think I have the bleeding stopped for good, it starts seeping again. I don't know what else to do."

Damon closed his eyes briefly. It took all his limited concentration to keep his mind relatively clear. At least he knew now it was early morning. "It's going to have to be stitched," he finally said. He watched her face go pale beneath the mud. "Did you clean it out yet?" He wasn't unsympathetic to her dismay, but there weren't a lot of options.

"Yes. We don't have any antibacterial spray or gel so I flushed the wound repeatedly with water. I hope that removed everything." Ravyn twisted her fingers around each other. She lifted her chin and added almost defiantly, "Warm water. I built a fire and boiled the water to get rid of any bacteria, and when it was cool enough, I used it to clean the cut."

If the pain hadn't been pounding at him, he would have smiled. He hadn't built a fire while they'd been on the run and he could see she worried over his reaction. Damon decided not to comment on it. "Get my vest," the weakness of his voice was all that kept it from being an order.

Ravyn frowned, but she retrieved the vest from the corner of the overhang and handed it to him. He couldn't remember exactly which pocket he'd put it in and it took him four tries to locate what he needed. Putting the vest aside, he held out the sealed package. Ravyn took it before she realized he had passed her a suture kit. "Damon, I can't do this."

The tormented expression on her face made him pause. "You have to, sweet pea. There's no one else. Closing it up will stop the bleeding and the thread is laced with antibiotics." He tried to keep his gaze steady, but his head hurt so damn much it was difficult. Damon wanted nothing more than to close his eyes and go back to sleep, although he knew he shouldn't.

She looked at him pleadingly, clearly torn between wanting to help him and not wanting to stitch him up.

"I can't do it myself."

When Ravyn finally nodded, he released the breath he'd been holding. Her hands shook visibly as she opened the package. He noticed they were the only part of her that was clean. How could he not admire this woman? He knew how much she hated being dirty, yet she'd used just enough water to get the muck off her hands. The only reason he figured she did that much was to make sure no more dirt went in his wound as she flushed it.

Her trembling increased as she held the needle and Damon swallowed hard. There was nothing to numb the wound and her unsteadiness was going to increase his discomfort. He gave her some instructions on how to proceed and then settled himself.

As he watched, she closed her eyes and took a deep breath. When she opened them again, her hands were steady. She never ceased to amaze him. Still, he knew her control was tenuous and Damon braced himself. If he so much as winced, Ravyn might lose her nerve. She appeared to be on the verge of tears as it was. To keep her mind off what she was doing, he started talking.

"My family lives in Connecticut," he told her, his voice unwavering even as the needle pierced his skin. "I guess you could call that my home, but I don't. I was shipped off to boarding school when I was six and was rarely there after that."

Ravyn didn't shift her focus from the stitching, but he knew he'd caught her interest. "Where was your boarding school?"

"The first one was in Massachusetts."

"First? How many did you attend?"

"Eight, I think." He barely suppressed the need to flinch as Ravyn tugged a little too hard.

"What? I can't believe you raised so much hell that you kept getting expelled."

"I didn't." Damon tightened his fists as she inadvertently jabbed him. She was so intent on her task, that he didn't think she noticed. When he was sure he could continue without revealing how much it hurt, he said, "My parents would hear about some great prep school and the next fall I'd be in a new school. I lived all over the eastern half of the United States."

She appeared shocked. And disapproving. "That's terrible. Children need stability."

Damon gave her a noncommittal grunt.

Ravyn stopped sewing him up and said, "You couldn't have liked all that moving around."

"No," he admitted slowly, "I didn't like it. It was tough, making friends and losing them year after year."

"And, after a time, it became easier not to let people close." Ravyn looked fierce and he knew it was on his behalf.

Damon started to shrug, but his body protested the movement. For the first time, he realized how stiff he was. "Maybe," he allowed, pushing aside the added twinge.

Ravyn huffed out a sigh, but kept her attention on the job at hand. He could feel sweat start to run down his face. She was over the heart of the wound now and the pain was sharper, harder for him to block out.

As if sensing this, Ravyn picked up the conversation. "At least you had your brother with you. Even though you say you weren't close, it must have been a comfort to know he was there if you needed him."

"He wasn't with me," Damon said, fighting to keep the pain from his voice.

"What?"

Damon hissed. He couldn't help it. The yank she gave the thread narrowed his vision to a tunnel. Resolutely, he fought the darkness bearing down on him. If he passed out, it would scare her. He swayed and felt her slip an arm around him. When the roaring in his ears subsided enough so he could hear again, he realized Ravyn was calling him "honey." Only the dizziness kept him from grinning broadly. When his head cleared a bit more, he realized she was crying. That cured any thought he had of smiling. His own hand wasn't quite steady as he raised his fingers to wipe the tracks from her cheeks.

"I'm sorry," she said, "I didn't mean to hurt you."

"I know." Damon shifted and rubbed his nose against hers. He kept the contact until he saw her calm down. "Can you finish patching me up?" he asked quietly. He didn't know what he would do if she said no.

"Yes." She gave him a squeeze before moving back to her original position. Her touch was exquisitely gentle, as if she could now sense the pain he tried so hard to mask. The tentativeness, however, increased his discomfort. He needed her to stop being so careful and do it. Instead of telling her this, he decided to take her mind off of what she was doing again.

"My brother went to St. Bart's. It's tradition the oldest Brody male attend that particular school."

"Why didn't you go there too?"

"I did the first two years. Then my parents heard about a school in Virginia. They weren't going to anger my grandfather by moving my brother, but there was no reason not to send me there." He shut his eyes, suddenly unable to keep them open any longer. At least Ravyn moved faster now.

Damon could hear Ravyn talking, but couldn't make out what she said. Her voice buzzed in his mind and he tried to focus, tried to pick out the words, but the effort overwhelmed him. He didn't resurface until he heard her calling his name.

"What?" he asked, not opening his eyes.

"I'm done. Should I find something to cover the stitches?"

He frowned as he tried to come up with the answer. It was in his head somewhere. His lips curved as the information came to him. "Bandage. Vest." He tried to connect the words, but the pounding in his head obliterated the idea before he could manage it. Damon groaned at the slight pressure near the wound. Then it ended. Hands rested on his shoulders, helped him back to the ground. It couldn't have felt better if he'd had a bed.

"Sleep, honey, I'll be here when you wake up."

With those soft words still ringing in his ears, Damon fell back into a place where there was no pain.

When Damon woke again, his head still hurt, but nowhere near as badly as before. From what he could see of the sky, he pegged it as late afternoon. He started to push himself into a sitting position and Ravyn was instantly there, her arm offering support.

"How are you feeling?" she asked, keeping her voice low.

"Better." His dry throat hurt. "I need some water."

She had the canteen uncapped and would have held it to his lips if he hadn't taken it from her. When he'd quenched his thirst, he returned it. He still felt weary even after sleeping all day, and Damon shifted until he could lean against the face of the rock. They needed to keep moving, but he knew it wouldn't be tonight. He didn't know where they were, didn't know what kind of protection Ravyn had found for them, but he had to trust her.

"You scared the hell out of me," she admitted, settling next to him. "You just went out. One minute we were having a normal conversation, the next you were barely coherent. I didn't know if that meant trouble or not." Ravyn took a deep, shuddery breath. "I didn't even know if I should try to wake you every hour or let you sleep. I decided to let you rest."

"I'm fine, Ravyn. Did the stitches work?" He opted not to tell her that standard first aid manuals recommended waking a concussion victim every hour and asking some basic questions. He was okay and it would just upset her.

"Yeah, you stopped bleeding. All I have to say is you better not get hurt again."

Damon smiled at her fierceness. "I'll do my best."

She smiled back, the cloud over her beautiful gold eyes lifting. "Are you hungry?"

He had to think about that one. "Yes." Maybe if he ate

something, this weakness in his body would dissipate. He might not be ready to run tomorrow, but they damn sure were moving out at first light. They couldn't stay here any longer.

It didn't take more than a few bites to realize he was starving. Ravyn kept supplying him with food, but didn't have any herself. He paused. "You ate already?" At her nod, he relaxed, sure she was taken care of, and resumed eating. When he'd finally had his fill, Damon closed his eyes and shifted into a more comfortable position.

"Any sign of the killer?" he asked. His voice was low in deference to the increased pounding in his head. He figured the answer was no, but he had to ask.

"No," Ravyn said. He sensed her shift so that she faced him. "Are you sure he trailed us?"

"He was there." He opened his eyes and turned his head so he could see her. "I felt him coming up on our backs."

Hesitation played across her face and then she must have decided he was strong enough to have a discussion. "I could hardly see you at one point and I had hold of your hand. Plus our tracks would have been obliterated almost instantly by that downpour. How could he follow us in that weather?"

Damon reached for her, linked their fingers. Her touch soothed something inside him. "I don't know, but he managed."

"Do you think he's still there, biding his time?"

It wasn't easy, but Damon focused on the world around them. He didn't sense the malevolence that he'd felt dogging their steps and the back of his neck didn't tingle. "I don't think so," he said, "but I don't know how we lost him. Things are kind of a blur after the tree came down."

Ravyn smiled at him. "You mean you don't remember knocking me to the ground and rolling around?"

"Well, hell, I always miss the good stuff. Was it more fun than the last time we took a tumble?" Her blush peeked through the mud and Damon grinned. He wondered why she started the teasing when she embarrassed more easily than he did.

"Hmm, no. It was more exciting last time when you were

fully conscious. Although, now that I think about it, I missed a great opportunity to take advantage of you."

Damon laughed, then winced as his body protested the noise and the additional movement. Her face had reddened so deeply that she looked sunburned, but he liked the fact that she didn't back down easily. There had been damn few women who could keep him on his toes and he bored easily with timid females. One thing he could admit readily, Ravyn was never boring. Even if she could talk a man's ear off.

"Sweet pea, any time you want to take advantage of me, you just climb aboard."

"Liar," she laughed at him. "You're too worried about distractions to mean that."

"You're right," he agreed, lifting her hand. He kissed her palm before teasing it with his tongue. Her pupils had dilated by the time he lowered it again, he noted with satisfaction. "Our time is coming, Ravyn, as soon as we're safe."

"The question is," she said seriously, "is what we're feeling for each other more than an attraction fostered by the danger and the intimacy of this situation?"

"I can't speak for you, but I've been in circumstances I consider more dangerous than this one." Damon reached with his free hand and tilted her chin up so she could see his eyes, see he meant what he said. "I've never reacted like this. It's you. It's us together. And it's not just physical."

"No, I know it's not." She put her hand over his where it rested on her face. For a moment, she studied him, then smiled. "Do you realize how filthy we are again? What would it take to talk you into stopping for a bath first thing tomorrow?"

Ravyn pulled back from him and moved to the vests. He doubted she was looking for anything in particular; she just wanted to end the conversation. Damon sighed silently and let her. He had read the confusion, the questions in her eyes and knew she wasn't ready to discuss their relationship yet.

"I think you're to blame. I've never been this dirty on a mission before," he teased to lighten the mood.

"Me? I'll have you know even as a child, climbing trees and sliding into third base, I remained nearly immaculate.

And I've been on Jarved Nine for eight months without getting covered with mud. It must be your fault."

Damon couldn't move fast, not yet, but he was swift enough to wrap his arms around Ravyn, keeping her own arms pinned at her sides. "Take that back," he demanded, his mouth near her ear.

"Never," she insisted, but was wise enough, he noted, not to try to wriggle free.

He took a deep breath and froze, all playfulness forgotten. Slowly, he released Ravyn and sat back, his mouth tightening. He raised his arm to his nose and breathed deeply again. *Yeah.* Realization momentarily distracted him from the pain in his head. A few things started to make sense that hadn't before. Too bad it had taken a whack in the head to get his brain working on something other than getting Ravyn out of her clothes.

"Are you okay?" Ravyn was at his side almost instantly, concern all over her face.

"You smell like dirt."

"Well, gee, thanks. I told you I needed a bath. And you don't smell so great yourself," Ravyn groused.

He looked at her, his expression sober. "Covered with all this dried mud, we both smell like dirt."

She began to look scared. "Is your head hurting you again?" She pressed her palm to his forehead, as if testing for fever.

"Ravyn," he said, taking her hand and lowering it away from his face. "I think he's tracking us by scent. When we're clean, he can follow us, but when we're coated with mud, we smell more like the land and that must confuse him."

"What makes you think that?" she asked, clearly not enthusiastic about his theory.

"Because he was on our trail yesterday. He should have caught up with us by now, but he hasn't. It wasn't the storm that discouraged him, it was our getting covered with mud again."

She still didn't seem convinced.

"The day of the mud fight, he must have crossed our path higher up the hill," he argued. "He should have been able to follow our footprints right to us, but he didn't. Because he isn't using his vision, he's using his sense of smell." He gave her hand a squeeze and said, "Maybe I'm wrong, but just in case, no more baths."

He thought Ravyn was going to cry.

Chapter Ten

Stacey didn't know why she'd ever believed Alex Sullivan to be her Prince Charming. She stared across the almost empty equipment bay at him, watching his throat work as he swallowed. She turned away, both regret and resignation in her heart. He treated her like a naive, stupid pushover.

Okay, maybe she was a bit naive. She'd grown up on a farm, the nearest town had been nothing but a blip on the map, and her high school graduating class had totaled thirty-five. The two years she'd spent in comm school hadn't given her much chance to experience big-city life. The demanding program left little time for anything save sleeping and studying. Joining CAT had put her right back in rural America. Kansas this time instead of Iowa. And, while CAT team members would take the flash train into Topeka from time to time, they'd always gone in groups.

She wasn't stupid, however, or a pushover. It took smarts to get into comm school, let alone complete the program with honors, and CAT only took the best of the best. And if she'd been a pushover, she'd still be living in Iowa. Married to her high school boyfriend, having his babies and helping him farm. Her family had expected it; her boyfriend and his family had expected it. It hadn't been easy to hold out against all the pressure she'd faced, to continue to commute seventy kilometers every day to her job at the granary. It had taken six years of hard work and ruthless scrimping to save enough money to pay for comm school. Her family still hadn't forgiven her for leaving.

She looked away from Alex before he caught her staring. There wasn't much to see in the converted equipment bay. One area had patched-up workout machines, a small punching bag and a larger, heavier bag. The side she and Attila used had a thickly padded floor to cushion falls and nothing else.

"Let's try that again," Alex said, ending the break.

Stacey bit back a groan. At this late hour, everyone but the flight crew on duty was asleep. She wanted to curl up in bed herself. It had been a long day. The sadist she'd once thought perfect had rousted her at some untenable hour and forced her to run laps. And do sit-ups, push-ups and other horrible things. She might never recover.

"Do you know what time it is?" she asked.

"Get this one move down and we'll call it a day," Alex said.

Stacey didn't know why she stayed. It certainly wasn't to spend time with Alex. Even though she had discovered what an arrogant tyrant he was, her body continued to react to his nearness. She wanted nothing more than to keep her distance, but she couldn't avoid touching him during these training sessions. He would grab her and she was supposed to execute some maneuver or another to get free. Only, when he held her close to his body, the last thing she wanted was her freedom. Her weakness left her angry with herself. I'm not a pushover, she repeated silently to herself.

"Ready?"

"Yes. Let's get this over with." She braced herself for Alex's assault on her senses and felt the small hairs on her arms stand on end as he came up behind her and wrapped his forearm around her throat. His scent teased her; the warmth of his body enveloped her. Stacey lost track of the move she was supposed to make.

"Don't worry about hurting me, I've got plenty of pads on," Alex said. "I want you to go all out."

Stacey felt his breath against her ear as he spoke. It took a minute for his meaning to register and she was grateful he attributed her hesitancy to a reluctance to injure him and not to her body running riot at his closeness.

"Okay," she said and tried to remember the first thing she should do. Was it something with her elbow? She tried to jab it into his stomach, but it lacked strength. His sigh of impatience skittered across her neck and raised goose bumps.

"You're never going to accomplish anything like that," Alex said. He kept his hold on her throat. "First, squat down and lean forward. Do it now."

Stacey was unable to move much in Alex's grip, but she did what she could. She noticed that if not for the padding he wore, her rear would be nestled against his groin. The thought distracted her. She imagined his touch, not at her neck but lower. His body hot and hard against hers. She pretended he wanted her too much to care where they were. Pushing clothes aside, too impatient to strip them off entirely. Needing to get his hands on her bare skin, needing her hands on his body.

"Pay attention," he barked at her and Stacey almost jumped. Thank God he couldn't read her mind.

"I am," she lied.

"No, you're not," he said, his voice carrying a note of huskiness. "You're off on some erotic daydream. Tell me, are we wearing any clothes?"

Stacey stiffened and tried to elbow him again, but he tightened his grip by a fraction and left her unable to do anything but flail about harmlessly.

"If you had taken what I was trying to teach you seriously," he told her, humor replacing the huskiness in his voice, "you would have been able to escape and get a few hits in."

"It's not funny," Stacey shot at him, twisting uselessly in his arms. It irritated her that she couldn't get free.

"No, it's not funny. What if this were real? What if someone really had hold of you like this? You would be helpless." Alex released her, but before she could react, he turned her so she faced him and grabbed her shoulders. "This isn't some damn game. We don't know what situation we'll be walking into on Jarved Nine. What do you think I'm going to do if someone grabs you and uses you as a shield?"

The way he leaned over her should have intimidated her, but it didn't. Even as aggravating as the man was, she knew she was safe with him. "Um, you're going to save me?"

Alex let go of her shoulders and stepped away. "I would try," he said, his voice less clipped, "but depending on the position of the assailant, I might not be able to get a shot off safely. I'd need you to help, either by freeing yourself or by exposing enough of the attacker to give me a better angle."

"I really don't think the situation will come up," she told him, taking a few steps back. She breathed a sigh of relief when he didn't close the distance. The man was too potent.

"You still like your fantasy of there being nothing wrong on J Nine that a little radio repair won't cure." Alex's lips quirked up in a sardonic smile. "I wish I could believe that myself."

"The odds are—"

"The odds are the CAT and Spec Ops teams are in deep shit," Alex interrupted. "You want to talk odds? What are the odds of all the CAT team's comm equipment going out? Not just primary, but backup and spares?"

Stacey gulped and pushed some hair that had escaped her ponytail away from her face. "Slim," she admitted reluctantly.

"Yeah, now figure in the Spec Ops team. They have comm equipment on their transport plus portable equipment they carry with them. What are the odds of their two systems going out at the exact time the CAT systems went down?"

"More than slim."

"Minuscule, I'd say." Alex began peeling the pads off his body. "And before you can raise some ridiculous argument about subspace interference, we both know that even if it affected the voice systems, the long range emergency beacons were designed to transmit through just about anything."

Stacey didn't reply for a moment, taken aback by the fact that the darn man still looked too perfect. He hadn't even broken a sweat despite the heavy padding he'd been wearing. Her own clothes were damp with perspiration and felt clammy and uncomfortable.

Reluctantly, she admitted Alex was right. The odds were something was wrong on the planet. Seriously wrong. Truthfully, she'd known all along, but she hadn't wanted to face it. She was closer to Ravyn than to her own sisters and the thought of anything happening to her was unbearable.

"What do you think we're going to find when we arrive?"

For a moment, Alex looked bleak, but the expression was gone in a flash. "Wounded. Maybe fatalities."

"But how? What? It doesn't make sense."

"That I don't know," Alex confessed. "The doctor doesn't think it's a virus, but she could be wrong. Maybe there was a fire or the planet has deadly animals the scout teams missed. There are all kinds of possibilities."

Stacey suddenly felt a hundred years old. Slowly, she moved from the center of the bay. Leaning against a wall, she slid to the padded floor. She closed her eyes and tried not to picture any of the disasters Alex had tossed out. He'd sounded emotionless, but she knew better. Ravyn talked about Alex a lot, and while her view was skewed, one thing was clear. His sister was the only person in the world the man loved. He had to be scared to death she was among the casualties.

Stacey's eyes popped open as she felt Alex settle beside her. She moved away from him and he raised his eyebrows in question. Ignoring that, she asked, "So is there anything Ravyn doesn't excel at?" She wanted to change the subject, to get both their minds off whatever horror awaited them on Jarved Nine.

A slow smile spread across his face. It transformed his whole demeanor from harsh and cold to heart-stopping sexy. She lost her breath at the sight. Good thing he didn't smile often, she thought, entranced.

"She can't shoot worth a damn," he said.

"What?" Stacey had been so busy enjoying his grin that she'd forgotten what they were talking about.

"Ravyn. She's scary with a pistol in her hand."

Alex said it with such indulgence, Stacey couldn't help smiling. Just when she'd convinced herself he was a nearly heartless son of a gun who wasn't worth her time, he would say or do something that left her wondering. Stacey shifted position, turning slightly toward Alex. "I didn't want to like Ravyn when I first met her," she admitted.

He smiled a shade ruefully, but he didn't look surprised. She assumed his sister had told him. She and Ravyn laughed over it now. But Stacey still had twinges of guilt over the envy she'd felt. Nothing had been average about her friend. Not her looks, not her intelligence and not her personality. People noticed her, responded to her. Ravyn had worked hard to build a friendship between them, and once Stacey had gotten to know her, once she'd realized the younger woman's life hadn't been a walk in the park, she'd let go of her jealousy. And found the sister of her heart.

"I didn't want to like her either," Alex confessed, drawing her from her memories. "I think I made it about a day before she had me in the palm of her hand."

Immediately, Stacey became suspicious. Alex Sullivan was not someone who shared anything personal, not voluntarily. "Why are you telling me this?"

"I need your cooperation. I need you to obey orders when I issue them without hesitating or arguing. Things will be easier if we are on friendly terms."

Stacey had to admire his honesty, but she wasn't sure what she thought of his motives. She didn't know if she could be friendly, not when she was trying so hard to kill her attraction to him. She had daydreamed about Alex Sullivan for years. In her fantasies, he'd treated her like a beloved princess. In the real world, he acted like she was an unwanted obligation.

"What do you think?" he asked. Somehow he'd edged closer without her knowledge. Not close enough to alarm her, but closer than she wanted him to be. "Want to be my friend?"

Cocking her head, she eyed him with mistrust. There was a thread in his voice that had alarm bells shrieking in her mind. He was up to something, she just didn't know what.

Stacey eased herself back a little more. "Define what you mean by 'friend.' "

Oh, he was good, she thought. He was careful not to overplay that wounded look, but she knew it lacked sincerity. There were a lot of words she'd use to describe Alex, but vulnerable didn't make the list. It hurt her in some indefinable way that he thought he could put one over on her. "If you want us to be on friendly terms, you'll cut the act," Stacey said.

"Act?" He feigned innocence, exaggerating so much that she knew he did it deliberately. She smiled reluctantly. An hour earlier she would have thought him incapable of this type of humor. It dismayed her to realize it added to his appeal.

"I grew up on a farm," she said. "I know manure when I see it. Right now it's at least hip deep."

"I thought I'd shoveled it deeper than that," Alex said and gave her a supernova smile.

He was too close again and Stacey put a hand on his chest to ward him off. His heart beat evenly. The warmth of his skin through the T-shirt made her fingers tingle and the urge to stroke his chest overwhelmed her. She might have spent the first twenty-four years of her life in a town of a couple of thousand, but Stacey knew trouble when it sat beside her. Too lethal, she thought, scrambling to her feet.

Alex rose with a feline grace. She watched him approach, his pace unhurried. Maybe that was what kept her lulled until it was nearly too late. He stalked her the way a panther stalked its prey. Temptation gnawed at her. It was the cocksure glow in his eyes that reminded her of his attitude problem.

"Back off, Sullivan," Stacey ordered. And took a deep breath when he complied. He still stood too close for comfort.

Alex didn't appear daunted, she decided. In fact, the man had the audacity to crook his finger at her. As if! With a growl of outrage, Stacey rushed him. Without stopping to think, she hooked a foot behind his leg and pushed. She felt justly rewarded when she saw him fall. It gave her even more satisfaction to see the amazement on his face before she stormed out of the bay.

Alex prowled the ship. To guarantee he didn't run into anyone, he stayed away from the bridge and the small galley just behind it. He couldn't keep the scowl from his lips. For a man who prided himself on his poker face, it was one more irritation in a night full of them.

Stacey Johnson had dumped him on his ass.

It still amazed him. He supposed he should be happy she could execute that simple maneuver. Except he knew damn well she wouldn't have brought him down if he hadn't been off balance. He'd expected her to throw herself into his arms.

Okay, so maybe he was a little spoiled. Women chased him. Had since he was a teenager. Even Lara had been the one doing the pursuing, at least until she'd found some rich sucker to tie herself to. Stacey couldn't hide her attraction to him. And when he issued an invitation to a woman who had already shown she wanted his attention, he'd never been turned down. Until today.

He was wound tight with no relief in sight. He couldn't figure out why he was all hot and bothered. She wasn't his type, damn it. He liked women who were sophisticated and glamorous. Stacey was wholesome. Everything she felt and thought was right there on her face for the world to see.

If he had any hope of sleeping, he needed to work off some of his frustration. With a grimace, he headed for the equipment bay and the gym set up there. If he had to pound the damn bag for an hour to release this tension, well, so be it.

He snarled quietly when he noticed the door to the bay was jammed open and light spilled out into the hall. Alex hesitated for a moment, curiosity warring with his need to be alone right now. Then he heard her voice. "Keep the weight on the front foot," she muttered loudly enough to drift into the hall. "Okay. Elbows in, fists in front of face."

Alex eased forward slowly, not wanting Stacey to see him. He needn't have worried. She had her back to the door and her concentration focused on a piece of paper fastened to the wall. It looked like she had printed out self-defense instructions from the computer. He felt his frustration lessen.

He watched her repeat the same move over and over. Each time she would read the instructions aloud, as if that made them clearer to her, and then try to put words into movement. It was tempting to make his presence known and correct all the mistakes she was making, but he remained silent. The woman was not a natural athlete. It took her nearly half an hour before she could snap kick without losing her balance. But she didn't give up and Alex admired that. He noted how hard she worked and how her damp T-shirt clung to her breasts.

The first observation pleased him and it meshed with what he'd heard from Ravyn. Until now he'd seen no signs of the determination his sister had mentioned repeatedly in reference to Stacey. The second image raised havoc in his own body once more. He didn't need to ogle the woman's breasts, but he couldn't seem to stop glancing in that direction. The lack of self-control had his temper fraying again.

He should walk away. Alex didn't know why he couldn't. Mentally, he took a step back and tried to figure out why Stacey tantalized him. She'd grown up in an area of the country that had been completely untouched by the wars. It had always amazed him how part of the United States had been so greatly affected while the rest of the country wouldn't have known a war was happening if not for the news. But that kind of ingenuousness left him irritated, not interested. Usually.

War had always been a reality for him. Before his parents' divorce, he'd lived near the front lines. Even the move to Arizona hadn't made the fighting more distant for him, not with his father in the thick of it. At fifteen, he'd found himself in California with his dad because his mother's new husband hadn't wanted another man's kid around.

Alex let out a silent sigh. The last of his childhood innocence had been shattered when his mother had chosen money over him. He looked at Stacey trying to coordinate her movements so she could throw a punch while she pushed off on her back heel. Her timing sucked. She was more naive at thirty-two than he'd been as a teenager.

He should just let her be, he thought. God knew what he'd been thinking when he'd issued his invitation earlier this evening. Getting sexually involved on a mission, even if they had nothing to do right now but wait and train, was the pinnacle of stupidity. He couldn't even lie to himself and pretend he'd done it to bind her to him. He'd wanted her, pure and simple.

He still couldn't believe she'd tossed him to the floor. His lips curled. He liked fire in a woman, and despite the red in her hair, he hadn't seen any signs of it till then. Yet there was something about her that reached him on a more than physical level, a sense of familiarity that had left him eager to spend the day with her, even if it was under the guise of training.

Alex shook his head at his own thoughts. He was imagining things. He needed to get back on track. And why bother taking the time and energy to pursue her? When he got back to Earth there would be plenty of other women vying for his attention.

He started to edge out of the room when Stacey stopped. Alex froze, not wanting her to see movement out of the corner of her eye and catch him. She stretched her arms over her head. Her soft groan of pleasure caused his body to tighten. Before he could shake it off and get out of there, she reached for the clip holding her hair back and released it.

This time he groaned, but silently. She ran her hands through the strawberry blond tresses, letting them fall carelessly down her back. Alex felt his blood heat. He wanted her hair trailing all over his naked body. The hell with it, he decided. To hell with complications and entanglements, he wanted her in his bed and if he had to pursue her to that end, so be it.

Damon watched Ravyn for a moment as she set up camp, then shut his eyes. He hurt worse than he wanted her to know. He suspected she had an idea, though, since she'd taken charge about midmorning. Aside from his having to point out which direction to go, Ravyn had been in control. Moving out at first light may not have been the best thing for his head, but the thought of remaining stationary one more day had made his shoulders itch.

When he felt better, he was going to ask her a few more questions about the training her brother had given her. Normally civilians as highly skilled as she appeared to be preferred to run the show. Yet Ravyn hadn't once challenged his leadership in their little expedition. She'd behaved more like a soldier, following orders and offering input when she felt it necessary.

He hated feeling helpless. He should be taking care of her, not the other way around. But just as she had obviously been trained to assume command when the situation warranted, he had been trained to relinquish command if the circumstances called for that. Yeah, he'd be asking a few questions tomorrow. He shifted position and winced. Or maybe the day after.

Thinking increased his headache, so Damon tried to empty his mind. He concentrated on his breathing, keeping it slow and even, but that quickly grew boring and his thoughts wandered. For a few moments, he listened to the soft sounds Ravyn made as she moved around. That didn't promote calmness either, not with the way he reacted to her. His injuries may have prevented him from acting on his attraction, but he wasn't dead.

The Old City popped into his mind then and Damon centered his attention on that. The images he had studied on Earth were indelibly imprinted on his memory, and he could recall them easily. He focused on an intricately carved fountain. There should have been water bubbling up, he thought, and almost instantly, his imagination provided it. He stared at the lion in the center. It almost looked real and he pushed aside the conundrum of why there was an Earth animal represented on an alien planet. It wasn't a puzzle he could solve now, and it would only increase his headache. Instead, Damon turned and began ambling down the wide street.

There were no vehicles of any sort, just people walking.

Some moved at a fast clip, some dawdled, but most seemed to have a purpose, a destination. Almost everyone was dressed in brightly colored clothes and the people were friendly, smiling or nodding to him as they passed. Damon returned the greetings. He liked it here. The peacefulness, the happiness, seemed to permeate the city. A melodious chime reached his ears and Damon picked up his pace. He hadn't realized it was so late already. Ravyn was waiting for him. His heart felt full as he neared their home.

He stopped short, absently apologizing to the man who bumped into him. *This is weird.* Damon drew a breath and splintered his concentration. This wasn't some odd dream. He was relaxed, but not asleep. He could still hear Ravyn setting up camp and yet he could see the people moving about the Old City. He could smell the scent of food roasting, hear the muted sound of voices, laughter. Yet there was an aura of transparency to what he sensed in the Old City, a certain lack of vividness. He reached out and touched the cool smoothness of a nearby pillar that didn't exist in his current location.

Before he could do more than question the extent of his head injury, Damon felt fear replace the joy. Although the sun still shone brightly, it was as if some dark cloud cast its shadow over the city. Ravyn! He started running then, dodging around slower pedestrians.

If he didn't get there in time, she would be forced to face him alone. He wouldn't allow her to do that. They were stronger together. The size of their home registered, but he paid little attention as he took the stairs two at a time. Damon didn't hesitate. He knew where he'd find her. He pressed the inset, impatiently waiting for the hidden door to open. Ravyn stood in front of the crystal obelisk, her hand already beginning to enter the slot linking her side to his.

"Wait," he ordered and hurried down the rest of the stairs.

Her eyes filled with such love that it nearly stopped him short, but there wasn't time to indulge himself. Damon quickly took his place opposite her and nodded. His hand met hers in the eye of the obelisk and their fingers linked.

The power racing through his body was familiar, yet he

knew he had never experienced this before. Not in this lifetime. It wasn't something a man would forget, even with a head injury, he thought wryly. Damon forced himself to close his eyes and focus. There were steps to follow, things they needed to do.

The feel of Ravyn's hand against his forehead startled him. There was no way she could reach him from her side of the crystal column. His eyes popped open.

"I'm sorry," she said softly. "I didn't mean to wake you. I just wanted to make sure you weren't running a fever."

It took Damon a moment to realize he was outside, not in some underground chamber. He let the disorientation wash through him without fighting it. A fever would explain a lot, he decided. Except he didn't feel too hot or too cold. His headache had even eased. As he looked at Ravyn, the feeling of being in two places at one time faded. He cleared his throat, uncomfortable as awareness returned. He wanted to share what he'd seen, but how did he explain a dream that didn't feel like a dream? Ravyn was already worried about how seriously he was hurt; if he told her, it would just add to her apprehension.

"Good news, Captain." His rank sounded like an endearment. "No fever. It's a miracle that wound didn't become infected considering how dirty you are. You feel up to eating?"

"Yeah," he said and started to sit up. Ravyn moved to help him. He wasn't surprised; she'd been fussing over him constantly since he'd been hurt. Part of him disliked being seen as weak, but another part of him enjoyed the attention, enjoyed that he meant enough to her to fuss over.

It was an effort to sit upright, and he shifted till he could lean against a tree trunk. Damon took a thorough look around their camp. Ravyn had picked a spot they could defend and he relaxed. She had her back to him and he tensed again as he noticed the bulge beneath her untucked shirt. She had one of the pistols and he didn't know when she'd taken it. He shook his head in disgust. How out of it had he been and for how long?

When she turned, Ravyn had the front of her shirt loaded

with food. She walked to him and slowly lowered herself to the ground. She sat facing him and said, "I don't suppose we get to wash our hands before eating?"

"You suppose right, sweet pea."

Damon reached out and took one of her hands in his. Pieces of dirt crumbled off and fell to the ground. He smiled; he couldn't help it. He knew how meticulous Ravyn was. More dried mud fell off as he rubbed his thumb against the heel of her hand. She hadn't complained once today despite the three different coats of mud she was wearing.

"When we reach the Old City," he said, the name bringing a sense of serenity back, "you can have all the baths you want. And in the meantime, a little dirt won't kill us."

Ravyn made a face at him. Freeing herself from his grip, she handed him a piece of fruit. "You really think we'll be safe once we reach the Old City?"

Damon shrugged. "I can't promise, but I think so. I'll fortify the gates and booby trap 'em. This thing, he may possess an incredible physical strength, but he's not supernatural. He has the same laws of physics to contend with as we do. We should be able to keep him out of the Old City."

After they finished eating, Damon lay back down. His head throbbed less when he was recumbent. He watched Ravyn walk around their camp one last time before she settled down near him. She pulled the pistol out of her waistband and placed it within easy reach. He wanted to put out his hand and touch her, but she wasn't close enough.

"What?" she asked, catching his frown.

Lifting his brows, he patted the ground beside him. She hesitated briefly, then shifted so he could hold her. He'd discovered something else since he'd been hit in the head. Ravyn kept a deep reserve buried beneath her friendliness. He didn't like it, but it undoubtedly was a defense mechanism she'd developed after losing so much of her family. He figured in time she would trust him enough to let him close the distance.

"I'll take that." He reached over her and grasped the pistol.

"Are you sure?"

"Oh, yeah," he told her.

Damon remained awake long after Ravyn had fallen asleep. He was cutting their wandering short and heading right for the Old City. There were answers there, he knew that, trusted that. Staring at the stars in the sky, he decided to put some credence in his earlier vision. He had few other options at this point.

He looked down at the dirt-covered woman he held. His heart swelled with a tenderness he'd thought foreign to his nature before finding Ravyn. There was a cloud of half truth hanging over their relationship. He had led her to believe they'd be safe once they reached the Old City. But he now suspected the murderer had killed many of the people who'd lived there.

Chapter Eleven

"You're smiling."

"I know."

"You're lying in the mud," Damon said, pointing out the obvious. He carefully scanned the area as he spoke.

"No. I'm at the luxurious and exclusive Lemuria Spa, where I am enjoying a mud bath."

Ravyn kept her eyes shut. Probably easier for her to imagine the spa that way, Damon decided. He crouched down just outside the mud pit and looked at her. Four days of keeping themselves covered in dirt had taken a toll on their clothes.

It wasn't easy making sure their body odor never overpowered the scent of dirt. In the high humidity and with the physical exertion, they both sweated a lot. Because of this, one coating of mud wasn't enough. Luckily, the constant rains made it easy to find new patches of muck whenever they needed them. He knew his sweet pea wasn't happy, but she hadn't complained, not once.

"What's after the mud bath?" Damon asked.

"After the mud is washed from my body, I'll be led into

this opulent room decorated in whites. Mozart is playing softly."

Ravyn's smile widened and her face beamed even through the grime. Damon grinned himself, enjoying the sight of her relaxed and content. They should be moving, but he couldn't find it in him to force her back to reality just yet.

"So what are you doing in this room? Sitting back in a plush chair with a glass of juice?"

Damon liked that idea. He would walk into the chamber, find her leaning back with her eyes closed. He could see her smile softly as she sensed his presence. Kneeling in front of her, he'd run his hands from her knees up to her waist and then tug her closer to him so that he could kiss her. He forced himself out of his daydream and swept their surroundings with his gaze.

"No," Ravyn said. "I'm naked, lying on my stomach on a massage table with just a little white towel covering my butt."

Damon's attention snapped back to Ravyn. The image that came to mind made him burn.

"I'm waiting for Thor."

"Thor?" he asked, his voice dangerous.

Ravyn apparently didn't notice. "Hmm, I always request Thor as my masseur when I go to Lemuria. The man looks like a blond god and the things he can do with his hands . . ." She sighed in pleasure and Damon growled. Her eyes popped open. For a moment, she stared at him, then propped herself up on her elbows.

"You're baring your teeth," she said.

"If you think some blond guy named Thor is going to be putting his hands on you, you haven't been paying attention."

"Thor is a professional. There's nothing sexual about it."

He could hear the laughter in her voice. Part of him realized he was making a fool of himself, but he couldn't seem to stop. "If that's the case, then you can find a masseuse named Inga who's about fifty and a grandmother."

Her lips twitched. She closed her eyes and lowered herself back into the mire. "Nope. I want Thor."

Damon sprang, launching himself into the mud. He

landed beside her and rolled, covering her. He pinned her hands over her head and trapped her legs under his, but she didn't struggle. Ravyn opened her eyes again and grinned up at him.

"You don't get Thor. From here on out, the only man putting his hands on your naked body is me."

Pursing her lips, Ravyn tilted her head and studied him. It took all his control not to shift uncomfortably under her stare. It began to sink in how stupidly he'd acted.

"I didn't realize you were so possessive," she said.

"Neither did I," Damon admitted. "I can't seem to help it." He took a moment to gauge her reaction before asking, "Is it going to bother you?"

"That depends," she said. "Are you going to act irrationally jealous every time a man talks to me?"

Satisfaction filled him at her casual acceptance that he would be part of her life once they returned to Earth. Damon put his pleasure aside and considered her question. She deserved a well-thought-out answer. He wasn't the jealous type, at least he'd never been in the past, but he placed himself in the situation and tested his response.

"Nah," he said after a moment, his smile sheepish. "As long as you don't plan on getting naked with other men, I'll be okay."

"Well," she said, pulling her wrists free of his loosened grip and wrapping her arms around his neck, "since I've never been naked with a man before, I don't think either one of us is going to have to worry about that."

For a moment, he stared stupidly at her, his brain trying to process what she'd said. It was the anxiety in her eyes that finally gave her words meaning. He couldn't have understood her correctly. "Did you say what I think you said?" Damon asked, amazed he could string together a sentence.

She looked over his shoulder, not meeting his gaze. "Yes."

He waited for her to elaborate, but she didn't. Damon shook his head, still unable to believe it. "You're a virgin?"

Ravyn took a deep breath. "Yes, I'm a virgin." The words were forced out between gritted teeth. She moved her hands to his shoulders and tried to push him off.

Damon refused to budge. "How is that possible?"

She shoved harder, but he'd been expecting that. "None of your business," she said and he could hear how mortified she was even if he couldn't see the color stain her checks.

"Come on, sweet pea, you trusted me enough to tell me, now trust me all the way." He kept his voice gentle although it wasn't easy. The thought of being her first made him so hot, he thought he might spontaneously combust.

Ravyn struggled a moment longer, then let her muscles go slack. He turned her face so their eyes met and she stiffened for a moment before conceding. "Alex scared the boys off when I was young enough to do it out of curiosity. And when I was in comm school, I was too busy to develop romantic relationships."

"What about after? Hell, there were seven women and thirteen men on Jarved Nine. I have to think you were pursued pretty hot and heavy the last eight months."

"No, not really. I'd become friends with all the men on the team before we left Earth. They were like honorary brothers and none of them ever tried to cross the line."

"I find that hard to believe. You're damn sexy."

"Me?" she asked, disbelief evident in her voice.

"Yeah, you," Damon said and pressed his body into hers. "All I have to do is get close to you and this happens, mud or no mud. You're bad for my control."

"I like that."

"You would," he said. "Our current situation is way too dangerous for distractions."

"I know."

"I swore to myself I wouldn't touch you until we were back on Earth. I won't be able to keep that vow. Unless you tell me no, you won't be a virgin when we get back home."

"I'm not going to say no."

Damon drew a shaky breath. He'd known that, but to hear her say it, nearly drove him past his limits. He fought off the need to take her here and now. "You're making it hard for me."

"I can feel that." Her smile was smug.

He crowded closer and pressed a kiss on her lips.

"Yuck! Damon! You got mud in my mouth." She made a face.

"Toughen up," he said without a whit of sympathy and pushed himself to his feet. "Time to leave the spa and start walking."

He helped Ravyn up and put on his vest. He settled the pack before he realized she was frowning at him. "What?"

"Why do you always start things and then pull away?"

"I start things because I can't help myself. I pull away because good sense finally rears its head. When we make love, I sure as hell don't want to be covered in mud and worrying about what's coming up behind me." Damon reached out and tucked her muddy braid behind her shoulder. "You shouldn't even have to ask. You're too aware of the danger we're in—and too well trained—not to understand."

Which had him frowning. He'd forgotten about quizzing her on her stepbrother and the training he'd put her through. He began to wonder just who the hell Alex was, but those questions were going to have to wait. He didn't want to take the time now. They'd already stayed here too long for his peace of mind.

Ravyn shrugged. "I needed to hear you say it," she admitted, her voice low. She fastened her vest and turned away.

He started to seal his own vest, but froze as a thought occurred to him. Damon groaned.

"What? Is it your head?" Ravyn hurried to him. He caught her hand and interlaced his fingers with hers before she could feel his brow.

"No, my head doesn't hurt. I just had a thought."

"The way you groaned," she said, "I thought you'd been hit in the head with a tree again."

"You're not using any birth control, are you?" He ignored her kidding, his mind focused on one thing.

"No, there wasn't any reason to. But you must be, right?"

Damon shook his head. "I haven't been involved in a long term relationship for years, so temporary measures have been good enough." He hesitated for a moment then added,

"Before we go any farther we need to consider the consequences."

The idea of making Ravyn pregnant made his chest ache with tenderness. Since she looked ready to bolt, he kept that to himself. Still, he couldn't leave it there. "If we take the risk and you become pregnant, I won't walk away from you or our child."

He stared at her long enough to make sure she knew he was dead serious and then started out. They had a long way to go and he wanted to reach the Old City as soon as possible.

For the first time in days, mud was at the bottom of Ravyn's priority list. She had too many other things on her mind to give more than a passing thought to how dirty she was. Her thoughts bounced, not settling on anything for long. It was a good thing Damon was back at full strength and in charge again. She trailed behind him the way she had that first day when she'd been in shock. Maybe this was just a different kind of shock.

She still couldn't believe she'd announced her virginity. He'd have found out at some point, but she figured she'd let him discover it on his own. Instead she blurted it out while they were rolling in the mud. Ravyn had never seen Damon at a loss before. She smiled reluctantly as she remembered the expression on his face. Not quite panic, but close. Then it had changed to something else, something she hadn't been able to name.

The smile disappeared. She knew she was an oddity. By the time she'd been out from under Alex's protection and finished with school, she'd known she wasn't going to go to bed with just anyone. She was waiting for a man who meant something to her, a man she couldn't say no to. It had taken her six more years to find Damon. She'd been relieved he hadn't pressed when she'd only answered half his question on why she was untouched. He'd probably figured out he meant more to her than any other man, but that didn't mean she had to admit it. She wasn't in love with him. Liked him, yes. Wanted him, yes. Love, no.

No way was she falling in love with anyone in Spec Ops. As hard as it was to watch her brother go out on assignments, she knew it would be a million times worse to watch the man she loved leave her time and again. There were no low-risk missions in his line of work, not with the tenuous peace that had been reached after the Third Oceanic War. Plus, the Alliance was stepping up its space explorations, and those often proved to be just as dangerous as war. Look at what had happened on a routine training mission. Six men had died. They'd probably told their wives there was nothing to worry about, that they'd be home in a few weeks, safe and sound. Only an ordinary training mission had gone to hell in a heartbeat.

Nope, she wasn't loving someone in Spec Ops. It was the situation that made her feelings seem so intense. Maybe if she were braver, she could kiss her man goodbye and trust he'd come home. Which led to another thing she had to consider. If she and Damon conceived a baby together, she just might end up raising the infant alone. Not that she didn't believe him when he said he'd be there. She was sure he'd try. But death would take him away from a child as surely as it took him away from her.

Ravyn shuddered. Just thinking about death reminded her of her friends, of Damon's men. For a moment, she saw nothing but blood, could almost feel it on her skin. Another, stronger shudder went through her. She'd worked hard at putting the tragedy out of her mind these last few days, and for the most part, had been successful. She had to do it again. With determination, she pushed their faces aside. She felt guilty doing it, but she couldn't deal with the loss now.

Instead she forced herself to focus on the pregnancy issue, latching on to it to forget the sight of the bodies. Life versus death. She'd never thought much about having children before, at least not concretely. That was more of a someday kind of thing. But now, she had to think about it.

A gust of wind reminded her she needed to pay attention to her surroundings. She looked at the sky, expecting to see clouds since the breeze had picked up, but it was still sunny. Ravyn had no doubt the rains would come. They always did.

For a moment she watched Damon move. She knew he'd made a big concession admitting he didn't want to wait till they reached Earth to make love. Although maybe the prospect of parenthood would shore up his resolve, she thought with a small smile of amusement. It certainly made her think twice.

Something drove him to put her protection above everything else. It was more than responsibility, more than honor, but she didn't know what. Someday, when the time felt right, she would ask, but for now, she just accepted it.

Damon checked on her frequently today. Maybe worried she would run the other way rather than take the chance on getting pregnant. Her lips curled. More likely, though, the lack of cover made him nervous. They were in the open, the trees and bushes few and far between. When she thought about it, it made the back of her neck tingle, as if she were being watched.

The soft ground sucked at her boots, but she was used to that. She must have stronger leg muscles now than ever before. She laughed softly, too softly for Damon to hear. Alex would be impressed. Maybe when she saw him, she'd challenge him to a run.

She tried to imagine her brother's reaction if she did end up pregnant. What came to mind wasn't pretty. He'd go after Damon, no question about it. Damon was bigger, but Alex was more intense. If they fought, both of them would end up hurt. Of course, knowing her captain, he might not fight at all out of some misguided idea of honor, and just let Alex pound him.

Okay, so desire said sleep with the man and take her chances. After all, the odds were she wouldn't become pregnant. She knew of couples who tried for years without conceiving. Her practical side said don't make love without some way of preventing conception. A baby would tie them together for life. Which, in Damon's case, might be shorter than average.

Her head began to ache from thinking about it. *The hell with it.* Ravyn tried to concentrate on how uncomfortable she felt with dried mud all over her body, but the sensation was nothing new. She was almost used to it now. She had to find something to keep her mind off of death, sex and babies, though.

Another burst of hot wind caught them and whipped the sides of Damon's vest open. Her eyes narrowed. He'd never left it unsealed before, but she bet he felt cooler in this heat. She wished she could do that, but with his size, he didn't have to worry about his vest sliding off if he left it open. She did.

With a sigh, Ravyn returned to her favorite thought. A bath. This time she imagined lukewarm water. That meant no bubbles, but she could live with that. Instead of champagne, she wanted a big glass of icy cold lemonade. Maybe lemon-scented shampoo to go with her drink and she'd stick with the Mozart from her spa fantasy. She imagined leaning back in the tub and stretching out. Part of Ravyn wasn't surprised to run into a set of masculine legs. Of course Damon would be sharing her bath. She could almost feel his big hands reach out and pull her on top of him. As she settled herself on him, she realized the swelling of her abdomen kept her from getting as close as she wanted.

Ravyn nearly tripped over her own feet. Well, she thought after regaining her balance, that answered the question. In the split second before her shock had knocked her out of the daydream, she'd been thrilled to be pregnant, to have a part of Damon within her. She *wanted* the bond.

She scowled at his back even though she knew it wasn't his fault. So she felt more for him than she meant to; it didn't mean it was love. She still had control, and she wouldn't allow herself to fall for him, no way, no how. Not when any day he could discover her cravenness. A man as brave and confident as Damon wouldn't be able to respect a coward. How long would he stay with her once he discovered the terrible truth? Not long, she bet. She brought her hand to her chest, pressing it over her heart. She didn't know if she could continue to hide her biggest weakness. The man saw far too much.

Damon had pulled ahead so Ravyn picked up the pace until she was just behind him. They neared an impenetrable patch of brush, and he altered their path so they could skim its outskirts. Ravyn heard a rumbling sound. She frowned in concentration, trying to remember why it was familiar. Damon was almost at the thicket when the noise came again. Her eyes widened as it dawned on her what it was.

"Stop!" she yelled, but even though he obeyed instantly, she knew it was a few seconds too late. She quickly assessed the situation, and without hesitation, put herself between Damon and the animal. Her vest was on and sealed; his wasn't. He was still recovering from a head injury; she was healthy.

The quill hurt like hell, and she staggered backward from the assault. She felt Damon's arm come around her, bracing her against his side. The pain remained too intense for her to form words, but she trusted he would figure out the creature was dangerous. When she heard the shot, she relaxed. He knew.

A burning sensation started where the spine entered her arm and pain swamped her senses. Her ears should be ringing from a gun fired so close, but if they were, she didn't notice. She couldn't see anything, couldn't smell the residue of the shot and she couldn't feel Damon, though she was sure he still held her.

Gritting her teeth against the pain, she hung on. It would have been easy to pass out, but she couldn't. She needed to tell Damon what to do. He wouldn't know. His team would have been in transit already when this unnamed animal was discovered and the information transmitted to CAT Command. Her voice came out low and harsh. "Get the quill out. Barbed."

If she could have managed it, Ravyn would have cursed.

Damon didn't realize how badly Ravyn was hurt until he heard her voice. He'd been busy studying the odd-looking animal, making sure it was dead. One look at her and worry replaced fascination. The last time he'd seen skin that color, his grandfather had been on his deathbed. The thought registered and then his training took over. He pushed aside the fear and lowered her to the ground. She was conscious, her teeth biting into her bottom lip. Using his knife, he slit the

sleeve of her shirt and exposed her arm. The area around the quill already looked red and swollen through the dirt.

Pulling the spine out of her arm would cause tissue damage, especially with the end barbed. Damon took out his camouflage shirt and ripped it so he'd have some pressure bandages ready. The wound would bleed as soon as he removed the quill. Her pulse was too rapid, her respiration shallow and she began to sweat. All symptoms of shock.

"Out. Poison." Ravyn's voice sounded like a croak.

He barely heard the words, but it forced him to act. He'd been worried about blood loss, but if the quill had some kind of venom, it had to be pulled. She flinched as soon as he handled her arm even though he'd been careful to touch her away from the puncture. Damon reached for the barb and noticed his hand shook.

"Steady yourself," he said. He'd directed the words to himself, but he realized Ravyn had taken them to heart. Her body stiffened slightly, her uninjured arm coming up to her face.

Focusing all his attention on the wound, Damon braced himself and yanked the quill straight up. Ravyn gave a muffled groan. Startled, he glanced up. She'd put her hand over her own mouth to suppress any noise she made. The woman continued to impress the hell out of him.

The bleeding began immediately, and he quickly grabbed a square of the shirt and applied pressure. Her breathing became easier and her hand slid to her chest. The blood seeped through the cloth and he added another pad. His number one priority was to stop the bleeding.

"Are you still with me, sweet pea?" he asked after a while.

He took the sound she made to be assent and added another compress. It felt as if the flow was slowing, but he didn't dare ease the pressure to look. Damon did a quick check. Her pulse still beat too rapidly, but her breathing seemed to be normal and her skin color was better. His worry about shock lessened.

"Ravyn. Ravyn," he said her name insistently until her lashes fluttered and her lids opened a fraction. "What symptoms are you going to be experiencing?" The silence dragged and Damon worried he'd left it too late. Her voice, when it came, was so soft he had to lean closer to hear her. He pushed aside his fear again, but he couldn't get the constriction out of his throat.

"Muscle weakness. Rapid pulse. Hallucinations." She left a long pause between each word. "Drunkenness. Headache."

Damon waited, but Ravyn didn't say more and her eyes drifted shut. The bleeding appeared to have stopped, and he added another pad before firmly securing all the bandages with a strip of fabric. Sitting back on his heels, Damon looked around. He knew it would be better not to move Ravyn, but he didn't have that option. The sound of the gunshot would have carried, and they'd been here too long already. Every instinct he possessed told him to get away from the area, that it was dangerous to stay.

Decision made, Damon donned the pack, arranging it toward one side. Ravyn hadn't moved and he frowned. He sat her up, put his shoulder into her middle and stood. She didn't respond in any way and that worried him. He shifted her body so she was balanced better and started walking.

Someone on the CAT team had to have taken a barb. The symptoms she'd rattled off were too precise to be speculation. Ravyn's muscles were completely limp, making her a dead weight. He had no information about the animal, but he guessed one spine couldn't kill a human. If the biggest animal on Jarved Nine was ninety pounds, it hadn't needed to develop a strong venom.

"What the hell did you think you were doing putting yourself in front of me?" he groused. Ravyn didn't respond, but he hadn't expected her to. "That thing had six more spines ready to fire."

Damon staggered at the thought. If he hadn't drawn his pistol and shot immediately, she could have taken another hit and that could have killed her. She'd been in a lot pain and hadn't been able to warn him.

Carrying Ravyn slowed his pace considerably and he required frequent rest stops. Sweat covered his body and dripped down his face. Because her muscles had remained limp, he hadn't realized she'd regained awareness until she'd started singing, mangling a bawdy drinking song almost beyond recognition. In the hours since, she'd alternated between singing, delirium and oblivion.

He blinked back the perspiration from his eyes and winced as Ravyn missed a note. The woman was remarkable in many ways, but she couldn't carry a tune. That didn't stop her from trying, though. She was singing "Ninety-Nine Bottles of Beer on the Wall" and kept losing count. Thank God, she couldn't produce much volume with her stomach resting on his shoulder.

Still, he preferred her singing to the hallucinations. It scared the hell out of him when she slipped into them. She talked to dead people. Her parents and stepfather liked him, she'd assured him after a long conversation with them. He'd only heard her side, but he'd gotten the gist of it without her passing on the information. What worried him was people on the verge of dying often saw deceased relatives. That was bad enough, but Ravyn had delusions that terrified her so badly, she'd emit shrieks of horror. They were muted by her position over his shoulder, but that didn't stop his blood from running cold.

"Damon!"

He hadn't realized the singing had stopped until he heard his name. "What?"

"Damon, where are you?"

"Oh, hell," he muttered. He'd rather hear two thousand more verses of the beer song than go through this again. He brought his free hand up and rubbed her bottom. "I'm right here, sweet pea," he said louder, hoping she could hear him.

She whimpered, and he knew she was deaf to anything outside her head. She shifted and he stopped walking. He was lucky her muscles were slack or she'd be thrashing right now.

"Help me," she called, her voice raising goose bumps on his body. "I need you. Damon, help me!"

His heart pounded and his legs went weak at the anguish her words betrayed. He put her down and sat, cuddling her in his arms. Ravyn's movements were weak, but her agitation was evident anyway. Her moan started low and became a wail.

That changed to one word repeated over and over. "No, no, no, no!" she cried.

Damon rocked her and made soothing noises. Nothing seemed to help. Then, as quickly as her hallucination had started, it ended and Ravyn went lax in his arms. Her eyes opened and she looked up at him. For a moment he thought she actually saw him, but the impression didn't last long. Her eyes still held a haze.

"You left me," she accused. His heart started to race. "You left me."

Closing his eyes, Damon tightened his hold on Ravyn. Somehow she knew he couldn't be trusted to protect her. Maybe she sensed his past failure. He didn't know. "No one's going to hurt you," he vowed. "I'll die first."

Chapter Twelve

The raucous screeching of some nearby lizards pulled Ravyn from sleep. Her head pounded, and although she willed them to be quiet, they didn't stop. Hoping to block the noise, she rolled on her side. She felt something scratchy as she moved, but forgot about it as pain slammed into her. Quickly, she returned to her back and took deep, calming breaths until the agony in her arm began to subside. Her relief was brief. The overly sweet smell of flowers made her stomach lurch.

Swallowing hard, she forced her eyes open and frowned. She was covered with leafy branches. Damon must have gone off, she guessed, and had concealed her the best he could. Ravyn pushed the foliage off with her good arm and then wished she hadn't. The rising sun lanced into her head like burning lasers and she squinted, trying to block out the bright light. Carefully, she sat up. She needed to find Damon, had to make sure the image of him going off to face the killer alone was only a nightmare.

Standing took effort and Ravyn swayed unsteadily. Her headache intensified. She knew should stay put, but she had to be sure Damon was okay. Looking around, she tried to find a sign showing which way he'd gone. She didn't see anything to tip her off, but she could sense him. Her hesitation was short-lived. She *knew* where he was and she *had* to see him. Now. She stumbled toward the rising sun, eyes narrowed against the glare.

Every step challenged her physically, her entire body protested the demands she made on it. Gritting her teeth, Ravyn made herself keep moving. Her watery eyes didn't make it easy to see where she walked and her sore arm brushed against a tree branch. The pain nearly dropped her to her knees, but she feared if she went down, she wouldn't get up. Instead, she clung to the branch until the burning torment stopped and she could continue.

It seemed like an eternity before she spotted him. He stood amid a group of trees, his arms crossed over his chest, staring off into the distance. Ravyn stopped short and sucked in her breath. Relief gave way to appreciation. The man made her knees sag in a way that had nothing to do with muscle fatigue.

"How are you feeling?" he asked quietly, turning his head and checking her out.

"Fine." At his skeptical look, Ravyn lifted her chin and tried to smile. It felt weak even to her and she changed the subject. "What are you looking at?"

For a moment she thought he would quiz her further about her health, but he said, "I'm trying to decide the safest route to the Old City."

When his attention shifted from her, Ravyn made her way over to him. He couldn't have seen her walking, yet as she pulled even with him, he slipped an arm around her for support. Giving up the pretense of feeling good, she leaned into him and followed his gaze. The sun was rising behind the Old City, giving the whole place a rosy glow. It was so beautiful, so radiant, she caught her breath in wonder. Ravyn thought she saw an enormous pyramid of energy emanating from the top of the walls surrounding the city, but she blinked and it was gone.

"Did you see that?" she asked in amazement.

"See what?" He sounded distracted.

Ravyn glanced over at Damon. He hadn't noticed anything, she decided. If she told him what she'd seen, he'd only worry. It hadn't been another hallucination; she was past those. "How the sun is making the city glow," she said. It wasn't a lie, it just wasn't what she had been talking about.

"Yeah, it's very impressive."

Okay, she could take a hint. "What's up?"

That finally garnered his full attention. "Where we're standing now, it's the last cover we'll have until we reach the Old City. It looks like the grass isn't even knee-high."

"And this is the most dangerous stretch for us."

Damon's frown deepened. "Yeah. All he has to do is wait and we could walk right into him."

"If we don't have any cover, he doesn't have any cover."

"Odds are he knows the area. We don't. There may be some place to hide that we can't see from here. Or he could just wait inside the Old City. Logically, this would be our destination."

"He can't enter the city. There's protection around it." Ravyn didn't miss Damon's concerned look. Darn it, that had just slipped out. She wasn't used to watching her words around him.

"Do you think you should lie down? That venom from the barb could still be in your bloodstream."

Ravyn shook her head carefully and relaxed against his body again. "I'm fine." And maybe if she said that often enough, it would be true. They were so close to their goal, but she didn't know how she'd make it the rest of the way. "Besides," she continued, "you'd sense him if he was close. You have before."

Damon grunted. A quick peek told her he had gone back to studying the terrain. She knew he wouldn't take any chances with her safety, wouldn't trust his instincts telling him the route was clear. She looked out over the land herself, trying to guess what Damon was considering. Her attention quickly drifted.

The early morning air held a hint of the sea. The Old City was built three kilometers inland from the largest ocean on Jarved Nine. Ravyn wished she could see it, but the ridge they stood on wasn't high enough for that kind of view. For a girl raised on the beaches of California, seeing the ocean only once in eight months had been torture.

The aura of the Old City seemed to intensify, pulling her thoughts away from the water. It had to be a trick of the sun, but it felt as if they were being welcomed. *All are safe within these walls.* Ravyn didn't know where the thought came from, but it wasn't hers. She shivered slightly, but not in fear. The energy from the city seemed to envelop her and she opened herself up, returning the embrace with joy.

"Sanctuary," she murmured, lost in the feeling.

Ravyn caught Damon's sharp glance and the way his lips tightened. He didn't comment on what she'd said, but she knew he wanted to. Then his expression changed and she knew he'd reached a decision. He pulled out one of the weapons, pressing it into her hand. "Stay here," he said. "I'll go get our stuff."

"I'll go with you." Her grip on the gun tightened.

"No, you won't. You'll be lucky to make it to the Old City without being carried. I don't want you wasting energy when we have to come back this way anyhow." His voice deepened as he added, "You'll be safe here, sweet pea, trust me."

Ravyn sighed. She did trust him, and he was right about her expending her strength. She hated that. "Okay," she agreed grudgingly, "but don't take too long or I'll come looking for you." The fear of something happening to him if he was out of her sight was too strong for her to put aside.

If anything, Damon's lips thinned further. "Yeah? And what are you going to do if I'm not back immediately? You can't even stand up without leaning against me."

Ravyn straightened. Of course, since she had to push off from him to do it, she doubted it underlined the point she was trying to make. "If I think you're in trouble," she told him, resolutely meeting his eyes, "I'll crawl if I have to."

"You would, too," Damon said, his voice a grumble of irritation. He looked seriously pissed for a moment and then his lips quirked. "What the hell am I going to do with you?"

She figured it was a rhetorical question since he didn't wait for an answer. As soon as he was out of sight, she made her way to the nearest tree. She didn't dare sit, but as she rested against the trunk, the black dots stopped spinning around her head. It was going to be a rough day.

It didn't take him long to return and Ravyn relaxed. The only thing troubling her now was how she'd make it to the Old City. One look at Damon and she decided to keep her concerns to herself. Exhaustion etched his face, leaving lines on either side of his mouth. Closing her eyes, she searched inside for a well of energy. She found a puddle. It would have to be enough.

He took her hand and squeezed it before starting out, and Ravyn wondered if she looked as scared as she felt. She stumbled along in his wake, unsure what pounded louder, her head or her heart. If only he hadn't reclaimed the gun. She swallowed hard, trying to rid her throat of the lump lodged there. Damon moved cautiously, but showed no sign of anxiety. *It's you, Ravyn. You're a coward.* She wished they were invisible and pictured a cloak shrouding them from the killer. The image became so real to her, she thought she saw a veil shimmer around them.

Eventually, tiredness overcame worry and it took all her determination to put one foot in front of the other. Her focus narrowed to the man leading the way. As the sun beat down mercilessly, her headache worsened and she found herself lagging behind. Then Damon stopped short, knocking her out of her lethargy. He signaled and she went still. She could reach him in a few strides, but the safety he represented seemed far away. She watched him look around, gun ready, and tried to control her trembling. Coward, the voice in her head mocked again.

He swung the gun around and she bit back a gasp. Then the tension left his body and she could breathe again. Ravyn moved to his side and found what had caught his attention. Some rodent-type animal, a grahlen she thought, struggled to drag a plant frond to its nest. Its beady brown eyes gave them a glare before it continued. She leaned her head on Damon's shoulder, following the animal's progress until it disappeared from sight. Now that the terror had subsided, Ravyn felt even more drained.

"Come on," Damon said. "I don't like standing here."

"Yeah," she agreed and straightened. Ravyn watched the world sway before it righted itself.

The Old City loomed like some unattainable mirage on the horizon, close, but never within reach. It became more and more difficult for her to stay upright. Her head reeled and her vision narrowed, but she blinked it back into some kind of focus. Just when she doubted she could continue, Damon put his arm around her, giving her some much needed assistance. Time lost all meaning, and when he stopped, she gave him a puzzled look.

"We're here, sweet pea."

Ravyn stared at him dumbly. When his words registered, she turned her head and saw the massive gray gate. There had never been a more beautiful sight and she nearly wept with joy. Her body threatened to collapse and she was grateful when Damon leaned her against the wall. The sun-warmed stone pressed against her back, keeping her upright. She could hear him struggle with the latch, then grunt in satisfaction. He steered her inside.

Sanctuary.

Ravyn smiled. They'd finally made it home.

Damon finished securing the last gate. He turned, stretching as he looked at the remarkably preserved city. He'd seen images, but nothing prepared him for the perfection of every detail. There should have been deterioration, but there wasn't. He'd searched some of the buildings near the gates for supplies to set the traps, and everything, right down to the most delicate cloth, looked as if it had been produced that day. It was eerie.

Hauling Ravyn around yesterday had taken a toll, and he still ached and felt fatigued. Thank God she'd managed to walk today. Not fast, granted, and she'd needed help most of the way, but he honestly didn't know if he could have carried her again. By the time they'd reached the gate, she'd been staggering. He didn't know which of them was more grateful to have arrived. At least inside the walls, he could relax. It was quiet inside the city. Not so much as a breeze blew, but it wasn't uncomfortable. If he didn't know better, he would swear it was temperature controlled.

After pocketing the supplies he hadn't used on the gates, Damon scanned the area where he'd left Ravyn. His brows pulled together in a worried frown when he didn't see her. She'd barely been able to stand by the time they'd reached the final gate. The first thing on the agenda was to take care of her wound. He should have cleaned it yesterday, but he had been too concerned with getting them away from the area where he'd fired the pistol.

When he finally spotted her, his heart stopped. He reached her side almost before it resumed beating. While he'd worked, he'd checked on her. Each time he'd looked over, she'd been sitting up, apparently alert. If he caught her eye, she would smile at him. Now she lay prone, her head propped up on the pack. Her eyes didn't open even when he knelt beside her.

Damon found himself oddly reluctant to touch her, afraid his hand would feel skin burning with fever. Afraid he'd failed again to keep someone in his care safe. How many times had the danger of infection been drilled into his head during survival training? Why hadn't he cleaned the wound before sleeping last night? He'd done nothing but stop the bleeding.

"Ravyn." He could hear the fear in his own voice.

Her face scrunched up and he said her name again, louder.

"What?" she said, testily. Her eyes remained shut.

Never before in his life had he been so grateful to be snarled at. Relief brought laughter and Ravyn's eyes did open then, so she could add a glare to her scowl.

"You had me worried," he confessed, sobering.

Her face softened. "I'm okay, just tired."

She was more than tired. He could see the listlessness in her eyes, and under the mud, her skin was flushed. Damon did reach out then and lightly touch her forehead. If his hand trembled slightly, well, he was entitled after the scare she gave him. Her skin was warm. "You're running a fever."

"Low grade," she agreed.

If his sweet pea wasn't denying the fever and insisting she was fine, then she was worse off than he'd realized. He pushed some of her dirt-encrusted hair off her face. Don't panic, he warned himself. She had enough energy left to be crabby, so she wasn't at death's door. Still, infection could be every bit as dangerous as the killer. "Think you can walk some more?"

"Of course," she said, the answer coming automatically.

She must have made her family, especially her overprotective brother, insane with her never-say-die attitude, Damon thought. God knew she made him crazy at times. And somehow, even when he didn't believe she could deliver, she managed to do whatever he asked of her. It amazed him how she pushed beyond her limitations. This time, however, it appeared her will wasn't going to overcome her body's weakness.

"Uh, Damon, will you help me up?"

"And you think you can walk?" he asked skeptically as he pulled her to her feet.

"I can walk," she insisted even as she wrapped her arms around him and grasped his waist.

He snorted. The only thing keeping her from landing back on the ground was the grip she had on him. "You're a trouper, but you can't do everything."

"It's not like you're asking me to capture an enemy platoon. All you want me to do is walk. I've been doing that for years."

Damon saw her feeble attempt at humor for what it was. "Distraction isn't going to work. You're not inexhaustible, even if you stubbornly insist otherwise."

Ravyn leaned back so she could look him in the eye. "Me? I'm not the one who insisted on lurching along for hours after getting hit in the head with a tree."

"It was a branch."

"Oh, well, that's different then."

Damon suppressed the desire to smile at her sarcasm. "Think you can stand on your own long enough for me to get our things?"

He knew better than to ask he realized belatedly. Her expression took on a mulish cast. "Of course," they said simultaneously.

Ravyn made a face.

"What can I say? You're too predictable, sweet pea."

He could see she didn't like that, but she didn't argue. Instead, she loosened her hold on him and steadied herself before letting go. Damon didn't waste any time grabbing his canteen and the pack. Ravyn's eyes were practically crossed as she struggled to remain upright. As soon as he had the pack settled, he slipped an arm around her. Judging from the way she immediately swayed into him, his support came just in time. He debated scooping her up and throwing her over his shoulder again, but his body protested at the thought. When he factored in Ravyn's reaction, he discarded the idea.

Their progress was necessarily slow, and though she continued to lean on him, her step never faltered. The sun hung low in the sky, the shadows beginning to lengthen. As they made their way through the city, Damon couldn't help but laugh.

"What?" Ravyn asked and he was heartened by her interest. She couldn't be too bad if her curiosity was engaged. He hoped.

"Just imagining the sight we must make. Both of us covered in dirt. You with your sleeve torn open, a camouflage bandage around your arm. Me with stitches in my head."

She chuckled softly. "We must look pitiful."

"The walking wounded," Damon agreed.

The smooth path didn't have so much as a crack or stray pebble to trip Ravyn up. The condition of their surroundings still stunned him. The environment was dust free. The areas of green, and they were plentiful, were perfectly manicured as if a team of gardeners had just finished work for the day. There was no sign that any kind of animal had made a home within the walls. It intrigued him. It was unnatural for an abandoned town to show no evidence of neglect. Despite everything abnormal about the place, Damon felt oddly at ease.

"You sense it too, don't you?" Ravyn asked.

"Sense what?" He felt her shift so she could look at him, but he kept his attention on the scene around them.

"The energy of the Old City. It's welcoming us."

Damon remained silent. While he might trust and follow his instincts, he wasn't fanciful enough to imbue something inanimate with human characteristics. And if he perhaps sensed acceptance at his presence, well, that was nothing more than imagination.

"For weeks after my first visit to the Old City, I dreamed of it every night." Ravyn smothered a yawn. "I don't remember much, except that I dreamed I lived here, that the people were gentle and kind. They had no knowledge of violence, no concept of war. It seemed like an Eden. Except there was some unseen threat and no one knew how to deal with it."

Damon couldn't imagine even dreaming about people unable to deal with a threat. One met menace with force or with stealth, whatever worked best to neutralize it.

"Which do you think is worse?" Ravyn asked, her tone thoughtful. "To be so used to peace that violence brings confusion, or to be so used to violence and war that it requires little thought on how to respond?"

"You picked a hell of a time to turn philosophical," Damon commented. They were both beyond exhaustion. Ravyn admitted to running a low-grade fever and was weak enough that she needed his support. Not quite the setting for abstract discussion.

Ravyn's shoulder moved in a shrug. "Sorry," she apologized, "my thoughts are wandering."

Intrigued despite his words, he gave the question some consideration as they moved through the city. "As a soldier, I can't accept being unprepared to defend my home, but there is a temptation to living in such complete tranquility."

The silence spun out around them, made even more obvious by the lack of wind. Perhaps being too perfect wasn't so great. He missed the sound of birds calling, the feel of the breeze against his skin. The rhythm of nature was soothing to him. This absence of it felt artificial. And yet, the city was not enclosed. There was no bubble or dome covering them.

"Damon, do you think we'll ever have that on Earth? Not an ignorance of upheaval, but an end to the incessant battles? An end to hate and murder and brutality?"

"No. Not in our lifetime."

"Too bad," Ravyn said in tacit agreement.

Damon continued to steer Ravyn along. He should settle them in a nearby building. Deep twilight had come upon them and he needed to tend her wound. They were far enough from the wall now, but something he couldn't name compelled him to keep moving. It wasn't right yet. Then they entered a square and he stopped, pulling Ravyn to a halt with him.

A large fountain sat in the center, empty of everything save a life-size stone lion. The carving was so detailed that every rippled muscle stood out. Its presence didn't surprise him. He'd seen images of it, so he knew it existed, but he swallowed hard. He knew exactly which way to go to reach the house he'd seen and he shouldn't. The CAT team hadn't mapped any farther than this into the Old City. Part of him hesitated at discovering whether his vision, for lack of a better term, had any validity. He wasn't sure what outcome he dreaded more, that it was true or that it wasn't.

Ravyn leaned more heavily into him and he started moving once again. The route felt familiar, as if he'd traveled it thousands of times. The hair on the back of his neck rose as he realized everything he saw matched his daydream exactly. They rounded a corner and there it stood. Damon stopped short in shock. He couldn't tear his eyes away. His heart pounded, but in excitement, not fear. The building had been constructed with nearly pure white stone, and it looked more like some ancient Greek temple than a house.

"Wow," Ravyn breathed.

Damon agreed. He shook himself out of his paralysis and headed for the door. Even in the encroaching darkness, the structure was impressive and the closer they got to it, the more incredible it appeared. It also had a lot of stairs they needed to ascend to reach the entrance. As they stopped at the base, he considered them, then studied Ravyn.

"I'm carrying you up the stairs," he decided. Before she could protest, he added, "It's not open to debate." He adjusted the equipment they wore and then hefted her over his shoulder.

"Ow! No wonder my stomach hurts." Ravyn shifted around, undoubtedly trying to find a more comfortable position.

"Yeah? Well, my whole body hurts. Hold still so we can get inside without breaking our necks."

She stopped moving, and taking a steadying breath, Damon started up. He didn't hurry. It hadn't been an idle concern about breaking bones if they fell down the narrow stone steps. He lowered Ravyn to her feet when they reached the landing. She rubbed her stomach and grinned sleepily at him. "I guess that wasn't so bad. I had a nice view of your rear end."

"Don't start more trouble than you can handle," he warned and brushed his lips across hers. Damon pushed the door open and guided Ravyn inside. It was dark, and he hesitated.

"Lights," she slurred, flicking her hand.

Damon gaped at her in the suddenly bright foyer. She sagged against him and he shook off his amazement. He closed the door. Hanging a right, they proceeded through an archway. Ravyn made the same flicking gesture every time they entered a darkened area. It wasn't until they stood inside the softly lit bedroom that he questioned how he'd known where to go. Ravyn pulled away, and still lost in thought, he released her.

She hadn't turned anything on here. The gentle glow came from four obelisks, set into niches in each corner of the room. One was pale blue, another some shade of pink, the third a dark green and the last a golden color that nearly matched Ravyn's eyes. His gaze followed the luminous beams until his attention was caught by an enormous bed. It seemed as if the light from the stones intersected over the center, forming a multicolored pyramid. He was shaken out of his fascination when he spotted Ravyn. She'd collapsed face down across the foot of the bed.

"Hell," he muttered, disgusted with himself. When it came to taking care of someone, he didn't do a great job. He rid himself of his pack, canteen, vest and boots, then made his way to Ravyn. Being careful of her injury, he rolled her onto her back. He took her boots off and unsealed her vest, but getting her out of it without causing her some pain would be difficult. Damon sat her up and tried to ease the vest off. It quickly became obvious that he needed her cooperation.

"Come on, Ravyn, wake up."

"Tired," she replied, not even batting an eyelash.

"I know you're tired, but don't you want to take a bath?" He thought the bribe inspired, but he received nothing save a small sound of agreement. It took some coaxing, but he managed to get her to sit up on her own. Her forehead rested against his shoulder and he used both hands to maneuver the vest off. As soon as she was free, she tried to lie back down.

"No," Damon said, "not yet."

"Wanna sleep."

"Just a little longer, sweet pea."

She grumbled, but complied when he urged her back on her feet. He swept her into his arms, making sure he had her good arm against his chest. The bathing chamber was mostly dark, just the slightest amount of illumination shining from some unknown source. He fumbled around looking for a light plate, the task not made easy with Ravyn still in his arms.

"Damn it. Where the hell are the lights?" All his frustration surged to the surface. They were both tired. He wanted to get her fixed up and go to sleep, but he couldn't take care of her in the dark.

Silhouetted by the dim glow, Ravyn lifted her hand, and again, the lights came on. It disconcerted him now as much as the first time. Damon didn't bother asking her how she did it. He moved his arm from under Ravyn's thighs and let her slide down his body until her feet touched the ground. Only she didn't stop. Her knees sagged and she nearly ended up on the floor before he tightened his hold. There was no way, he realized grimly, that he could let her fend for herself in a shower or tub. She'd probably drown.

The enormous bathing chamber appeared to be made of smooth crystal tiles. They were mostly gray, but splashes of color here and there caught his eye. Finally he spotted a door that looked like it might lead to a shower. It had no handle and he had difficulty feeling around one-handed for some sort of latch, but at last he opened the portal. It *was* a shower. Complete with what looked like some kind of soap in a clear, crystal decanter. Too bad he couldn't figure out how the hell to turn on the water. Nothing even remotely resembled a faucet. "Shit." He looked down at the woman resting against his body. She *had* turned on the lights. "Can you get the water running?" he asked.

She nodded and in seconds water streamed out of a white stone conduit into the tiled enclosure. Damon stuck his free hand into the flow. The temperature was perfect. He shook the drops off his hand, but didn't want to wipe it off on his filthy clothes. He was tired enough not to care about their weird surroundings, and Ravyn's eerie knowledge.

"Towels," Ravyn said, her voice slurring the word. "In there." She gestured weakly.

"Where?" he asked. He saw nothing but a blank wall.

Turning a bit in his arms, she reached out and pressed one of the crystal tiles. There was a steady increase in the glow where her hand rested. It dissipated and the wall slid slowly open, revealing a linen closet.

"Well, I'll be damned." Ravyn was spooking him. He pulled out a few towels and placed them on the counter. He spotted a chair in the corner and eased her onto it. For a moment, he worried she'd slide to the floor, but she slumped back and stayed put. He dug among the towels some more and found a smaller one to spread out as a bath mat, but he couldn't locate a single washcloth.

Damon looked at Ravyn and sighed. He couldn't put it off any longer. He stripped off his T-shirt and tossed it out of the way. He pulled off his socks, pants and shorts before turning to her. The buttons on her shirt didn't want to slip through the stiff fabric, but he forced them. When it hung open, he considered the problem of how to get it off her.

Untying the bandage, Damon removed the squares of blood-soaked fabric. As he'd feared, the last pad stuck to her injury. Since pulling it off would undoubtedly reopen the wound, he soaked a small towel and used water to loosen the bandage. When he finally got it off, he studied her arm. It looked too red to him and the skin around it felt a little too hot.

Damon finished undressing her, and while he tried to be a gentleman, he couldn't keep from staring once he had her naked. Swallowing a groan, he forced himself to move. He lifted her from the chair. Her bare skin slid against his bare skin and his body reacted. Gritting his teeth, he ignored it the best he could. He stepped into the shower, closing the door behind them.

The water felt good. He stood there, holding her, and let the cascade wash over them. Rivers of dirty water flowed down their bodies, and he made sure Ravyn's head tilted in a way that kept her eyes out of the stream. He turned her so her back rested against his front and reached for what appeared to be liquid soap. Damon put a little dab into his hand and rubbed it between his fingers. He brought his hand to his nose. It felt and smelled like the sap from the soap plant they'd used.

Satisfied with his tests, he used it generously on Ravyn's hair. It took three applications before the water stopped rinsing out dirt. Lathering soap between his hands, Damon carefully cleaned her face. That seemed to revive her and her legs supported her, although she still had to lean against him. It made things a little easier not to have to hold her up.

He took a deep breath and braced himself. Now came the part that would really torture him. Gingerly, Damon brought his hands around and started washing Ravyn's body. At first, he stayed in areas that could be called innocent. It didn't matter. He'd been hard since he'd stripped her, but now, with his soapy hands sliding over her body, his erection became painful.

Cleansing the wound took extra time, but too soon he had

to move onto the places he'd skipped. With great reluctance, he cupped her breasts. She fit his hands perfectly, and he sucked in a sharp breath as desire lanced through his body. He could feel Ravyn's nipples peak, could hear her soft hum of pleasure and then she about killed him. She wiggled her gorgeous little butt against his hard-on. Damon groaned and pressed himself tightly against her before he realized what he'd done.

Cursing, he put his hands on her shoulders and shifted her away from him. He worked faster now, wanting to finish as soon as he could. She's hurt, he reminded himself, but he still nearly lost it when he slipped his hand between her legs. She was hot and wet. He wanted to stroke her until she came apart for him.

Damon jerked his hand away as if he'd touched fire. He couldn't take anymore. She was clean enough, he decided and hustled her out of the shower. He wrapped her body in a towel and used another one to dry her hair. The thin, short cloth did nothing to deter his desire. He could still feel the slick warmth of her skin against him.

"Ouch," Ravyn complained without heat. "You're pulling my hair. I can do it myself."

"Okay." No way was he going to argue with her. Damon only stayed long enough to put her in the chair and make sure she didn't topple out of it, before he returned to the shower. If there had been faucets, he would have cranked the cold water up, but he had no clue how to adjust the temperature. He washed his own hair and body and then stood under the streaming water, his head resting against the cool tile. He wasn't moving until he had his control back.

Nearly twenty minutes passed before he thought he could handle the sight of Ravyn. Opening the door, he stepped back out and froze. Any ground he'd gained was lost as he drank her in. She'd combed her damp hair away from her face. Somewhere she had found a slinky little nightgown and the material clung to her curves before ending way too soon. His gaze traced the line of her long legs, appreciating each inch of bare skin.

Damon moved his eyes back up her body and noticed

there were spots on the fabric where she'd missed drying herself completely. Only the thinnest threads of self-discipline kept him from pulling her to the floor and moving his body over hers. In an effort to beat back the overwhelming arousal, he shifted his attention to what she was doing. On the counter sat a small jar of ointment and Ravyn was dabbing it on her wound.

His eyes widened in alarm. "What the hell is that?" he demanded. Didn't the woman have any sense? For all she knew, she could be putting rat poison on her arm.

"Salve," she answered calmly.

He realized she was totally oblivious to both his arousal and his frustrated anger. Damon took a deep breath, and noticing he stood naked and dripping, wrapped a towel around his waist. She wiped the excess unguent on the side of the jar and reached for a cup sitting at her elbow.

"Ravyn," he said, moving toward her as fast as he could. It wasn't fast enough. She finished the contents of the cup before he could grab it away from her. She released it easily. The bottom held a fine coating of sediment. He brought the cup to his nose and sniffed. Definitely not water.

Alarm ran through him. What had she consumed and how much? If he got her to vomit, would that get enough of it out of her system? He closed his eyes and pushed his dripping hair off his forehead. She could have ingested the first of it shortly after he returned to the shower. It might already be too late.

Damon ignored the sound of the water shutting off, but when he felt movement, he opened his eyes. Ravyn had walked past him and had nearly reached the bedroom. "Where are you going?"

"To bed," she answered easily and left him where he stood.

He chased after her and held her wrist to stop her. "That stuff you drank, we have to get it out of you."

"You're so sweet to worry, but it was just a healing powder. Nothing in it is going to hurt me."

"You don't know what you ingested," he insisted.

"I knew how to turn on the lights and the shower. Trust me to know what I used." She pressed her lips to his chin.

"Why don't you finish drying off and come to bed?"

Damon let her walk away from him. Something inside told him Ravyn did know what she'd taken, that it wouldn't harm her. And she moved better, looked better than she had earlier. It scared him, but he would trust her knowledge and his instinct against all logic. He returned to the bathroom, rinsed out the cup and recapped the jar before running the towel over his hair and body.

By the time he reached the bed, Ravyn slept. Her breathing appeared normal, and he relaxed just a fraction. Damon tossed his towel on a nearby chair and crawled into bed beside her. If she had any difficulty during the night, he would deal with it.

Chapter Thirteen

Stacey hesitated outside Alex's cabin, unsure of how to proceed. She should announce her presence, but knocking and awaiting permission to enter didn't fit the mood she wanted to project. She decided to just open it and boldly walk in. Although, if he'd secured it, that wouldn't work.

For the last few days she'd tried to avoid temptation, but she couldn't outdistance her thoughts or feelings, and running brought out the hunter in Alex. The man sought her out with the single-minded determination a predator showed for his chosen prey. Their training sessions remained all business, but afterward all bets were off. His attention left her flustered and aroused. A brush of his hand across hers and she forgot why she shouldn't have a quick, hot affair with the man. When it ended, her broken heart would eventually heal and at least she'd know what it felt like to be with him. Her body told her it would be very good.

It didn't help that every day she discovered different facets to him, each more enticing than the last. She found the real Alex Sullivan to be far more appealing than her fantasy of him, although she wasn't sure why. Even making an effort to be agreeable, the man was no Prince Charming.

It was time to settle things. Somehow. Taking a deep breath, Stacey depressed the plate. To her surprise the door opened. Without pausing she raised her chin and strode into the room, prepared to have it out with the darn man. All thoughts of confrontation slipped from her mind when she saw him. Alex sat on the edge of a couch, a small picture cradled in his hands. He looked up at her entrance and the anguish in his expression pained her. For an endless moment, his despair was there for her to see. Then, in the blink of an eye, it disappeared to be replaced by his usual, neutral mask.

"What is it? What's wrong? Have you heard something?" Stacey moved deeper into the sitting room with each question.

"No."

Just one word, no explanation. Typical, arrogant Sullivan. She wondered whether he'd deny the hopelessness she'd seen on his face if she asked him about it point blank. But she knew better than to do that. It would be like prodding the panther with a sharp stick and hoping he didn't lash out. "Then why are you sitting here like this?" Stacey gestured toward him with her hand.

He gave her a long look and she held her breath, sure he wouldn't say a word. Then he sighed, sat back in his seat and placed the picture on the table beside him.

"Just thinking," he finally said.

"About Ravyn."

Alex didn't answer, but he didn't need to. She could see the picture he'd put on the table. In it he wore his Western Alliance uniform and Ravyn wore the CAT uniform. Both were smiling. Stacey recognized it as the photo Ravyn had insisted on having made before she left for Jarved Nine. People commonly carried mementoes, but she would never have pegged the austere man in front of her as one of them.

Stacey sat beside him; she placed a hand on his forearm. She felt his muscles tighten before he relaxed. He didn't pull away from her touch, but except for that involuntary movement, he didn't respond either. "You're playing the 'what if' game," Stacey said, keeping her voice low. "What if Ravyn is dead? What if Ravyn is injured? What if her injuries are bad enough that she's dying as we make our way to Jarved Nine? What if we're too late?"

His muscles tensed again beneath her hand—heck, his whole body tensed. Stacey knew she'd hit the nail on the head. It explained why he hadn't come searching for her tonight and why he'd looked so miserable when she'd entered. "What if" could be a dangerous game.

"How about this, Alex: What if Ravyn is fine? What if there is a logical explanation why contact was lost with both the CAT and Spec Ops teams? What if everyone is waiting healthy and whole for the rescue team to arrive?" This was her dearest hope.

He turned his head and studied her. "Not likely," he said, voice like gravel.

"Wrong. My 'what ifs' are every bit as likely as the scenarios you've been running through your head." Since she didn't believe this herself, Stacey had a hard time injecting her words with confidence.

"No, they're not. I wish to hell they were. I've been a soldier for a lot of years. When contact is lost that abruptly and not reestablished it's never a good sign, Stacey."

For a moment, she reveled in the sound of her name com ing from his lips. He tended to not address her by name at all if he could help it, and when he had to, he usually called her Johnson. She disregarded the pleasant warmth in her chest when he moved away from her and leaned forward again, his forearms braced on his knees. His stoicism didn't fool her. Even with his face impassive, she knew he'd gone beyond worry. He'd never struck her as someone given to melancholy, and she had to wonder why he chose to wallow in it now. And why he didn't do a better job of concealing it.

"I think you just want to feel sorry for yourself, Sullivan." She tossed the words out there like a gauntlet and waited for his response. It didn't take long to get one. He leaped to his feet as if he'd been zapped with a cattle prod.

He turned, glared at her and said with enough ice to freeze hell, "You don't know what you're talking about."

"Oh, yeah?" Stacey got to her feet and squared off against him. "I know you're sitting all alone in your cabin, thinking about how you're going to deal with Ravyn's death. You told me yourself that you trained her. How can you write her off this easily? You've held her up as a shining example for me to follow, but when it comes right down to it, you don't believe in her or her abilities. Makes me wonder why you're bothering to train me. It won't make any difference in the outcome, right?"

Alex opened his mouth and shut it without saying a word. His jaw tightened so much, she was surprised it didn't crack. "Lady," he finally said, "what the hell did I do to deserve you?"

She knew he didn't mean it as a compliment, but she said, "I don't know. I guess the angels are smiling on you."

His lips quirked in a smile he couldn't suppress and Stacey let out the breath she'd been holding as she felt his mood lift.

"Alex," Stacey said, moving closer, "if anyone can take care of herself, it's Ravyn. And she has an entire Spec Ops team there to attend her. I hope they're not so busy protecting her that they forget about the others."

He laughed, a rich, full sound she felt in every cell of her body. "She does have a way of wrapping the biggest, toughest men around her finger." Sobering, Alex slipped his hands into the front pockets of his fatigue pants. "I just hope Brody can handle her and the situation."

Something about the way he said the other man's name caught Stacey's attention. "You don't like him, Brody, do you?"

"No."

"Come on, Sullivan, I know Ravyn taught you better. One-word responses are unacceptable. *Why* don't you like him?"

He took his hands out of his pockets, the look in his eyes colder than she'd ever seen it. Nervously, she twisted a strand of hair that had escaped her ponytail and tried to find some of the bravado that had lead her to his cabin. Alex folded his arms over his chest and leaned against the wall. One booted foot crossed the other at the ankle. "A friend of mine from West Point was wounded on a mission during the Third War. It fell to Brody to get him out of enemy territory safely. Brody got Sam out, but not before he was injured further. The injuries were severe enough to end his career."

"That was Brody's fault?"

Alex nodded once, sharply. "He made some bad decisions."

"So," Stacey said slowly, trying to think while she spoke, "you're worried that he'll get Ravyn hurt?"

"No." Stacey glared at him until he continued. "Brody knows what he's doing now. Hell, he was little more than a kid when that whole mess transpired."

"Why do you dislike him then? Obviously he's competent if you aren't concerned about his abilities now. You can't blame him for being inexperienced back then."

"It's his fault Sam's career is over."

"Does Sam blame him?"

Alex shook his head and straightened. Her laying siege to his shaky logic made him nervous, she decided. That wasn't her purpose, she just wanted to understand him, but the conversation interested her too much to drop. "Come on, Alex," she coaxed, "there's more to it than that. Let's hear the rest of it."

His lips tightened stubbornly. He shifted as she came closer, and Stacey shadowed his movements. She couldn't believe *she* put *him* in a sweat, but for every step she took, he moved away. He didn't stop until she had him in the corner with no place to go. The rabbit had trapped the panther. Confident now, Stacey moved forward. It was a mistake. She realized it the instant she came within reach. He pounced. Before she had time to react, he had her backed into the same corner he'd been in. His body crowded hers as he loomed over her.

"Why are you really here, Stace?"

She looked up at him, unsure what to say. All she could think about was the heat of his body pressed into hers. The sound of his voice was like hot fudge flowing over ice cream. Smooth and rich and oh, so sinful. She stared into his eyes and knew he had well and truly caught her.

He laughed, not in amusement, but in pleasure. His hands came up to her shoulders before running down her arms and catching her wrists. Alex brought her arms up so that they went around his neck. "Take what you want," he told her.

She did. She pulled his mouth down to hers and kissed him. She kissed him the way she'd been dreaming of for six years. His lips were warm and incredibly soft for such a hard man. He didn't try to wrest control from her, but followed where she led. She took the kiss deeper. She knew she'd have to make a decision soon on whether to stop this, but not yet. Not yet. An urgent need seemed to emanate from him and Stacey found herself responding to it, becoming desperate herself. She held on tighter as the mating of their mouths became savage.

Stacey gasped as his calloused hands covered her bare breasts. Alex had taken over although she wasn't sure when it had happened. He had her so lost in sensation that she hadn't felt him unbutton her blouse or open her bra. He pulled back and looked down. His harsh breathing sounded loud. She followed his gaze and was mesmerized by the sight of his hands on her. She should stop this, she should stop this.

Their eyes met and she read the want in him before he lowered his head and replaced one of his hands with his mouth. Stacey's head fell back as she arched into him. She heard the rasp of a zipper, then felt the roughness of his fingers as he slid his hand between her legs. He knew just how to touch her, and she couldn't stop the sounds that escaped her lips. She hit the peak so fast she cried out as much in surprise as in pleasure. The feeling of cool air where his warm hand had been forced her to open her eyes.

Do something, she told herself when she realized he was baring the lower half of her body. Stacey tightened her grip on his shoulders as Alex crouched in front of her and freed a leg from the restriction of her clothes.

As he stood, his hands opened the fly of his fatigues and pushed them down over his hips. Stacey's eyes widened, but before she could decide what to do, his mouth covered hers again. This time he teased her, and with a sigh, she surrendered. She reached for the buttons on his shirt, opening them with haste. She barely registered the heat of his skin on her fingers before he moved between her thighs and she lost herself in the feel of his hardness sliding against her. There were no words spoken. He led and she followed. When he lifted her, she wrapped her legs around him and guided him home.

Alex slid in slowly and stopped, letting them both get used to the feel of him inside her. He couldn't help but groan. It felt good. Too damn good. And then he had to move. He meant to be gentle, but he felt his control slipping away. He grabbed for it, but it danced outside his reach. He retained just enough presence of mind to make sure his hard thrusts didn't hurt Stacey. When it registered that she enjoyed his possession, he let go completely.

The noises she made pushed him closer to the edge, but he'd be damned if he was going over alone. He adjusted her position slightly and continued to stroke into her. It didn't take long before he felt her entire body tense and then she screamed. The last thread of his restraint snapped, and with a groan that felt torn from his soul, Alex allowed his own climax.

It took him a long time to regain awareness. Her fingers toyed with his hair. Her mouth pressed kisses into his throat, causing little ripples of response throughout his entire body. His arms quivered from holding Stacey's weight, but he wasn't ready to pull out yet. He could stay this way forever. The instant the realization registered, he tensed.

Forever? Alex separated their bodies and eased her down until Stacey's feet touched the floor, but he couldn't quite let go of her yet. She'd already made him lose control, something he'd never done before, not even with Lara. Now she had him thinking of forever and he knew better than that. Anger gave him the strength to close the holes she'd made in his wall.

When he pulled back, he was able to keep his face impassive although it wasn't easy when he got a look at Stacey. He tugged up his pants, tucked himself away and zipped up again. Alex swallowed hard. She stood there alone and disheveled, making no move to cover herself. He felt his body begin to come back to life and even took a step toward her before he stopped himself. Self-preservation came to his rescue. "I'll see you tomorrow morning for training," he said with seeming indifference. The stricken look on her face nearly felled him, but he walked away, closing the door to his sleeping area behind him. He fisted his hands against the wall, fighting not to go back to her.

Alex heard her leave a few minutes later. It was only imagination that made him think he'd just made a huge mistake.

Ravyn padded out of the bathing chamber, her bare feet making no sound on the stone floor. Stopping, she flexed her toes on the smooth surface. It should have been cold or at least cool, but it wasn't. Like just about everything else in the room, the floor was gray. Only the bursts of bright color throughout the chamber kept it from being depressing.

With a shrug, Ravyn resumed walking. She normally had little interest in how a place was decorated, but she couldn't seem to stop herself from studying her current surroundings. The carpet that covered most of the floor was a mishmash of pale blue, pink, deep green and gold. Instead of being ugly, it seemed perfect. She knew it had been made to match the obelisks that occupied each corner of the room.

Tired of the dim lighting, Ravyn waved a hand toward the outside wall. Fascinated, and with a bit of surprise, she watched it transform from opaque stone until it was clear as glass. Bright sunshine streamed in and she blinked several times as her eyes adjusted. Unable to stop herself, she went to the wall and reached out a hand. It felt like plain, ordinary stone. Ravyn laughed quietly in delight. This place amazed her. Movement caught her attention and she focused on the grounds beyond the wall. For a moment, she didn't see anything and then the small lake churned as Damon broke the surface.

Part of her relaxed. She hadn't been worried about him; they were safe within the walls of the Old City, but she'd gotten accustomed to him being nearby when she woke. You better get used to his absence, she told herself. She knew if they stayed together once they returned to Earth, she'd often be waking up alone. He'd be gone on missions for days, weeks, months at a time. The reminder sobered her.

Ravyn sighed. If she were smart, she'd reconsider her decision to deepen their relationship and run for the hills. Well, figuratively. He waded out of the lake then, completely naked and too gorgeous for words. And she knew it was already too late to play it safe.

She watched the water stream from his body and wished the lake were a bit closer to the windows. She couldn't quite see as well as she would have liked, but that didn't stop her body from reacting. When he reached for a towel and started drying off, she realized she was ogling him and shook her head. The man deserved his privacy, she thought and crossed to the bed.

Pushing the blankets down a bit, Ravyn settled herself against the pillows. She sat with her legs crossed and tugged the thin night slip down as far as it would go. She was decently covered, but barely.

The sunlight seemed to play off the obelisks, sending prisms of color throughout the room. Ravyn looked from crystal to crystal. Aquamarine for knowledge, rose quartz for love, green tourmaline for abundance and citrine for optimism. She cocked her head and considered those four qualities. Images flashed through her mind in a dizzying kaleidoscope that had her planting her hands on the mattress for balance.

Nothing she saw made sense to her, but when the visuals stopped, she knew the characteristics of the gems were important tenets of the society that had lived here. Ravyn shook off her disorientation. She knew one other thing. This room belonged to the leaders of the Old City, a man and a woman who had loved one another beyond reason.

She looked up at the sound of the door opening and smiled at Damon. "Hi," she said.

"Hi yourself. I see you're finally awake. How are you feeling?"

"Great." Ravyn couldn't take her eyes off him. One hand

held the gun, the other the straps of the pack. All he had covering him was a towel tied around his waist. Suddenly she felt more than a little warm. God, she was so shallow, she thought unrepentantly. Instead of admiring him for his intelligence or his honor and integrity, she was drooling over his body. But what a body. *Hmm.*

"You sure?" he asked.

"I'm sure," she said. Her voice had a breathless quality to it that had her blushing, but at least she wasn't panting. Yet.

"Let me check that arm now that there's enough light in here to see something." He looked pointedly past her, his tone dry, but he didn't comment on the see-through wall.

He bent and put the pack aside, leaning it against the wall. Ravyn noticed then that he was wearing his boots with the towel. She couldn't quite suppress a laugh at the sight. He grinned back at her. "I know, I look ridiculous," he said. "I just couldn't see putting on dirty clothes again." Since the boots weren't laced up, he stepped out of them easily. "Better?"

Ravyn nodded, not trusting her voice. His towel had parted as he'd removed the boots and she had gotten an eyeful.

He advanced toward her, all masculine grace and power. She loved the way he moved, loved the sight of all that bare, tanned skin. She loved his strong face, his dark hair falling over his brow where it had started to dry. But most of all, she loved the way he looked at her. Not just with desire, but with tenderness.

Damon put the gun down on the stand next to the bed. She sat in the middle of the enormous mattress, just out of his reach. "Slide over here so I can get a look."

Ravyn shook her head. "You come here," she told him, her voice thicker than usual.

He raised both eyebrows, but didn't argue. When he sat facing her, he softly clasped her arm. Ravyn watched him study the wound, noticed his brow scrunch in puzzlement. She knew what he saw, she'd examined it herself after she'd showered this morning.

Damon looked up at her. "Your arm has healed so much,

that if I didn't know better, I'd swear it's been at least a week since you took the barb."

"I know. Maybe we should put some of that salve on your injury too." It stunned her that she sounded halfway normal.

He reached out with his other hand, his index finger tracing a circle on her skin around the wound. The hardness of his hands, their strength, contrasted with the gentleness of his touch and Ravyn shuddered.

"Did that hurt?"

"No."

His eyes found hers, his gaze sharpened and then he smiled. His hands moved to her legs, his thumbs rubbing the inside of her knees. Ravyn could feel her world narrow to this man and the bed they shared. She leaned into his chest and whispered a kiss across his mouth. Damon turned his head, keeping the contact and tightened his hold on her.

His taste, his scent, his heat surrounded her. Ravyn took his hands, moved them so that she could go up on her knees and get closer to him. She gasped against his lips as his calloused fingers trailed across the nape of her neck. As close as she was, it still wasn't near enough. She shifted again so she straddled his thighs. His hands slid to her hips, squeezed briefly and then he went still.

Damon's grip tightened, keeping her from her goal. He broke their kiss. "Ravyn, no."

"No?" she asked, surprised.

Ravyn opened her eyes and looked at him. Damon wanted her, she had no doubt about that. His skin held a flush of arousal; his eyes were dark and hot. A surreptitious glance downward told her just how excited he was. He'd left her hands free and she slid them from his shoulders to his pecs and flexed her fingers.

"Stop that," he said, sounding anything but resolute.

She stilled, but didn't move her hands away from his chest. "Why, Damon?"

"You know why. I can't let you make this decision while you're caught up in the moment."

It was then, her eyes locked on his, that Ravyn stopped fighting her emotions and let herself fall all the way in love with Damon. Later, she told herself, she'd worry about the ramifications, but for now, she just allowed herself to feel.

"Honey," she said, "I decided before I got hurt. But you're right, I don't want to do this if you aren't sure. We both need to go into this with our eyes open."

He growled, there was no other word for it, and Ravyn found herself on her back, Damon beside her. Startled, she laughed before his mouth covered hers. "Trust me, sweet pea," he said when he finally let her up for air, "I'm very sure."

"But," she started, stopping when he put a finger over her lips.

"It's always been up to you. I made my choice before we ever talked about birth control. So, if you're sure . . ."

Ravyn smiled. "Anyone ever tell you that you talk too much?"

He laughed, she presumed at the absurdity of that statement coming from her. After all, she'd been the one to press him to talk more. His chuckle cut off when she reached for the knot in his towel. She, who had never been bold with any man, found herself taking the lead. As soon as she loosened the towel, he tossed it off the side of the bed. Ravyn stared, transfixed at the sight of him. Suddenly she felt self-conscious, unsure. She looked up at Damon, her eyes holding a mute plea.

"It's okay," he assured her, his voice quiet. "I'll take care of you. I'll take care of everything."

His kiss was gentle, his tongue stroked the inside of her mouth lazily, as if they had all the time in the world. She could feel the restraint he exercised, realized how difficult it must be for him to take it slow, but she trusted him absolutely. Ravyn let herself relax into him.

She wrapped her arms around him, held on tight. He burned her wherever their skin touched, but she wanted that heat, craved it. She ran her hands across his back, tracing a path over his shoulder blades and spine. One heavily muscled thigh nudged between her legs and slid upward, taking the skirt of her night slip with it. Ravyn gasped, breaking the kiss, as he pressed against her core. Her eyes opened at the gentle stroke of his fingers against her jaw. It took a moment for her to focus. She darn near dissolved at the look of untempered need on his face.

"Okay?" he asked.

"Yes. Don't stop." Ravyn slipped her hands beyond his waist and tugged him closer.

His thumb traced her bottom lip and Ravyn opened her mouth, pulling it in, laving it with her tongue. She smiled as she felt Damon shudder. He pulled free, planted a quick, hard kiss on her lips and then his hands swept down her sides. He came up underneath the thin night shift, cupped her bare bottom, pressing her even more tightly against him.

Ravyn rocked against him, his hard length hot against her belly. Suddenly even the thin material of her nightgown was too great a barrier. She wanted it off. She reached for the fabric bunched at her waist, but couldn't move it, not with his body so close to hers. "Damon," she said impatiently, knowing he would understand what she wanted.

He smiled slightly and eased back so he could help her draw it up and off. The slinky cloth caressed her sensitive skin and she caught her breath. When she would have squeezed herself against him once more, Damon held her away. Ravyn's murmur of protest died in her throat as he raised his eyes back to hers. There was such reverence in his gaze that she felt tears gather.

"Do you have any idea," he said slowly, "just how beautiful you are?"

Ravyn would have shaken her head in denial, but she couldn't doubt his sincerity. She brushed a kiss to his chin and her heart seemed to expand until she thought it would burst from her chest. She watched him as he continued to drink in the sight of her. In a detached sort of way, it amazed Ravyn that she didn't feel self-conscious as he looked his fill. It aroused her to know she pleased him, to know he couldn't tear his gaze from her. A part of her wanted to take the time to study him as well, but the awe she saw on his face held her mesmerized.

His hand trailed up her rib cage, cupped her breast. For a moment they were both still and then he ran his thumb over her crest. Ravyn tightened her hands in his hair before pulling his mouth to hers. She nibbled at his bottom lip, nipping, then soothing with her tongue.

Ravyn lost herself in sensation. His hands and mouth seemed to be everywhere at once and she couldn't keep her own hands immobile. She touched every inch of his body she could reach. Well almost. There was one part of him shyness kept her from stroking. She didn't realize how crazed that made him until he raised his head from her body.

"Damn, Ravyn. Touch me."

"I am."

He growled. Taking her wrist, he guided her to where he wanted her caress. He stopped short, releasing her within a hair's breadth of his goal. "Please."

As much as he needed to feel her touch, she knew he was leaving it up to her. That he wouldn't force her to do anything she was uncomfortable with even if it killed him. She closed the gap he'd left, running the backs of her fingers up his length. His body shook by the time she reached his tip. She turned her hand, curling her fingers around him, and glided back down.

His groan started deep in his chest and rumbled to the surface. It amazed Ravyn that arousing Damon raised her own level of passion. She gave him a small push and he took the hint and lay on his back, one arm behind his head so he could watch her. Ravyn knelt beside him and tried different amounts of pressure, different ways of touching him. He had a smile on his face as she experimented, and she realized he took almost as much pleasure in her discovery as in her caresses. She continued to gauge his reaction to everything she tried until she felt she had a good idea of what pleased him most.

She could see the sweat on his body, feel the tenseness of his muscles and Ravyn knew he kept a tight leash on himself for her. It humbled her to know he cared so much. She smiled back at him and leaned forward, brushing her hair across his groin. She heard him suck in a breath and her smile widened. The thick curtain of hair hid her from his view, and he jumped in surprise when she pressed her lips to the crown of his erection.

"Stop," he ordered, reaching for her.

"You didn't like that?" Ravyn had been sure he would.

"Too much, sweet pea, too much."

He guided her over his body. Ravyn gasped at the heat of him between her legs and arched back. His hands on her hips kept her from doing more than subtly rocking. With a groan he choked off before it could fully emerge, Damon loosened his grip, and sliding his arms up her body, pulled her down to his chest. Kissing her, he rolled until she was on her back and he was above her. For a moment, they froze, staring at each other. His eyes were so dark with arousal that she could see only an outline of green. She brought a foot up, sliding it from his ankle to the back of his knee. The coarse hair of his leg tickled her toes.

"I can't wait any more, Ravyn." His voice was soft, gentle despite the gruffness, the huskiness.

She knew he was giving her one more chance to change her mind and love for him surged through her body. "I don't want you to wait."

The feel of him slowly entering her left her gasping. Ravyn gripped his biceps and tried to remain relaxed. She'd led an active life, she doubted she still had a physical barrier for him to breach, but the strangeness she felt as he sank deeper had her fighting the need to tense. She heard him murmuring reassurance as he inexorably joined their bodies.

When he stopped, her gaze flew to his in surprise. His eyes were tightly shut and sweat all but dripped from his brow. Some instinct had Ravyn bringing her legs up and wrapping them around his hips. With a groan, his entire body went rigid. "Damon?"

He rested his forehead against hers and looked down at her. "Just don't move," he grated out.

Okay, she thought, she could do that. But as the minutes passed, the only sound the raggedness of their breathing, Ravyn began to wonder how much longer he wanted to wait. The minor discomfort she'd felt had dissipated, leaving her burning for him. It became more and more difficult for her to remain still.

She pressed kisses to his chin and jaw line, her legs tightened around him. "Honey, please," she urged, "please."

Ravyn watched him study her, then his lips quirked up at the corners and he rocked just a little, as if testing the waters. He must have been satisfied with her response because he didn't hesitate any longer. He stroked into her, his pace measured and unhurried. At first, his hands guided her into his thrusts, but, as she caught his rhythm, he let go.

There were no words to describe the feelings within her. This didn't just involve her body, but her heart, mind and soul. All of her felt joined to all of him. Just Damon, only Damon. She moaned as the sensations wound tighter inside her. As if waiting for that signal, Damon's movements became firmer.

She lost herself in him. In the intense exultation of his body moving within hers, in the slightly salty taste of his skin as she pressed her lips to his shoulder. She could see only him, smell only the scent of their arousal in the air. Neither of them was capable of forming actual words, but the sounds he made, the sounds she heard coming from her own mouth, pushed her to the edge. Everything conspired to bring her to fever pitch.

She rode the swell of excitement as it continued to build. Then the wave broke, bringing her into a shore of such intense pleasure that all Ravyn could do was hang on to Damon and moan his name. Even lost in her own sensations, she felt him thrust harder. Once, twice, a third time and then he, too, reached the paradise he'd brought her to.

For a long while, they both remained still, gasping for breath. Ravyn mumbled a complaint when Damon separated their bodies, but she subsided as he pulled her against his side. Her head rested on his shoulder, his arm firmly around her waist, keeping her close. His hands were gentle, stroking her with such care that she smiled. Her fingers slipped from his chest to his stomach, but she didn't have the energy to move them any farther.

"Damn, sweet pea," he said, his voice low, "that was incredible."

Lost in lassitude, Ravyn slowly opened her eyes. "Yeah," she agreed, her voice still husky, "it was."

He kissed her then. A kiss so soft, so gentle, so full of feeling that tears of emotion welled in her eyes. Slowly, almost reluctantly, he pulled back and silence enveloped them again as they continued to hold one another. His hand absently stroked up and down her arm and Ravyn sighed and settled herself more comfortably against him.

"I can't believe your brother could frighten off all the guys. Not as beautiful and passionate as you are," he said a long time later.

"Believe it," she assured him calmly. "I almost never got asked out, and when I did, there was never a second date. Somehow, Alex always managed to be outside when they'd come to pick me up. I guess there was something about him dressed in fatigues with a knife strapped to one thigh and wearing his Spec Ops beret that scared the boys off."

"Your brother is Spec Ops?"

"Sure, I told you that."

"No, you didn't."

Ravyn shrugged, her shoulder sliding pleasantly along his skin. "I meant to. I was curious if you knew each other."

"I don't remember meeting anyone named Verdier."

"Verdier is my dad's last name. Alex is a Sullivan."

Ravyn felt Damon stiffen and she circled her fingers lightly on his stomach to soothe him.

"Your stepbrother," he finally said in a tone she couldn't decipher, "isn't Colonel Alexander Sullivan, is he?"

"You *do* know Alex," Ravyn said, thrilled.

Damon carefully freed himself, sat up and dropped his head into his hands. "Shit," he muttered, "I'm a dead man."

Chapter Fourteen

Of all the people in all the world, why did Ravyn have to be related to the colonel? Without much effort, Damon visualized the man's reaction when he found out about the two of them. It might be a blessing to be killed outright. It would be a damn sight better than being made a eunuch. He winced at the thought.

Somehow Damon couldn't quite reconcile Ravyn's beloved brother with the man he knew. The colonel made an arctic winter feel warm. It seemed beyond comprehension that the Alex who doted on Ravyn and the rigid, remote Colonel Alexander M. Sullivan were one and the same.

Movement caught his attention. He turned in time to see Ravyn crawl under the blankets and pull them up to her chin. She appeared more than a little ill-at-ease and uncertain. Damon immediately put his worries about the colonel's reaction out of his mind. He'd deal with that when the time came. Ravyn was more important. Getting under the covers himself, he shifted so he faced her. "Come here, sweet pea."

She hesitated and his heart skipped a beat. He wanted to close the distance between them himself, but refused to force her in any way. She didn't move, just looked at him and his pulse rate picked up. With a stunning burst of clarity, he realized he felt something akin to desperation.

When he didn't think he could stand it any longer, Ravyn eased over until she lay beside him. Damon couldn't help it. He reached over and touched her. He put his hand on her hip and ran it down the back of her thigh to just above her knee. His fingers continued to gently knead her flesh as she stared at him. Apparently she reached a decision. Ravyn smiled tentatively and cuddled into him. Something inside Damon relaxed and he wrapped his arms around her. He kept his hold loose even though every instinct he possessed urged him to clasp her tightly to him.

"You don't like Alex," she said, sounding sad.

"I don't dislike him, but it's hard to be friendly with someone who hates you." Damon held his breath. Please, he thought, don't let her pull away because of this.

"Why would Alex hate you?"

"For one thing, my brother married the woman he was seeing."

"Your brother is the poor sap that got stuck with Lara?" She looked abashed as what she said appeared to sink in. "Um, sorry, I didn't mean it quite that way."

"Don't worry about it," he said. "To be honest, I'm not sure what Royce sees in Lara myself."

"You can't? She's very beautiful."

"No, she's not. Well, I suppose she's attractive enough if you don't notice how cold her eyes are."

Ravyn rested a hand on his chest just below his dog tags. "I didn't think things like that mattered to a man."

"They do to me." Damon had been chased by too many women who were interested in his family's money, not in him. Avarice had marred the beauty of more than one woman in his view, but he didn't share that with her.

"Why else do you think Alex doesn't like you?" Ravyn asked, pulling him out of his thoughts.

Damon grimaced. Well, hell, he'd known the time would come when he'd have to tell her about his greatest failure. He let go of her and rolled onto his back, unable to watch Ravyn's regard for him seep out of her eyes. He put an arm behind his head and stared up at the ceiling. His other hand fisted at his side.

"Before I joined Spec Ops my first assignment," he told her, without inflection, "was under Major Sam Benning."

"Sammy is Alex's best friend."

Damon braced himself at the obvious affection he heard in her voice. He knew it was going to hurt when Ravyn hated him too. But maybe he deserved it. It *was* his fault. All of it.

"During a real ugly battle in the Third War, five of us were cut off, separated from the unit. Me, Major Benning and three privates. The major was injured. Not severely, but he lapsed in out and of consciousness, so I had command."

"How long had you been commissioned?"

"Long enough," he said. He didn't want her to think he was excusing himself in any way.

"How long, Damon?" she demanded.

"Two months." Ravyn didn't say another word. He didn't have to close his eyes to remember the chaos, the roar of weapons being discharged, the screams and moans of the injured. The smell of gunpowder still burned his nostrils. Get on with it, he told himself when he realized he'd been lost in thought. For a moment, he wanted to forget about telling Ravyn and pretend it had never happened, pretend it wouldn't make a difference.

"The first bad decision I made was when I opted to rejoin our unit. There were other Alliance forces close by that didn't have as many enemy soldiers in the way. The second bad decision was putting Conway on point. She had more time in than the other two privates, so I thought she could handle it."

"But she couldn't."

"No," Damon said. "We ran into a little trouble. She should have helped us. We would have been okay if she had."

He forced himself to back up, to explain everything in sequence. "We took cover while Conway went ahead to collect information on what was in front of us. A group of enemy soldiers practically stumbled right into us. I don't think we even took a breath until they started moving away. Major Benning had been unconscious for a while and I didn't think he would come to right then. He kind of made a grunting noise, just enough to call attention to us. Then all hell broke loose."

Carefully, he unclenched his fist. His knuckles ached. He ran his hand over his mouth, wiping away some of the perspiration above his upper lip. It had been eight years and his body still reacted to the memory. He had a feeling if he lived another eighty years, he'd still be sweating when he remembered that day.

"We exchanged fire. I thought there were six of them and we took them all down. There were eight. Two of them came up on our flank. A twig snapped or something, but it gave us a couple seconds of warning."

Damon took a few deep breaths. He wanted to sound calm and reasonable when he related the events of that day. He could feel Ravyn's eyes on him, but he didn't look at her. That she stayed so silent didn't bode well, he decided. He took another breath.

"I could see Conway standing beyond the two men," he continued, his voice steady. "She had a clear shot without endangering us. Because it would be easier for her, I didn't shoot. Almost as soon as I made that decision, I realized she was terrified. Instead of helping us, she turned and ran. The enemy opened fire and her cowardice cost two men their lives and the major his career and his mobility."

Ravyn made a small noise and Damon closed his eyes tightly for a moment. He'd known his actions were unforgivable. He lowered his arm from behind his head and stroked the mark furrowed high across his bicep.

"You've had your other scars removed," Ravyn said, sounding subdued, "but you kept that one. Why?"

"So I never forget that bad choices cost lives. This is the only hit I took, a minor flesh wound. The two men who died had more than a dozen bullets in them. Major Benning, who was on the ground, took three bullets. I received one little graze. My mark of shame," he finished, his mouth twisting.

"What happened to Conway?"

"She ran right into a full-scale engagement. She took so

many bullets from both sides that she was nearly unidentifiable."

Another life lost for which he was responsible. He'd gone to her funeral. "I went to all three funerals. I watched their parents and families grieve. All of them thanked me for coming. Thanked the man who had gotten their child killed." Damon swallowed hard to clear his voice. "So that's why the colonel hates me. I caused his best friend to be permanently disabled."

"Tell the rest of the story, Damon."

He looked at her then, too startled not to. She appeared sad, but not accusing. "There's not much to tell," he said with a shrug.

"Tell me how you and Sammy got back to our side."

"We walked back."

Ravyn shook her head. "Sam couldn't walk. You put him over your shoulder and carried him. Kilometers from what he's said. And that graze on your arm, your mark of shame, caused you to lose enough blood that the doctors all agreed you should have been unconscious yourself."

"It wasn't kilometers," Damon said, not quite sure what to make of the information Ravyn had. How much had she known before he'd said a word?

"I didn't know it was you," Ravyn said, as if picking up on his thoughts, "and I didn't know much of the story. Both Alex and Sammy tend to shield me, but I overheard them arguing when Sam was staying with us right after his discharge. He credits you with saving his life."

"Major Benning is a generous man. If I had made other choices, things would have been different."

"Maybe," Ravyn conceded, "but maybe not. You can't know what would have happened."

He started to turn away, unable to accept her absolution. She touched him then, tangling her fingers in his hair and holding him steady so that he had to look at her.

"You were twenty years old, Damon, and as green as the grass in Ireland. You did the best you could."

"I should have done better," he insisted. It was hard for him to meet her eyes. She didn't know; she hadn't been there. He should have gotten everyone out alive and healthy.

"The army doesn't agree. They gave you a medal. I bet you never wear it though, do you?"

He couldn't contain a small, mirthless chuckle. "You know me too well."

"I know you care too much, take too much responsibility for things you have no control over. Events have a way of happening, people make decisions you can't predict. Tell me, do you blame yourself for what happened to your team at the CAT facility?"

"No." He'd gone over this time and again in his mind.

"Why not? Why is what happened here different?"

"This time I made the right choices. I'd make them again in the same situation. They just didn't work out right."

"So you made the best decisions you could at the time." She waited for his nod before continuing. "Eight years ago you did the same thing. There is no difference. You just have more experience now." Ravyn moved until she leaned over him. He suspected she did it for emphasis, but it didn't have the intended result. He found himself distracted by her nakedness.

Her hand hit his shoulder hard enough to get his attention. "Stop staring at my breasts when I'm trying to make a point."

It surprised him to feel his mood lighten. He even managed a real smile for her. "Sorry, sweet pea. I can't help it. You might want to cover up if you plan to continue with your point."

With a half laugh, half growl, she pulled the blankets around her. And ended up baring him, which seemed to distract *her*. Her battle with the covers continued solo until she glared at him and said, "You could help me here."

When the blankets were more or less fixed and they were more or less covered again, Ravyn unexpectedly straddled him. Shock held Damon still and her hands captured his wrists, imprisoning them next to his head. For a moment, he tensed; then he relaxed as another part of him began to tighten. She kept the lower half of their bodies separated, but he swore he could feel her heat. It made him crazy for that touch of her.

"I don't know how to tell you this, but you're all but guaranteeing I won't hear a word you say." He arched his hips slightly to explain why, but she moved, preventing contact.

"I know, but you weren't listening to me anyway. We're going to try something different. Repeat after me, 'I am not responsible for Sam Benning's injuries.' "

"Ravyn," he protested. He tried to move his hands, but she squeezed his wrists harder and he subsided.

"Say it."

He stayed silent. It wasn't true; he couldn't say it.

"Don't you want to be inside me? Feel my body surrounding yours, all wet and hot? It's getting me excited just remembering what it was like. The feel of you so big and hard. Mmm. It was so good, Damon." Her voice had a breathless quality to it that added to the torridness of her words.

She licked her lips and gave a little shimmy that made her breasts jiggle. It took every ounce of willpower he had not to break her hold and roll on top of her. He wasn't even sure what stopped him. "What game are you playing?"

"Positive reinforcement."

She didn't sound very much in control herself and Damon smiled, figuring he could hold out longer than her. "Oh, yeah?"

"Yeah," she drawled. "Let's try this sentence, since the first one is too difficult for you. Say, 'I made the choices I thought were right at the time.' "

Damon considered her words as much as he was able with all the blood rushing south from his brain. He decided they were true enough. "I made the choices I thought were right at the time."

She lowered herself until her moist heat rested on his erection and then she slid up and back, stroking him. He arched his hips and this time she didn't pull away. "Say, 'I did not fire the weapon that hurt or killed any member of my team.' "

"I might as well have."

Ravyn separated her body from his and he groaned. He

could see it cost her, but it just about killed him.

"Wrong answer. Wanna try that again?"

He grit his teeth, but the words seemed to come out anyway. "I did not fire the weapon that injured or killed any member of my team."

He could barely keep his eyes open as she rubbed against him once more. The feel of her sliding on his shaft was just too good. It took him a minute to recall he should be watching for her to lose control and end this game. She didn't say a word for a long time, long enough for him to not care about anything but what she did to him.

" 'I did the best I could.' "

Damon hesitated and Ravyn halted, albeit reluctantly. He noted she all but panted, but he couldn't take advantage of her arousal. Not when her dead stop left him feeling frenzied. His fingers twitched. Though she'd slackened her hold enough that he needn't worry about hurting her, he didn't try to twist free.

"I did the best I could," he said, each word pulled from him. "Now keep moving." She did and he groaned his thanks. Right now, he didn't care about anything but release.

"You like this?" she asked, breathless.

"Oh, yeah, sweet pea, but I want inside you."

"Not yet."

"Ravyn," he objected, but she swooped down, cutting off his protest with a kiss that demanded his total compliance.

" 'I am not responsible for Sam's injuries or anyone's death.' "

"That's not fair." Damon knew now that she wasn't going to let him find his pleasure until she got the words she wanted.

"Neither is blaming yourself for something that wasn't your fault. I can hold out longer than you can."

"Just because I say the words, doesn't mean I believe them." But he knew she was right about outlasting him. As close as he was, he would say just about anything to join his body with hers.

"I know that. I'm betting, though, that just saying it will be enough to get you to start thinking. Get you to forgive yourself. No one blames you but you." Her voice had a thready quality to it that did not diminish the vehemence of her belief.

"And the colonel," he pointed out.

"Sammy doesn't blame you. The parents of those who died don't blame you. Alex's opinion doesn't count. He's not necessarily reasonable when it comes to people he cares about."

"That's good news," he commented with as much dryness as he could manage given that he was so hard he didn't know if he would live through the experience. "He finds out about us, he *is* going to kill me. You realize that, don't you?"

Ravyn smiled down at him. "Don't worry, honey. I won't let my big brother hurt you."

His laugh came out sounding pained. She moved just enough to keep a fine edge on his need. He didn't know why, but Ravyn managed to reach a part of him no one else had ever touched. He felt a warmth for her he couldn't name. Never in his life had he seen a more beautiful sight than the woman straddling his hips. "Ravyn, please. I need you."

"You know the magic words, and I don't mean 'open sesame.' "

She had him laughing again, even though he didn't have the breath to spare. "It's not my fault. Not that the major got injured or that the others died." He might have said it, but it lacked sincerity. Ravyn hadn't asked for that though. "Now, sweet pea. You promised."

She shifted enough for him to slide home in one smooth thrust. This ride wasn't going to be slow and easy, not with his control shattered. He was so close. "Harder," he told her. Her inexperience showed in the timidness of her movements. He freed his hands then, moving them to her hips and guiding her into his strokes. His pace was fast and furious, and she braced her hands against his chest. Each finger burned her brand into his skin. He released one of her hips, finding the center of her pleasure. He'd be damned if she wasn't coming with him.

"Oh, Damon. Yes!"

And she was there. He could feel it. He exploded inside

her with a power he'd never experienced before. His. She was his. He might have even muttered that when he pressed his mouth against the long, elegant line of her throat as she lay over him.

He didn't know how long they stayed that way, but he was nowhere near recovered when she said, "That's why you went Spec Ops, isn't it?"

"What?" It took all his concentration just to breathe, how could Ravyn be ready to talk?

"What happened that day. It's why you applied to Spec Ops."

He forced his brain back to work. "Yeah," Damon admitted with more than a little reluctance. He thought they were done with this conversation. "I figured if I had more training, learned more, I wouldn't make those kinds of mistakes again."

She lifted herself up just enough to scowl down at him. With a smile, he rubbed her bottom in a gesture of surrender. He wouldn't survive a second go-round of Ravyn's positive-reinforcement technique. She settled herself against him again with a sigh that sounded contented. He could have stayed like that forever, their bodies joined, but Ravyn's stomach growled. She tensed, probably in embarrassment, but Damon smiled. "I brought food in the pack," he told her, giving the cheek his hand rested on a small squeeze.

With more than a little reluctance, Damon lifted her off him and left their bed. By the time he turned around, pack in hand, Ravyn had donned her nightgown again. "You didn't have to dress for dinner on my account," he said.

She blushed, but didn't answer. He sat beside her on the bed and spread out the food he'd gathered. Ravyn seemed oddly pensive, like she'd put a wall of reserve between them. He didn't like the idea that she'd distanced herself emotionally from him. Damon could only come up with one reason why. While he'd been relaxed and relieved that she didn't blame him for the fiasco eight years ago, he'd forgotten her beloved Alex hated him. What were the odds she would anger the stepbrother who'd raised her for a man she'd known such a short time?

Usually Ravyn chattered to fill a silence, but today he found himself doing it. "As soon as we get back home, I'm going to have myself a big, inch thick steak, rare. Green beans and a baked potato on the side. You dream of baths, I dream of beef." Granted, his words weren't haha funny, but Ravyn managed only a weak smile of acknowledgment.

He hadn't felt a panic like this since he'd seen Conway run and knew he and the others were sitting ducks. Damon swallowed hard and tried a different subject. "How did you know the way to turn on the lights and the water? And to do this?" He gestured to the clear wall off to the side.

Ravyn swallowed the food she chewed and shrugged. "I don't know. I just knew."

Damon frowned. He wanted something more concrete than that. After all, he hadn't forced her to throw up last night because he'd trusted she knew what she had done. He didn't want to hear she'd just *known*. "What? You're psychic?" His trepidation made the words come out harsher than he intended. Ravyn finally looked at him again and her eyes had a snap to them that relieved some of his worry. He swallowed the apology he'd been forming.

"I've always known things. Not anything useful, like a luxury hotel having a structural collapse or that a killer would wipe out the CAT team, but other things. It's gotten stronger since I arrived on Jarved Nine and stronger still since, well, what happened." The temper seeped from her to be replaced by shadows, and he knew she was remembering the massacre. She looked away for a moment, and when she finally met his gaze again, he noticed she looked beaten. A sound of protest escaped him.

His tough little sweet pea suddenly seemed fragile, as if one careless touch or comment would shatter her. Damon wished he knew how to help her, to breach the chasm between them. "Finish eating, Ravyn," he said with care. "Even if you're not hungry any longer, you need to keep your strength up."

That she followed his directive without a discussion first didn't bring him any pleasure. The woman who knelt beside him now was not the same woman who had climbed on top of him and insisted he repeat after her. He wasn't sure who this new person was, but it wasn't the Ravyn he knew.

His fear went soul deep. He'd been alone since his birth, untethered to anyone. He'd tried to find a home in the army, had made some good friends, but they'd had their own ties, their own parents, brothers, sisters, wives, children. Damon had about given up finding anyone he belonged to. Then he'd met Ravyn. She sat with her head bent, silently eating. If she severed the connection between them now . . . He swallowed hard, something inside bleeding at the loss he knew was coming.

Maybe it was better this way. He could focus on keeping her safe until the rescue team arrived. And when he faced the killer, well, it wouldn't matter so much if he walked away from the encounter. Not as long as he took the murderer down with him. A man could be overly cautious when he worried about returning to his woman. With nothing to lose, he could fight better. Yeah, he thought, her rejection made him stronger.

He put a hand to his heart. It still hurt. One side of his mouth tilted up derisively. He couldn't even lie to himself. If Ravyn wanted to pull away, he'd let her go, but only so far. He'd woo her back or court her or whatever the hell he needed to do, but he wasn't about to concede defeat. Not yet.

Damon knew he could never atone for his actions eight years ago, but maybe if he avenged the deaths of her friends, she'd be willing to put up with the colonel's displeasure at their involvement. At least enough to stay with him. He needed her in a way he didn't fully understand. It went beyond sex and even beyond feeling connected to her.

Ravyn stared at her hands as he returned the uneaten food to the pack. He couldn't identify her mood. If he didn't know better, he'd think it was dread. Damon couldn't stand it any longer. Before he could say anything, however, Ravyn finally raised her head and looked at him. Her gold eyes appeared even more haunted, and he tensed to keep from tugging her to him and offering comfort. She wouldn't welcome his touch, he could tell from the set of her jaw.

She bit her lip, hesitated and he braced himself for her rejection. That he wouldn't accept it didn't mean it wouldn't hurt. She probably was trying to find a way to let him down gently. She was that kind of woman. He saw Ravyn square her shoulders as if she'd shored up all her reserves to do what needed to be done. Damon kept his eyes on her and waited for her to speak. Her words, when they came, were so far from what he'd been expecting that she stunned him into silence.

"Damon," she said, her voice, though clear and firm, still managed to hold a note of hesitance. "I'm a coward."

Chapter Fifteen

Ravyn thought she'd prepared herself for any response Damon might make to her confession, but she hadn't imagined him staring at her blankly as if she had spoken in an unknown language. She wished he'd say something. The stress of waiting strummed at her nerves. For some unfathomable reason, he had yet to discover how cowardly she was. As soon as she'd heard him talk about Conway, she'd realized she couldn't keep quiet any longer. She didn't expect him to take it well. Ravyn hadn't missed the derision in Damon's voice as he'd spoken of the fainthearted soldier.

"What?" he finally asked, still looking blank.

It had been hard enough to say it once. She didn't want to repeat it, but she did anyway. "I'm a coward."

He laughed. She hadn't expected this response either. He laughed so hard he fell backward on the bed. She began to get mad. She hadn't said anything funny. He propped himself up on his elbows, looked at her and laughed again. The man was damn lucky, Ravyn decided, that the pillows were out of reach.

"You're serious, aren't you?" he asked when he managed to contain his mirth.

Ravyn thought his realization a bit belated, but she nodded.

He sobered and sat up. "*This* is what's been bothering you for the last half hour or so?"

Again, she nodded, not quite able to speak around the constriction in her throat. She grew queasy at the thought of his warm regard turning to distaste. She looked away, knowing it wouldn't be long now.

"Why do you think you're a coward?" Damon sounded only mildly curious.

Ravyn couldn't believe he needed her to enumerate her failings. But she would. "You found me hiding underneath my bunk, for a start." Her fingers plucked at the ridge of blanket beside her hip.

"What do you think you should have done?"

The carefully neutral tone he adopted didn't fool her for a second. She had to swallow hard before she could force the words out. "I should have retrieved one of the weapons and gone after the killer."

"You think that would have been the brave thing to do?"

A slight edginess slipped past the evenness as he spoke. Ravyn noted it immediately. Obviously he'd begun to see her true colors. She watched her fingers tighten around the soft blanket and forced herself to say, "Yes, it's what I should have done."

"You think you would have had a chance against a murderer that had already killed nineteen people?"

Confused, she lifted her gaze. Damon looked like a storm ready to break. She couldn't figure out what she'd said to anger him. Then she realized if she'd taken care of the killer instead of hiding, his team would still be alive.

"I'm sorry," she said, her voice barely above a whisper. Her hands shook and she hid them behind her back. "I know it's my fault your men are dead. I'm sorry."

"What?"

That one word flayed her with its sharpness. She looked away again, not wanting Damon to see tears fill her eyes. *You're such a baby.* She didn't even have enough courage to face his censure and he had every right to show his displeasure.

"Ravyn, look at me," he said, his voice tender.

The tears she'd struggled to contain slipped free at his gentleness. *Why couldn't she be braver?* Blinking furiously, Ravyn forced herself to look him in the eye.

"You wouldn't have stood a chance," he told her.

"Alex trained me."

"There's a big difference between the training you have and the training you'd need to face this killer. Six very experienced Spec Ops soldiers appear to have been helpless against him. You couldn't even take me the day we fought in the mud, and I didn't want to hurt you. Going after the killer wouldn't have been brave; it would have been foolhardy."

Something in the way he spoke dried Ravyn's tears. She studied him for a moment and realized he meant exactly what he said. He didn't think hiding that day made her weak. "I still should have done something," she insisted.

"Like deploy the emergency beacon?" One side of his mouth quirked up, almost derisively. "You saw how much good that did."

Ravyn stared at him for a moment and let his words sink in. What could she have done differently? What would have changed the outcome? Damon was right; she hadn't been able to take him. Oh, she'd put up a good fight, but in the end, his skills had far outweighed hers. It didn't take much reasoning to realize his men would have been as proficient and they'd gone down when faced with the killer.

"I get scared every time you're out of my sight," she announced almost defiantly. So he was right about one thing, that didn't mean she wasn't a coward.

"So? You think I don't worry when I can't see you?" He sounded as belligerent as she had.

That knocked the wind right out of her sails. "You do?" she asked, all warm inside. Lord, she had it bad for this man.

"Hell, yes. Do you think I'm a coward?"

"No!" Ravyn blurted, not wanting him to believe for one instant she thought him less than courageous. Not when he had all those doubts about himself and his abilities. She knew how torn up he still felt about Sammy and the others.

"I rest my case."

Ravyn frowned. He'd tricked her. "Damon," she said, "I know what I am. I lived with brave people. I never saw them scared the way I get. Gil, Mom, Alex fearlessly did what needed to be done. I've known my whole life that I'm not like them."

Damon cupped her face and ran his thumb along her cheekbone. "Sweet pea, maybe you didn't see them scared, but that doesn't mean they didn't feel it. I sure as hell wouldn't want to go into battle with someone who was completely unconcerned. A little anxiety keeps you on your toes, makes you a better soldier. Courage isn't being fearless. Courage is feeling the fear and doing what needs to be done anyway."

Ravyn wrapped her fingers around his wrist, not to pull his hand away, but because she needed to touch him. "But I haven't done what I needed to."

"No? You fought me when I pulled you out from under the bunk and you didn't know who I was."

"I was so terrified, I didn't remember any of the things Alex had taught me. I was ineffectual."

"You still tried. You never lost your head no matter what we faced, which was a big help." He smiled. "You threw mud and wrestled me, and I'm much bigger and meaner than you are."

"You might be bigger," Ravyn said, returning his smile, "but I knew you wouldn't hurt me. Besides, you made me mad."

"And when the killer stumbled past us, you didn't scream or go running off in a panic. When I got knocked in the head, who jumped in flood waters to pull me out?"

"Anyone would have done that," Ravyn insisted.

Damon shook his head. "You stitched me up even though I could tell you didn't want to do that. You slept between me and any possible danger when I was out of it."

Ravyn opened her mouth to argue with him, but Damon

moved his thumb so the pad rested on her lips. She subsided reluctantly.

"You took control when my head pounded so bad I couldn't think. And who jumped in front of me and took that barb? You think these actions are cowardly?"

She nipped at his thumb to get him to remove it. "I didn't think about jumping in front of you, I just reacted. That doesn't mean anything."

"The hell it doesn't," he told her, leaning forward. "I can tell you right now most people wouldn't have done it."

She gave his wrist a squeeze. "Honey, I know you're trying to make me feel better, but . . ." Her words trailed off when his hands went to her waist and she smothered a yelp as he pulled her next to him. Before she could react, he had half her body covered with his and a leg thrown over hers.

"Repeat after me, 'I am not a coward.' "

The smirk on his face irritated Ravyn almost as much as having her own methods turned back on her. "Damon," she said. Her voice held warning. Instead of looking concerned, the man had the nerve to shoot her a smile that made her toes curl.

"I'm trying some positive reinforcement," he told her.

Unable to help herself, she laughed and reached for him. "I like the way you think, Captain."

Alex never apologized. He'd learned young it didn't change anything. Still, he felt nearly compelled to ask Stacey to forgive him. Hell, if any man ever treated Ravyn like that, he'd kill the son of a bitch. And Stacey was his sister's best friend. Ravyn would have his ass for this.

If Stacey told her.

What was he thinking? Of course Stacey would tell Ravyn all about what happened. Women shared everything with their best friends. Today he refused to believe his sister wouldn't be alive to hear about his transgression. Last night had been the anniversary of his mother's death. Although he'd never been close to her, it reminded him of all the people he'd lost in his life whom he had been tight with. The number had been too high.

Of course, that didn't excuse the way he'd treated Stacey. Not the taking her against the wall part; she'd been right there with him for that. No, it was the look on her face as he'd walked away afterward that ate at him. Maybe he had grown too accustomed to women who didn't expect more from him than sex. Women who expected him to walk away exactly like that after they'd finished. But he'd known from the start Stacey wasn't someone who took sex casually.

Alex groaned and ran a hand across his chin. He hadn't shaved this morning and the stubble abraded his palm. He wondered if Stacey waited in the equipment bay or if he'd have to track her down. It was a good fifteen minutes past the time their training sessions usually started, but he couldn't force himself to move. He knew he couldn't avoid her forever, though.

The door opened then and Stacey exploded into his room. He saw beyond the temper sizzling from her body. He noticed the sallowness of her complexion, the puffiness of her eyes that she hadn't quite been able to conceal, the dark circles that spoke of a sleepless night and he felt even worse than he had earlier.

"You're late," she informed him. Her anger held flame and heat. "You may not think much of me, but I thought you respected your precious schedule. Didn't you say we didn't have any time to waste when it came to training?"

"Stace," he began only to stop uncertainly. This was a new experience for him, not knowing what to say to a woman. Her hazel eyes, normally so clear and bright, appeared muddy. Alex began to get a better idea of how deeply he'd hurt her.

"What?" she snarled at him.

He opened his mouth and shut it again. Two little words. How could it be so hard to say them? It wouldn't begin to make up for his behavior, but at least she'd know he regretted it. People said those words all the time, why couldn't he?

"You're a jerk, Sullivan," she said as the silence dragged.

"I know," he admitted.

"You had no right to treat me like that."

"I know."

"You know, you know. You just know everything, don't you?"

He reached for her then, wanting to comfort her, but she evaded him with ease. Alex knew he could catch her, but he didn't try again. He didn't blame her for not wanting him to touch her. He turned from her and drove both hands into his hair. He tightened them into fists, pulling enough to be uncomfortable and then dropped them back to his sides. There had to be some way to make this right, he thought desperately. Some way that didn't involve those two words he couldn't say.

"Look at me," she ordered. "Don't you ignore me like I'm beneath your notice."

Alex pivoted sharply, disbelief filling him. He was displaying more agitation, more emotion than he had in years and she thought he was ignoring her? No wonder men and women had so many communication problems.

"I wasn't ignoring you," he told her, but she fluttered her hand as if waving aside his words.

They stared at one another across the length of the room. He didn't know what she saw, but something had her setting aside her temper. He knew she could hit flashpoint again in a second, but, for right now, her anger had abated.

"I never knew you were a coward," she said with the same amount of emotion she would use to state the time.

That pronouncement lit Alex's fuse. "You want to repeat that?" he asked, his voice low and dangerous.

"Oh, not physically," Stacey said. "I bet when it comes to physical risk, you're brave as can be. Emotionally is another story. You're afraid to feel anything for anyone. You said it yourself, you didn't want to love Ravyn. My guess is it's easier for you not to care about anybody."

Alex grabbed for his control with both hands. "You're pushing me."

"It's time someone did. You stay so safe and untouched while us mere mortals struggle with human emotions. Remaining uninvolved makes you feel superior, doesn't it, Sullivan?"

Anger had crept back into her voice, but Alex battled his

own indignation. "Who are you to judge anyone else? You grew up in some hick town, untouched by war. I watched my father go out on missions so dangerous it was a miracle he came back alive. Did you fear for anyone in your family? No," he answered before she could. "Did you ever think about the people who were affected every day by war?"

"And that's why you're emotionally crippled? Because you grew up near the front lines? That's a cop-out. Ravyn grew up the same way and she doesn't hold people at arms' length."

"You don't think so?" Alex knew how cold his voice sounded, but he didn't try to warm it. "Ravyn is exactly like me. We just go about it differently."

Stacey stepped forward, her eyes narrowed. Alex took a minute to appreciate the sight she made. She looked magnificent, furious and ready to do battle for a friend. "That's not true. She has lots of friends. Everyone loves her."

"Yes, Ravyn has lots of friends. She's everyone's buddy. Aside from you, how many others does she confide in, share herself with?" Alex didn't wait for her to answer. "No one notices because she treats everyone with the same apparently open friendliness. What you don't realize, what no one seems to realize, is that's her wall, her way to keep herself separate." As soon as he finished speaking, Alex regretted what he'd said. He felt as if he'd betrayed his sister in some way. If people couldn't see past the front she put up, he had no business pointing it out. He understood completely Ravyn's need to keep herself safe. It hurt when people died or left you.

Stacey appeared stunned. "Oh my God," she finally said, her voice sounding as astonished as she looked. "You're right, that's exactly what Ravyn does. I don't understand. Why?"

Alex shoved his hands in his pockets and shrugged. "Her father died when she was little more than a baby. She lost her mom and my dad at fourteen. After that, I raised her and she had to live with the knowledge that some day I might not come home either. It's understandable she doesn't let many close."

"You and I are the only two, aren't we?"

"Yes. She doesn't love easily," he offered, trying to make Stacey feel better, "but when she does, it's for keeps."

"What about you? Why are you so closed off?"

Alex contemplated answering her question for a moment. He couldn't manage to force "I'm sorry" out of his mouth, but maybe if he talked about his past, she would know he felt remorseful even if he couldn't articulate it. His gut knotted at the thought. He'd have to find another way. Years of protecting himself were impossible to toss aside.

"My job requires distance," he said, with a shrug. He knew from the expression on Stacey's face that she didn't buy his story. Alex kept talking, hoping to distract her. "Dad and Marie's deaths really left Ravyn reeling."

"Of course," she said, sarcasm dripping from her words, "their deaths didn't affect you at all. You wouldn't have been expecting anything to happen to them while we were at peace, but you didn't falter for a moment, did you?"

"No, I wasn't expecting it." He kept his voice even, his face impassive. It was second nature to hide emotion. Alex wouldn't admit to being shaken at the loss, but he had been. He'd become complacent, so sure his father and stepmother would always be there. Fate had shown him differently. When he surfaced from the bleakness of remembered loss, he saw Stacey glowering at him again. Anger had left her face suffused with color and he found himself curious about where the blush started. Her chest? Lower? He shoved his hands deeper into his pockets to keep himself from reaching for her. He might want a repeat of last night, but she didn't.

"How did the ice goddess get past your walls?"

"You mean Lara?" Alex watched Stacey's temper soar higher, the red on her cheeks deepen, and wondered what he'd done now. Although she'd remained scornful, he'd thought her rage had been cooling. Or at least been under control.

"I bet you never treated her the way you did me."

Alex watched Stacey's ponytail swing as she tossed her head. Why hadn't he loosened her hair last night? Hell, he'd been dying for the feel of it and he'd missed his chance. He had definitely been in too much of a hurry.

"Look, I didn't mean to walk away from you the way I did last night." He knew that was inadequate as an apology, but it would have to do.

"Oh, yeah, I bet you didn't mean to." She huffed out a breath that had her bangs flying. "You accidentally fastened your pants and strolled away as if nothing had happened. Why don't you at least admit the truth? We both know it didn't mean a thing to you!"

Alex pulled his hands from his pockets, took hold of her shoulders and lowered his head until they were nose to nose. She didn't try to break his grip, but glared up at him. "It meant too damn much," he said, his tone atypically heated.

He wasn't sure who was more surprised by his words, Stacey or himself. He never meant to admit that. It gave her power over him and he'd sworn he would never give another woman a chance to shatter his heart. Abruptly, he stepped back and moved to the cabin door. "We need to get going," he said when he had his usual dispassionate voice working. "We still have a lot of ground to cover before we reach J Nine."

"What do you mean 'it meant too much'?"

Alex ignored her demand. "Come on, Johnson, let's move."

"You really don't think I'm a coward?"

Damon quit playing with the water and groaned. "Are you trying to kill me?" he asked, turning away from the shower to look at Ravyn. She worked absently at a knot in her damp hair.

"I'm serious."

"So am I. Any more positive reinforcement and neither one of us may be able to walk for days."

Ravyn reached for him and sharply tugged some chest hair. He caught her hand and pressed her fingers flat against his pecs. "Okay, okay. No, I don't think you're a coward."

She bit her lip and he knew she had yet to be convinced. It would take time for her view to shift. He tugged her body against his own, just holding her. She moved easily into his arms, returning his embrace without hesitation and he knew a peace he'd never felt before. It lasted until she pressed her mouth against his chest and gave a little lick. Conscience battled with baser instinct and won. Reluctantly, he took a step back. He knew Ravyn had to be sore and he had no intention of adding to her discomfort. Damon put her away from him.

"Finish getting dressed, sweet pea." The sight of her in a top that clung to her breasts and pair of panties that showed off her long legs played hell with his determination that they make it out of the suite today. She pulled on a pair of pants, but it didn't help him any. They were red and fit much too close.

He turned his back to her and started switching the water on and off again. Ravyn had shown him how to manage the lights and water with a flick of his wrist and focused concentration, and he remained fascinated by the technology. At first, he hadn't been able to make any of the controls work; then Ravyn had told him to quit analyzing his actions. After he'd stopped thinking, it had been easy. Still, Damon couldn't keep from trying to figure out the process. Near as he could tell, they pulled up minute amounts of energy from the planet, directed it toward, say the showerhead, while imagining water coming out of it. He hadn't figured the whole thing out yet, but he did know the process was more deliberate and time consuming for him than for Ravyn.

"Damon, are you going to play with the water the rest of the afternoon?" she asked, sounding amused.

"Sorry." He turned the shower off and left it that way.

"I think we should destroy our clothes," she said. "We have a whole closet at our disposal anyway."

He looked at the pile of mud-encrusted garments on the floor and then shifted his gaze to the closet door. Ravyn had opened it after their shower. The thing was huge, bigger than a lot of rooms he'd seen, and loaded with clothes, both men's and women's. Damon tugged at the black pants he wore. They were about three inches too short. "I don't know," he said, "at least my pants, dirty as they are, fit me."

Ravyn glanced down at his ankles and sank to her knees. "I can fix that," she told him.

Only one thought filled his head at the sight of her kneeling before him and it had nothing to do with the length of his trousers. The image of her mouth on him had the crotch of the borrowed trousers becoming uncomfortably tight. She tugged at one leg and the material stretched. While he stood, amazed, she moved to the other leg and repeated her actions until he had a pair of slacks that appeared made for him.

"How—? Never mind." Damon shook his head and fastened the shirt he wore. The sleeves were too short and he pulled at them. Nothing happened. He tried drawing energy from his surroundings as he imagined the cuff reaching his wrist. A small thrill of elation shot through him when the fabric began to lengthen. By the time he finished altering the shirt, Ravyn stood, watching him with an indulgent smile on her face. His lips twitched. Okay, so he was like a little boy with a new toy, Damon admitted to himself, but it was different to be able to adjust things by thought alone.

"Come on, let's get some shoes on. There's something I've been wanting to check out."

Her grin widened, but she followed him into the bedchamber without comment. He grabbed her boots and handed them to her.

"Oh, wow. Thanks for cleaning them."

"I had to do something while you were sleeping."

She wrinkled her nose at him, but otherwise ignored his comment and sat on the bed. He had his own boots on and tied before she managed to get one foot shod. Damon watched her meticulously work the laces of her boots. It didn't matter what she did, he never tired of observing her. He doubted he ever would. That brought a thought to mind.

"Ravyn."

"Yeah?" She looked up from her task.

"The colonel really won't like the idea of the two of us."

She didn't say anything for a moment. When she had both her boots tied, she walked to him. Her toes almost touched his before she stopped. "I've never let Alex pick my friends. I'm certainly not going to let him tell me whom I can have as a lover. If he doesn't like it, he'll just have to get over it."

Damon took exception to being referred to as her "lover." What they had went far beyond that, but he let it pass. After studying her, he decided she meant what she said about the colonel. For now, at least. Things might be different when she faced her brother's disapproval head on. He dropped the subject and took her hand. "Come on."

He led her unerringly through the hallways to a wall. There were symbols embedded in the stone with brightly colored gems. It was so familiar and yet not quite. Ravyn linked her fingers with his, and when he glanced over, he realized she had the same interest in the pattern that he did. Her free hand reached out and touched it, tracing the swirl that went through the center of the figure. Without warning, she jerked her hand back.

"What is it?" His body tensed, prepared to defend her.

"There's incredible power there. I don't know if it's in the image itself or behind that wall, but I've never felt energy like that before in my life."

He touched the wall himself, not expecting to feel anything, but he did. And he understood why Ravyn had pulled her hand back so quickly. A force seemed to fill every cell in his body, making him hum with electricity. He loved the sense of invigoration, but, at the same time, it made him uneasy. Whatever the force was may have started out natural, but it had been formed and guided by the people who had lived here.

Raising his hand, he pressed a number of stones in a sequence he remembered from his daydream. The wall opened as he'd known it would. Damon could have explored while Ravyn slept, he'd passed this spot on his way out of the building, but some intuition told him to bring her with him.

He led the way down the stairs, Ravyn close on his heels. Her hand was cold and he knew she was scared. He also knew she berated herself for feeling that way. "Turn on the lights for me," he told her and almost instantly the stairway lit up.

These stairs were not gray like everything else, but clear as if they walked on ice. The bottom tread had an inclusion that made him think of a star burst. He stopped and stared at the stone beneath his feet.

"Did you know clear quartz puts human energies in sync with the universe?" Ravyn asked, but she didn't wait for an answer. "It's a powerful stone used to increase telepathic and psychic abilities. I wonder what the inclusion is?"

Uneasy with the idea of getting in sync with the universe, Damon stepped onto the milky white floor and pulled Ravyn with him. He hoped she didn't tell him anything about this white stone that he would be happier not knowing.

The glow from the stairway didn't go far into the room and he mentally felt for lights and brought them up. Ravyn sucked in her breath and he followed her gaze. There on a clear dais stood the blue obelisk he'd seen in his vision of the Old City. White walls made the crystal column the focal point of the room. Ravyn broke his hold and went to it. Resting her hands on the stone, she closed her eyes. She stood that way for a long time before her eyes opened and she smiled at him. "Touch it, Damon."

As if compelled, he moved forward. He stood close, pressing his body against her, and placed both hands beside hers on the obelisk. The stone seemed to hum beneath his fingers, stronger than the sensation he'd felt at the wall. Damon could sense Ravyn's arousal and his own body grew hard. They were getting turned on from touching a big rock, but he couldn't pull away.

"Greetings and salutations to you on this very fine day."

The voice, though sweetly feminine, did not belong to Ravyn.

Chapter Sixteen

Ravyn drew a quick breath. The voice startled her, but didn't scare her. Still, she took comfort in the solid warmth of Damon's body surrounding her. She knew with all her heart he would never let anything harm her.

"Telepathy?" Damon's murmur tickled her ear. His calm acceptance had her glancing over her shoulder in surprise.

"Has to be," Ravyn said, just as quietly. This lost society couldn't have spoken English. That went beyond the realm of possibility. A shimmering behind the teal obelisk caught Ravyn's eye. She couldn't take her hands off the stone to point it out to Damon so she used her chin. "Look over there."

"Damn."

She understood the awe in his voice. She felt it herself. There, real as life, stood a man and a woman on the other side of the column. Ravyn felt a shiver go down her spine. The other couple seemed to be looking right at them, waiting for the shock to wear off. It had to be an illusion. Another tremor went through her body as she realized she and Damon wore this couples' clothes, slept in their bed. The woman smiled as if sensing her thoughts and Ravyn leaned into Damon a little bit harder.

She couldn't tear her gaze away from them. They were both humanoid. In fact, they could stroll down the street in any town in America and no one would give them a second glance. Except for their eyes. Their irises were gold. Not the golden brown Ravyn saw when she looked in the mirror, but the yellow-gold cats had. Even their pupils were shaped like a cat's. It should have been eerie, but it wasn't. Something about it seemed familiar.

"You realize," Damon said, "we're the first to see what these people looked like."

"We'll be the only ones." Ravyn didn't know where the knowledge came from, but it resonated within her. She studied them, trying to memorize everything. The same part of her that knew nobody else would see this couple and she and Damon would only see them this one time.

Their dress seemed formal considering most of the closet held casual clothes. The woman wore a flowing gown of the lightest, most gossamer fabric Ravyn had ever seen, yet she was covered more than adequately. The dress was the palest of blues and pinks. Aquamarine and rose quartz, she realized.

The man stood protectively at the woman's side. His pants were black and fit closely to a very impressive pair of thighs. Not quite as impressive as Damon's, Ravyn decided loyally. The shirt he wore should have made him look like a court jester, yet it did not. The green and gold fabric draped a broad chest and massive shoulders. It explained why Damon could wear the man's clothes, even if they were too short for him.

The woman raised her hand and pushed her long, midnight hair away from her face. She looked back at the man, caught his nod and turned to her and Damon once more. "Allow me to perform introductions. I am called Meriwa and this is my mate, Kale." The man inclined his head, his dark hair falling in front of his shoulders. Meriwa paused and Ravyn wondered if she and Damon were expected to reciprocate. This had to be a recorded message, yet it was so lifelike it felt rude to stand there.

Meriwa smiled again, giving Ravyn goose bumps. Millennia-old images were not supposed to read the minds of people in the here and now. Thankfully, the woman continued before the sensation grew more pronounced. "We are the gatekeepers of this planet. If you have been here for any length of time, you are aware this world harbors a menace to all sentient beings."

"Oh, yeah," Damon said dryly, "we noticed."

"This threat is not of our people." Meriwa's "voice" shook slightly, but it was hard to tell whether it was a fault in the message or high emotion. "Many died and many more returned to our home world before we learned who committed the mutilations. The being is exiled here from a distant planet. It was difficult to scan his mind without him discovering the intrusion, but we felt we had no other choice if we hoped to neutralize the threat. We learned he believes his goddess requires the sacrifice of sentient beings. He arranges their bodies in her symbols, the lightning bolt and the flower, as a tribute."

Ravyn felt Damon tense.

"He began this method of worship on his planet of origin and was angered when he was banished to an uninhabited world, unable to honor his goddess properly. Then our people arrived to colonize this place."

Ravyn's hands started to tingle and she flexed them against the stone. At first she thought they were falling asleep, but as her fingers slid against the smooth surface, she realized the pulsing came from the monolith. A second image began to form. Her heart started to pound wildly and her breathing became fast, shallow. Instinctively, she tried to back up, but only succeeded in plastering herself against Damon. She was shocked to feel his arousal pressing into her bottom, but then the figure solidified and she couldn't concentrate on anything except the alien.

He was tall. Taller than Damon by at least a foot and quite easily the most muscular creature Ravyn had ever seen. His blue skin had yellow stripes and dashes, giving him a patterned look. In the center of his forehead was a large, lime green lump with blue wavy lines. The colors merged and blended so well it was difficult to tell which was the primary hue. Trousers and a vest were the only clothing covering his hairless body.

Meriwa had started speaking again, but Ravyn tuned her out, trusting Damon would pick up what she missed. She couldn't stop staring at the alien. His shoulders were yellow with a red, labyrinthine pattern. She wondered if it was a tattoo. The image turned his head, startling her, and Ravyn locked gazes with him. His big eyes had no white in them, only blue. There was a swash of green around the iris, which was an even more brilliant blue and a twist of fluorescent yellow around the black pupil. She hadn't thought she'd be able to sense a soul within him, but she could. It was twisted and dark, cold. Malevolent.

With a violent shudder, she closed her eyes and tried to put the sight of him out of her mind. She felt Damon's breath tickling her neck and gratefully concentrated on that, on the feel of his body, the beat of his heart.

"You can open your eyes now," he whispered and Ravyn flushed as she realized Damon had picked up on her cowardice. When she finally managed to look again, the image of the killer was gone.

"Now only four of us remain here," Kale said, picking up the tale. Ravyn felt a tingle of sexual awareness at the richness of his tone. "Soon Meri and I and our guardians will face this killer. Our plan is to capture and hold him within a pillar of onyx. Since you are seeing this message, our attempt failed."

As Ravyn watched, Kale and Meriwa linked their hands. A moment of silence laden with unhappiness spun through the chamber and they held on to each other tightly, as if marshaling strength from the other's touch. Ravyn could feel their emotions and realized the message had elements of empathic communication as well as telepathic. They shared a glance so poignant, she couldn't help smiling sadly. She imagined how she would feel if she stood with Damon, recording information for others in case they failed, but praying it would never be seen.

When Meriwa spoke again it was with an urgency, a quickness that had been missing earlier. "You, children of the future, must succeed where we have failed. Imprisonment could not be accomplished, so the only option is to kill this creature. We hope you are better prepared for this mission than we." She paused for an instant. "This message would not be triggered if there were not two of you, and you must be joined in all ways before you face this alien. We have tuned the stone you touch to assist your connection. Inside the eye of the obelisk, you will find two amulets of the same stone. Wear them at all times."

Ravyn flexed her fingers again. The eye was just inches from her right hand and she longed to reach in and pull out the amulets. Her hands, however, still would not obey the command to move and she knew they wouldn't until the message played out.

"If you do not face this threat together," she continued, her face intent, "you will be defeated. Only when you are joined can you overcome the alien's mind-control abilities. He is stronger than any individual. You, woman yet to be born, must be the one to pull up vast amounts of energy from the planet. Your man cannot. And you, mate to this woman, must wield the energy as your weapon. Your woman cannot."

"A word of caution," Kale said, his "tone" grave. "You must ensure your guardians are at your side when you face him. You will need their protection more than you can imagine. But above all, whatever happens, do not allow the alien a means to leave this world. If let loose, he will wreak untold havoc before someone can quell him."

Meriwa held out her free hand beseechingly. "Do not discount our guidance because we have failed. It is trustworthy and sure. We offer you our prayers and hope you are able to bring peace to this beautiful planet. *Shalohmah.*"

With that last, unknown word still lingering, Meriwa and Kale flickered out of existence. Ravyn didn't move until she felt Damon step away. Slowly, as if coming out of a trance, she lowered her hands and moved off the dais.

"Well, that was interesting," Damon said, casually reaching into the eye of the column. He sounded nonchalant, as if things like this happened to him all the time. Ravyn could only admire his poise. When he pulled his hand back out, he held two miniature replicas of the teal obelisk. Each was suspended from a black cord and perhaps five centimeters long.

Ravyn reached for one, cupping it in her palm while Damon continued to hold the cords. The base of the obelisk fastened into the vale, leaving the pointed end hanging down. Set horizontally across the top were four tiny stones. Aquamarine, rose quartz, tourmaline and citrine. The gems vibrated pleasantly against her skin. Carefully, she untangled the cord of the stone she held from Damon's fingers and slipped it over her head. It fell to the top of her breasts and rested near her heart. She cupped her hand over it, in awe of the thrumming power she felt. "Aren't you going to put yours on?" she asked.

Damon grimaced. "It's a necklace."

Ravyn tried to keep from grinning. "You wear dog tags."

"That's different."

"Of course it is, honey," she said, not making any effort to hide the fact she was humoring him.

He shook his head and then jerked the cord down around his neck. "Only for you," he told her as he tucked it inside his shirt. "And don't you be spreading this around either once we get back to Earth. I'll deny everything."

"It's our secret," she promised, concealing her laughter.

Damon ignored Ravyn's amusement and considered things. Then he grinned. The situation was beyond bizarre. "I think I missed the day of training when we covered how to handle telepathic messages about exiled alien serial killers that use mind control to subdue their victims."

"Of all the days you picked to skip." Ravyn shook her head, her expression somber.

"I know," he said, adopting the same grave tone. "What was I thinking?"

"Obviously, you weren't using your judgment or you'd have known that class would be indispensable." She couldn't quite hold on to her solemn mien and she finally gave up the attempt, throwing her head back and laughing.

Damon pulled her into his arms and pressed a kiss to her forehead. His body still throbbed with arousal. It didn't take a genius to figure out one of the ways he and Ravyn were supposed to be connected was physically. The reminder wiped the smile off his face and he considered the obelisk.

He knew precisely what Meriwa wanted of them when she'd spoken of tuning the stone to assist them. They were to join their hands in the eye of the pillar. Damon hugged Ravyn tighter to him. He'd checked out the hole when he'd reached in for the necklaces and there had been nothing in there to cause him to hesitate about this next step. But still he felt unsure. Ravyn must have felt his tension because one of her hands began rubbing his back in a soothing motion. Taking a deep breath, he forced himself to relax. Even if they completed the process that would join them on all levels, he still wouldn't let her face the killer.

He didn't care if some dead ancients claimed there was no other way to defeat the alien. His number one priority was keeping Ravyn safe. It had been since he'd found her and nothing had happened to change that.

"You realize," Ravyn said, her voice muffled against his chest, "that whatever they tried to imprison the killer didn't work. That Meriwa and Kale died in the attempt."

"I know."

"What if we aren't any more successful than they were?"

Damon eased Ravyn back just enough so he could see her face. "You aren't going with me. I'm leaving you with the rescue team and taking care of him myself."

"The hell you are!" Ravyn grabbed his shirt by the collar and pulled his head down to hers so she could glare at him eye to eye. "You heard what they said. We have to face him together."

"You don't want to confront this killer."

"Of course not," Ravyn said much more quietly. "You know I'm terrified at the thought." Her lips twisted in self-disdain.

Oh, hell. He pressed his lips to each corner of her mouth. "That's not what I meant, sweet pea." He kissed her again, this time square on the lips. "It's just that taking him down could get ugly. You don't need to see that."

"Uglier than falling over the body of a teammate in the dark? Uglier than being covered in the blood of my friends? You know I'm a coward." Ravyn clapped a hand over his mouth before he could interrupt. "I'm a coward, but I'm more afraid of staying cocooned in the Old City and having something happen to you. We'll meet him together or not at all."

With one hand, Damon pried her fingers from his shirt and with the other, he uncovered his mouth. He kept hold of both her hands. "I bet you drove the colonel insane," he commented.

"He claims I'm responsible for every gray hair on his head."

"I'm not surprised. I feel myself aging right this minute."

"Damon," she said, turning her hands so she could lace her fingers through his, "I can't stand the thought of you dying. When the rescue team arrives, we can just go."

He shook his head. "I can't walk away and leave the killer unpunished. What happens the next time someone lands on Jarved Nine? And he murdered my friends and your team."

"You want revenge."

"Justice," he disagreed.

"Then I'll be at your side."

Damon read the determination in her eyes. Something inside him unfurled at the certainty that Ravyn cared for him. She might be scared about a showdown, but that wasn't going to stop her. How had she ever come up with the idea she was a coward? "Stubborn," he said, but it came out like an endearment.

"You like that about me." She smiled faintly.

"I like everything about you," he said and kissed her before she could respond. Her lips trembled against his, then parted as his tongue teased the seam. Another connection seemed to be forming between them. He could almost feel

Ravyn reaching for him with her heart before some door seemed to slam shut.

Damon stepped away from her and shook his head. He felt hurt being closed out so abruptly. It reminded him that he'd always been an outsider. Freeing himself from her grip, he walked behind the column. Checking for the source of the image was something he should have done immediately although he didn't expect to find anything. Now he used it as an excuse, a way to buy some time until he had the ache safely hidden. Crouching down, he ran his hands over the pillar. There were no protrusions or indentations, not so much as a small pit to signify where the projection could have come from. He straightened and studied the walls and ceiling, all with the same results. Nothing.

He sensed Ravyn come up behind him. Felt her nuzzle his back before her arms snaked around his waist. "What's wrong?"

"Nothing." Damon put his hands over hers, rubbing her fingers before he broke her hold and turned to face her. She looked honestly confused and concerned. She didn't know what she'd done, he realized. Maybe he'd imagined what had happened during their kiss. It had just felt so real.

For a moment, he thought she would challenge his assertion that nothing was wrong. Instead, she said, "I wonder what we need to do with the obelisk before we can take down the killer."

Damon studied Ravyn for a moment, then said, "We stand on opposite sides of it and join our left hands in the eye."

He waited for her to ask how he knew, but she didn't. It restored his good humor to have that much of her trust. Damon doubted he could have accepted the same statement, even from Ravyn, without asking a few questions.

"Shall we try it?" she asked.

Ravyn moved to the other side of the monolith from where they stood, taking the place he had seen her occupy in his vision without being told. That gave him pause, then he shrugged it off and took his position facing her. *What could happen?* He raised his hand and centered it palm up in the eye. He felt her tentatively rest her hand on his.

All hell broke loose.

Flashes of light burst from the walls, ceiling and floor like they were in a retro dance club. At first, he instinctively narrowed his eyes against the brilliance, but found it didn't hurt. As soon as he registered that sensation, energy strong enough to make him feel woozy started flowing through his body. He tried to withdraw his hand, but, like earlier, he couldn't move.

"Damon?"

"I'm here, sweet pea," he said and tightened his hold on her. Her fingers trembled, but he didn't know if fear or the incredible power caused it. He met her eyes over the top of the stone. "Don't fight it. Just go with it."

She nodded, keeping her eyes locked on his.

The roaring noise seemed to come from within his own body. It deafened him to everything but the pounding of his heart, the raggedness of his breathing. He wanted to close his eyes against the intensity of everything going on, but he refused to relinquish Ravyn's gaze. Not when she needed him.

There should be wind, he thought inanely, to go with the storm crashing around and through them. He felt nothing but the energy and Ravyn. Her skin hot where it touched his, her fingers quivering against him. He inhaled deeply, trying to regulate his respiration. It helped, quieting something inside, and his eyes widened as he realized their breathing patterns were in sync. The beat of their hearts changed then, matching exactly. Their bodies were in rhythm. That he noticed this with everything else going on in the room amazed him. He couldn't hear the sound that Ravyn made, but he felt it anyway. Her eyes slipped shut and he allowed himself to surrender to the need to do the same.

Damon became aware of warmth filling his body. Without his sight distracting him, everything became magnified. The heat in his heart intensified until it burned. Although it didn't hurt, he wanted to rub his chest to try and ease the unfamiliar feeling. His free hand remained heavy, almost as if his arm had been weighted.

It felt as if an invisible door on the top of his skull had

slid open and the sensation startled him. Before he had full awareness of what was happening, he found himself suspended in midair. He looked down and "saw" himself standing at the pillar, his hand linked with Ravyn's. What started to unsettle him wasn't that his consciousness was hanging out near the ceiling, but that it didn't seem abnormal to be outside his body.

Ravyn, he thought, and in the next heartbeat he sensed her beside him. The essence of their beings brushed against each other until the edges, the separation, seemed to blur. Joy surged through him at the union. No sooner did that register than he returned to his physical self. Not abruptly, but similar to a leaf drifting from a tree, he floated back.

He wondered what she felt. Ravyn was so much more sensitive to energy than he was. What continued to happen disconcerted him, affected him in ways he could barely comprehend. What did she think? How intense did this feel to her?

His heart went supernova. Before Damon could even think about opening his eyes, he felt it retracting, returning to his chest. Something had changed, though, become different. He frowned, trying to figure out what. He didn't have much opportunity for thought. Something began to drill into the center of his forehead. This brought real discomfort and he struggled to stop it. He couldn't. Fighting it increased the pain so he surrendered to it. Immediately, the ache lessened. He remained seemingly powerless and that frustrated him, angered him. Damon hated feeling helpless.

His own worries became secondary. He could sense Ravyn warring against the required submission. She fought even harder than he had, and the more she battled, the more intense her pain became. He could feel her agony as if it were his own. He couldn't speak, couldn't tell her to relax, to relinquish herself to the flow. It took all his concentration, but Damon squeezed her hand, trying to reassure her. He thought she returned the pressure, but she didn't stop resisting the energy. She knew better; he was sure of it.

Damon managed to open his eyes. The view dizzied him as the lights from the walls, ceiling and floor flashed even faster than they had earlier. He wanted to shut it all out again, but he focused his gaze on Ravyn instead. A grimace twisted her face and rage flooded through him. Meriwa and Kale had no right to do this to her, to them. If he had known it would cause his sweet pea torment, he never would have told her what to do. Gradually, he became aware that the frenetic flare of the lights had slowed. It appeared almost lazy now. The energy filling his body seemed to ebb and the roaring sound receded, letting him hear just how harshly they both were breathing. Ravyn opened her eyes then and she looked shell-shocked.

Like his mother's antique music box winding down, the sequence ground to a halt. Damon knew he could withdraw his hand now, but he held on to Ravyn until he saw her start to sink to the floor. She was on her knees when he reached the other side of the obelisk, and he dropped behind her, bracing her with his body.

"That," she said, "was not fun."

"You shouldn't have fought it," Damon said. "It wouldn't have caused you so much pain if you'd just let it happen."

She didn't comment. He was right, but then he didn't know why she had tried so hard to stop the joining. If he understood how completely they were bound together, she didn't think he'd be quite so calm about the whole thing. He'd find out soon enough, and she couldn't help wondering what his reaction would be. The pain surged then, nearly overwhelming her, and she quit thinking about it.

Ravyn leaned against Damon, grateful for his support. Her head felt like it would fall off if she so much as winced. Although, the way she was suffering, that might be a blessing. She'd had psychic headaches before, but never one that had hurt this bad. Closing her eyes again, she let her head rest against his chest. She'd brought this ache on herself by trying to prevent what was happening, but the knowledge gave no comfort.

Damon's arm went around her waist. The simple gesture echoed through her, and she carefully moved to rest both her hands atop his. Ravyn concentrated on bringing green healing energy down to surround her head. She slowed her breathing, deepened it. Ten minutes should take care of it, she figured.

As the stabbing pain in her temples eased, it became harder for her to keep from acknowledging the situation. And she wanted to; she really wanted to. She . . . No, she corrected, *they* were going to have to deal with the repercussions of what had transpired. Ravyn sighed and felt Damon bring his other arm around her. He remained silent and she knew it was because that's what she wanted. She wondered if he realized the source of his actions.

After the headache disappeared, Ravyn kept her eyes closed. Discreetly, methodically, she built a wall. She needed to do it now while they were still tired. Later would be too late. Once he experienced the full effect of their connection, she wouldn't be able to erect the barrier without him knowing. Even now, she had to be cautious so Damon wouldn't realize what she was doing.

"You okay?" he asked.

Although her headache had left, Ravyn appreciated that he'd kept his voice quiet. She opened her eyes and turned so she could see him. "Better," she offered with a faint smile. She tried to straighten, but he tightened his hold.

"Take a few more minutes," he told her.

"Damon, I'm kneeling on a stone floor. In a few more minutes, I may be unable to walk."

"Sorry." Grinning sheepishly, he helped her to her feet.

Her knees protested the movement. Even once she stood, Damon didn't release her. To be honest, she didn't want him to. It was another facet of this connection they shared, the desire to remain in some kind of physical contact. It was also about the only part of the link that didn't alarm her.

She ran a shaky hand through her hair, pushing it off her face. Her strong reaction had come instinctively and Ravyn didn't know why she had such a negative response to their bonding. Why *was* she so opposed to letting Damon discover how she felt about him? Why did she need to keep herself protected? It was completely irrational considering she loved the man.

A shiver went through her as she felt Damon nuzzle her neck. She moved back, fitting herself to him. Her eyes slipped to half mast as she noticed he was still hard. Her body went from zero to a burning inferno instantly. Not instantly, she realized as she rubbed her bottom against him. She'd been aroused for quite some time, but hadn't been conscious of it. Ravyn smirked at how oblivious she'd been. Too concerned with bonds of the heart and mind to notice how excited she was. Now that was concentration, she thought, amused at herself.

The notion was short-lived as his hands and mouth incited her past the point of thinking of anything but him. Ravyn reached back and held on to his hips, grinding herself against him. "Damon." She barely found the breath to gasp his name.

"I know," he told her, his voice rougher than she had ever heard it before. "Now, sweet pea. I can't take it slow."

A part of her realized his desire fed hers and she mirrored it back until they were nearly insensible with it. Another aspect of the bond they shared, she noted before the realization flowed out of her head. She couldn't wait any longer for him. Leaning forward, Ravyn took hold of the obelisk.

Damon needed no further invitation. She felt him tug her pants to her thighs. She parted her legs as far as she could manage and then he was there, broad and hot. He entered her and she moaned her approval. Nothing had ever felt this good, this necessary before. She climaxed on his first stroke, but he didn't last much longer. It didn't matter. The fever didn't abate. Damon stayed hard, kept moving, and Ravyn met his every thrust. They were beyond words, communicating their enjoyment with noises that sounded far more animal than human.

She wanted to feel more of him. Damon's chest covered her back, and she felt his teeth nip at her neck. That was all it took for her to reach the crest again. Ravyn let loose with a yowl that vibrated through the stone she clasped. He roared as he reached his own release and his big body sagged against her.

Ravyn wrapped her arms around the obelisk and let it support both their weight. She panted, trying to pull in enough air, but trapped between a rock and a hard male body, it was difficult to calm down. He didn't pull out and she wanted him to stay inside her. The intensity of their coupling left her reeling. Why? she wondered. Why had they both gone so out of control so fast? It hadn't been lovemaking. It had been so far beyond that, Ravyn had no name for it.

You must be joined in all ways.

Ravyn's eyes widened as she remembered Meriwa's words. *Joined in all ways.* He nudged her and she sighed, her body immediately ready for more. Her hiss of pleasure became a gasp of surprise as knowledge suddenly filled her head. There was one bond left the stone couldn't be programmed to forge. One tie between them that only she and Damon could create.

It was up to them to conceive a child.

Chapter Seventeen

Ravyn sank back in the hot water and closed her eyes. She'd already added a powdered version of the healing ointment to the bath. Thank God she'd found the huge tub tucked behind another sliding wall. She and Damon had spent a fair amount of time soaking in it. They'd needed to. The last day and a half was a blur of sensation, of arousal, and if they hadn't had the healing waters, she doubted either one of them would be able to walk by now. She barely had time to stretch before her senses told her she wasn't alone. "You get out of here, Damon Brody," Ravyn told him, not opening her eyes.

"How about if I promise to stay on the other side of the tub?" He sounded cajoling.

Ravyn raised her lashes just far enough to shoot him a doubtful look. She didn't believe him.

"Sweet pea, I couldn't get hard again even if I wanted to."

"That's what you said last time!"

"I know, but this time I really mean it."

At least he had the grace to look embarrassed. With a sigh, Ravyn relented and nodded her agreement. He settled in on the opposite side of the tub as promised. It didn't matter.

With Damon's long legs, their feet tangled together. As if her body had been missing his, something taut within her eased. She felt the simmering begin again and tried to ignore it. Ravyn watched his eyes heat and nudged him with her toe. "Stop it."

"I'm trying," he said, looking rueful.

She pulled her legs to her chest and wrapped her arms around them. The teal stone between her breasts vibrated pleasantly. She'd tried to remove it before her bath, but something inside her had balked at the idea. Damon's amulet, she noticed, rested just above his dog tags. Looking at his chest was a mistake. Her temperature shot upward, but she couldn't tear her eyes from him. She wanted to bite him, lick him, kiss him. Hugging her knees harder, she fought the urge.

"You're not helping things."

"I know." She dropped her head to her upraised knees and breathed deeply. When she had her restraint back, she looked up again and met his eyes. "I've been wondering, what do you think Kale and Meriwa meant about having our guardians by our side?"

"I'm not sure. They said *their* guardians remained after the others left, so I'm guessing they were real people." He shrugged and her thoughts shifted abruptly as she watched his muscles flex. This preoccupation with his body was almost humorous.

"Have you given any consideration," she asked, "to why we can't keep our hands off each other?"

"You mean aside from the fact you're sexy as hell and I've been fighting the need to make love to you almost since the day we met?" His voice carried the smokiness of arousal.

Ravyn swallowed hard. "Yes," she said, "apart from that."

"No."

"You don't think it's odd?" Her body yearned to touch his.

"Now that you bring it up, yeah." He cleared his throat, but it didn't dispel the thickness. "It's like I'm insatiable."

"*We're* insatiable," she corrected.

"You have a theory?"

Ravyn couldn't fight the need to touch him any longer.

She stretched her legs out again, sighing in relief when they came into contact. "I do have a theory," she said. She lost her train of thought briefly as Damon trapped her feet between his. "I think we'll be out of control like this until I'm pregnant."

"Yeah?" He didn't sound unnerved or worried in the least.

"That doesn't trouble you?"

"No." He leaned forward and ran his palm from her ankle to the back of her knee. Ravyn grabbed his hand and held on to it.

"You don't feel manipulated by that damn obelisk?" She'd meant to sound outraged, not breathless.

"Look, Ravyn, we both knew going in pregnancy was a possibility." He stopped rubbing his thumb over her wrist. "That's not what's bothering you, though, is it?"

She pursed her lips and remained silent. He studied her for a moment, his eyes too sharp for her peace of mind. Of all the times for Damon to be able to bank the fire burning between them, why did it have to be now? She knew the instant he'd reached a conclusion.

"You don't like being out of control." His voice held dawning realization.

"Maybe," she allowed slowly. Ravyn considered it for a moment. Okay, so needing to be in control explained a few things. Like why she didn't want Damon to know she loved him. It would be giving him power over her in a way. She trusted him, but she didn't want to be dependent on him, to acknowledge her emotional state to a large degree was now tied to his actions.

"You're frowning. It's not that bad, so don't worry."

"It's cowardly," she disagreed. Ravyn didn't put up a fuss when he reached over and moved her until she sat astride him. He'd lied about not being able to get hard again, she noted. With a small smile, she wrapped her arms loosely around his neck.

"No. Sweet pea," Damon said gently, "it's natural. Even before you lost your family, you knew their jobs held danger. Of course you want to control as much as you can."

Ravyn rested her forehead against his. The stiff thread of

his stitches poked at her skin and she frowned. "We're putting some salve on that before we leave this room." Damon squeezed her waist and she got his message without him saying a word. "I need to think before we talk about it, okay?"

"Yeah, okay." He slid his arms up her back, pulling her against him. Ravyn rested her head on his shoulder, trailing her hands down his sides. There was no urgency to their caresses, just a need to feel the slide of skin against skin.

He was hers. Even before that stupid stone had linked them in ways that disconcerted her, she'd known this. She nipped at his neck where it joined his shoulder before kissing away the sting. They'd been born for each other.

And if that knowledge didn't sit quite comfortably yet, at least it didn't terrify her any longer.

Damon woke up feeling as wrung out as if he'd run ten klicks in full gear. Through Death Valley. In August. He groaned silently, not wanting to disturb Ravyn, who needed the rest. If he hurt this bad, she had to be worse off. Still more asleep than awake, he turned his head to look at her.

She lay on her back, one hand over the amulet, the other at her side. Her lips appeared slightly swollen, probably from a few too many hard kisses, he thought regretfully. She had faint circles under her eyes, but then neither one of them had done much sleeping the last two nights. He turned on his side, propping himself up on his elbow so he could study Ravyn a little closer. Damon's lips quirked up at the corners. He doubted he'd ever get tired of looking at her, being with her. Even asleep, she was more vibrant than any other woman he'd known.

Carefully, he pushed her hair off her face. It amused and charmed him that even after all they'd done with and to each other, she retained the need for modesty. He must have pulled that nightgown off her a hundred times and she still insisted on wearing it while she slept. The pale blue color made Ravyn appear exotic and Damon fisted his hand to keep from touching the silky material covering her body. Somehow, despite his best intentions, he found himself running a knuckle across the crest of one breast. He craved contact with her.

He opened his fist, his palm barely touching her as he ran it down her torso. With a sleepy smile, he lightly splayed his hand over her abdomen. Their baby was busy dividing cells. Damon jerked his hand away, no longer drowsy.

He pushed the blankets down, and with a tentativeness that had his fingers trembling, he reached out again, both with his hand and his senses. This time he wasn't surprised to feel the pulsing that marked the presence of their child. Ravyn had been right, he noted absently. She'd said the unquenchable desire would last until he'd gotten her pregnant. He still wanted her—he couldn't imagine a day when he wouldn't—but the need wasn't out of control any longer.

As the idea registered, a huge grin broke out across his face. He was going to be a daddy! Afraid of spooking her, he hadn't told Ravyn he wanted her pregnant, wanted this lifelong tie between them. Softly, he rubbed her tummy, saying hi to his baby. It nearly overwhelmed him, the idea of going from having no one to being half of a couple and now part of a family.

Logic said he couldn't tell whether Ravyn was pregnant; she probably wouldn't even know this quickly herself. But logic meant nothing. He *knew*. For the first time, he began to glimpse their connection. It had been there while they'd made love, but he'd been too aroused to pay attention.

Before he could think about that any further, Ravyn's hand covered his where it rested on her stomach. Damon finally took his gaze from her belly and looked up to find her watching him, her eyes slumberous. Damn, he thought, the knowledge blind-siding him. He loved Ravyn. His heart skipped a beat. Damon shook his head—talk about being slow on the uptake.

He linked his fingers with hers so both of them were cupping her abdomen. "You're pregnant," he said into the quiet.

"I am?" He watched Ravyn's eyes go out of focus and felt her consciousness probe her body. "I am," she agreed.

"Are you okay with it?" He couldn't quite read her tone.

"I'm fine. How about you?"

He couldn't keep the idiotic grin off his face. "Will it scare you if I admit I'm excited?"

"No," she said, smiling up at him. "That makes me feel better. I want our baby to feel loved, not like an obligation."

"That's not a worry. I love him already." Damon cleared his throat, uneasy with the thickness emotion put in his voice. Now would be a good time to tell Ravyn how he felt about her, but something had him hesitating and the moment passed.

"I'm glad," she said, freeing her hand from his. She reached for him, trailing her fingers just below the wound on his forehead. "I didn't do a good job mending you. This almost looks worse now that the stitches are out."

"Don't fuss, sweet pea. I'll have a doctor remove the scar and no one will ever know I was hurt."

"I'll know."

She sounded serious and that concerned him. "Ravyn, are you really okay about the baby?"

She sat up, dislodging his hand and didn't stop moving until she knelt facing him. Damon slowly shoved himself up so they were eye to eye. He could sense something bothered her and his gut clenched at the idea that she didn't want to be pregnant.

"I'm scared, Damon," she admitted softly. "It's not just us facing the killer anymore. I mean that was frightening enough, but now, if something happens, it affects our child too." He watched her circle her fingers over her stomach, as if offering comfort to the small being now within her womb.

Damon didn't bother telling her she wasn't facing the killer, Ravyn would only argue with him about it, but her concerns reaffirmed his decision to keep her safe. "I promise you," he said, "nothing is going to harm this baby."

"You can't promise that," she said. "I wish you could."

"Trust me."

"I do trust you, but you know there's no telling what will happen. Neither of us has ever worked with this energy before. What if we don't become good enough with it to win? What if we win, but something happens to the baby anyway?"

Ravyn's tone became more and more intense as she talked

and Damon covered her mouth with his to quiet her. She terrified herself more with every word she spoke. Hell, she was scaring him. When he felt some of the tension leave her body, he eased away from the kiss, but kept his arms around her.

"I'll take care of the two of you. Trust me," he repeated.

She was quiet for a moment, then smiled faintly before settling against him. "Is it too early to claim hormones made me overreact?"

He traced his fingers down her spine. "If it makes you feel better, you can blame anything you want."

"You know what, honey?"

"What?"

"Our baby is damn lucky to have you for a father."

Damon stopped breathing for a moment. Squeezing his eyes shut, he tightened his hold on her. No one had ever really cared much one way or the other if he was around, let alone considered his presence lucky. He knew she didn't realize what those words meant to him. When he finally found his voice, Damon said, "I'm the lucky one, sweet pea. I'm the lucky one."

Damon wished now he hadn't suggested this. His curiosity about using energy as a weapon and his desire to keep Ravyn from becoming suspicious about his plans to face the killer alone, had led him to make an error in judgment. He'd thought it would be simple, certainly no more difficult than turning on the lights.

He was wrong.

When they'd started, Ravyn had been upright. Then she'd sat on the grassy hillside. Now she was lying on her back, face scrunched up in concentration. He sat, forearms braced on his bent knees, and took another survey of their surroundings. This place was the most unique firing range he'd seen. Three sides were steep, artificial hills, as was three quarters of the last side. The entrance was in a stone wall that ran the last quarter of the way along the fourth mound. The narrow enclosure seemed to be bubbling with power, although they had yet to fire a shot.

Damon stretched out beside Ravyn, propping himself up on his elbow, and watched her with concern. Sweat beaded her skin and ran into her hair. Her face was red with exertion, yet beneath the flush, she seemed drawn. Frowning he said, "Ravyn, I think we should quit for the day."

"I've almost got it."

"That's what you said an hour ago."

Her face smoothed out and she opened her eyes, turning her head to look at him. "I really almost have it. Pulling up the energy is easy enough, but it comes in vertically and I need to flip it horizontal to pass it to you. That's where I'm running into the problem. I lose my grip on it then."

Reaching over, he pushed her damp hair off her forehead. "We can come back and try again tomorrow, you know." He'd find an excuse to avoid it then. Damon knew the answer without her saying a word. He recognized that stubborn look.

Turning on his back, he linked his hands behind his head. Although he wasn't watching her, he kept himself tuned to his sweet pea. If it appeared she was in any kind of distress, he'd step in and stop her whether she was ready to quit for the day or not. He watched the clouds drift past and let his mind wander.

His heart felt full as he considered the future. He wouldn't bring it up yet, not until he'd taken down the killer, but they had plans to make. Did she want to stay on the CAT teams? And if she did, how would they manage a relationship if she was off world? Then there was his job. Things were heating up again, and he knew he'd be out in the field a lot. He wasn't sure he wanted to fight in another war or be away from Ravyn and his child for months at a time. They'd work it out somehow, he decided. Loving Ravyn made him too happy to let his career, or hers, get in the way.

Her gasp yanked him from his thoughts. "What?" he demanded, sitting and facing her.

Ravyn grinned up at him. "I did it! I turned the energy." Her smile faded. "But I got so excited, I dropped it again."

"That's great! Why don't we wrap it up for the day."

"You keep suggesting that," she groused. "I want to complete an energy exchange before we head back in."

"I keep bringing it up because you look exhausted." Damon knew that fact wouldn't influence Ravyn. She'd forge ahead no matter what it cost her personally. "What about the baby?"

"I'm fine, honey, and so's the baby. You know I wouldn't do anything to hurt him."

Damon looked away for a moment and took a deep breath, before focusing on Ravyn again. "Half an hour," he conceded.

"Okay."

He knew she'd agreed too easily, but he didn't call her on it. Ravyn sat up and shifted so she partially faced him. It didn't look like she was working quite so hard now, although she was clearly concentrating. It didn't take long before she grinned at him again. "I've turned the energy a dozen times without losing it. I want to try passing it to you now, okay?"

"Yeah, let's do it." Damon centered himself and opened his mind to receive the energy. He wasn't quite sure how he knew what to do, but it felt right somehow. Instinct, he guessed.

He felt Ravyn pull the energy from Jarved Nine and gather it within her. She shifted it and started to direct it toward him. Only the energy never made it. Damon frowned. It was as if some barrier prevented it from reaching him. "What happened?"

Ravyn shrugged, but she looked decidedly uncomfortable.

"Let's try again."

"Um, you're right. I am tired. Let's call it a day."

"The half hour isn't up. Try it again."

She opened her mouth, but shut it without saying a word. Damon stared at her intently, but Ravyn wouldn't meet his eyes. He had a bad feeling about this.

He sensed her go through the process again, and he opened himself even further. Again, the energy was blocked as she tried to send it to him. Damon closed his eyes and let himself "see."

There was a fortress around Ravyn. It was so high, he couldn't locate the top of it and his gut told him it was far too thick for the energy to make it out. He'd known Ravyn protected herself, he just hadn't realized how impenetrable her barriers were. Expectantly, he looked at her and waited for her to raze the wall. Or at least let him inside.

Minutes passed and she did nothing. She wouldn't even look at him. It dawned on him then that the wall wasn't something she'd created unconsciously or had forgotten existed. This barrier had been deliberately erected and she *wanted* to keep him out. For an instant, he was stunned into numbness; then pain deeper than anything he'd known before ripped through him. It couldn't hurt any worse if the killer had reached in and torn out his heart.

Damon turned his head, hiding his devastation. His luck hadn't changed. Here he'd been thinking about them being a family, about finally having someone of his own and it had been nothing but an illusion of his own making. It hadn't taken very long for the bubble of his imaginary utopia to pop. And his sweet pea was the one holding the pin.

Not *his* sweet pea, he corrected. Ravyn.

He was stupid, he berated himself. Just because he loved her, didn't mean she felt the same for him. How many more times would it take before it sank in that he'd always be an outsider? Even Ravyn didn't want him. Not really.

Damon pushed himself to his feet. *To hell with her.* He stalked off, leaving her in the grass.

Ravyn couldn't believe how fast things had gone wrong with Damon. He'd changed from ebullient and happy to cold and remote. And the fault rested squarely on her shoulders. So far she'd endured two days of his excessive courteousness without a break. She didn't know how to fix it, though, not without letting down all her guards. The very thought made her desperate.

"Why don't we go outside and get some air?" she suggested.

Damon glanced at her and then went back to cleaning one of the guns. "Why?" he asked, in an oh-so-polite tone. "It's just as artificial out there as it is in here."

Ravyn winced. *Ouch!* She could handle one completely

pissed off male, she'd done it before, but beneath the anger was hurt. Hurt she'd caused. Her heart ached with remorse.

Sprawling back in the chair, she propped her bare feet on the table in front of her. The large sitting room off the bedchamber allowed him to put a lot of space between them and she didn't like it. She watched him with longing as he methodically worked on the weapon. His hair had grown out enough to look shaggy and very unmilitary-like, making it easier for her to forget he had a dangerous career.

As if feeling the weight of her stare, he looked up, green eyes pinning her. "You have something you want to say?"

"No," Ravyn said, shaking her head.

"I didn't think so."

She shifted her gaze away from him. He'd slept beside her without touching her, not even wrapping his arms around her in the night. He'd remained nearby during the day, but couldn't have been more distant if he'd been on Earth.

Ravyn traced the aqua squiggles on her purple pants with her index finger. The pants fit like a second skin, as did the matching aqua top which ended at the waist of the pants. Each time she lifted her arms, it bared her midriff. It was the sexiest outfit she'd been able to find. The plan had been to entice Damon into making love, sure once they did, all would be forgiven. Only he hadn't shown any interest.

Okay, so maybe it wasn't the best method of conflict resolution she could have come up with. Especially since it seemed to have made him angrier. Ravyn flexed her toes against the table surface and swallowed a sigh. She wanted things back the way they'd been before.

"So what are we going to do today?" she asked, forcing her voice to sound cheerful.

For a moment she didn't think Damon planned to answer. He generally didn't start ignoring her until he'd had enough of her compulsively perky chatter, and she hadn't said much yet this morning. On the other hand, he had been doing a good job of pretending she didn't exist.

Finally, not bothering to look at her, he said, "We're going to the edge of the city and deploying the short-range beacon."

"We are? The rescue ship would be here already?" Oh God, Ravyn thought, scrunching her eyes shut. She had almost no time left with him. As much as she wanted to leave this planet, she feared there would be no way to fix things with Damon once they were surrounded by others. Pressing her fists to her face, she tried to beat back the panic. She refused to lose him. Taking a deep breath, she lowered her hands and let her eyes devour him. The idea of never again feeling his touch on her body, of never again seeing him smile just for her, scared her to her soul.

"I doubt it," he said, without inflection. "This is the first day help might be here, but it's unlikely. I'd say two or three more days." Seemingly oblivious to her, he put aside one gun and started the cleaning process on the other.

Ravyn let her head fall to the back of the sofa. What kind of coward hurt the man she loved, and let him go on hurting, because she was afraid? She made herself sick. The silence lengthened and she couldn't bear to think of her cowardice any longer. She'd toyed with an idea since she'd first fixed the short-range beacon and maybe now would be a good time to try it. Quietly, she retrieved the beacon and set it on the table across from Damon. "Can I have your knife?" she asked, her voice small.

Without a word, he dug it out and slid it across the smooth surface. He didn't ask what she had in mind even when she started taking apart the housing of the beacon. Ravyn wasn't sure if that was a measure of trust or indifference and she wasn't going to ask. While she worked, she forgot the antipathy he felt for her. She tested the changes she made and frowned. Not quite right, she determined and went back to her task. The fifth time she tested it, Ravyn grinned. *Perfect.* She closed the housing once more, happy with her accomplishment.

"I set up the beacon," she said, "so it transmits our location. Without satellites to triangulate by, the rescue team might have a hard time finding our position. With this basic code telling them where to find us, it should be easy for them."

"Fine."

"It isn't as simple as it sounds," she prattled on. "The beacon isn't set up to do that, but with a few little tweaks here and there . . ." She broke off at Damon's glare.

"Why don't you cut the bullshit, Ravyn? For two days you've been trying to pretend nothing's wrong. I'm not playing that game so leave off." With a last, hard look to underline his words, he went back to the gun.

Ravyn had to hurry to keep up with Damon, but she didn't think he was moving as fast as he wanted. Even as angry as he was, he wouldn't forget his responsibility to keep her safe. Or maybe he was just worried if she fell, she'd hurt his baby. It depressed her to think that was his chief concern. She hadn't said a word since he'd told her to be quiet. What could she say? She'd hurt him badly and deserved his contempt. If she wanted to fix things, she was going to have to work up her courage and drop her defenses. The problem was, she didn't have a clue how.

Damon stopped when he neared the wall of the Old City and swung the pack off his shoulder. He set the beacon on a nearby ledge and deployed it as she caught up with him. Ravyn stood close, just wanting to be near him, but he moved away from her. After a few minutes, he stopped the signal. "Why aren't we leaving it on until help arrives?" she asked.

Before he could answer, Ravyn felt a presence. Cold and ugly, it made her shiver. "I think something's out there," she said quietly. When she got no response she looked away from the wall and gasped. The blankness in Damon's eyes, the lack of animation in his body made her heart leap into her throat.

"Damon!" she barked at him. Not so much as a blink of his lashes. When he'd been hit in the head, she remembered, he'd responded to her sweetness, not her sharpness. "Honey," she said coaxingly, "come back to me."

Still no response. Ravyn swallowed hard and reached for him. The muscles in his forearm were rigid. She ran her hand up and down, stroking him, murmuring his name, pleading with him. All to no avail. Before she could come up with another idea, Damon started walking. The movement was jerky, so unlike his usual grace, that Ravyn could only stare for a moment. It was as if he were a marionette. Her eyes widened as realization dawned.

"Damon!" She ran and planted herself in front of him, trying to stop him. He walked around her and she darted in front of him again, grabbing his biceps. This time he picked her up and put her aside before he continued on. Terror rose up so strong that she wanted to curl up and cry, but she couldn't. She had to do something. Somehow the killer had reached in and was controlling Damon's mind. She was sure of it. Now he was being steered inexorably toward one of the gates. She didn't need to be precognitive to know what would happen when he got there.

Putting herself in front of him a third time, she wrapped her arms around him and jumped up, hooking her legs around his waist. She knew Damon wouldn't hurt her even if he had become a zombie and he didn't, just peeled her off and put her aside. He'd nearly reached the gate and time was running out.

Two linked minds. The killer could overcome an individual, but not the pair of them if they joined. She didn't have time to debate the idea or worry over it. Damon's life was in danger; protecting herself counted for nothing. Her decision didn't take even a split second of thought.

Ravyn put herself between the gate and her love, took a deep breath and opened a portion of her wall, reaching out to grasp Damon and pull him through the gap. In the flash of vulnerability, she could feel the malevolence, the wrongness of the killer outside the Old City. Then her barrier was sealed off again, and she had Damon safe within.

She'd expected him to recover instantly. He didn't. He'd stopped moving, but his body remained rigid. His eyes stayed empty. Oh, God, what if she'd left it too late?

"Damon!" Ravyn sounded alarmed.

He shook his head, taking in his dual surroundings with a frown. Physically, he stood near a gate to the Old City without a clue how he'd arrived there. But in his head, he was inside the impenetrable walls of a fortress. "What happened?" he asked.

"He had you. One minute you were here; the next you were like a puppet. I couldn't stop you from walking to this gate or snap you out of it." Ravyn's voice shook.

Damon frowned as memory, of a sort, returned.

Ravyn reached out took his hand, both in the city and in the fortress. At her touch, it finally dawned on him what had happened. She'd put her bulwark around him too. She'd let him inside. Interested, he looked around again. Her protection was strong and even more impressive than he'd imagined.

He no sooner had the thought then the walls started to waver. The bastard was trying to get in. Without hesitating, he joined with her and reinforced their shield. In the physical world, the silence hung eerily, but within the fortress he could hear the roar of outrage from the killer. "Can we hold this fortification in place," he asked, "and get away from this wall?"

"Yes, but it'll take both of us to keep him from breaching it. He nearly broke through before you added your support."

"I'll manage. If you feel it slipping, we'll strengthen it before we continue." Damon didn't wait for a response, but went to the ledge where the beacon sat. It seemed odd to be walking in one dimension and stationary in another, but he didn't let it distract him. If she hadn't wrapped this protection around him, he would have opened the gate, walked out of the city and been killed. He had no doubt of that. And Ravyn would have followed him in death. She hadn't been exaggerating the precariousness of her wall. It had been seconds from crumbling. *Shit.*

He put the beacon in the pack, grabbed Ravyn's hand and hustled them away from the edge of the Old City. Damon didn't stop moving even after they were out of range. He had felt the killer's mind pounding at the gates of their protection until they were nearly a quarter of the way to the heart of the town.

When they arrived at the fountain near the city center, he put the pack down and pulled her against him. "Thanks," he said. She didn't reply, just held on to him tightly. Almost afraid to hope, Damon reached for Ravyn with his senses.

This time no barrier kept them apart and his hurt ebbed away. She did love him, he realized, slowly smiling.

"Why did you shut me out?" he asked.

Ravyn shrugged her left shoulder. "I was scared, what else? And I didn't want you reading my mind."

"Why would you think I'd be able to?"

"The message from Kale and Meriwa was telepathic."

"So you assumed we'd be communicating that way too."

"More than communicate. I thought we'd be in each other's minds at will. I wasn't comfortable with that," Ravyn said.

"I wouldn't be either, but you never bothered finding out the link is empathic, not telepathic." He ran his fingers along her jaw to the underside of her chin and tipped her face up to his. "You're not comfortable with that either. Why?"

She didn't want to meet his gaze, but he shifted until their eyes met, unwilling to let her evade a conversation they should have had two days ago. At last she stopped trying to avoid him and said, "I told you I was a coward."

"So I know how you feel about me. You know how I feel too. What's scary about this?"

"I'm afraid you'll find out who I really am and won't want me anymore." She held up a hand to keep him quiet. "I'm afraid even if we get back to Earth okay, that something will happen to you because of your job. Just thinking of you being injured or killed terrifies me. I know it doesn't make sense. Keeping you out wouldn't prevent it from hurting if anything happened, but fear isn't always logical."

Damon swallowed hard. He could actually feel how scared she was at the thought of anything happening to him. No one had ever cared for him this deeply. He couldn't lie to her even if he wanted to. She knew too much about Spec Ops to be fobbed off with half-truths. Her lips trembled and he shifted his hand so he could run his thumb across them. She pressed a kiss to the pad of his thumb as it reached the center of her lips and smiled at him tremulously. He replaced his fingers with his mouth.

"I need to hear you say it," he said, lifting his head.

She swallowed hard, nearly a gulp. "I haven't said that to anyone since I was six, maybe seven."

"Why not?"

"I don't know. I guess because it made my family uncomfortable. After I'd tell them how I felt, they would all mumble something along the lines of 'me too' and run off."

Considering how closed down the colonel was, Damon wasn't surprised. What did astonish him was why he hadn't guessed Ravyn would be carrying around some of the same baggage. The man had raised her from the age of fourteen and no one would ever accuse Colonel Sullivan of being open with his emotions.

"I promise I won't mumble and run off. Say it, Ravyn," he encouraged. He did need to hear the words. After the last couple of days, sensing it wasn't enough.

She opened her mouth, but only a kind of squeak emerged.

"You want me to go first? I love you, sweet pea." And now he had an idea why she was scared. He felt vulnerable.

"Damon," she said, her voice thick and shaky. When she continued, she spoke fast, as if trying to spit it out before her courage deserted her. "I love you too."

Chapter Eighteen

If Alex could have gotten out and pushed the ship to make it go faster, he would have. His gut churned. Ravyn needed him and she needed him *now.* From the time she'd been a little girl, he'd always sensed when his sister was in trouble. It had never been this strong before, however, and never at such a great distance. He didn't believe in psychic links, but he believed in his connection to Ravyn.

The sound of running feet had him turning. Stacey slid by the entry, not able to stop in time. Her arm shot out, wrapping around the jamb and halting her forward progress. She scrambled into the equipment bay with more haste than grace. "Ravyn's in trouble," she said, panting. "We have to do something!"

He didn't know why, but he wasn't surprised to discover she shared a link with his sister too. "What do you suggest? You come up with something we can do from here and I'll do it." All the icy rage Alex felt at his helplessness filled his words.

He watched her recoil at his tone before she regrouped. "Can't the ship go any faster?"

"No. If it could, I would have given the order days ago.

We're at maximum sustainable speed and have been from launch."

Terror shot through him and it took all of Alex's training not to react. Stacey gasped. He knew in his soul they felt what Ravyn felt and right now she was scared out of her mind. His hands tightened into fists, the only outward sign of the impotent fury raging through him. He'd kill to keep his sister safe and here he sat, days away from J Nine, unable to do anything but wait.

Part of the frustration involved not knowing what frightened her. Ravyn didn't jump at shadows, but he knew spiders made her scream. It could be that simple or as terrible as running for her life. But even as worried as he was, he also felt relief. This was the first sign he'd had that she was still alive.

The intensity decreased and Alex took a deep breath. Uneasiness remained, wariness, but the terror had abated.

"What do you think is happening?" Stacey asked.

He almost snapped at her. Did she think he had a crystal ball he could gaze into and come up with the answer? Alex reined in his temper. This was the friendliest Stacey had been with him since the showdown in his cabin and he didn't want her to put her back up again. Just because he was scared and wanted to lash out, didn't mean he had to do it.

"I don't know," he said, fighting to keep his voice neutral.

They stood there without saying anything as the apprehension ebbed until it became little more than a suggestion, something he could easily have written off if he didn't have a history of sensing when Ravyn was in trouble. He monitored the feeling, keeping close tabs on it. When it changed to a nervousness, his brow furrowed with confusion. What was going on?

Stacey sucked in her breath at the next emotional surge. Her eyes met his and she looked as baffled as he felt. "It feels like joy." Her voice held a trace of question.

"Yeah," he muttered, his voice hoarse. "To me too."

Then, without warning, the link was severed. Alex wanted to punch something. Illogical though it may have been, he wanted to maintain the tie, hold on to it so he could reassure himself when he needed to. The swiftness with which he'd lost contact alarmed him. Time stood still for one endless moment as he tried to assimilate the experience.

"I guess I'll go back to lunch," Stacey said, breaking the spell.

"Wait." He wasn't ready to let her go yet.

She paused, clearly eager to leave. "Yes?" she asked, with the cold formality Alex had grown accustomed to.

He had no real reason for stopping her other than an uncomfortable need to win back her regard. He searched for something to say and grasped at the first thought that came. "Has that ever occurred before between you and Ravyn?"

"No. Why do you suppose it happened now?"

Alex relaxed a bit. He'd engaged Stacey's interest. She still spoke to him with a politeness that rankled, but at least she wasn't running off. He shrugged. "I don't know. I've never felt anything this strong from her before."

"Something could have changed Ravyn, allowing her to broadcast to us."

"Or maybe she's never been this scared before."

Stacey shrugged one shoulder. "Another possibility," she said coolly and turned to leave once more.

Alex knew he should let her go. It was no secret she didn't want to spend more time with him than she had to. He should be grateful she was professional enough to continue the training. It would have been easier on her if he'd arranged for one of the other men to take over the sessions, but he didn't like the idea of anyone else touching her. So he tortured them both. It felt wrong for them to be at odds. An ache had developed within his chest, an ache he couldn't rid himself of and it had everything to do with the distance between them. His weakness bothered him, but Alex hadn't found a way to overcome it.

"Maybe we're the ones who changed and let Ravyn connect to us," he said, his words sounding nonchalant despite his turmoil.

He heard her take a deep breath before she turned around and walked to him. "What's up with you?"

"What do you mean?" He tucked both hands into his back pockets to keep himself from reaching for her and hanging on until she would take him anyway she could get him. Once hadn't been enough. Or maybe it had been too much.

"We could speculate all day about why we suddenly have such an intense connection to Ravyn without reaching any conclusions. That's not your style. So why are you keeping me here?"

"I want us to be friends," Alex said.

Stacey laughed. It sounded bitter, not amused. "Too late," she told him. "Do you really think I'm so pathetically eager for your attention that I'll forget your behavior and be friends?"

He cleared his throat and said, "That isn't how I would put it. For the good of the mission, we need to get along."

"Good of the mission. Ha! You just want more sex."

She jabbed her finger into his chest and he captured her hand, pressing it flat against his body. "You have to admit," he said, voice deepening, "it was damn good between us."

It had been damn good, but Alex realized he should have kept his mouth shut. Stacey's toe found his shin with enough force to make him wince. He'd probably end up with a bruise.

"Just because I came, doesn't mean it was that good. My high school boyfriend lasted longer than you did." After shooting him one last derisive sneer, Stacey stalked out.

It was perverse, but Alex found himself grinning. He'd made some progress. Miss Manners had been replaced by a fiery-eyed hellion. Oh, yeah, things were definitely looking up.

Damon concentrated on the target in front of him, trying to tune out everything else. He'd discovered manipulating Jarved Nine's energy, using it as a weapon, required total focus. The slightest waver in his attention and the energy would seep harmlessly back into the planet.

He imagined a line from his body to the target and sent the energy hurtling down it. Bull's-eye! Ravyn cheered and he allowed himself a small smile of satisfaction, even though he knew better. If it turned out they had to defend themselves this way, he and Ravyn would be in a world of trouble.

Ravyn sobered and looked at him. She tilted her head as she studied him, a dark curtain of hair falling over her shoulder. His thoughts derailed as he remembered the feel of her hair sliding over his body, of it fanned out on the pillow as he lost himself in her. Damon watched her eyes darken.

It didn't surprise him that Ravyn picked up on his less than enthusiastic response to their energy practice or his mental detour into what they'd done this morning in bed. He'd nearly gotten used to their heightened connection in the two days since she'd let him inside her walls. It may not have been telepathic, but the empathic bond between them was so strong there were times it did feel like mind reading. It still scared Ravyn when it occurred, but she didn't try to close him out any longer.

"Why the mild response?" she asked. "You hit the target dead on."

Damon crossed his arms over his chest. She knew so much about military practices he sometimes forgot she didn't know everything. "From the time you drew the energy until I shot at the target took too long. More than three minutes."

"We're still learning. Your first couple of days using a gun at the firing range, you couldn't have been very fast. The speed came with time. Two days ago I couldn't even pass the energy without losing my hold on it and you couldn't hang on to it long enough to use it. We've made excellent progress."

Damon shrugged. "You've got a point," he conceded.

Ravyn crossed her arms over her own chest, mimicking his stance. "Why the rush? Why are you feeling uneasy?"

"I don't know."

She narrowed her eyes.

His lips twitched as he suppressed a smile. He couldn't get away with anything. "Time is running out. It's like we're on a collision course with destiny or something." Damon shrugged again, uncomfortable with what he said. Gut instinct was one thing, but this strong sense of presentiment was something else altogether. He didn't like it.

Ravyn wrapped her arms around his waist and he returned

the embrace, hanging on to her more tightly than necessary. He reached for her with the essence of who he was. She met him halfway and their spirits intermingled effortlessly. Serenity filled him. Three weeks ago he hadn't known she existed and now he couldn't imagine a day without her. Losing Ravyn would destroy him and the killer remained near, remained a threat.

Her fingers splayed in his hair, gently rubbing his scalp. Damon knew she'd picked up on his disquiet and tried to soothe him, but he couldn't relax until he had Ravyn safe. He pressed his mouth against her throat and took solace from the pulse he could feel beneath his lips. Proof that she lived, that it wasn't too late. Not yet.

"It won't be like last time," she murmured against his ear.

He didn't know if she referred to the last time someone faced the murderer or the last time he had been responsible for another life, but it didn't matter. This connection allowed him to feel how deeply she believed in him. It was humbling.

Suddenly, without warning, Ravyn's knees sagged and she gasped as she gripped him firmly. It took him a split second longer to feel the strong emotions that buffeted her. Anger. Unreasoning, barely controlled fury. He didn't have time to identify the rest of the jumble slashing at her.

"Damon!"

"I got you. Help me get the wall up," he told her. Caught in the backlash, Ravyn couldn't do it. She threw her head back and he could feel the echo of her pain. He had always done the support work for the wall, but this time he had to take the lead. Once he had it visualized, the maelstrom she was trapped in eased until she could focus with him.

He sank to the ground and cuddled her on his lap. Damon wiped the perspiration from her forehead and pressed a gentle kiss to her temple. Another mistake. He'd made another mistake in trying to protect someone. They didn't bother guarding themselves in the center of the city, believing the killer's reach didn't extend so far. From now on they would keep the barricade up all the time, no matter how tiring it became.

Ravyn's breathing remained ragged and he stroked her back, quietly waiting for her to relax before he asked some questions. He used the connection between them to send her tranquility and to try to heal any lingering discomfort. It seemed to take a long time before the tension eased out of her muscles and she sank against his chest, letting him take her full weight.

"Are you okay?" Damon asked, his voice nearly soundless.

"Yeah," Ravyn said, drawing in a shaky breath.

"What happened?"

"I'm not exactly sure. I know we've felt the killer every morning when we head to the edge of the city to deploy the beacon. His anger batters against us, but this was different. This rage penetrated everything."

"From now on we're keeping our defenses in place."

Ravyn pushed herself up so she could look him in the eye. "Damon, I had the wall up. It's always there. The fury pierced it, disintegrated it."

He frowned. "I didn't feel any wall."

She shifted, cupped his face with her hands and smiled at him. "That's because I keep you inside with me and you don't think about it except when we leave the center of the Old City."

"It doesn't make sense," Damon said slowly. "If he could bore in this deeply, why wait until now? Why not do it as soon as he realized we were in here? Or the first day we deployed the beacon and escaped him?"

"Nothing about this killer makes sense," Ravyn said, skating her hands down his cheeks and over his shoulders. "Why did he wait eight months before attacking? Why did he wait so long when the settlers of the Old City began building?"

Damon kneaded the tautness in her neck. "It's a big planet and there's no indication he has any kind of transportation. If he moves around, doesn't stay in this area, it might have taken him eight months to discover the arrival of the CAT team."

Ravyn considered what he said and then nodded, her expression thoughtful as she stood. She held out a hand to help him to his feet and he took it, curbing the desire to pull her into his arms. This incident left him even more positive that despite all his plans, fate had something else in mind. Something was rushing toward them head on.

"Then we'll practice, honey," Ravyn said, enfolding him in her love. "We'll keep practicing until we're as fast as you think we need to be."

Damon smiled grimly. Maybe there was a drawback to this closeness after all. If he couldn't keep anything a secret, how could he slip away to hunt the killer without her?

The mood of the Jarved Nine rescue team had descended somewhere south of grim. Stacey pushed her damp hair off her forehead and tried to keep her mind on her job. Not an easy endeavor since she didn't have much to do. She'd put aside her animosity toward Alex. Not that she'd forgiven him or forgotten what he'd done, but neither of them could afford to be distracted as they dealt with this unknown threat.

Her excitement at landing on an alien planet had been short-lived. J Nine looked so ordinary. No purple moss or lime green sky or anything else that screamed, "I'm off world." Never mind that she'd studied the images sent back or that she'd known the Western Alliance favored the most Earth-like planets for possible colonization, it had still been disappointing.

Sweat rolled between her breasts and dampened her hair, but inside she felt icy. She hadn't seen the bodies, didn't want to see them. These weren't strangers who'd died, and right now she was functioning by pretending it hadn't happened. She'd known something had to be seriously wrong on the planet. Her heart, however, had continued to hold out hope. Maybe that's why she'd been stunned by what they'd discovered inside the CAT facility.

To be fair, she didn't think any of them, even Alex at his pessimistic worst, had expected the extent of the carnage they'd found. He'd gone pale with what she pegged as fear before fury quickly replaced it. Even that emotion had been brought under control, although it had taken him a few minutes.

A noise had her whirling, her eyes straining to see into

the brush that surrounded the clearing. She stared, unblinking until Alex said quietly, "It's just an animal. Relax."

"You're sure?"

"Yes." The headset crackled with one of the search teams checking in and Alex responded, ignoring her again. Stacey monitored the transmission, but nothing new had been discovered.

The facility stood in the center of the clearing, the prefab walls looking a sinister gray, and she repressed a shudder that wanted to work itself from the inside out. She was glad to be standing outside. Glad it was Dr. Mitchell in the building with the bodies and not her. And glad Alex had appointed himself her babysitter. His presence comforted her, kept her from running, screaming back to the transport.

Stacey felt the hair stand up on the back of her neck, but forced herself not to whirl again. She'd been jumping at shadows all day. Despite finding pools of dried blood on the floor and nineteen body bags in the facility freezer, everyone else on the team had remained steady. She couldn't give in to her fear. Alex already considered her a liability; she wouldn't prove him right. Slowly, cautiously she turned her head. A small, furry animal looked back at her, its head cocked in curiosity. Her shaky laughter had a worrisome edge to it. She stared at the animal until it scampered away.

After thoroughly searching the facility and finding all the comm equipment damaged, the Spec Ops team had begun a sweep of the surrounding area. They hadn't located any signs telling them which way the men had gone with the lone CAT team survivor. Instead they had found the remains of more bodies.

Stacey shifted until she could see the abandoned transport leaning mournfully to one side. Holes had been punched into the fuselage and the interior looked even worse with all the control panels and circuitry destroyed. She didn't need Alex to tell her the military transport had been built to withstand enemy attack, not to mention entry into a planet's atmosphere. Whatever had damaged the vehicle had inhuman strength.

Another prickle of unease rippled across her skin. The

flight crew guarded their transport, she reminded herself. They wouldn't be stranded on Jarved Nine. She couldn't help thinking of Ravyn, and anyone else who'd survived, fleeing with almost nothing but the clothes on their backs. Stacey knew her friend was the lone CAT survivor, even though Dr. Mitchell hadn't run the DNA tests yet. The sensation she'd had the other day still resonated strongly within her. She'd been connected to Ravyn; she couldn't doubt it.

A beeping noise made her jump before she remembered she'd set the alarm as a reminder. Alex had ordered hourly reports to the ship orbiting Jarved Nine. Stacey tried to collect her thoughts so she would sound professional, not completely out of her element and scared out of her mind.

"Johnson."

Stacey jumped again and felt stupid when it registered Alex had been the one speaking. He hadn't missed her display of nerves, but he didn't look condemning. No, she thought, he appeared sympathetic. She must be seeing things.

"Tell the ship the number of casualties has reached twenty-five and get an update on that damn storm. Also tell them we'll be leaving the surface at dusk and spending the night aboard."

"We're leaving?" Stacey asked. She couldn't have been more shocked if Alex started flapping his arms and flying.

"Yes. We'll return tomorrow at first light, but it's too dangerous to spend the night here." He put his hands on his hips and looked at the sun riding low in the sky. Stacey watched his mouth tighten and knew he didn't want to leave without his sister. His desires, though, took a backseat to the safety of the rescue team.

Alex moved off, quietly issuing orders in his headset to the men combing the area, and she began her transmission. Somehow she managed to sound cool and concise, but as she disengaged after sending the sign-off code, she noted her hands trembled. Stacey leaned her head back and took a deep breath. She couldn't wait to return to the ship. It wouldn't be much longer till dusk, maybe another hour or so. She just wasn't looking forward to being confined in the transport with the remains of the dead.

* * *

The day already felt hot and oppressive and the sun had barely risen. Alex tried not to let this sense of time running out interfere with what he knew needed to be done. Dr. Mitchell and Stacey stood together, talking quietly. Both looked tired, but then their duties had kept them from getting all the sleep they needed.

It had been late last night when the doctor had completed the identification of the bodies. Stacey had sent the information back to Earth using the most complex encryption program the military had devised. They didn't want news of the dead getting out in the media before the families had been notified. The encryption program bought CAT and Alliance Command time to send out representatives while the news media worked furiously to break the code.

They had remains for everyone except Ravyn and Brody. Of course, there was no guarantee something hadn't happened to them farther from the facility. Alex pushed a hand through his hair. He'd bet money Ravyn was still alive. Or at least she had been three days ago. He couldn't write off what he'd felt, and he didn't want to. It gave him hope.

He had mixed emotions about Brody being the other survivor. On one hand, he'd become a top officer in Spec Ops. On the other, Alex couldn't forget how he'd screwed up eight years ago. Sam still didn't have the use of his legs despite all the operations and advances in medicine.

Alex frowned, but he was glad Ravyn wasn't alone. He thought he'd given her all the training she could need, but he'd been wrong. He should have tried harder to discourage her from joining the Colonization Assessment Teams. His lips turned up slightly at the corners as he imagined how that discussion would have gone. Ravyn could give lessons in stubbornness, and she'd been able to talk him into things with alarming ease.

Three weeks had passed since the emergency beacon had been activated. The odds that tracks remained to tell them which direction Brody and Ravyn had gone were slim. They'd spend a few hours making sure the pair wasn't hiding in the vicinity, but Alex doubted they'd find anything here. His internal clock continued to tick, winding him tighter.

He heard the beep that signaled it was time for Stacey to transmit an update to the ship. He strode over to her and waited. When she finished, he asked, "What's the latest on the hurricane?"

"It looks like it will make landfall this afternoon," she told him. "The best guess is in the vicinity of the Old City."

Alex muttered an expletive. The storm bearing down on the coast made his blood run cold. Something he couldn't name told him they had to find Ravyn and Brody before it hit, that if they had to search afterward, it would be too late. If he were in Brody's position, he'd head for the Old City. The wall made it easier to defend and there would be places to hide and take shelter. Alex wanted to forget his training, put the team in the transport and head right for the city.

"Do you remember the time," Dr. Mitchell said gently, breaking into his thoughts, "when Ravyn was about seven? You'd gone sailing with your friends and wouldn't take her with you."

"I remember," Alex said. It wasn't a good memory. His father had been out on a mission. Marie had been busy with the wounded from one of the last battles in the Second War. For once Alex had stood firm against Ravyn's pleas to be included and had dropped her off at the childcare center on his way to meet his friends. Only he hadn't made sure she'd gone inside.

"What happened?" Stacey asked.

Alex remained quiet, letting the doctor tell the story. He didn't know why she'd brought it up. He still got the shakes if he thought about the incident too long. He turned away, trying to close out the doctor's voice, but not wanting to miss the point she undoubtedly had.

"Ravyn followed Alex. She didn't get to the marina in time to talk herself onboard. He and his friends had already set sail so she decided to go after him. She managed to find a little boat with a motor and get it started."

"Ravyn stole a boat?" Stacey's voice rose in shock.

"She was just a baby," Alex tossed over his shoulder, the instinct to defend his sister too ingrained to put aside.

"This seven-year-old," Dr. Mitchell said, "was so determined and resourceful, that though she knew nothing about boats, she was able to start it and drive out of the marina."

Point taken, Alex thought, but the doctor had left out a big part of what had happened. He turned back to the women. "That seven-year-old didn't know how to swim and wasn't wearing a life vest. She saw a sailboat and thought I was on it. As soon as she got close, which took some doing with her lack of skill, she stood and jumped up and down, calling my name."

Stacey gasped. It had been the first time he'd felt the connection with Ravyn and known she was in trouble. Alex closed his eyes briefly and took a deep breath. He couldn't let an old memory rattle him when the current situation required all his attention. "She capsized the boat. Luckily, the people onboard the sailboat saw her go under and someone jumped in to save her. She wasn't breathing when they pulled her on deck."

"She survived, Alex," Dr. Mitchell said.

"She easily could have died," he replied, voice tight. He pivoted and stalked off until he couldn't hear anything else the doctor might say. He wanted to be out searching with the team, but knew he needed to organize the effort and keep an eye on the women. Dr. Mitchell carried a sidearm and knew how to use it, but Stacey had no weapon or any skill with one.

Time dragged. Every hour he returned to get a report on the storm, but he didn't hang around long enough for any more trips down memory lane. His body became more and more tense, but Alex couldn't prevent it. It was as if some voice in his head kept whispering, "Hurry, hurry, hurry."

It was midmorning when Alex heard Stacey transmit on the rescue team frequency. "Colonel Sullivan, you're needed here."

The tone of her voice made him hurry to where she stood. "What is it?"

She held up her hand, silencing him. He watched her frown in concentration for a moment and then he turned to Dr. Mitchell. "What is it?" he asked quietly so he wouldn't disturb Stacey.

"A short-range beacon is sending a signal," she answered, her voice every bit as quiet as his.

"Frequency?" Alex asked, but the doctor shrugged. He leaned over and read the numbers on Stacey's equipment. Not only was it a military frequency, it was one Spec Ops used. He tuned his own comm unit so he could hear it. He frowned as he listened. Short-range beacons were supposed to give out steady, regular beeps. This one emitted short and long tones in some pattern he couldn't identify. Without warning, it ceased.

"How long was it broadcasting?" he demanded.

"About three minutes," Stacey answered.

She started to say something more, but Alex cut her off. "That means Brody is still alive."

"So is Ravyn. The message was in code. It's a rudimentary one we learned early in our studies at comm school, but it's not used anymore and hasn't been for decades. Out of everyone who was on this planet, Ravyn is the only one who could know it. She's also the only person I'm aware of who could tamper with a short-range beacon and get it to broadcast in code."

Alex barely registered Stacey's excitement with his own running riot. "What was the message?"

"The Old City. It was repeated for the three minutes."

Alex allowed himself a quick grin, then flipped his comm unit back to the frequency of his team. He relayed the info, then added, "Come on, let's move." He looked in the direction of the Old City, noted the dark clouds in the sky. "Stace, transmit this info to the ship. Tell them we're heading to the Old City, and get a weather update."

He wasn't surprised to hear the hurricane still appeared headed for the settlement. At least now, if the storm hit before they found Ravyn and Brody, they didn't have to leave J Nine. They could hole up in one of the buildings and wait it out.

"Hurry, hurry, hurry," hummed through his head again and his gut tightened. He herded the two women to the transport. The flight crew already had it fired up and ready to go. Alex stood outside the hatch until the final man boarded. He took one last, lingering look at the horizon and then got on himself.

Time was definitely running short.

Chapter Nineteen

Ravyn stood inside the doorway of a little shop off the square and watched Damon. He had barricaded a part of himself off from her and she didn't like it. Knowing what she did about warriors, she suspected he was up to something, but if she asked what, he'd work harder to keep her in the dark. She had a good idea about his plans anyway.

Pushing herself away from the doorjamb, Ravyn joined him at the fountain and put her hand over his. He linked their fingers, but didn't turn from his study of the sky. She looked up. The sun was eclipsed by a thick cover of roiling black clouds. Lightning flashed, stabbing viciously across the horizon. Rain sheeted down. Yet the Old City remained dry and the wind calm. Bright light glowed from some unseen source as if the late afternoon sun continued to shine. She understood now what had captured Damon's interest. She found it mesmerizing herself.

"The Old City is encapsulated," he said.

Ravyn nodded absently. "By a pyramid of energy. Isn't that why we go to the edge of the city every morning to deploy the beacon instead of doing it from home?"

"I had a feeling the beacon wouldn't be able to transmit

out of here if we weren't by the wall, but I didn't know why." Damon turned his attention to her. "The atmosphere has always felt artificial. Why didn't you mention the pyramid?"

With a shrug, Ravyn said, "I saw it the morning after I took the barb. If I'd said anything then, you would have thought I was hallucinating. You were already worried about me."

He opened his mouth, but shut it again without saying anything. Instead he closed his eyes and tilted his head back, as if looking to heaven for strength. Ravyn bit her lip to keep from smiling. She knew he had a problem with her keeping something like that to herself. If she really had been hallucinating, he would have wanted to know.

"You and Alex are a lot alike," Ravyn said, stretching the truth. She knew exactly what effect her words would have. Sure enough, Damon's eyes snapped open and his head whipped around. His look of outraged disbelief made it impossible not to smirk. She rubbed her thumb over his hand and added, "Except when he looks heavenward, he usually mutters a request for help."

"I believe it. Next time tell me all the information you have. I'll decide whether or not to worry." Damon sounded irritated.

Ravyn arranged her expression so it was appropriately sober and said, "Okay, honey, next time I will." She added just the right note to her voice to make it sound as if she humored him, but not so much he could call her on it. He clenched his jaw hard enough to make a muscle start jumping. Bulls-eye, she thought, veiling her eyes with her lashes to hide her satisfaction. Served him right for keeping secrets.

He should have been able to feel her playing games with him. Yesterday he would have. But then yesterday, the man hadn't distanced part of himself from her.

"Do you think the rescue team will be here soon? I hate going to the wall and feeling the killer trying to get into our heads." Ravyn's skin crawled at the thought.

Damon shifted, his free hand coming up to cup her face. "You could stay here tomorrow. We can hold the wall even with physical space between us."

She turned her head, pressing a kiss into his hand. "No. I

won't let you go alone!" She hadn't meant to sound so savage. "I love you, Damon," Ravyn added more gently. The words still didn't flow easily from her lips, but she could say them now without having a panic attack.

He softened in some indefinable way. "I know. I love you too." He brushed his lips across hers. "Always, Ravyn."

Damon stared, as if memorizing her face, and Ravyn felt her level of anxiety rise. Her heart started to pound. She had a sense of time running short, of Damon's presence slipping away. *No!* Nothing was going to happen to him. She wouldn't let it.

She freed her hand and threw herself against him with enough force to drive him back a step. Damon's arms went around her to steady both of them, but he looked confused. She pulled his head down and took his mouth. Breaking off the kiss, she looked at him. Satisfied with the stunned heat in his eyes, she pushed him until his legs hit the end of the bench behind him.

"Sweet pea?"

A second shove forced him to sit and then she climbed on him, straddling his hips and grinding against his burgeoning erection. She fisted her hands in his hair, tugging his head back so he met her eyes. "You're mine, Damon Brody, and I'm not losing you now," she said fiercely. "You let anything happen to you and I'll hunt your soul down to the ends of heaven and kick your ass. Are we clear?"

"Yes, ma'am," he said, lips twitching.

Ravyn stopped his laughter by devouring his mouth again. She wasn't quitting until he realized she meant business.

Stacey doggedly continued to trail after Alex. They'd split up into teams of two to cover more ground inside the Old City, but hours had gone by with no one finding a trace of Ravyn or Brody. The last sign of their presence had been the booby-trapped gate they'd carefully disarmed to gain entrance.

As the gate had been rearmed, Stacey had watched the transport leave Jarved Nine to return to the ship. Sullivan had made the only choice he could, she knew that. The wind had tossed the vehicle as they'd landed and the storm would only intensify. To protect the ship from damage it had to leave the planet, but it made her uneasy to think of being stuck here.

The original plan had been to land within the Old City, but there had been some kind of force field surrounding the settlement and they hadn't been able to set down inside the walls. She continued to glance up from time to time, unable to stop herself. There was a storm raging furiously over her head, but not a drop of rain or gust of wind touched her.

Alex stopped and Stacey pulled even with him. The city remained eerily empty. Then he started taking check-ins from the other teams and she realized another hour had passed. Again, no one had found anything. She sighed. "We could search for days and not find any sign of them."

Alex tucked the stylus into the side of the electronic map and looked at her. "We'll find them."

"How? If they're moving and we're moving, we could keep missing each other." Stacey tried not to be discouraged, but the sheer number of buildings and streets made the search daunting.

"Brody knows this is the time frame within which a rescue team would arrive. He won't move unless he has no other choice. Stace, we've been leaving markers." He opened his hand revealing little yellow blobs. "Brody knows how to read them. He sees them, he'll find us if we don't find them first. Trust me."

"I do." She knew nothing took precedence over finding his sister. Stacey watched Alex take a last look at the map and then put it away. She waited until he had the pocket fastened before she pointed up and asked, "Don't you find that odd?"

He glanced up. "You mean that a force field we can't see is keeping the storm out? Yeah, it's odd, but I'm glad it's there. We would have had to stop searching hours ago if it weren't."

Stacey's thoughts left the storm and returned to the search. "I think we should try to raise them again on the radio."

"We've run through all the military frequencies a dozen

times. Either his comm unit is broken or Brody managed to leave that somewhere the same way he left his assault rifle."

Finished with the discussion, he walked away. Stacey had to hurry to keep up with him. He was still ticked off about finding Brody's rifle propped up in the corner of Ravyn's room at the facility. She didn't understand how they could tell it was his. It looked no different to her than the one Alex carried, but Carmichael had identified it as the captain's gun. She'd been told each man made personal adjustments to his weapon.

It didn't take Sullivan too long to slow down. Stacey was relieved. She huffed from the pace he'd set and couldn't have kept up with him much longer. The only sound in the Old City was her breathing and the crunch of her feet on the stones. Even with the clunky, heavy-looking boots Alex wore, he moved silently.

They had another ten minutes till check-in time when Alex stopped short. She'd been looking at the sky again, but he didn't even sway as she plowed into his back. Puzzled, Stacey moved beside him and followed his gaze.

They'd found Ravyn. And Brody.

Brody sat on a bench beside a fountain and Ravyn sat astride him. Even from this distance, Stacey could see Ravyn had her hands buried in his hair and he had hold of her hips. The kiss they shared was so carnal, it was hard to believe they still had on all their clothes.

Stacey looked at Alex. She knew how he felt about Brody and how overprotective he'd always been with Ravyn. Especially when it came to men. He bared his teeth, his face feral, and snarled faintly. As involved as Ravyn and Brody were, she didn't think they'd hear it. But the instant Alex's rumble started, Brody stood, put Ravyn behind him and drew his gun. He scanned the area, his body tensed for battle. When he saw them, he began to lower the weapon. He hesitated before he put it away and she guessed Brody had noticed the look on Alex's face.

Alex stalked forward, stopping about four meters away from them. For an instant, she stayed put. Then it dawned on her she better catch up and try to prevent a murder.

When she got to Alex, she put her hand on his wrist and dug in her fingers. Her grip had no noticeable effect. Stacey watched Ravyn step from behind Brody's back. She waited for her friend to run to Alex and throw herself in his arms.

She didn't. Instead she stood beside the captain and laced her fingers with his. "Hi Alex. Hi Stacey."

Alex was busy glowering at Brody, so Stacey answered, "Uh, hi." It seemed surreal after what had happened to hear Ravyn greet them so nonchalantly. Or with seeming nonchalance, she realized belatedly. There had been a warning note in her friend's voice as she stared at her brother.

Ravyn was sending Alex a message.

From the tenseness of the muscles under her hand, Stacey knew he'd received it and didn't like it. Not one bit. Ravyn looked determined, Brody looked wary, Alex looked murderous and she searched futilely for a way to lower the tension level.

The break in radio silence as the hourly check-in began relieved Stacey. Alex ignored the radio so she took over. She announced their discovery and told them to stand by for coordinates. When Alex didn't supply them, she looked to the captain. For a moment, she didn't think he would answer either, but then he rattled off a set of numbers. She relayed them to the waiting rescue teams.

"That's not where we are," Alex said, his voice sounding about as warm as the ice age.

"That's where we've been staying. There's enough room there to put up everyone until the storm blows over," Brody answered. He didn't sound conciliatory, but he did keep his tone neutral. It was better than nothing, she decided.

Nobody moved.

Stacey stopped herself from blowing out a breath of frustration. Alex's behavior bordered on idiotic, but at least he had enough sense not to try to order Ravyn to him. She knew her friend wouldn't budge from the captain's side. If Alex issued that edict and Ravyn ignored him, the tension would only escalate further. And it was explosive now.

"Sullivan," Stacey hissed under her breath, "play nice."

He ignored her, but her words did have some effect. Ravyn

and Brody shared a glance and evidently reached a decision. That they could communicate with a look underlined how close they'd become. It had to nettle Alex, but he didn't visibly react.

"You should see the house we've been staying in," Ravyn said with what had to be forced perkiness. "It's incredible." She and Brody began walking, still holding hands. They were so in sync, it was as if their every move was choreographed.

Stacey allowed herself a moment of envy, then gave Alex a light push. He turned his glare on her, but at least he moved. At the rate they were going, everyone else would arrive at the destination before they did. She knew the showdown between Brody and Alex had merely been postponed, but maybe by the time it became inevitable, Alex would be more reasonable.

Or maybe not, she thought, watching him bare his teeth again as Ravyn leaned up to whisper in the captain's ear. Stacey sighed. Things could only get better, right?

Damon kept his eyes on the colonel. He knew better than to turn his back on a dangerous predator. Ravyn hovered nearby, prepared to put herself in front of him if she felt it necessary. Good thing he had a healthy ego, he decided, his lips quirking. Part of what kept him on edge, though, was her worry.

The colonel didn't seem to care that the rest of the rescue team found the situation humorous. No one said anything, however, and the silence seemed to grow more and more strained. Even his sweet pea remained quiet. His smile grew. Ravyn caught his amusement and turned to him, a question in her eyes. He broadcast his love for her and felt it returned. The communion ended when the last duo arrived. He nodded at Carmichael; they'd worked together before, but he didn't recognize the woman with him.

"Doctor Gwen!" Ravyn crossed the room and hugged the other woman.

"Ravyn," Colonel Sullivan barked, "you go with Dr. Mitchell and let her check you out. Brody, I want a report."

"Damon should go first," Ravyn argued. "He was hurt worse than I was."

"You were hurt?" The colonel's voice sounded deadly. The glare Damon received looked even more lethal.

"Hardly at all," Ravyn lied easily.

Sullivan stared at her a moment. "Take the doctor to a room where she can check you out. Brody, you come with me."

Ravyn glanced at him and he nodded, telling her to follow orders. Sullivan looked surprised for an instant before a fierce scowl distorted his face. Damon knew his sweet pea wanted to be sure he'd be fine left with her brother, but the colonel did not like her seeking another man's okay before obeying his orders.

No one moved until Ravyn and the doctor had left the room. "Brody, now," the colonel thundered and Damon followed. The redhead trailed after him. Sullivan stopped. "Johnson, stay here. I want you to contact the ship. Bring them up the date."

"If I go with you, I'll have more information to report," she said. Despite the bravado, Damon sensed her anxiety.

"I'll summarize for you later. Stay."

For a moment, Damon thought the woman was going to pick up the small green obelisk sitting on the table to her left and chuck it at the colonel's head. Fire shot out of her eyes, but she pivoted and stalked off. He was glad she wasn't mad at him.

It wasn't until Colonel Sullivan stood pointedly in the doorway of the small room off the great chamber, that Damon moved again. He wasn't looking forward to this confrontation.

The door closed with an ominous click and he stood rigidly at attention. He had a brief glimpse at the raw fury in the colonel's eyes before a shutter came down. Damon was grateful for his superior's iron control. The older man's hands knotted into fists. Then he moved away, putting the desk between them.

"I don't like you using my sister," Sullivan drawled softly.

"I'm not using her," Damon denied between gritted teeth. "Sir," he tacked on belatedly.

"You took advantage of her."

"No, sir."

"You can't deny you're sleeping with her."

Damon was surprised the colonel's voice didn't cause icicles to form in the corners of the room. "With all due respect, Colonel, it's none of your business."

Sullivan's knuckles went white. Damon braced himself, but the colonel regained control.

"The hell it isn't. She's my sister."

The man had a point, Damon conceded. The animosity had to be put aside. "You and I, Colonel, need to declare a truce. I don't want Ravyn to feel torn between us. It's not fair to her."

"We don't have to declare anything, Brody. You're not going to be around her long enough for it to matter."

"You're wrong, sir."

"No, I'm not. Adrenaline and fear forge relationships that don't last once things return to normal."

"Ravyn and I have more than that. Sir."

"Ravyn was the only survivor of a massacre," Colonel Sullivan said. "She needed to feel safe and looked to you. That's all it is. Gratitude. Dependence. It won't last."

"You don't know your sister very well, sir, if you believe that." Damon watched the colonel's eyes narrow, and a muscle began to tic in his jaw as he battled for control.

"Are you telling me after three weeks, you think you know Ravyn better than I do? I raised her after our parents died."

Taking his life in his hands, Damon said, "Sir, you know her as your sister. I know Ravyn as a woman."

Sullivan grabbed the edge of the desk with both hands, but Damon didn't move his attention from the other man's eyes. A flicker in his gaze might be the only warning he had before the colonel attacked.

"Ravyn can do better than some rich kid playing army."

"Yes, sir," Damon agreed. Ravyn could do better, but it was too late. She was stuck with him now.

"You hurt her and you might as well shoot yourself because I'll hunt you down and kill you."

"It's a deal, sir." Damon saw Sullivan's lips tighten and realized he'd given the wrong answer. Again.

"Of course," the colonel said, sarcasm dripping from each word, "you'd have to hang on to your weapon. Would you like to explain why I found your assault rifle at the CAT facility?"

"No, sir, I would not."

The colonel looked ready to leap over the desk, and Damon wished he could take the words back. Sullivan probably thought he was being flippant. He wasn't. He didn't want to admit he'd forgotten it. Damon opened his mouth to give a more politically expedient answer, but didn't get the chance to speak.

"Brody," Sullivan said, his voice sounding strangled, "I want your report now." He didn't add, "before I kill you," but it was implied.

Damon went along with the change of subject. He didn't want to get into a fight with Ravyn's brother and Sullivan's control was hanging by a thread.

Leaving out everything of a personal nature, he filled the colonel in on the events since his team's arrival on the planet. They were on the familiar footing of a subordinate reporting to a superior officer, but the tension didn't ease, not with the man firing questions at him every other sentence.

"This is one helluva mess," Sullivan commented evenly when Damon managed to finish.

"Yes, sir." Damon knew the colonel wouldn't be receptive to a request from him, but he'd made a vow to his dead friends and their families. "Sir, once the non-military personnel are off the planet, I'd like permission to take a team after the killer."

"Permission denied."

"Why, sir?"

The colonel leaned forward, hands flat on the smooth wood of the desk. "I don't have to offer you any explanations, Captain."

"No, sir, you don't." Damon realized if he didn't drop it, he'd be getting himself in even deeper trouble, but he couldn't let this one slide. He knew the Western Alliance would send in Spec Ops teams in an attempt to capture the alien. He also knew it would be a slaughter. If he kept quiet, he was as responsible for the deaths of those men as the murderer. "But, sir, I believe right now is our best chance to destroy the killer."

The colonel straightened, put his hands on his hips and studied him. "Explain, Brody."

How did he explain the alien's mind-control abilities? How did he tell Sullivan he was able to protect himself because Ravyn helped him hold an imaginary wall in place? How did he tell the colonel he wanted to try to expand the wall to encompass the entire team currently on Jarved Nine? The man didn't exactly look like someone open to this kind of thing.

"Let's just say, Colonel, I have an advantage later teams won't have."

"Let's just say I don't buy that, Captain." Sullivan crossed his arms over his chest and drilled him with a glare. "We both know Command won't allow you to return to J Nine. You're too involved. I think you're looking for excuses to carry out your own plan for revenge and it isn't going to happen. The mission is to rescue the CAT team. The bodies are recovered; the survivor is rescued. We're going home. End of discussion."

Damon glared right back at the colonel. He remained at attention, but his hands clenched into fists. No one else was dying if he could prevent it. No one.

"Sir—"

"Not one more word, Captain," Sullivan warned, voice low. "Just so you understand, this is a direct order. You are not taking a team to hunt the murderer. Is that clear?"

"Yes, sir," Damon ground out. It was splitting hairs, but the colonel had not forbidden him to hunt alone. It would be easier in a team, but he could do it himself without disobeying the order of a superior officer.

He wasn't leaving until he'd taken out the killer.

Chapter Twenty

Ravyn wanted to run, but she knew better. Damon and Alex were used to her and wouldn't flinch if she burst into a room, but she didn't want to startle the rest of the Spec Ops team. Given the situation, their reflexes would be set on a hair-trigger. Sure enough, each man reacted when she entered. Ravyn paused, letting them identify her, and scanned the common room. Everyone was accounted for with two notable exceptions. Instinctively, she stretched her senses, reaching for Damon.

It didn't take long to zero in on his location, but he'd closed off his emotions enough so she couldn't tell what he felt. With a worried frown, Ravyn started for the door on the far side of the room and then stopped. Neither Damon nor Alex would appreciate her interference. They needed to work this out themselves. She just hoped no one got hurt.

Reversing course, she headed for the corner Stacey had claimed. She was busy, so Ravyn leaned against a nearby table and waited. When the opportunity arose, she said, "You're not going to be able to transmit through the energy shield over the city."

"So I'm discovering."

Ravyn lifted her brows at the anger she heard in Stacey's voice. "What happened?"

For a moment, Ravyn thought Stacey would play dumb. With a sigh, her friend removed her headset and tossed it on the table next to the comm unit. "I don't know how you've kept from killing your brother all these years. The man is such a jerk!" Stacey said with feeling.

"What, specifically, did Alex do?"

"He mistook me for an Irish setter. He ordered me to stay!"

Ravyn pursed her lips to keep from smiling. She'd known for years about Stacey's fascination with her brother, but she'd also known her friend held an idealized view of Alex. It seemed the blinders had come off. If Alex had riled her up with one word, something was going on between them. Ever since Lara had exited his life, Ravyn had talked them up to each other, hoping Alex would be interested and Stacey would still like the "real" man.

"He does tend to a bit be autocratic," Ravyn said with care.

"Autocratic, arrogant, bullheaded, heartless."

Stacey's voice rose with each word and Ravyn noticed they'd managed to catch the attention of everyone in the room. That wouldn't do. To get down to the nitty gritty, they needed to lose the audience. If Stacey believed Alex to be heartless, she'd gotten much closer to him than she knew. Close enough to make her brother lash out. "Is there anything else you need to do here?" Ravyn barely waited for her to shake her head. "Good, let's go." She grabbed Stacey's hand and gave her a tug.

"Where are we going?" she asked as they left the room.

Ravyn ignored the question. "These are all bedchambers," she said, as she continued to lead the way down the long, wide hall. "There are enough rooms for everyone to have their own. If they want. Damon and I are in the largest suite."

They reached the sitting room. Ravyn pushed the door open, gestured for Stacey to enter and then closed it behind them. Since she and Damon didn't spend much time here, nothing looked too out of order. She couldn't say the same about the bedroom.

She'd taken no more than a couple of steps away from the door when she found herself wrapped in a bear hug. It took her by surprise since Stacey wasn't one to display affection, but she recovered and returned the embrace. Tears gathered in her eyes as she clung to her friend. It began to sink in that she and Damon had help now. They weren't on their own any longer.

"Do you know how scared I was?" Stacey asked, sounding choked.

"Probably not as scared as I was," Ravyn said quietly. She didn't try to hide the thickness of her voice.

"No, probably not, but, good grief, Ravyn, I felt what you were feeling a few days ago and you were terrified. Do you know how insane that made us?"

For a moment, Ravyn froze. She didn't realize Stacey could pick up on her fears too. There were times she didn't even like *her brother* knowing how she felt. Slowly, she released the breath she'd been holding. She couldn't do anything about the connection, but she found it interesting how her friend aligned herself with Alex. It made her even more curious about what had gone on between the two of them.

"And then," Stacey continued, tightening her hold, "when we went inside the building and found all those bodies. . . ."

A violent shudder went through her friend and Ravyn found herself offering comfort and reassurance even though the reference to her teammates brought back her own pain. She blocked it. She needed to hang on a little bit longer, then they'd be home and she could let loose, but not yet. Not yet.

Finally, Stacey pulled away, and with obvious self-consciousness, turned her back to wipe at her eyes. Ravyn knew the show of emotion made her friend uncomfortable and she gave her the space she needed to recover. Crossing the room, she settled on a sofa and tucked her legs beneath her. She waited silently until Stacey sat in a chair across from her, but Ravyn didn't get the chance to speak first.

"So, what's with you and Brody?" Stacey asked.

"I thought that was obvious." She knew a diversionary tactic when she heard one, but decided to go along. Sometimes the fastest way to get answers involved a circuitous path.

"Judging by the way you aligned yourself with the captain when we showed up, you know Sullivan doesn't like Brody. Are you aware of the reason?"

"Reasons," Ravyn corrected. "And yeah, I know those too. Damon and I talked about it."

"I only heard about Brody messing up."

Ravyn's feet hit the floor as she leaned forward. "Damon didn't mess up," she said fiercely. "He did the best he could. Even men who had more than a couple of months in uniform might have made some, if not all, of the decisions he made. I don't know what Alex told you, but Damon isn't to blame."

"You're in love with him." Stacey sounded amazed.

Letting some of the tension drain away, Ravyn leaned back. "Of course I am," she said simply.

"I wondered what kind of man would hold your interest. I should have guessed it would be someone in Spec Ops like your brother."

Ravyn shrugged. "Damon and Alex aren't that much alike. They share some core values, but Damon is a lot more laid-back." She grimaced. "Except when my safety is the issue."

Stacey's expression became intent. "Does Brody feel the same way about you?" she demanded.

"Yes." Ravyn hid another smile as the lines on Stacey's face smoothed out. She didn't know if she should feel grateful she inspired such overprotectiveness in others or insulted that everyone felt she needed to be protected.

"I hope Sullivan doesn't try to come between the two of you. He's cold-blooded enough to attempt it."

For a moment, Ravyn didn't respond. "Alex won't try to break us up. He'll grumble and threaten Damon's life, but he won't go beyond that." She hoped.

"You're dreaming," Stacey replied.

Oh, yeah, Alex had done a number on her, Ravyn decided. After a brief, internal debate, she said, "I can guarantee Alex will make a complete turnaround and insist Damon stay with me."

Stacey snorted in disbelief. "You wouldn't say that if you'd heard how your brother talked about Brody."

"Doesn't matter. Once Alex finds out I'm pregnant, he'll handcuff Damon to me if he needs to."

Ravyn watched Stacey's eyes widen. Her mouth opened and shut several times with no sound emerging. Taking pity on her, Ravyn said, "The doctor confirmed the pregnancy, but Damon and I already knew and we're both happy about it." She paused and then added, "I'd appreciate it if you wouldn't say anything to Alex."

"Of course I won't. He's not going to be thrilled, Ravyn."

"I know, but Alex is nothing if not pragmatic. Besides, it's time he got over some of the things he's holding against Damon. Like the fact his brother married Lara."

"Sullivan should be thanking his lucky stars someone else married that ice goddess."

Ravyn lowered her lashes, hiding her amusement at Stacey's obvious jealousy. "You know I agree with you," she said with careful neutrality. "The other problem is Damon's family has money. Alex doesn't like rich people."

"Why not?"

Ravyn didn't respond. Instead she rose and walked over to the table, studying the food there. Before she decided whether to divulge one of the major factors in the development of Alex's defenses, she wanted to know how serious Stacey was. Did she love the man behind the image she'd created? Stacey huffed impatiently, but Ravyn didn't hurry. Settling on a fruit, she wandered back to the sofa and began peeling the pink rind.

"Well?" Stacey prompted.

"How long have you and Alex been spending time together? Three weeks?" Ravyn asked, keeping her gaze on her hands.

"Just over two weeks," Stacey clarified.

"Not easy to avoid each other onboard ship."

"He insisted on training me." Her tone was bewildered.

Ravyn's lips twitched, but her expression remained sober. She knew her brother well enough to understand that meant the two of them had been together nearly every waking minute. Alex was intense at the best of times. She could imagine how over the top he'd seemed to Stacey while he was training her. Ravyn finished peeling the fruit. She carefully sectioned it and offered half to Stacey. She waited until they were done eating before she asked, "What happened with you and Alex?"

Stacey sputtered for a moment before collecting herself. "I told you. He trained me."

"I'm not talking about that," Ravyn said. "Something personal is going on between the two of you."

"Have you ever considered it's none of your business?"

Ravyn smiled both at the tartness of her friend's words and at her defensiveness. "Nope. We're best friends. You know you want to tell me all about it."

Stacey looked down at her lap, her fingers tightening into fists. "He's your brother."

"That doesn't mean I can't be objective. Besides, who knows Alex better than I do?"

There was a lull. Ravyn could almost feel the words building up behind a dam. Stacey would have had no one to talk to for the length of the voyage. Who was she going to seek advice from? The Spec Ops team? Doctor Gwen, who had known Alex since he was a teenager? Ravyn didn't think so.

Sure enough, the dam broke and the story came tumbling out. Ravyn listened, only making a sympathetic murmur or two. When her friend started blinking back tears, Ravyn sat on the arm of her chair and gave her a quick hug. Her lips thinned as she heard how her brother had walked away from Stacey. She understood why he'd behaved like a boor, but that didn't make it right.

As she finished, Stacey wiped away the few tears that had escaped. "I shouldn't have said anything," she said.

"Of course you should have told me," Ravyn said firmly. "Do you want me to beat Alex up for you?"

Stacey's laugh sounded shaky. "Now that I'd like to see."

"I can take him. The man won't lift a finger to hurt me. With that kind of advantage, I can inflict plenty of damage."

"I don't want to be the cause of any trouble between the two of you. I know how close you are."

"Stacey," Ravyn said, dropping to her knees in front of her and taking hold of both her hands. "Do you love Alex?"

"How can you ask a question like that? Only a masochist could love him. No offense," she added quickly.

"If you want him, Alex is yours."

"What?" Stacey's head came up in shock.

"No matter how attracted he was to you, do you think if he all he wanted was sex, he would have given in to it?"

"It doesn't mean anything. Everyone has lapses."

"Not Alex. Not on a mission. And certainly not on a mission to rescue me." As her friend shook her head, Ravyn added, "Colonel Control didn't even make it to the bed. Doesn't that tell you something?" Stacey stilled and Ravyn noticed a small glint of hope appear in her eyes. "Alex wouldn't have pulled back so hard and cruelly if you hadn't gotten too close."

"He didn't shut the ice goddess out," Stacey argued.

"Oh, yes, he did. They fought about it often. Alex likes to blame Lara completely for two-timing him, but he wouldn't let her in, even though she begged him. Between that and his frequent absences, it's a wonder they lasted as long as they did."

Stacey broke her hold and walked across the room. Ravyn kept quiet, knowing her friend needed time to absorb what she'd heard so far. She sat back on the sofa and waited.

"Why?" Stacey asked, keeping her back to her.

"You don't know about Alex's mother. He never talks much about her. From the time he was small, she used him as a weapon against Gil. I know she never spent much time with him, but when she and Gil divorced, she fought for custody. And when she met a wealthy man who wanted to marry her if she got rid of her son, she couldn't ship Alex back to his father fast enough."

Stacey shifted and asked, "That's why he hates the rich?"

"Yes. Lara marrying Damon's brother sealed those feelings. Do you know how many times Alex saw his mother after she remarried? Once. For about an hour. When she died, she was a stranger to him."

Stacey remained quiet.

"He was devastated by our parents' deaths. Alex stayed strong for me, but he had no one he could let go with. He didn't trust anyone else enough." Ravyn saw Stacey's brow furrow.

Maybe nothing she said would make a difference. Maybe Stacey wouldn't risk herself again. Maybe, even if she did, Alex would still blow it. She wanted them to have a chance. She knew they'd be good together. If Alex could let Stacey in. "If you want Alex," Ravyn said, "you'll have to do most of the work. He won't meet you halfway. Probably not even a quarter of the way."

"He doesn't love me."

With a shrug, Ravyn said, "I don't know. I do know he feels more for you than he has for anyone else in a long time. It's your decision if that's enough for you to gamble on."

Stacey didn't respond and Ravyn scrunched down on the sofa, making herself more comfortable. She'd stuck her nose in as far as she intended to. The rest was up to Stacey and Alex.

Stacey kept replaying what Ravyn had said as she waited for Alex. She hadn't gotten to ask any questions because her friend had changed the subject and then Damon had arrived. Recalling how Ravyn lit up when she saw him made her envious. Just a bit. The man was great looking even with the scar on his forehead, but it was the way the two of them couldn't stop touching each other as they'd talked that made Stacey smile.

The sound of a door opening pulled her back to the present. Dr. Mitchell walked across the room with more poise and confidence than Stacey figured she'd ever have. "Night, Doc."

"Good night, Stacey."

Stacey's nerves pulled taut as the doctor disappeared down the hallway. Alex could walk into the room any minute now. She twisted a lock of hair around her finger and bit her lower lip. If Ravyn had it wrong, she'd feel so stupid. The sound of thunder was little more than a distant whisper in the well-built house. Before the noise faded, Alex appeared.

He stopped, looking around the empty room. "Where is everyone?" he asked with seeming indifference.

Stacey stood, not fooled by his tone. There were only two people he wanted to locate. "They went to bed," she told him. Let him guess whether she meant everyone or just Ravyn and Damon.

His brows drew down. Stacey felt his intensity level shoot skyward and sighed. She hoped Ravyn appreciated what a good friend she was. Trying to appear casual, she placed herself between Alex and the hallway to the bedchambers.

"Which room is Ravyn in?"

"The big suite at the end of the hall," Stacey said.

"And where's Brody?" There was no more pretense. Alex's soft voice sounded lethal.

"Same place."

Stacey raised her hands, palms up, and caught Alex as he surged forward. He tried to move around her, but she fisted her hands in his shirt and did her best to hold him there. "You can't just burst in on them," she said, trying to penetrate his anger.

"The hell I can't."

He tried to free himself again and Stacey tightened her grip. She raised her chin defiantly. "Ravyn is an adult and she loves him. It's none of your business."

"It's not love. What they have won't last long once they're back on Earth."

"Alex, you better accept their relationship. They *are* in love with each other and Damon *is* going to be part of Ravyn's life for a long time. You'll only hurt her if you insist on hanging on to your animosity."

"She knows how I feel about him."

"No kidding. You haven't exactly tried to hide it." Stacey took a deep breath unsure how to make the idiot see how selfish he sounded. "I thought you and Damon reached an understanding. That's what he told Ravyn."

"I told him he was as good as dead if he hurt her. I didn't say he could sleep with her."

Stacey would have laughed at how irate he sounded if the

situation weren't so volatile. When he put his hands on her waist and started to lift her, she knew time had run out. "Did you know Ravyn never liked Lara?" she said, the words rushing out.

"You're wrong," he told her.

"Every time Ravyn came back to school, she'd vent her feelings about Lara. As sorry as she was you got hurt, she was just as relieved the two of you weren't together any longer." She felt Alex's fingers spasm against her waist in reaction.

"If Ravyn didn't like Lara, why didn't she say something?"

Stacey released his shirt, and gripping his arms, she said, "Because she loves you and she knew how you felt about her. Can't you do the same thing for Ravyn that she did for you?"

With a scowl, Alex broke her hold. Instead of moving toward the hall, he turned the other way and drove both hands through his hair. "I don't want my sister hurt," he said, facing her.

"Damon would never deliberately hurt her."

"You don't know him," Alex ground out.

"And you do? Have you ever talked to him as a man and not a lower-ranking officer? Have you ever watched the way he looks at Ravyn? Touches her? Talks to her?" Stacey threw up a hand to keep him from answering. "I mean without thoughts of murder."

Alex grunted and looked away. "She's still my sister."

"And you want to protect her. That's admirable. But he's her lover," Stacey ignored the growl, "and he's taken over that job. It's time for you to step aside."

Alex didn't argue with her, but he still appeared mutinous.

"You knew this would happen someday," she told him gently. She knew this rite of passage wasn't easy for him. Maybe it was harder because he wasn't Ravyn's father.

"He's not good enough for her," Alex said gruffly.

Stacey laughed. "You'd never think *anyone* was good enough for your sister. It doesn't matter, though. It's not your choice to make. It's Ravyn's, and she's made it."

"Hell," he said. But it was grumbled, not snapped and Stacey knew she didn't have to worry about him charging down the hall anymore. One explosive subject defused. Time to ignite another. If she had the courage.

Stacey felt a tingly sensation and looked up to see Alex studying her. At first she thought he appeared indifferent, but upon closer inspection, she detected speculation and a banked heat. It gave her the boldness she needed to dive in. "You're afraid of me, Sullivan."

He got an infuriating smirk on his face. "Anything you say," he agreed, humoring her.

She ignored him and continued. "I scare you because you want more than sex with me."

"If I say yes, do I get to get back in your bed?"

"As I recall, you were so hot for me, we never made it to a bed," Stacey tossed out sarcastically as her heart sank at his lazy impudence. It *was* only sex. Why had she believed, even for a moment, it had meant more to him? She almost turned to leave when she heard Ravyn's voice in her head. *Alex wouldn't have pulled back so hard and cruelly if you hadn't gotten too close.*

"It's not going to work. You can't drive me away. I mean more to you than a quickie against the cabin wall and nothing you say or do will convince me otherwise." That sounded good, she decided. Truthfully she didn't believe what she said and he wouldn't have to work too hard to make her surrender the battlefield in full retreat. Stacey waited for his attack.

It didn't come.

Instead Sullivan looked like *he* wanted to retreat. Stacey blinked hard to clear her vision, but it didn't change what she saw. Unless her eyes played tricks on her, he'd gone pale.

"I don't love you," he said.

"I never said you did." She remained calm and unhurt because she sensed she had him on edge. "But you wouldn't have touched me if it was only lust. I come with complications. For one thing, I'm your sister's best friend." She stared him down, half expecting him to have a crushing rejoinder. Instead, he glanced away as if he couldn't meet her gaze any longer.

"I'm a distraction you don't want or need on a rescue mission." Stacey stepped closer, and this time, when he took a step back, she knew it wasn't part of some trap he wanted to set. "I shatter your control," she said, taking another step as she kept trying to close the distance. "You hate losing control."

"What do you want from me?" he asked, voice low and tight.

"I want you to admit it, Alex. Admit I mean something to you. Admit you want more than a quick encounter."

Stacey moved another pace forward, and as Alex stepped back again, he ran into a table. She watched his eyes widen in surprise at the obstacle, and for the first time, she honestly believed she did mean more to him than he felt comfortable with. The man always had a handle on his surroundings, yet she had him so unnerved, he hadn't realized there was a table behind him.

"What's gotten into you?" He couldn't quite pull off the derision he tried to fill his voice with.

In that instant, Stacey knew his secret. The man tried to appear unfeeling, but the truth was he felt things too deeply. That was why Alex lashed out. She *had* gotten too close and he didn't want to care for her that much. Only it was too late. He did care. She could see it now that she knew what to look for.

"Nothing. I can see beyond the smoke screen you keep throwing up now, that's all. You can't say anything to make things easier for you. I'm not going to avoid you or do anything to help you keep your distance. It's all on your shoulders."

Alex swallowed hard and sidled to his right. She moved with him, in awe of her power. Leaning forward, she rested her hands on the table to either side of his hips. She wasn't quite touching him. If he inhaled deeply, though, they'd be in contact. She smiled, watching the shallow breaths he took.

"You're running, Alex. I knew you were a coward at personal relationships, but even I thought you were braver than this."

"Stop pushing me," he gritted out.

"If I don't, you'll keep right on running." She leaned forward, her lips a hair's breadth from his, and stopped. He warred within himself, she could see it in his eyes. The part of him that wanted to remain safe against the part of him that wanted more than one night with her. "Life's all about risk, Alex. There are no guarantees. Either of us could die tomorrow. The secret is to make each day you're alive mean something."

"I want you," he said, his voice guttural.

"I know you do, but I need more." Please, she thought, find the courage to say the words.

He groaned, his hands taking hold of her hips and pulling her against his erection. She didn't fight him, but she didn't respond either. At least outwardly. Stacey gripped the table harder, reminding herself this meant nothing if she didn't get him to acknowledge what there was between them.

"Don't do this," he protested at her stillness.

Stacey looked into his eyes. "Don't be a coward," she urged quietly. Her voice shook with the effort it took to resist him. As she watched, she could almost see a hole develop in his wall.

"You're right," he said, sounding rough. "It's not just sex." Alex closed his eyes briefly, marshaling his strength. "I'm not an easy man to spend time with. I never will be."

"I'll consider myself warned," she said, trying to pull his mouth to hers. Alex resisted her efforts.

"No," he said, "this time we're finding a bed."

Chapter Twenty-one

Ravyn reached for Damon and found nothing but an empty mattress and cool sheets. Instantly alert, she leaped out of bed. Their rooms felt empty, but she checked the sitting room and bathroom anyway. Nothing. An image from her nightmares popped into her head. Damon laid out on an altar. Dead. "Nooo!" She ran to the hall door and threw it open. "Damon!"

Doors opened up and down the corridor. Her attention was snagged for an instant by the sight of Stacey and Alex coming out of the same room. Then, as she felt the stares of five strange men, it dawned on her how little cover the tiny night slip provided. Flushing, she slammed the door closed again and ran to get dressed.

Damon had gone off in search of the killer. She knew it. Her body trembled, making it difficult to pull on a pair of pants. She had to get to him in time. She couldn't be too late. Couldn't be. If anything happened to him . . . She cut off the thought, knowing she wouldn't be able to function if she didn't.

"Damn it," she cursed, shrugging into her shirt, she hadn't meant to fall asleep. The way he'd made love to her last night, she'd known something was up. She didn't think they'd gotten a solid hour of rest, not the way he kept reaching for her as if every time might be the last. "Damn it, honey," she muttered hoarsely, "you weren't supposed to go off alone!"

With impatient fingers, Ravyn brushed the tears from her cheeks and extended her senses, seeking Damon. She couldn't find him. Panic built until she recognized she was too upset to focus. Taking a few deep breaths, she tried again and got the slightest of inklings. He hadn't gotten too far yet. And he'd have to stop to disarm the gate. That gave her a little time.

Racing back into the bedroom, she frantically searched for her boots. She didn't worry about Damon sensing her agitation. He'd closed himself off enough that he wouldn't know she'd discovered him missing, wouldn't know she followed him. Finally, she found the boots and stepped into them. She considered not tying the laces, but figured a sprained ankle would slow her down more than the minute it would take to secure them.

With a sob of relief, Ravyn pulled open the door and ran down the hall. She heard Alex calling her name, but ignored him. Nothing mattered but finding Damon. She struggled with the front door before she managed to get it open and dashed down the stairs. She paused just long enough to sense which direction he'd headed and then sprinted after him. After a few minutes, Ravyn was gasping for breath and knew she had to slow down. If she didn't pace herself, she'd never make it.

Once, as she stopped to get her bearings, she thought she heard footsteps behind her. But when she tried to verify it, she lost the whisper hold she had on Damon and she shut out the sounds. If Alex and the others followed her, good. If they didn't, she and Damon were the only ones who could deal with the killer anyway.

Finally, the city wall loomed over the top of the buildings. Almost there, she thought and moved faster. What she saw when she reached the edge of the city stopped her cold. A growl of dismay escaped as she studied his handiwork. She wasn't sure how Damon had managed it from the other side of the wall, but he'd rearmed the gate. Precious seconds flew by while she tried to think. Fear crushed her chest. She couldn't afford to wait for Alex, but she didn't know how to undo the security and she didn't want to set it off.

She knew it involved some kind of snare and she could just imagine herself hanging by her ankles until her big brother cut her down. Wouldn't that be fun? Alex would never let her out of the city. Too bad she hadn't thought to ask Damon what he'd done. Not that he would have told her. She scowled. He'd undoubtedly been planning this one man mission for a while.

Finally, in desperation, Ravyn drew energy from the planet, tossed it at the trap and pictured it coming undone. The gate eased open.

"It worked," she said in soft amazement. As she left the city, a wall of hot, humid air hit her and nearly knocked her back a step. Ravyn pushed forward, her eyes scanning the area. She spotted him halfway across the clearing.

"Damon!" she called, her voice filled with equal parts relief and irritation.

He stopped and turned, a startled look on his face. It quickly changed to frustrated anger. Too bad, she thought, making her way to him. The going was tough. Most of the storm had moved on, but it had left the ground sodden, and she grimaced, muddy. She had a stitch in her side and was close to gasping for air, but she didn't slow her pace.

The man was dressed for battle. Black pants, black shirt with his vest on, and somehow, he'd acquired an automatic rifle. Despite the frown on his face, his eyes were flat and shuttered. Warrior mode, she knew.

"You shouldn't be here," he said.

"If you think you're facing this killer on your own, you better think again."

"You'll only get in the way."

"Because I'm a coward."

"No, because you lack the training. Because," his eyes lost their remoteness, "I'll be too worried about you to fight."

Ravyn reached up and touched his chest. She could feel

the amulet under his shirt and vest, and with her other hand, she touched her own stone. An arc of energy zipped between them and the distance he'd created disappeared. Although she'd once shied away from this link, she now welcomed its return. Closing her eyes briefly, she let his emotions wash over her. She sensed his edginess, his anticipation and his fear.

"We have to face him together. You heard Kale and Meriwa."

He blew out a harsh breath and glanced heavenward, before lowering his head to stare her down. "Go back to the city and stay there," he said, his voice implacable.

Raising her chin, she returned his glare. "No."

The showdown continued until Damon figured out he couldn't sway her with intimidation. "Sweet pea," he said gently, moving until he could put his arms around her, "please, go back."

Ravyn wanted to capitulate. She heard the anxiety in his words, but she knew she had to be with him. "Together, Damon," she whispered, resting both hands against his chest.

"I want you safe," he said, leaning closer. "I want our baby safe."

Ravyn ignored the snarl she heard behind her. She knew it was Alex. She had no idea when they'd gained the audience and she didn't care. Her discussion with Damon had precedence. "And I want our baby to know his father. That means either we face the killer together or we both leave the planet."

"Colonel Sullivan," Damon said, lifting his head and looking over her shoulder, "will you please take Ravyn out of here?"

Ravyn was about to protest vehemently when she felt a presence. The air became oppressive as tendrils of evil snaked toward them. "Damon," she whispered, in warning and in fear.

"I know," he said. Grimly, he raised the muzzle of his weapon. She watched him measure the distance to the Old City and knew when he decided she wouldn't make it in time. They had no cover and Damon moved, using his body to protect her.

Apparently, the others felt the presence too. She found herself in the middle of a ring of soldiers along with Stacey and Doctor Gwen. The circle remained loose, so each man had room to maneuver if the need arose. She couldn't tell which direction the alien approached from even after her nose picked up an overwhelming stench. Ravyn swallowed hard to keep from gagging.

She felt the tension level rise, but what amazed her was the fear she sensed. Everyone present, including the entire Spec Ops team, was scared. Even Alex. She looked at their faces. None of them showed a hint of this as they scanned the area for the killer. Stacey was the only one who appeared alarmed. Maybe Damon was right. Maybe she wasn't a coward. Maybe others were better at hiding their fears.

Ravyn reached for Damon with her mind and reinforced their mental wall. He didn't glance her way, but he added his support. Too bad only their minds were shielded and not their bodies. They needed physical protection. Belatedly, she realized the others were defenseless. Despite the stifling heat, she shivered. Her brother, her best friend, Doctor Gwen, the men who had come to rescue her, they all were in danger. Could she safeguard the others? Did she have the ability? She wrapped her arms around herself and bit her lip. She had to try.

The attempt was partially successful. She could completely surround Stacey and Alex, but not the rest of the team. Maybe it was a matter of emotional connections because proximity had no bearing on who she could shelter. She wished she understood her new power better.

Unwilling to leave them vulnerable, Ravyn enclosed the others in an egg of protective energy. She didn't know if it would do any good, but it was better than nothing.

A flash caught her attention and Ravyn turned to see a glowing ball of energy zinging toward them. The trajectory would take it between Damon and Alex, right to her. Her heart pounded wildly as she stared at it. Both men shifted, but it was Damon who put himself squarely between her and the fireball. She didn't need any special connection to know why. He was her champion, her protector. He took the hit meant for her.

She gasped at the pain, but it wasn't hers, it was Damon's. Although he grunted and his knees sagged, he did not fall. Her captain was hurt! Fear and fury raged through her.

"Damon!" He had to be okay. He had to. Ravyn rushed forward, reaching for him, but he shook her off. His body was unmarked by the energy and she moved until she could see his face. She detected no signs of agony. For a moment, she stared. She'd seen him in warrior mode before, but not to this degree. Intensity came off him in waves.

Bracing himself, Damon began shooting in the direction the ball had come from. The sound of gunfire was loud, but it should have been louder. No one else was firing. Alex shouted orders, but received no response. She looked at the Spec Ops team. They were frozen, rigid.

Her brother wheeled around and Ravyn took an involuntary step back. She'd never seen Alex like this before. He eyed the team wrathfully as he barked out more orders. The anger morphed into grimness as he understood the men were not ignoring his orders, but were unable to obey. He grabbed the weapon from the man standing next to him and added his firepower to Damon's.

"Ravyn," Stacey hollered to be heard, "what's going on? Why aren't they moving?"

"I'll explain later," she said. It would take too much time to go into it now. Damon might need her. She returned her attention to the battle. Both men continued firing, but she didn't see anything worth shooting at.

She had to do *something*, so she tried to reinforce the cloak around the Spec Ops team and the doctor. She felt the killer trying to dismantle it and her eyes widened in alarm as she realized how strong his mental powers were. Ravyn began to worry he would use the team against them. If he did, they were beaten. She redoubled her efforts to shield them. Sweat covered her forehead by the time a stalemate had been reached. While she couldn't break the paralysis they were in, neither could the alien lure them to him. A part of her relaxed at the knowledge.

Suddenly, a volley of radiant balls streaked toward them from several directions. Before she could react, Damon pushed her into the mud and lay on top of her. She felt several balls crash into the planet and was relieved they missed everyone.

The energy traveled through the ground and her stomach churned as her body absorbed the heavy vibration. Ravyn was glad for the solid warmth of Damon's body along the length of hers.

He moved slightly and she felt his warm breath at her ear. "Do you see those boulders at two o'clock?"

Ravyn shifted her gaze. She didn't see anything she would call boulders. "Tell me you don't mean those small rocks."

"They're the only cover we have a hope of reaching. When I give the word, stay low and run for them."

"What about everyone else?"

"He's aiming for us and ignoring the others. As long as he can keep the team in limbo, they should be fine. The colonel will take care of Stacey."

Ravyn crouched when he shifted off her. Protectively, Damon put himself in front of her and fired a burst of rounds. "Now, sweet pea," he ordered, grabbing her hand and pulling her along.

They didn't make it far before blazing orbs of energy flew at them. The balls seemed to be hitting everywhere like embers sailing out of a roaring fire. Damon yanked her to the muddy ground and again covered her with his body.

"Brody, can you see where the hell he is?"

Ravyn turned her head and mud oozed over her face from chin to cheek. A sharp rock dug painfully into her hip. Alex was near them, his body pressing Stacey into the wet soil. Her friend looked about as petrified as she felt.

"No, sir." Damon muttered, then added a one word curse as another ball streaked toward them.

This one didn't miss and Ravyn felt his body jerk. Panic filled her. "Damon?"

"Give me a minute," he ground out. He was mentally

blocking her once more and she knew he didn't want her to feel how much he hurt.

Ravyn didn't dare move for fear of causing Damon more pain. She watched Alex kneel, spraying the area the fireball seemed to have come from with bullets. The stench got stronger and she was grateful she hadn't eaten anything since the night before, sure she would have thrown up if she had. She felt Damon's body tense.

"What the hell is that?" Alex asked above the gunfire.

Stacey yelped.

Slowly, Ravyn turned her head and looked forward.

The alien came toward them.

She bit back a gasp. Even though she'd seen what their quarry looked like in Meriwa and Kale's chamber, it didn't prepare her for his presence. His colors were more vivid, his size more intimidating. He had an air about him that made her wonder if he could be beaten.

Damon put himself in front of her and fired his weapon, but he moved stiffly and Ravyn knew he was hurting. Despite two men shooting at him, the killer continued forward, unfazed.

As he closed the distance, her heart rate picked up. He absolutely towered over Damon. Ravyn watched the bullets stop and fall harmlessly to the ground before they reached the murderer, as if they hit some invisible force field. His gaze met hers for one, endless moment. In that time, she saw ancient knowledge and power like she had never before imagined. And she saw death. The deaths of the three people she loved most. She saw herself alone, as she waited for him to finish her.

"Look away, Ravyn," Damon ordered.

She broke eye contact and the feelings of hopelessness receded. The monster had been creating the images, Ravyn realized. Somehow it seemed scarier than outright mind control. She stayed prone in the mud and watched as the alien causally lifted one blue hand and directed another sphere of energy toward Damon. He evaded it by a hair's breadth.

Unreasoning fury coursed through her, pushing aside the fear. The killer had tried to influence her emotions and now he was trying to inflict more pain on the man she loved. Like hell. She reached for the rock pressing into her leg, and standing, tossed it at the murderer's head. As soon as it left her hand, she realized she was an idiot. Why did she think a stone would have any effect when the bullets didn't?

"Get down," Damon growled, standing half in front of her.

Ravyn couldn't. She was too shocked by the monster to move. Her assessment came from what she sensed, not his appearance. She'd never felt evil like this before. They weren't living beings to him, but offerings. The killer turned his attention to her. She was careful not to look him in the eye, but it didn't matter, she felt the pleasure he took in their predicament. He grinned at her. Caught in the pointed yellow teeth were shreds of flesh. She shuddered as the idea of him eating hearts and tongues flashed through her mind. With a gulp, she looked away.

"Are those eyes?" Stacey asked, standing beside her.

"Both of you, get down." Alex joined Damon in shielding them. "Now!" he thundered when he didn't get instant obedience.

Unable to stop herself, Ravyn looked back at the murderer. Dangling like fringe from the hem of his vest were eyeballs. Human eyeballs. He must have preserved them in some way because they stared back at her with unblinking perfection.

She felt wooziness swamp her. She didn't want to speculate whose eyes looked back at her, didn't want to guess if those blue eyes belonged to Sondra or to Pyle, but it was hard not to. Her knees buckled and Damon's arm went around her waist, holding her up. The wall of protection she created started to waver and the alien's grin widened. *Pull it together, Ravyn. Now!*

"Sweet pea, I need you."

She nodded and took a deep breath. The smell just about choked her, but it brought her to her senses. If she couldn't do better than this, she should have stayed in the Old City. Determined, she hardened the wall. Her composure was threatened again when the killer ran a hand over the eyeballs, lightly brushing them and causing them to swing, but she shook off her horror and gathered her strength.

After firing more rounds and getting the same, useless results, Damon slipped the safety on his weapon and tossed it to the ground. "Ravyn, pull up the energy." His voice was grim.

Nodding, she started to draw from the planet when the alien lifted his hands. Flustered, she dropped the energy. The burst hit Damon again, driving him back a step. Squeaking with dismay, she wrapped her arms around him to keep him from falling. His body shook and she tightened her hold. The alien grinned once more, but she ignored him and concentrated on her job. By the time Damon was steady, she was able to pass him a wave of energy.

He fired it, but it seemed to expand and dissipate before it reached the alien. "Keep it coming," he ordered and she realized she shouldn't be standing there, watching.

Hurriedly, she drew from Jarved Nine and managed to hold on to all the power even when the killer raised his hand to fire. She watched in helpless rage as the flare headed toward Damon, but this time it stopped short of its target, splattering out like a snowball hitting a window. Out of the corner of her eye, she saw Stacey move beside Damon, hands raised. She turned her head to the other side and saw Alex in a similar pose. He raised his eyebrows as their eyes met, but didn't say anything.

Guardians. The "voice" seemed to be both hers and Meriwa's. Now some of what the ancients had said made sense. While she and Damon could protect their minds, they were physically vulnerable. Stacey and Alex were their guardians, their sentinels.

Like two gunslingers meeting at high noon, Damon and the alien stood only meters apart, shooting energy at each other. Ravyn struggled to keep up. It seemed her captain could fire a lot faster than she could draw. The killer managed to get off four or five shots to every one of theirs. She concentrated only on pulling, holding and passing the energy. The murderer couldn't score any hits, not with their guardians in place, but they weren't striking the alien either.

No one gained an advantage. How much longer could the

standoff last? The energy work left her drained, and it was worse for Damon. Not only was he hurting from the hits he'd taken earlier, but his part of the process required more effort. The murderer seemed unaffected by fatigue and able to continue indefinitely. His shots retained their speed and precision and she could detect no signs of weakening.

She took a deep breath, wiped the sweat dripping from her face and reached for more energy. Swaying with exhaustion, she passed it along the channel to Damon. It amazed her, but the conduit between them remained open. Fatigue had always caused it to collapse when they'd practiced, yet they were more wiped out now than they'd ever been before. It puzzled her.

Ravyn handed off more energy and sent her consciousness inside herself. She traveled to the passage leading to Damon. They weren't the ones holding it open, she realized, her eyes widening in shock. Their baby was doing it. It couldn't be possible, she thought. The baby was little more than a group of cells at this point. She searched deeper, going beyond the physical, and met his essence. He was beautiful, powerful, and she couldn't prevent a sappy smile as it dawned on her that she and Damon were going to have their hands full raising this child.

"Ravyn," Damon barked, forcing her to focus on the battle.

Quickly, she drew more energy, and as she transferred it, she put a hand on her abdomen and lightly rubbed. She sent all the love she felt to the baby. Damon fired, and for the first time, this shot didn't fade before it reached its target. Ravyn had started drawing more energy, and in surprise, she lost her hold on it. Ignoring the curse Damon muttered, she passed him another round. She was on to something here.

On the next pull, she opened her heart. She sent Jarved Nine love, and she wrapped the energy she passed to Damon with all the love she felt for him. She felt his surprise, but he was so used to opening to her, that when he fired, his heart was brimming with love for her as well. This shot not only made it to the target. It hit. Full force.

The creature bellowed in pain and outrage. Something

changed on his face, making Ravyn think he had been toying with them, but was done with the games now. The next volley from him came fast and furious. It amazed her how he could direct the energy balls in multiple directions. She knew Alex and Stacey were hard pressed to keep up, but somehow they managed.

Adding love slowed down the energy transfer even more, but it worked. As shot after shot hit, inflicting damage on the alien, he moved closer. Ravyn wondered if he thought it would give his blasts more power. Frustration made him angry and more hate filled every fireball he aimed their way. The greater his malice toward them, the weaker his flares seemed to be.

Despite this, they had no advantage. She and Damon grew more weary with every shot they fired, and Stacey and Alex grew more tired with each blast they blocked. Retreat wasn't an option. Maybe the four of them could get back inside the city, but they couldn't leave the rescue team behind.

The impasse continued. Ravyn looked around, her body trembling with fatigue. Damon swayed, his breathing rougher than usual. Stacey's eyes were slits, as if it would take too much out of her to open them completely. Alex appeared drawn and pale. She tried to shake off the lassitude and focus. If any one of them faltered, the alien would pounce. She couldn't let Damon or Alex or Stacey die. There had to be something else she could do, Ravyn thought desperately. There must be more!

More. That was it! More love.

The love she injected to the energy increased its potency, but not enough. What if she found more feeling within her?

She called upon all the love she had ever felt and filled the energy with it. Damon looked startled again, as if sensing something different, but he fired. The alien staggered back two full steps and seemed to wobble a moment before righting himself. This was the most damage they'd managed to inflict so far.

"What did you do?" Damon asked and she could hear total exhaustion in his voice.

"I remembered all the love I've felt in my life."

He nodded thoughtfully, took the energy she passed him and shot it. This time the alien went to his knees. He got up slowly, shaking his head.

"Interesting," Damon commented.

Ravyn tried to pull the energy faster so they could get off a one-two shot. She was unable to add any speed to the process. The killer, as if mocking her inability, shot off three quick bursts. The shield their guardians held appeared to flicker briefly before solidifying once more.

"Would you guys please do whatever it takes to finish this," Stacey said wearily. "I don't know how much longer I can keep this up. I'm dead on my feet."

"Better than dead, period," Alex told her. He ignored Stacey's attempt at a glare.

"You know," Ravyn paused as another attack by the killer was deflected, "I'm filling the energy with love as I pass it over. Then you're filling it with love as you fire. What if we entwine our love together for the whole process?"

Damon nodded again. "Worth a try."

Ravyn drew the power from Jarved Nine. She felt Damon weave his love with hers and she brimmed with the beautiful vibration. Only half aware of what she was doing, Ravyn reached for Stacey and Alex. They were linked, although not as strongly as she was joined to her captain. She found cords running amid the four of them. Almost tentatively, she opened to her brother and friend and asked them to join their feelings of love to her and Damon's.

There was a brief hesitation from both of them before she felt their compliance. Four strands of love meshed into one and Ravyn added the planet's energy. Nothing had ever felt so wondrous. Reluctant to lose the sensation, she slowly passed it over. It built further as it flowed by the baby, and surprised, Ravyn almost lost the hold she had. Damon turned to her as he began to receive the power. She read his own amazement easily. "Conceived in love," she whispered reverently.

His lips turned up slightly as he rested one hand atop hers over the baby. "Damn right."

The energy, filled with love, continued to stream to him.

In her peripheral vision she saw so many bursts of light heading toward them, it looked like the Fourth of July. Still, the three of them remained within their peaceful bubble.

"Excuse me for interrupting your little tête-à-tête," Alex said, irritation evident, "but we need you to pay attention. Things are getting a little dicey here."

They separated, but the energy continued on its path. Alex wasn't exaggerating. The shield he and Stacey held was a solid wall of light as the alien inundated them.

She passed the last of the energy.

Damon fired.

The alien dropped.

The noise he made raised the hair on the back of Ravyn's neck. She knew she'd never forget the pitiful sound. He tried to stand, but only made it to his knees before falling back to the ground. For the first time she saw something akin to pain cross his face. He managed one more shot, but it fizzled before it covered half the distance to them.

She and Damon held their link long after they felt the alien's life force leave. Remorse at causing his death choked her and it didn't seem to matter he had been evil. Later, she decided. She'd deal with this later.

Ravyn's knees gave out. Damon caught her and they sank to the ground together. They held each other, breathing shakily as they tried to recover. Stacey already lay flat on the ground. The team, Ravyn noted, remained frozen. Alex was the only one upright and functional. Semi-functional, she corrected as she watched him stagger to the alien and verify the threat had ended.

"Brody," Alex said when he rejoined them. He had the weapon Damon had used in his hands. "I don't appreciate you appropriating my assault rifle."

"Colonel," Damon said, not opening his eyes, "would you like to explain why I found your assault rifle in the common room?"

"Insubordination," Alex accused without heat. He sat down hard beside Stacey.

* * *

Alex knew he should check on the team, but he couldn't move. He'd never been this tired before. Every muscle in his body quivered with fatigue, even his brain. Later, he'd have to think about what had happened. How Stacey had known she could throw a shield to protect Ravyn and Brody. How he had known he could connect to her and help her hold the wall. He frowned. Hell, if it hadn't been for Stacey, his sister might have been seriously hurt. Or killed. He hated having to admit her presence on this mission had been a good thing.

Movement caught his attention. He watched Brody stand and help Ravyn to her feet. They leaned on each other as they started to walk.

"Brody," he called. For a moment, he thought the captain planned to ignore him, but then he stopped and looked over.

"Yes, sir?"

"You better plan on marrying my sister long before the baby arrives," he said, making his voice as threatening as he could.

Alex wasn't reassured to see both Ravyn and Damon look shocked by his suggestion. It didn't appear as if either one of them had given marriage a moment's thought. When they started weaving their way back to the Old City, he let them go. He'd said his piece and if Brody didn't follow through, well, he had his rifle back. He caressed the stock.

"Nice, Sullivan," Stacey commented. She struggled to sit up and he reached over to help her. "A shotgun wedding. Just what Ravyn's been dreaming about all her life."

"Since you're so sure they love each other, I shouldn't need the shotgun."

He half-expected Stacey to jerk out of his arms after the exchange, but she didn't. His hold tightened, pulling her a little closer to his side. The woman had him all tied up in knots. Almost idly, he noted it wouldn't be long before it began raining again. Finally, Alex said, "You did good today, Stace."

"Do you mean that?"

"I wouldn't have said it if I didn't mean it." He couldn't

stop there. "But I ordered you to stay inside the city." She should have listened to him, but Alex had to admit it was a damn good thing she hadn't.

"You know what, Sullivan? You're a pain in the neck," she said, sounding aggravated.

"I know that. So," he said, trying to sound like it didn't matter, "you want to give us a chance when we get back to Earth? See where we end up?"

Her eyes were big when she stared at him. He could almost feel her trying to measure how he felt about it. Alex bit his tongue. He wouldn't beg or explain. She'd have to make up her mind without that.

"You're so romantic, I could just swoon," Stacey said dryly.

"I don't do romance."

"No kidding." She paused, tilted her head. "What the heck, might as well give it a shot."

Alex smiled with satisfaction and kissed her. He knew he should have been relieved when he heard the troops return to life, but instead he cursed the timing. Steeling himself, he broke the kiss and pushed to his feet to see how they'd fared.

Damon made it to the first square inside the Old City. This fountain didn't have any extraordinary features, but it did have benches. He and Ravyn collapsed together onto the nearest one, and he breathed a sigh of relief. They could have stayed with the others, but he knew the pyramid over the city would recharge them faster than their bodies could on their own.

Ravyn looked wiped out, her face pale except for the dark circles under her eyes and the smear of mud covering her right cheek. He imagined he looked about as good. Battle took a lot out of a person, but the clash they'd won had drained him in a way he'd never felt before. He couldn't read Ravyn. He was so tired, he didn't know what *he* felt aside from relief. All he wanted was to crawl into bed beside her and sleep for about twenty hours. Maybe longer. She slipped her hand into his, linking their fingers and he sighed, content.

"So," he said after the silence had spun out a while, "do you want to get married?"

"We don't have to just because Alex demands it."

"I know. Hell, sweet pea, we're already committed to each other heart and soul. Might as well appease your brother and the government and have a wedding. I don't think the Alliance bureaucrats need to know anything about our joining ceremony."

Ravyn laughed softly, her eyes taking on a bit of heat. "Especially what happened after the light show."

"That was my favorite part," Damon protested with a smile.

"Mine too, but that's between us."

Sobering, Damon cupped her face in his hands. "I love you, Ravyn. Whether you accept my proposal or not, you're stuck with me."

"I'm counting on it," she said. She leaned forward, pressing her lips to his briefly. "You know I love you too."

"I know," he assured her. Damon also knew it still wasn't easy for her to say the words, but she made the effort because of what they meant to him.

"So," Ravyn said, "what do you think about having the ceremony on the beach?"

Damon grinned with satisfaction. "The beach sounds good. Think you can get everything ready to go in a month?"

"How hard can it be?" she said, shrugging. "And if I need help, I'll draft Stacey."

Damon stood, pulling Ravyn to her feet and into his arms. She was laughing in surprise when he pressed his lips to hers. She deepened the kiss and desire flowed between them. He eased back.

"I guess that seals it," Ravyn said, smiling up at him.

"Not quite. Something as important as an engagement calls for more than a kiss."

"Yeah?"

"Yeah. Let's go home, sweet pea."

Epilogue

Damon sat up, going from sound asleep to alert in a nanosecond. "What the—?"

Music blared from the sitting room. With a groan, he rubbed a hand over his forehead. The sax that had sounded so sultry and sexy last night while he'd held his wife in his arms, seemed obnoxious at, he squinted at the clock, two A.M. He reached out with his mind and turned it off.

It came on again in less than thirty seconds. His sweet pea whimpered quietly. He didn't blame her since she'd been up less than two hours ago. Because he was so tired, it took a great deal of concentration, but he maneuvered the energy until he'd disconnected the player from the grid. Blessed silence filled the suite and Damon settled back beside Ravyn.

He ran a comforting hand down her back as she snuggled against him. Drowsily, he enjoyed her nearness. At least until the music returned, louder this time. They both groaned.

"Your turn," she muttered sleepily against his chest.

"It can't be Cam."

Damon felt her reach out mentally and extinguish the sound. "Who else can it be? And he does know how to turn the lights on and off."

"Yeah, but a disconnected entertainment system is harder than the lights." His last word was obliterated as a wailing riff rattled the framed images hanging on the walls. With a curse, he climbed out of bed. Even if it wasn't Cam, he had to turn it off so they could get some sleep. The glowing pyramid emitted by the four obelisks gave him enough light to find his jeans. Damon yanked them on, fastening them as he walked across dimly lit hall. He turned the music off. It switched on once more. Off. On.

Off.

He reached his son's crib and looked down. Cam grinned happily up at him. The music came on. Again. Ravyn was right. It was Cam playing with energy. He decided he preferred the lights flashing to this.

"You have your mother's stubborn streak," Damon told him.

The baby's grin widened and he made a noise that sounded suspiciously like a giggle. Damon couldn't help smiling back, even as he mentally flipped off the player.

"You know," he said, as he scooped up Cam, "most babies cry when they want something. Even you did for the first three months before you learned to manipulate energy."

His son didn't look the least bit chastised, and Damon sighed. He had a feeling he and Ravyn were in for more earsplitting wake-up calls.

After changing Cam's diaper, Damon pulled a bottle through the warmer and settled down in the rocking chair with his son. There was a gurgle of pleasure; then, with the exception of a few slurping sounds, silence reigned as the baby drank, his little hands resting against the bottle.

It never ceased to amaze him how tiny Cam was or how perfect, but it was the absolute trust in his son's eyes as he fed that left Damon feeling awed. Holding him, even if it was in the middle of a very long night, made his heart swell with love. Damon cuddled the baby a little closer.

He knew how lucky he was. Just a year ago, he and Ravyn had almost lost it all and now he had everything he'd always dreamed of. A wife he loved more than life, a fantastic son and time to spend with them. Sometimes he wondered what he'd done to be so blessed.

For three months after he and Ravyn had left Jarved Nine they'd talked about what they would do and where they would live. She'd resigned from the Colonization Assessment Teams within days of their landing on Earth, and he'd turned in the papers to resign his commission the day he'd returned to his base. It took six months to become effective, but then he'd be out. They could move anywhere.

As for a career, he'd been toying with the idea of starting a foundation to assist disabled veterans because the Alliance wasn't doing nearly enough. Then he'd been summoned to the base commander's office.

The army was reluctant to accept his resignation, claiming he was too vital to the Western Alliance. They proposed sending him to Jarved Nine to assist the military operation in the Old City. The teams based there since the alien had been defeated hadn't found anything of use, and the army believed Damon would be more successful.

Damon had needed to call in every favor he'd been owed, but he'd managed to get Ravyn assigned to Jarved Nine with him as a civilian consultant. It wasn't the future either of them had envisioned, but they were together and that was the important thing.

Cam pulled his mouth off the bottle's nipple and made a smacking noise with his lips. It yanked Damon back to the here and now. Putting the bottle aside, he tossed a towel over his shoulder and lifted his son. He had lots of practice at burping and it didn't take long before Cam issued a series of noises better suited to a linebacker than a fourteen-pound baby.

"Some day, Cam, you're really going to impress your frat brothers," Damon told him, pressing a kiss to his temple. He put the baby back in his crib. Cam's mouth twisted into an angry pout and the lights flashed on and off. With a sigh, he picked him up again and settled into the chair. Rocking gently, he held his son against his chest. He'd just have to wait until Cam fell asleep.

* * *

Ravyn yawned as she slid her toolbox under the bed. Damon had been broadcasting thoughts and emotions at top volume while he'd tended to Cam, and since she couldn't sleep and block him, she'd decided to take preventative action. She'd disabled everything that produced a loud noise. Heaven knew Cam would be awake in another two hours and playing with energy again. He'd circumvented the lack of power, but she didn't think he could get around the missing components. At least she hoped not.

She smiled to herself at the odd precautions she had to take as a mother on Jarved Nine. It certainly wasn't traditional parenting. But then there was nothing traditional about living on another planet, surrounded by hundreds of military people looking for advanced alien technology.

In the short time they'd been back on Jarved Nine, though, Ravyn had come to like their rather strange existence. She loved living in Kale and Meriwa's old house, the place where she and Damon had first declared their love. From what she'd heard, the full-bird colonel in charge of this mission had tried living in the grand house before she and Damon had arrived, but the vibration the crystals emanated was too high. The colonel hadn't been able to tolerate it. In less than a day, she'd moved to a smaller, but still opulent, home nearby.

Ravyn pushed her hair off her face and decided she'd better find Damon. He'd been quiet for a while now. She crossed the hall and stopped in the doorway to the baby's room, a sappy smile spreading across her face as she noticed her two guys asleep in the rocking chair.

Softly, she padded over to them and ran a gentle hand over her baby's silky, dark hair. He didn't have a lot yet, but what he did have was just right. Ravyn smothered a laugh as she studied her husband and child. The two had identical expressions on their faces. Cam was most definitely his father's son.

She reached for Cam, carefully trying to separate him from Damon so she could put him to bed. Her husband's grasp tightened—so protective, even while he slept.

"Honey," she said, her voice just above a whisper, "let me have Cam. He needs to be in bed."

Damon's eyes partially opened and then his hold relaxed. She shifted her son into her arms and headed for the crib. Cam squawked and Ravyn stopped, swaying slowly.

"Shhh, sweetie, it's okay. Mommy has you." She pressed a kiss to his cheek. "I'm putting you to bed, that's all. You can't sleep on top of Daddy, he's tired too, okay?"

When Cam didn't protest anymore, Ravyn resumed walking. She kissed him again, squeezing him closer for a moment, before laying him down. He settled in with barely a blink, one tiny fist curling near his chin. She couldn't help but stare. It still amazed her to know she and Damon had created this perfect little boy. She blinked back the tears that filled her eyes, but she couldn't stop the sappy smile from showing up again.

She sensed Damon approach, felt him slip his arms around her waist. He pushed her hair aside, pressing a kiss to her bare shoulder and Ravyn leaned back against his chest. She rested her hands atop his, enjoying his touch.

"You should be sleeping," he told her, voice still thick.

"I couldn't," she answered every bit as quiet as he'd been. "You were thinking too loudly."

"Sorry, sweet pea. I'm not used to this telepathy thing yet or the way it comes and goes."

"Me either, but then it's been growing since we returned to Jarved Nine. I'm sure we'll adjust to it like we have to everything else." Ravyn also sensed it would gradually become a full-time connection, but the idea didn't worry her a bit. She stroked his fingers with hers, loving the feel of his warm skin.

"Cam did well at the Peace Day picnic yesterday," Damon said, resting his chin against her temple.

"He did, although we almost had some explaining to do. When Colonel McNamara spilled her water and it splashed Cam, I felt him start gathering energy. For a minute there, I thought he was going to reverse the stream and send it back to the colonel. I don't know if he changed his mind or couldn't figure out how to do it, but it was a close call."

"I felt that. I didn't realize what he was trying to do."

Ravyn sensed her husband's amusement and bit back her own laugh. It really wouldn't have been funny if the baby had shown his abilities to a meadow full of people. Little Cameron Julian Brody, named for Damon's maternal grandfather and her father, was proving to be the handful she'd predicted before he'd been born.

Ravyn loved Peace Day. She always had. Started by people in the New Age movement at the end of the 1990s, it had originally been called Peace in a Day and the goal had been an end to all wars by the turn of the millennium. It hadn't worked, but still, for one day a year, everyone was supposed to visualize world harmony. She'd always wanted peace very badly, but now that she was a mother, that wish had taken on new urgency. And maybe, just maybe, something they found here on Jarved Nine would help.

Thinking about her desire for peace brought something else to mind. "What were you and Alex talking about at the picnic?"

Her brother had pulled strings to get assigned to Jarved Nine with her and Damon. She still didn't know how he'd convinced his superiors to send Spec Ops teams here for security or to get himself appointed as the officer in charge of them. Or how he'd gotten Stacey assigned as CAT liaison for the project. No one else from CAT was here.

They both froze as Cam shifted and made a little noise. When he settled back into sleep, they breathed a sigh of relief. Damon and Alex mostly got along. Now. But Alex continued to watch over her, hell-bent on ensuring her husband treated her right, and that led to an occasional flare up.

"It wasn't about you, sweet pea," Damon said, his voice even softer than before. "He and McNamara have been butting heads and he wanted my opinion, that's all." He must have felt her surprise. "Yeah, I know. Sullivan asking for my take on something is rarer than lamordite. What about the intense conversation you had with him?"

"That was about Stacey. I suggested he marry her since they've been living together for almost a year now."

"Bet he loved that."

"He told me to mind my own business."

Damon snorted. "Yeah, right. The same way he minds his. Your brother might be mellowing, though. He only threatened my life twice yesterday."

Ravyn laughed and turned her head so she could see Damon's face. "You just need to keep me happy, honey, and you're safe."

"And are you happy?"

Like he needed to ask. The bond between them was so strong, he sometimes knew what she felt before she did. Now, with this telepathic link appearing and starting to grow between them, he'd probably know what she was thinking before she did.

"I could be happier," she told him, trying to hide a smile.

"Yeah? Anything I can do?" He nuzzled the place where her neck and shoulder met.

"You're on the right track."

"Well, let me know when I reach the station."

Ravyn wiggled her bottom against the front of his jeans. He went still for an instant and then one hand came up, cupping her breast through the silky fabric of her night slip. His other arm tightened across her waist, pulling her more firmly against his body. "Sweet pea, why don't we go rest."

Ravyn didn't need a telepathic link to know what Damon meant by *rest.* She pressed herself more firmly into his hand. "Honey, I like the way you think."